D1483894

THE PARTY
LONDON PREP: BOOK 5

THE PARTY

LONDON PREP: BOOK 5

JILLIAN DODD

Copyright © 2021 by Jillian Dodd

All rights reserved.

This book is a work of fiction. Any references to historical events, real people, or real locales are used fictitiously. Other names, characters, places, and incidents are the product of the author's imagination, and any resemblance to actual events or locales or persons, living or dead, is entirely coincidental.

Editor: Jovana Shirley, Unforeseen Editing

Jillian Dodd Inc.
Madeira Beach, FL

Jillian Dodd, The Keatyn Chronicles, and Spy Girl are Registered Trademarks of Jillian Dodd Inc.

ISBN: 978-1-953071-22-4

BOOKS BY JILLIAN DODD

London Prep
The Exchange
The Boys' Club
The Kiss
The Key

The Keatyn Chronicles®
Stalk Me
Kiss Me
Date Me
Love Me
Adore Me
Hate Me
Get Me
Fame
Power
Money
Sex
Love
Keatyn Unscripted
Aiden

That Boy
That Boy
That Wedding
That Baby
That Love
That Ring
That Summer
That Promise

THURSDAY, OCTOBER 17TH
Jam your toast.
6:30AM

I WAKE UP, crying. My fingers are digging into the sheets, and my chest is heaving from my dream. Everything feels off. *Wrong.*

My shirt is sweaty and sticking to me. There are tears on my cheeks.

I wipe them off, upset with myself.

Because I dreamed about Noah last night.

And it wasn't a good dream.

I shut my eyes, trying to clear the images from my mind.

I was at Noah's house.

I don't know exactly what we were doing, but we were laughing. He dragged me into his room, pushed me onto his bed, and I thought I knew what was going to happen. *We were going to kiss.*

But then the dream changed, and suddenly, I was at school and saw Noah in the hallway. I smiled at him. He smiled back. But instead of stopping to talk to me, he moved past me. I tried to keep up with him, but he kept going into different classrooms. And somehow, all the classrooms connected into a large maze, and I couldn't keep up with him. Every time I found him, it was like he was gone again, through the next door. I eventually caught him though. I reached out and grabbed his arm.

Suddenly, we were back in his room. *Finally*. I can't remember his words exactly. And I'm not sure we even spoke. But it felt like I heard him.

Or understood him.

We were lying in his bed, happy. Noah propped himself up. He pushed my hair behind my ear, but as he did, his smile shifted.

It lessened.

It was like he was reflecting on the memory of us. Even looking at me there, right in front of him, he looked nostalgic.

Like he had moved on.

Like he had let go of me.

Like we were already over.

I wrapped my fingers around his wrist, trying to show him that I was still here. I shook him, trying to get him to really look at me. *To see me.* But his expression didn't change. His smile slowly faded, and he got out of bed. I tried to speak, but I couldn't. My mouth moved, but no words came out. He couldn't hear me.

And then Noah left his room.

I got up to go after him, but when I got to his door, it was locked. I shook the handle over and over, but I couldn't get out. I was trapped. I tried to scream, but I didn't have a voice. I slammed against the door, but there was only silence. My fists didn't make a sound. I started crying. I could feel the tears, I could feel the burning in my throat, but I couldn't hear myself. I couldn't hear anything. No one came to the door.

And then I woke up.

A shiver rips through me.

"What the hell?" Mohammad mumbles from the floor.

I cover my eyes with my hands, trying to forget my

dream.

"You're soaked through," he whispers, sliding next to me in bed.

I glance over to see that Olivia and Naomi are curled up on my other side, still asleep.

"Bad dream," I reply, trying to shuffle through my thoughts. I need to separate what was real and what was a dream. "A nightmare."

"Well, you're okay now. It was just a dream," he says.

I nod, pulling my legs up to my chest, and stare at my toes. Mohammad's right. It was just a dream. I close my eyes, trying to forget the way Noah looked at me and wondering if it was some kind of premonition.

"You're shaking." Mohammad pulls me toward him, and I lean my head on his shoulder.

"I'm cold," I whisper.

"Here." Mohammad pulls up the comforter, covering both of us. "Better?"

I nod.

"Was the boogie monster chasing you?" Mohammad asks with a yawn.

"It was terrible. I was locked in a room, and I couldn't get out," I reply. "I kept trying … I wanted to so badly, but I couldn't." A tear escapes, rolling down my cheek.

"It's all right. It was just a dream," Mohammad says again, rubbing my shoulder.

I nod against him, wiping my eyes.

It was just a dream.

Mohammad rubs my shoulder for a few minutes before speaking. "Why don't you go take a shower? You'll feel better after."

"Okay," I reply. But I don't move. My chest aches, and my body feels lifeless.

"What was the dream about?" Mohammad asks.

I swallow, my throat hot and scratchy.

"I don't want to talk about it," I finally say.

"Who's talking over there?" Olivia mumbles from the other side of the bed. Her face is smushed into her pillow, and her blonde hair is everywhere.

"Sorry," I whisper. I wipe at my eyes, not wanting them to see me cry. "I'm going to go shower."

I start to crawl over Mohammad, trying to get out of bed. But he gets up with me and follows me into the bathroom.

"What was it about?" he asks, closing the door behind us.

I sit down on the bench as Mohammad turns on the shower. He makes sure a towel is next to it before looking back at me.

"It was terrible. I couldn't ever get to him. Over and over, I followed him, and he always slipped out of my fingers. When I finally found him, well, it didn't matter. I could see it in his eyes. I was a part of his past. And he was happy about it. I wasn't his future, Mohammad. I wasn't anything, except a memory that had lingered for too long." Tears escape my eyes, and I bury my head in my hands. My body shakes as I relive the dream.

The nightmare.

"Shh." Mohammad's palm finds my back, and he pats it gently. "It's okay."

"But it's not," I snap. I look up at him and shake my head.

"Was it about Noah?" Mohammad asks, his forehead creasing.

My cheeks flush at his question, but I still nod.

"You're not only part of his past," Mohammad says, crouched in front of me.

I look down at the floor, embarrassed.

"You were right. It was just a dream," I say, looking up to Mohammad. "*It was only a dream.*"

"I'll order us food. Then, we can watch the sunrise, okay?" Mohammad puts his hands on my knees and holds my gaze.

"Sure." I nod.

"Take a shower. You'll feel better. And if not, I'm sure a coffee will cheer you up." Mohammad gives me an encouraging grin before walking out of the bathroom and closing the door behind him.

I sit for a moment, letting the bathroom fill up with steam. When the mirror starts to fog, I peel off my damp clothes and get into the shower. The water is hot against my skin, but it feels nice. I squeeze shower gel into my hand and rub it down over my arms, and then I cradle my arms, comforting myself.

Because that dream really got to me.

And normally, they don't. I know they're dreams. I know they're a part of myself. They're my interpretations, my worries, my insecurities. They're all about me, coming from me. But in the moment, it didn't feel like that. It felt like I was going crazy. I felt stuck.

And I guess, last night, I felt like that with Noah. I felt like we weren't going anywhere. I felt like he was slipping out of my grasp.

Again.

I sit down on the shower floor, bringing my knees up to my chest, and let myself cry. I have to get it out now, before I go back out to the girls. To Mohammad.

Eventually, I stand back up. I feel shaky, but I wash and condition my hair anyway. When I'm finished, I pat myself dry with a towel.

I brush through my hair and pull on a robe, looking at my reflection.

I look tired.

I have dark circles under my eyes.

I break my own gaze, flip off the light switch, and walk out of the bathroom.

"Mohammad's ordering breakfast," Naomi sings when she sees me. She's sitting up in bed, and she looks wide-awake.

"Good for him. Some of us are *trying* to sleep," Olivia grumbles next to her. She's curled into a ball in the middle of the bed. And it doesn't look like she's going to get up anytime soon.

"Feel better?" Mohammad asks, joining us in the bedroom. He's still shirtless and in his basketball shorts, like he was last night. But his shorts are sitting lower on his hips this morning, and he has bedhead.

"Yeah," I say, trying to sound convincing as I force a smile on my face.

"Good. Food's on the way," he replies, walking back into the sitting room.

I turn my attention to Naomi.

Oh my god, she mouths to me, fanning her face.

Apparently, I wasn't the only one to notice Mohammad was still shirtless this morning. I smile at her just as Mohammad pops his head back in.

"Come on, you have to come see this."

Naomi springs out of bed and laces her arm through mine, dragging me into the sitting room. As she does, I look over my shoulder at Olivia, who is still facedown in her pillow.

I turn my gaze from Olivia toward Mohammad. He's parting the curtains that run along the entire wall to reveal the pink horizon.

"Wow," Naomi breathes out when we get to the sitting room.

We take a few steps closer to the window and look out across the park. It's aglow in the morning light.

Pink and perfect.

Like nothing can taint it.

And I instantly feel sick. Because all I can think about is my dream. About Noah. And how wrong it is that in the midst of this beauty, my heart aches.

Naomi releases me and presses her palms against the window.

"It's stunning," she gasps, turning to me brightly.

I force back tears.

"It is," I agree.

I wrap my arms around my waist, holding on to myself.

"This is mad. Who knew the sky could look like this?" Mohammad says, walking over to me.

He drapes his arm over my shoulders, pulling me to him. I wrap my arm around his waist and let out a deep breath. Mohammad stands strong and firm, and I fold into him. He exudes energy and warmth, and I know that I need some of both this morning. So, I let myself relax in his embrace.

"Come on, Naomi," I say. She's still plastered against the window, looking out in awe. "You're missing out."

"On what?" she replies, not breaking her gaze from the window.

"On our moment."

When she turns to look at me and Mohammad, I wave for her to join us. She comes to stand on the opposite side of Mohammad, lacing an arm around his waist. He puts his arm over her shoulder, so we're all three wrapped up together. Naomi tickles against my arm and gives me a warm grin.

I smile back at her before looking out at the horizon. At the rising sun.

I take in the color of the sky. The love I feel, holding on

to Mohammad. The happiness that Naomi radiates.

And it's perfect.

"I feel like someone should wake up Olivia for this. She's missing out," I say, feeling better.

One glance up at Mohammad reveals a wide grin on his face. His eyes flick down to meet mine before he looks over at Naomi.

"Haven't you heard the expression, *Don't wake the sleeping beast*?" Naomi giggles. "If you're going to wake her, you're on your own for it."

Mohammad lets out an easy laugh.

"Not a morning person?" I ask.

"She only becomes a morning person when there's food involved. It's a general rule that I don't wake her without the promise of food arriving soon."

"Well," I say, unwrapping myself from around Mohammad, "I think I'll chance it. It's too beautiful for her to miss."

I walk into the bedroom, leaving Mohammad and Naomi alone. She still has her arms wrapped around his waist. I smile at them before turning my attention to Olivia.

One glance at her in bed shows she's back asleep.

I walk to the window, peeking out. It's the same view as the sitting room and equally as beautiful. I drop the curtain, letting the sliver of pink light disappear.

"Olivia," I whisper, crawling next to her in bed.

She stirs, letting out a quiet groan.

"I know that you're sleepy, but the sunrise this morning is worth waking up for. I promise." I tentatively place my hand on her shoulder, wondering if she's going to wake up and start swatting at me. But before I have a chance to think better, I shake her gently, hoping to ease her awake.

"Go away." She bats her hand out at me, rolling in the opposite direction.

I lay my head back against the headboard with a smile.

"Not a chance. You won't win this one." I laugh.

"Have you met me?" she mumbles back, sounding more awake.

"Have you met *me*?" I question.

She peeks over her shoulder at me, looking annoyed. "Fucking Americans. You never quit," she mutters. But at the same time, she sits up.

And I know that I've won.

"We do have a never-quit spirit," I agree, perking up.

"Where are Naomi and Mohammad?" she asks, glancing over to me.

"Watching the sunrise in the other room. It's slightly romantic."

"That is romantic," she says groggily. "And you want to interrupt it?"

"It's actually the same view from the window in here. I just figured I should let you wake up before pulling the curtains open."

"Smart decision." Olivia rubs her hands across her face. She blinks a few times, looking more awake. "All right, let's see it."

We both slide off the bed and move to the window. Olivia sits cross-legged on the floor as I pull back the curtains. She closes her eyes briefly at the light, but they slowly flutter back open.

"Wow," she exhales.

"I know."

I sit down next to her on the floor, both of us looking out at the skyline. We sit in silence, watching the sky turn from a light-cotton-candy pink to a deeper shade of purple. It's mesmerizing in its innocence.

In its newness.

The entire day is awaiting us, and it makes me grateful that I'm sitting here, experiencing this with Olivia.

I glance to her.

"Thank you for being there for me this week. Letting me sit with you at lunch. The birthday party last night … I really appreciate it," I tell her.

Because Olivia has been by my side since the moment she told me what Noah said to Harry.

That he *loved me*.

Maybe that's when she finally realized that I wasn't trying to steal Harry from her. That I wasn't playing some game.

Harry. Noah. Olivia. Me.

It's all just been a collection of events and moments that wound us up together and somehow resulted in one big, complicated disaster.

"Don't worry about it. We've been through a lot together," she reflects. "Plus, Naomi always gets what she wants. And she wanted us to be friends …"

"It always surprises me how much you own up to these things," I say, knowing that's probably the best I'm going to get from Olivia.

Olivia lets out a laugh. "What can I say? Naomi's my best friend. Her opinion matters to me. And usually, she's right. So …" Olivia shrugs.

"She does always provide unique insight."

A knock comes from the other side of the hotel room door, and I listen as either Naomi or Mohammad answers it. A few seconds later, Mohammad pops his head into the bedroom.

"Food's here," he says excitedly.

He quickly leaves us and starts talking to whom I assume is room service. Olivia stands up, pulling me with her. We both go into the sitting room, the smell of coffee lingering in the air.

"Yum." My mouth waters at the scent.

And the thought of some caffeine.

Mohammad rolls the cart toward the couch with a wide grin.

"It smells *amazing*," Naomi says, falling down onto the couch. And she's glowing.

I raise an eyebrow at her, wondering if it's the food she's flushed about or the fact that Mohammad is pretty much serving her breakfast, shirtless. She just grins back as I walk over to the cart.

It's loaded with toast, jam, butter, and honey. There are eggs, meat, and tomatoes. But there's also a single sliced banana on a plate with a cup of almond butter sitting next to it. I blink, wondering if it's just my mind playing tricks on me.

"Mohammad, how did you know?" I ask, looking between him and the banana.

"I'm your best friend. It's my job to know," he replies proudly.

My mouth slips open as I stare at the banana. Because the only person who knows that my favorite breakfast is toast with almond butter, honey, and banana on top is Noah.

And Noah isn't here.

I'm not at his house, having him make this for me.

I'm with Mohammad and the girls at a hotel.

"But …" I start.

"Know what?" Naomi asks with interest from the couch.

"What her favorite breakfast is," Mohammad says brightly, handing me a piece of toast.

"What's your favorite breakfast?" Olivia asks, grabbing jam and a slice of toast for herself.

"Um, I really like toast with almond butter, banana, and

honey," I explain.

"That sounds disgusting." Olivia laughs, her nose scrunching up. She pours herself a cup of coffee from the pot and takes her plate and cup over to the dining table.

"You have no idea," Naomi says from the couch. "When I slept over the other week, she and Noah were eating these bananas he'd sautéed on the stove without anything else! It was mad."

"Hey," I cut in, eyeing her. "You ate some too. And if I remember correctly, you *liked* it."

"I was being polite," Naomi disagrees.

I raise an eyebrow at her as she takes a sip of her tea.

"Fine, it wasn't the worst thing. But it was still strange," she admits.

"Noah's like that with his food," Mohammad says, dumping eggs and sausage onto his plate. He puts two pieces of toast on either side of the mound, like they might somehow hold it all in.

I watch him in amazement.

He glances at me excitedly. But when he sees the toast he gave me still in my hand, he looks confused. I set it down on a plate and look across the spread again, trying to decide what I want.

"Mohammad, would you mind putting jam on a piece of toast for me, please?" Naomi asks.

"I would *love* to jam your toast," Mohammad replies with a smirk.

My mouth practically hits the floor with his response.

Because he did not just say that!

Mohammad's eyes are sparkling, and I watch him slide jam across a piece of toast, looking way too happy about it. I glance over at Naomi, wanting to know what she makes of the situation. But she doesn't seem to have noticed his play on words.

"Mohammad ..." Olivia coughs, setting down her cup of coffee.

She rubs at her temples, looking weirded out. And part of me is right there with her.

I shake my head and refocus on breakfast. I start to build my toast, watching as Mohammad takes their plates to the couch. He hands Naomi hers first, and she grins up at him. He smiles and then sits down. A second later though, he's inhaling his food.

I shake my head again, looking back down at the cart. I end up making a variation of my almond butter and banana toast. I decide to put the almond butter directly on the banana instead, and then I jam the toast, topping it with eggs.

I don't know why I force myself to make it differently, but I do. It's probably because Noah told Mohammad it's what I like. And for some reason, knowing that he told Mohammad but isn't here himself ... well, it makes me want eggs on my toast instead.

After breakfast, Mohammad goes to shower while Naomi, Olivia, and I drink our coffee and tea. Mohammad doesn't take very long, and when he joins us again, he's in his uniform. I check the time, seeing we don't have that long before we need to head to school.

"I'm going to go change."

I put my empty plate back on the cart as I head into the closet. I change quickly, and when I join them again, Naomi and Olivia are both in my bedroom.

"Bloody hell. I forgot my skirt," Olivia says, shoving her pajamas into her duffel with force. She has on her uniform top and jeans.

"Do you want to borrow one?" I offer.

"Thanks, but I need to stop by my house anyway. I forgot

my yoga gear as well," she replies, flaring her eyes.

Naomi presses her lips together before pulling out her phone and checking the time.

"If we leave right now, we won't be late," Naomi says, collecting her things. She puts everything into a large tote before pulling it onto her shoulder.

"All right," Olivia agrees, opening up the bedroom door. She grabs her bags before putting on her coat and walking out into the sitting room with Naomi.

I glance around the bedroom, looking for my bag for school. I finally find it under a pillow that got tossed onto the floor. My room's a disaster from the festivities last night, but the mess will have to wait until later. I remember what Olivia said about yoga and make sure to throw in my change of clothes for class.

"What's up?" Mohammad asks Naomi and Olivia when I get into the sitting room. He already wheeled the dining cart out into the hallway and is standing with his backpack in hand.

"I need to stop by my house," Olivia answers, raising her eyebrows. She looks annoyed with herself.

"Gotcha. We will have to meet you at school. Mia wanted to show me something before class," Mohammad says as I grab my coat.

"Mia?" I ask, confused.

"I didn't know you and Mia were friends," Naomi chimes in as we make our way to the door.

I check my bag, making sure I have my phone, room key, and homework.

"She knows I'm the hottest DJ in town. Wanted to show me a new artist," Mohammad boasts.

"Hottest DJ?" I question, grinning at him.

"You know I am. Besides, if I recall, you've danced many

a dances to songs I've selected. So, really, all your fun has been because of me and my brilliant music selection," he says, opening the door for us.

"Sorry I suggested differently." I chuckle.

"Anyway, we'll just see you at school then?" Mohammad asks, looking directly at Naomi.

"Yeah." She flushes, looking down at the floor with a smile. "See you at school."

"Cool," Mohammad says, looking a little red himself.

He awkwardly glances at Naomi and then away from her as we wait for the elevator. I look between them and have to bite my lip to keep from cooing. I notice Olivia watching them too. But instead of looking happy, she looks almost spooked by their interaction.

When the elevator dings, I'm pretty sure I hear Olivia mumble, "*Finally.*"

"HEY!" I CALL out to Mia when we get to the common room at school.

"Ah, you're here!" she says, rushing toward me and Mohammad. She gives me a quick hug and nods at Mohammad.

"Your hair is still purple," I say, looking her over. "Helen must have given in?"

Mia grins. "Noah guilted her into letting me keep it. Isn't it amazing?"

"Wicked," Mohammad says, taking in her hair.

"It is," I agree. "So, what's going on? Mohammad said you messaged him about music?"

"My friend Aaron is a fantastic artist. He's going to release his first album next month, and he sent me a few of his songs early. You have to hear them! He's ridiculously talented," she says, dragging me to the couch.

I glance back at Mohammad. He gives me a smile and

looks genuinely interested.

It's not until Mia's pulling me down onto a couch next to her that I see Noah. He's seated opposite us, his left leg crossed over his right. I barely have a chance to register his presence before Mia is shoving an earbud into my ear. She puts the other in hers, turning toward me excitedly.

"Are you ready to have your mind *blown*?" she asks.

At first, I want to laugh, but she looks so serious that my smile fades, and I nod in agreement. She turns on the music, and I make sure to really pay attention.

My first thought is that Aaron has got a great voice and that I like his style—a mix of rap and pop. I bob my head along, smiling over at Mia in encouragement. She's silently singing along, and I watch her lips move with each lyric. I smile at her again before glancing across to the other couch.

Mohammad sat down next to Noah, but their attention is on us. Mohammad is watching Mia. Noah keeps his head straight, his eyes moving between me and his sister. Every few seconds though, he leans toward Mohammad, telling him something.

I pull my eyes away from them.

After three songs, I take out the earbud and give it back to Mia.

"It's really good," I admit.

"I know." Mia nods, her eyes glowing with pride. "He's so talented. A true storyteller."

"I like the way that he mixes genres too. It's cool to hear that."

"That's what Noah said," Mia replies, her eyes moving to her brother and then to Mohammad, who's getting up from the couch.

He comes over and pulls me up.

"Trade spots. I want to hear," he says, taking my seat on

the couch. "I'm always looking for new music."

"You and your music," I comment, feeling slightly abandoned. I consider just standing there, but I know that would be silly. And it would probably freak him and Mia out.

I turn around, eyeing the empty spot next to Noah. It's the obvious option unless I want to move to a different section, which would just be weird.

Noah looks up at me, waiting to see what I'll do.

I step away from Mohammad and Mia and take a seat next to him. I look across at Mohammad, who's totally into the music. Mia looks thrilled, and when I glance over at Noah, I see that he's watching Mohammad too. He lets out a chuckle before greeting me.

"Morning," Noah says with a smile.

"Morning." My voice is full of hesitation as I fold my hands into my lap.

I keep my gaze down, trying to ignore the heat coming off of Noah. It's hard enough, sitting next to him in class, but sitting next to him on the couch? It's even worse. We're closer than usual. And after being pressed against him last night and my dream this morning …

"You all right?" Noah asks, his hand coming down onto my arm. I glance over at it, feeling his fingers burn into my skin. "You don't look very good."

I break my eyes away from his fingertips, moving them toward his face.

"Oh, really?" I ask.

Noah shakes his head. "I mean, you look tired," he clarifies.

"I am. Late night and all that."

"That's not it," he disagrees.

He searches my face, his forehead creasing. I try to hide from his prying eyes, but I can't. My face falls. I know he isn't going to drop this.

"I had a nightmare," I say.

"Do you want to tell me about it?" he asks. And I can hear the concern in his voice.

I glance around, seeing more students pouring into the common room. And with Mia and Mohammad sitting straight across from us, I feel like I'm under a microscope.

"Not right now."

Noah must understand because he gives me a small smile. I want to smile back, but instead, I look down at my hands in my lap. Because every single cell in me is confused.

Noah bumps his shoulder against mine. "We can talk anytime, you know. That's what friends are for, right?"

"Friends?" I repeat. Because is that what last night was to him?

Us being *friends*?

"I know what your problem is," he says.

"You do?" I ask, looking toward him. Because maybe he actually has the answer that I'm looking for.

"Mmhmm." Noah nods. "You're missing the battle of the bathroom, I think."

His brown eyes are all over me, making me extremely nervous.

"I can't do this with you, Noah."

"Do what?" he asks.

"This." I point between him and me, shaking my head.

I've never felt so … off. After last night's interaction with Noah and my dream, I don't know if I want to smile at him or start crying. My emotions are everywhere right now. I feel all over the place.

I feel like a mess.

Noah watches my hand move between us, his golden-brown eyes growing flat.

"Are you trying to say that the battle of the bathroom wasn't a thing?" he finally asks.

His response lessens my tension, and suddenly, my chest feels lighter.

Because this—here, with Noah, the lightness between us—is real.

I roll my eyes at him and play along. "Please. Competing for bathroom time with you is the *last* thing I miss about your house."

"Maybe so," he replies, leaning toward me. "But I know you *have* to miss seeing me in only a towel."

I can't help but feel happy when I see the sparkle in Noah's eyes and the silly grin on his face. He raises his eyebrows at me in question.

"Noah. Williams."

"Yeah?" he replies, his gaze never leaving mine.

"Are you flirting with me?" I narrow my eyes at him.

Noah shakes his head, but it isn't convincing. And his silly smile turns into a full-blown grin. He lets out a deep chuckle. "Never. I wouldn't dare."

I feel stuck, looking at him. I can't imagine what my face looks like right now, but it has to be a funny sight to see. I'm so confused. And annoyed. And kind of happy. And annoyed that I'm happy. A smile grows on my own lips.

"You are." I laugh.

I give his shoulder a push, my cheeks flushing before I glance over at Mohammad and Mia. They're watching us, but the second I catch them, they quickly look away.

"And if I am? Is that really so bad?" Noah looks at me through his dark lashes, his neck jutting out as he tilts his head back.

And I know the look well. It's his *are you really going to argue with me* look.

"Um …"

"Besides, I'm not flirting. I'm just telling you a truth from our past experience."

"Why bring it up then?" I cut in.

"Because you looked sad when you got here. And you *always* look happy when you're yelling at me. Banging on the bathroom door. Calling out my name." His voice drops as his eyes flick up to mine. "Finding me shirtless … and wet."

I think my heart stops. Or maybe it rips out of my chest and flees. Or maybe it hops straight into his hand. I have no clue. All I know is that my chest feels like it just broke open and my heart has left me.

Practically flew out of me.

Because Noah isn't just flirting with me. He's *majorly* flirting with me. And right here, in front of his sister. *His sister!*

And Mohammad.

He's gone from joking and occasionally flirting to something way different.

He's being unfair. And direct. And hot.

Really, really hot.

And I am not about to question it.

"You really think you have such a huge effect on me, don't you?" I say, trying to keep my cool.

"I know I do." Noah's eyes crease at the corners as he smiles. "You know what I was thinking about?"

"What?"

"Do you remember me mauling you that one day?" he says, his cheeks flushing.

"*Almost* mauling me," I correct. "I made it out, un-scathed."

Noah nods. "That's true. I know you liked it though."

"What exactly did I like about it?" I push, thinking back

20

to how Noah's head was tucked into my neck. How his breath was warm and his teeth were all over my skin.

"Being slobbered on." Noah laughs.

My lips pull into an amused frown, and I shake my head. "You're disgusting."

"Whatever I am, you love it."

Noah holds my gaze, and it feels like the whole world is looking back at me in his eyes. And I don't understand it. *How is this possible? What's going on with him? With me? With us?*

"What happened to you between last night and now?" I ask, trying to figure out the change.

"Well, you asked—" Noah says, sounding unsure of himself.

I cut him off, "It's a good thing."

"It's what you want, right?" Noah's brows draw in with his question.

"Is it what you want?" I ask.

"This, with you, is easy. It's the friends part that I might have a bit of trouble with," Noah answers.

"Being friends is asking too much?"

"Too much?" Noah repeats, blinking a few times. But then he refocuses. "Did you … like my gift?"

"I wish you had stayed."

"Stayed?" Noah repeats, looking more cheerful again. "You had a pretty full house, birthday girl."

"Full hotel room," I correct. "But what does that have to do with it?"

"Some things are private," Noah says.

The school bell rings out, cutting off our conversation.

Mohammad pulls the earbud out of his ear, nodding his head.

"So, are you into it?" Mia asks him excitedly.

"Totally," Mohammad says, still tapping his foot on the ground. "He's got some great tracks."

"Well, he's got a gig in a few weeks. We should all go," Mia says, looking between the three of us. "It's at a shit place, and we'll probably be the only ones there, but seriously, he's going to be a star someday."

"I'm so down," Mohammad agrees, pulling his backpack onto his shoulder.

Mia and Noah are both looking at me, apparently waiting for an answer.

"Yeah, I'd love to," I reply.

"Great." Mia grins, shoving her phone into her bag. She's glowing, and it's easy to tell she's happy about other people liking his music. "I can't wait."

"It will be fun," Noah agrees, glancing at me as we walk to class.

Weasel my way.
STATISTICS

"SO, IF I had been alone, what would it have been like?" The question is out of my mouth before I can stop it.

Because Noah is so talkative and flirty this morning that I'm hoping he can clarify a few things from last night. A few things from this morning. Like what he meant by privacy. We were alone out in the hallway last night.

Was that not private enough?

"We would have ... celebrated," he replies, sliding into his regular desk.

I drop my bag onto the ground and look at him. "My birthday?"

"Of course." Noah laughs.

I shake my head at myself. Of course he meant my birthday.

What was I thinking?

It's just that something about him is making me nervous. Usually, I'm relaxed with him. We've always been able to talk. We've never set boundaries because I never thought that they were necessary. But now, I feel like I'm floating in a pool of whens and ifs. There are too many paths, outcomes, possibilities. And the probability of what is going to happen is so unclear.

I flip open my stats textbook, my hate for the subject returning.

"What?" Noah asks.

"I just feel aimless this week. Like I don't know up from down," I admit.

"All you have to do is check your feet," he quips.

"I can't look at my feet," I say to my textbook. "I'm distracted. And confused."

"By me?" Noah asks.

"Well, yeah."

"I can't be your fixed point, Mal," he says, drawing my eyes up from my textbook.

"I'm not asking you to be."

"Even if I wanted to be, you have to find your own footing first."

I swallow. Because he's right. I know he's right. "It's just—"

"You're a romantic," Noah finishes.

"I am not," I say way too fast, feeling like my eyes are about to pop out of my head.

"You are. And you're flushed again." Noah's holding back his smile as he looks toward me.

"And you're annoying," I reply. "I hate to break it to you, but you are not about to weasel your way back into my life, okay? You made it very clear this week how you felt about me. And you made it very clear last night that you didn't—"

Noah doesn't let me finish. "Weasel my way back in?"

"Yes. Weasel. Your. Way. Back. In." I point my finger at him with each word for emphasis.

Noah licks his lip as he watches me, and it breaks my concentration. It sends a small crack through my frustration. I don't know why his mouth always catches my attention or why I find so much interest in his lips. Their shape. Their color.

"And I ..."

"Don't get distracted," Noah says quietly.

"I'm not," I reply, trying to collect myself.

Trying to remember what I was even saying.

"You were," Noah disagrees, shaking his head. "But I'll let this one slide."

"What do you want?"

"I want to know if you thought about me over the weekend," he says.

"You never crossed my mind." I stick my chin out at him, willing my eyes to become glass. To become impenetrable.

"I don't believe that," Noah says, his eyes growing playful.

"You can believe what you want." I cross my arms over my chest in defense. "Your beliefs don't bother me."

"Hmm." Noah pushes out his lips, seemingly not convinced.

"What did you think? That I was just lying in bed, dreaming about you? Yeah, right."

"You're a terrible liar," Noah says, looking me over. "You know I can see right through you."

"I'm not lying."

"And I'm not Noah," he deadpans back.

"And does *Noah* have a point?"

Noah's face shifts, his expression growing serious. "I wondered what your thoughts were this weekend. That's it."

And it kills me that he pronounced weekend like it was two separate words. He slowly drew it out.

The words.

His statement.

Everything about Noah is slow and decisive.

"I thought about a lot of things," I say as the tardy bell goes off.

Mr. Johnson passes out an assignment for us to work on during class.

"So, you thought about your time here?" Noah asks, apparently not done with the conversation.

"Yeah."

"What about that time you saw me naked?" Noah whispers.

"*Mostly* naked," I clarify.

"Did you think about that?"

"Of course not."

"What about when you sat on my lap in bed?" he asks, his eyes finding mine.

"Are you seriously asking me that?"

"Yes," he replies.

"It didn't come to my mind."

"What about yesterday? You asked me about … wings."

"Consider it irrelevant. Nothing will change things," I say, shaking my head.

"And what about last night?"

I suck in an unsteady breath, not sure what last night meant. The sweats. The tears. The dream. The … *hug*.

"I don't know, Noah. Do you?"

Noah bites the inside of his cheek, his lips pulling to the side. "Well, what about the thought of having me fully? Now that you're staying." Noah's brows weave together in uncertainty.

My mouth slips open at the thought of having Noah. Fully having him.

I can't even imagine it.

"It hasn't crossed my mind," I say back.

"Pity."

"Is it? Why would I want someone who only wants me because it's convenient?" I growl.

"I wouldn't call these circumstances convenient," Noah says, exasperated.

"What would you call them?"

"Predetermined," Noah replies.

I raise my eyebrows at him before pulling my attention back to our assignment.

I keep my head down and focus on the assignment—*and not Noah*—until the bell goes off. I look up as it rings out, not sure how that even happened. It felt like we were only in class for maybe fifteen minutes. I close my textbook, putting it into my bag.

"I can see that you're frustrated. You've got a lot of tension in you," Noah says as we walk out of class.

"Is it that obvious?" I ask as I make my way to my locker.

"Yes. It's very clear. Especially when you spend the entire class ignoring me."

"I wasn't ignoring you."

"No?"

"No. And no amount of flirting or teasing me is going to change that."

"You're just saying that because you're tense," Noah says, his hands coming down onto my shoulders. He rubs his thumbs into my skin, quickly finding a knot.

A moan escapes my mouth. Noah's hands on me feel amazing, and I have to focus all of my energy on not letting my eyes roll back.

"See," he says, spinning me around to face him. "Two seconds with my hands on you, and you've already loosened up."

"That little nervous knot was put there by you!" I try not to shout.

Noah grins. "Nervous knot. I like that. I might have to start calling you my nervous knot." He's beaming, and it makes it hard not to smile back at him.

"It's kind of fitting," I agree with a laugh.

But then I catch myself.

"This nervous knot is fine on her own. Okay? Like you said, stand on my own feet."

"I know what I said. But think about it, Mal. Two seconds with my hands on you, and your eyes are rolling. Imagine what might happen if you gave me a few more seconds. Or minutes even. I think I could work out a lot of that tension," Noah says, towering in front of me.

"In my shoulders?"

"To start with." Noah gives me a lopsided smile and then walks off down the hall, leaving me in a puddle. An unwound, loose, knotless puddle that can't feel her legs.

Messing with me.
LATIN

I CAN STILL feel Noah's hands on my shoulders as I sit down in class. It amazes me how he manages to somehow find the center of my problem. And he makes fixing it so easy. If I'm struggling with classwork, he helps me. If I'm sad, he tries to cheer me up. If I'm angry, he finds ways to get the energy out of me. And apparently, when I'm nervous, his hands on me really do help.

But I kind of wish that they didn't.

And that he wasn't always right.

But somehow, Noah always finds a way to fix things. I just don't know if he realizes yet that so many of my problems would be fixed if things were different between us.

"I can't believe you cried last night. And this morning. It sort of feels like all my efforts went to shit," Mohammad says, sliding into the seat next to mine.

I push Noah out of my mind, focusing on Mohammad.

"Wait, you knew I cried last night?" I ask, connecting our eyes.

"It was obvious after you said good-bye to Noah. Your eyes were all red."

"You never said anything."

"I didn't know if you wanted to talk about it with Olivia and Naomi there," Mohammad replies.

"I'm sorry if I put a damper on your efforts. I didn't mean to."

"Are you two good now? I mean, this morning, you were talking. You looked uncomfortable though," Mohammad asks as he pulls out his notebook.

"He's messing with me again," I confide, pursing my lips.

Mohammad lets out a sigh. "He wants you."

I shake my head.

"He wants to play with me," I clarify. "At least, I think he does."

"Kinky." Mohammad grins.

"Not kinky," I disagree.

Mohammad's eyes move up toward the corner, like he's working through his thoughts. "Well, you aren't dating Harry. You aren't dating anyone."

"Thanks for the reminder."

"It's a good thing. Get kinky with Noah. Sort things out. See what happens. Just be sure before you do," Mohammad warns.

"Be sure of what?" I tilt my head at him.

"Well, preferably wait until after Harry's thing tonight, seeing as you agreed to be his date. And be sure. You don't want to fuck around with them. Despite the whole *date who you want* agreement, I don't believe it will last."

I let out a sigh.

"You're very encouraging today, and I appreciate that. But you also just contradicted your previous advice," I point out.

"All right, maybe a bit," Mohammad admits.

"A bit?" I laugh.

"Look, get kinky with whoever. Just make sure it's only with one of them," Mohammad insists.

"Says the guy with two dates tonight!" I cry out. "And seriously, you know I wouldn't hook up with both of them." I flare my eyes at him, annoyed he'd even think I would.

"I know you have feelings for both of them," Mohammad says pointedly.

"It's not the same."

"Then make that clear," he insists. "Besides, if there's going to be any kink in your future, you'd better figure it out."

I frown because Mohammad's right. Despite their whole *date who you want* and *take time to figure things out* agreement, the second I kiss one of them again, everything will change.

"I've always thought of Noah as a friend. Even when I wasn't confused about how I felt, I never imagined him as …"

"As what?"

"As ... I don't know. Mine. As a boyfriend. As someone who could be only for me. Does that make sense?"

"Nope," he replies blankly.

"We've been close. But it's been as friends. But at the same time, he's hot. Really hot. And right now, it's pretty upsetting."

"His hotness?" Mohammad asks, trying to piece together what I'm saying.

"Exactly. Wait, no. I'm upset that he's being unclear about his sexy comments."

"Sexy comments? Give me an example."

"*Do you think about when you saw me naked*?" I state, repeating one of Noah's many questions.

"I haven't seen you naked," Mohammad starts, but then the lightbulb goes off. "Oh shit ..."

"Yep." I nod in agreement. "Anyway, I really loved last night. I appreciate you and Naomi planning it. I was surprised in a really good way."

I lean over my desk and give Mohammad's arm a heartfelt squeeze.

"It was bomb. I'm pretty jealous you get to live in a hotel," Mohammad says as the bell goes off.

"Well, you're practically living there with me," I say with a laugh. Because Mohammad might *actually* be in the hotel room more than me.

"Speaking of which, we need to talk about tonight."

"What do you mean?" I ask, confused.

"I've been thinking about what we should do after Harry's thing," Mohammad whispers to me as class starts.

"I didn't know there would be an after," I whisper back.

"Oh, for sure. I'll tell Mum I'm staying over with Harry or Noah, but I thought I could crash at your hotel. That we all could."

"Harry would probably be fine with it. I mean, depending on how his talk went with his parents last night. But Noah? I don't know. He wouldn't even stay last night."

Our professor pulls up lecture slides, flipping off the lights and turning on the projector.

"I wanted to check with you first before bringing it up at lunch," Mohammad whispers, looking between me and the front of the room.

"I'm fine with it as long as you're there," I agree, refocusing my attention on our professor.

Mohammad nods back in agreement.

Starfish bras.
ART

"I THINK MOHAMMAD is a bit salty about you ruining your farewell party last week," Noah says when I get to class.

I drop my bag onto the ground, sliding onto my stool. "What?"

"He was messaging me earlier about tonight. Wants to do something after Harry's," Noah explains.

"We just talked about it in Latin. I'm not sure if it's a good idea though." I look over at him. "Are you planning on staying at Harry's? Or is Harry staying over at your house?"

"We haven't talked about it." Noah shifts on his stool, turning his legs toward me.

"Hmm. I guess we can just figure it out at lunch. But I think Mohammad wants us to hang out at the hotel after," I say, basically repeating Mohammad. But then what Noah said comes to my mind. "Wait, what did you mean, Mohammad's upset with me?"

"He said last night that I should have stayed and turned it into a party. Apparently, he didn't get the kind of … time he wanted with Naomi."

I roll my eyes.

"Come on. He's just too chicken to ask her out. If he did, he'd get all the alone time with her that he wants. See, problem solved."

Noah lets out a warm laugh. "Have you met Mohammad? He has his own playbook and rules."

"Why won't he ask her out? I don't get it. He never has trouble with anyone else. He gets girls. You said it yourself," I point out.

Noah nods, his lips pulling to the side. "I think it's because he fancies her. It's different than what he's used to."

"Maybe," I agree.

"Besides, I think a little fairy promised him that there would be starfish bras and mermaids at your farewell party. Can you blame him for being upset about that being canceled?"

"I said that as an idea," I correct.

"Well, I liked the idea," Noah replies.

"Could you imagine? Me in a starfish bra? Mohammad would probably find a trident or something. He'd be so into it." I chuckle.

"Oh, I could imagine it." Noah smirks.

"The only problem is, I don't have long red hair. And I'm not curvy, like a mermaid. Aren't they supposed to be bronzed and beautiful, sitting on rocks, distracting men or something like that?"

"No, silly. That's a siren. Mermaids are just mermaids."

"So, they just go about their day underwater? No calling to men or wrecking ships involved?" I grin.

"Luckily for them and the men, no."

"Hmm." I glance around the classroom, trying to imagine what it would be like if this were all underwater. "So, I could be a mermaid?"

Noah rests his chin against his palm, bringing his elbow onto the table. "If you could breathe underwater."

"And had a tail," I add, going through the mermaid requirements.

"Exactly," Noah agrees.

"And you could be a merman!" I smile at him.

"Oh, fuck no." Noah vigorously shakes his head.

"Oh, yes. If I have to be one, then you have to be one too," I insist.

"Is that right?"

"Come on. If not, who would I argue with? I'd die of boredom," I say as Mrs. Jones closes the door.

I glance at Noah, and he shakes his head, disagreeing with me as Mrs. Jones starts speaking.

"Open up to chapter twelve. We're going to start reading about ceramics." She walks over to the far wall of the classroom, motioning to a shelf filled with various clay figures. "I'd like for you to read through the chapter today and tomorrow during class. I'm also going to pass out clay and sculpting tools for you to practice with. When we're back from break, you will each start a ceramics project."

Mrs. Jones is beaming as we all flip open our textbooks. She waves a few students out of their seats, instructing them to pass out pieces of clay and tools to each table.

"So, you'd want me in the sea with you?" Noah asks while examining the clay while I flip through the chapter, finding a picture showing the various tools that we will be using.

"Well, yeah. I'd need someone to talk to, right?"

"You'd have the entire sea at your disposal. Seahorses to

play with. Starfish bras to make. I think you'd keep plenty busy."

"A girl could only play with seahorses and weave together starfish bras for so long before getting bored."

"Can you imagine us arguing underwater?" Noah laughs, his eyes sparkling.

"It would be just a bunch of bubbles coming out of our mouths. It would be so funny."

"I can't imagine myself with a tail," Noah admits, shaking his head.

"Really? I can. You'd make a good merman. I mean, you could always be shirtless. You could float around as you pleased. You'd get to see me every day, wearing a starfish bra *and* playing with seahorses." I tilt my head, pointing out the obvious appeal.

"Are you trying to convince me to become a merman?" Noah's chest vibrates as he laughs.

"Pretty much. Didn't you ever used to play in your bath?"

"Are you asking me if I used to pretend to be a merman in the bathtub as a child? Because I feel like you should know the answer to that."

"And what's the answer?" I tease.

Noah raises his eyebrow and shakes his head.

"Aw. No fun." I pout.

"Did you?"

"Not at all," I admit, grabbing the clay from Noah's hands. It sticks on my fingers, and I wrinkle my nose. "I wasn't big into imaginary games."

"You're too literal for that, huh?" Noah asks, studying me.

"Pretty much. Even as a child, I was practical and pretended to have a job—playing doctor. Teacher. Chef. I couldn't even come up with being a mermaid. Isn't that sad?" I look at Noah, dropping the clay back onto the table.

"Nah. Everyone has different talents."

"Mine just aren't art-related. Unlike you and Mia," I say, the drawing Mia gave me yesterday coming to mind. "Speaking of which, want to see one of your sister's creations?"

I glance back at Mia. She's got her head down in the textbook, looking between the book and our tools with determination. I turn back to Noah with a grin and open my notebook.

I pull out the sketch and hand it to him. Noah's eyes widen as they scan across the sheet. He snaps his head toward me.

"Is this what you think of me?" Noah asks, gaping at the drawing.

"Mia drew it!" I laugh, grabbing it back from him. "It's pretty accurate, don't you think?"

Noah rolls his eyes. "Apart from the hair," he states. "Did you ask her to draw you this?"

"No. It was a gift. But I might have provided the inspiration," I admit.

"Really?" Noah asks with interest.

"I was comparing you to Medusa on one of your off days," I explain. "And Mia thought it was so funny that, apparently, she had to draw it."

Noah brings his eyes to mine. "So, that's what I look like when I get upset, huh?"

"Basically." I nod.

Noah frowns at the paper. "Attractive. Very attractive."

"At least the snakes have matching scowls," I offer, looking at the little snakes as his hair. "They're kind of cute."

Noah weighs his head back and forth, like he thinks my comment was actually serious.

"I suppose at least I'm not the only one scowling," Noah agrees.

I slide the drawing back into my notebook for safekeeping.

"I think you should give me that. You shouldn't be allowed to hold on to something that portrays me in such a negative light."

Noah holds his hand out to me. I look between his hand and his serious expression and laugh.

"I am *never* giving this up. Besides, I could use her drawing as inspiration for our sculpting project."

"Are you mocking me?" Noah asks, his mouth slipping open.

"*No*," I tease. Even though I completely am.

"Well then," he says, rolling up his sleeves as he picks up the clay, "maybe my sculpture will be of a mermaid who has a striking resemblance to you. Dark hair. Seahorse companion. Starfish bra and all."

Noah smirks at the clay, looking way too devious. And very, very serious.

"You wouldn't."

Noah looks up to me and smiles.

"Would you?" I ask.

Noah doesn't say anything. He just pulls open his notebook and spends the rest of class sketching out mermaids.

Made my demands.
LUNCH

"YOU CANNOT MAKE me into a mermaid," I beg when class is over.

"I'm not making any promises." Noah shrugs, looking way too amused.

"Noah, that's mortifying," I groan.

"And you having a drawing of me, made by my own sister, insinuating that I'm Medusa isn't?" He holds my gaze, wanting to prove his point.

"Fine. If I cough up the drawing, then you have to promise not to make the mermaid sculpture. Or any other sculpture related to me for that matter. Deal?"

I extend out my hand, holding my pinkie finger up in the air. Noah glances at my hand before looking down the hallway.

"No deal. But it was a good try." He smiles.

"Do you get pleasure in torturing me?" I mumble, pulling back my hand. I try not to stomp next to him, but it's hard when he's being annoying.

When he won't just do what I want.

"Yes. I get an enormous amount of pleasure out of teasing you," Noah says, raising his eyebrows at me as we get to the lunchroom.

Mohammad and Harry are already at our usual table. Mohammad is seated on the other side of the table though, opposite where he usually sits.

When we get to the table, Noah sits down next to me instead.

"Finally," Mohammad says, looking up from his tray. "Okay, so here's the plan."

"I thought we were supposed to decide on a plan together?" I cut in, looking between Mohammad and Harry.

Harry shrugs, taking a drink of soda.

Mohammad ignores me. "I'm going to come by your hotel before the party. I'll bring my uniform for tomorrow. I already talked to Mum. She's fine with me staying the night." He grins.

"With me?" I ask, my forehead creasing.

"No. With Harry," Mohammad corrects.

"Why are you bringing your uniform to the hotel?" I ask, trying to follow along.

"Because staying at Harry's is just an excuse," Mohammad replies.

"Wait, Noah, are you staying?" Harry asks, looking up.

Noah looks back and shakes his head. "Mum texted me. They've decided they aren't going, and she said she wanted me back home after, as it's a school night. Mia's been throwing a fit about us getting equal treatment or something," Noah says, pulling out his lunch.

I quickly remember that I need to go get my own, but Noah pulls out two sandwiches, handing me one.

"But she did invite you all to stay at the house."

"We'll just figure it out later," Harry says, popping open his bag of chips.

"How are things at the house?" Mohammad asks Harry.

Harry's blue eyes slip to Mohammad. "It's a fucking nightmare. They were already setting up this morning. Our house smells more like a floral shop than a house. It's like they think if they woo everyone with champagne and hors d'oeuvres, then they might suddenly forget about the small fact that my dad's abusive."

Noah looks concerned.

"Maybe your dad thinks the smell of flowers will cover his tracks," Mohammad offers.

I set down my sandwich, not feeling good about tonight. Not feeling good about any of it.

"Harry, are you sure you want to be there tonight?" I ask.

"I *have* to be there," Harry replies, bringing his eyes to mine.

"I'm sure Helen could call your mom. She could tell your parents this is ridiculous. Mohammad's parents have to agree,"

I say, looking to Mohammad for support.

Mohammad swallows his food before hesitantly looking at us. "I haven't mentioned all of that to them exactly."

"What?" I almost shout.

"My parents wouldn't take the news well. I wouldn't be allowed over there anymore," Mohammad replies.

"Thank you for thinking about me," Harry says to me. "But it will be fine. Maybe it will bring us closer as a family or something."

"Do you actually believe that?" I ask seriously.

"Who knows? The worst that can happen is I don't let my parents down, and we get some free champagne and then bail when my parents turn their attention away." Harry looks at me like he's waiting for me to agree.

"Okay." I nod.

"Good," he says, grabbing his soda. "Speaking of the party, I told my parents not to invite Olivia."

"Really?" Noah asks with interest.

"Look, this whole thing is a fucking charade. I don't even want you lot there, honestly. I find it repulsive, what my parents are doing. But I know that I'm going to need you there. All of you. But I don't need her there," Harry says seriously.

"We'll be there to support you," Noah replies.

I nod in agreement.

Harry's eyes flash with pain, causing Mohammad to pat his shoulder.

"Sorry I've been talking about it like it's just some party. I was being a prick."

"Nah," Harry replies. "I'm just nervous."

Noah speaks up. "You know Mia will be there as well. She's going with Sophia and her parents."

"You had your talk with your parents last night, right?"

Mohammad asks Harry.

"Yeah. I'd rather not spoil lunch with talk of it." Harry pushes his tray away from him. "Let's discuss it tonight. What time are you supposed to come round?"

"Half past seven," Noah answers.

"Right. Come at seven o'clock. I'll explain everything then," Harry says.

"Sounds good," I reply.

"You should have seen the sunrise this morning," Mohammad says, changing the subject.

Noah extends out part of his sandwich, offering it to Harry. He won't take it at first, but Noah doesn't pull his hand back. Finally, Harry accepts it and takes a bite. He chews a few times before swallowing it down with a gulp of soda.

"You were up early enough to see it?" Harry asks with disbelief.

"Yeah, Mallory woke me up," Mohammad starts, but I cut him off.

"To watch the sunrise. I've got a great view overlooking the park."

"Yeah …" Mohammad says, his forehead creasing. "Anyway, it was spectacular. I could get used to that hotel."

"What are you going to do when I move?" I tease.

Mohammad rolls his eyes, clearly not thrilled with the idea. "Just let me live happily in denial for now, okay?"

"When are you moving out?" Harry asks me.

"I'm not sure. Whenever my parents buy a place, I guess."

Noah slides me a bag of carrot sticks as he pulls out an apple for himself.

"So, what color was it?" Noah asks.

"What color was what?" Mohammad says, looking up from his chicken.

"The sunrise," Noah says.

"Pink," I answer, thinking back to this morning. "Almost iridescent. Beautiful."

"It was." Mohammad nods his head in agreement.

"Bollocks," Harry declares. "Now, I'm jealous. Why couldn't I have been invited round to see the pink sunrise?" He pushes out his lips and tries to look between Mohammad and me with pathetic puppy-dog eyes.

But it takes everything in him not to crack a grin.

"Would you have woken up if we'd called you?" I raise my eyebrows at Harry, bringing a carrot stick to my mouth.

Because I'm pretty sure I know the answer.

"Probably not. But I could have at least seen the missed calls and felt included," he replies, placing his hand over his supposedly crushed heart. He must not be too upset though because there's a smile resting on his lips.

"I promise to call next time." I laugh.

"And what about now? I'm gutted about missing out." Harry continues to pout.

Mohammad just laughs at him. "Let's plan on watching it. All of us, together."

"Let's do it," Noah agrees as the lunch bell goes off.

We clear off the table, and Harry and Noah walk next to one another down the hallway. I wrap my hand through Mohammad's arm, walking in step with him.

"I heard that you were upset about the farewell party being canceled," I say, bringing up what Noah told me in Art.

"I wasn't upset," Mohammad says, his voice faltering.

"Why didn't you tell me?" I ask.

"Do you and Noah have to talk about everything?" Mohammad whines.

"Apparently. Why didn't you tell me you were upset?" I ask, holding his arm tighter.

"Because I didn't want to upset you more. I was looking

forward to us all being together before you left. And since Friday, things haven't been the same. But after the weird drop-ins last night, I was over it. Shit needs to go back to normal," Mohammad says firmly.

"Yeah, but, Mohammad, you told me I needed to give them time. And Harry wouldn't have stayed anyway because of his family dinner."

"Doesn't matter. I talked to them about it," Mohammad says when we get to his locker.

"Seriously? And how did they take it?"

"Who knows? I just made my demands," Mohammad answers as he opens his locker and gets out a textbook.

"You didn't wait for an answer?"

"Of course not," Mohammad replies, closing his locker. "I made my demands, and they were final. No questions."

I tilt my head at him, trying to imagine Mohammad demanding *anything*. Let alone from Harry or Noah.

Normal isn't good.
GEOGRAPHY

I WAVE AT the girls before I sit down, and then I turn back to face Harry in Geography.

"Did Mohammad demand that things go back to normal?" I ask, butterflies forming in my stomach.

Harry's blue eyes flash up to mine. "Don't worry about that."

It's all he says, but it's answer enough.

"I never want you to feel pushed," I reply, immediately feeling guilty.

"Trust me, I never do anything that I don't want to do,"

Harry replies with a cocky grin.

"Even for Noah or Mohammad?" I question, not convinced.

"All right, maybe for them," Harry admits. "But I was glad when he brought it up."

"You were?"

"Yeah." He nods. "I'm glad that you're going to be there tonight. And thank you for agreeing to be my date."

Harry doesn't drop my eyes, and my heart speeds up at his gaze.

"Don't worry about it," I reply, clearing my throat. "Honestly, I'm happy that I can be there for you."

"Speaking of that ..." Harry says, biting his lip.

"What's wrong?"

"About the whole Olivia thing. My mum *did* want to invite her family, but I asked her not to. I sort of said that it would be weird for you, as my girlfriend, having my ex there."

"You told your parents I was your girlfriend?" I ask, my voice rising in surprise.

"I know I shouldn't have lied. I just felt cornered," Harry replies. He nervously taps his fingers against his desk.

His eyes come back up to mine.

"You know that this has nothing to do with Olivia, right?" I ask quietly. "It has to do with you blaming her for things that happened in the past. That isn't fair, Harry."

"I know. And I talked to her about her family, like you suggested."

"How did it go?"

"It was hard."

My eyes want to slip over to Olivia, but I keep them on Harry instead. "Why?"

"We were together for a while. Of course I feel bad that she's hurting. But it also doesn't feel like my place anymore."

"Since you're not together?"

"Yeah."

I nod, understanding where Harry is coming from.

"But you *could* be friends. You could talk and be there for one another without being together," I offer.

"That's what you think we should do?" Harry's eyes come up to mine, his jaw setting in place.

"Yes," I answer.

Harry glances in Olivia's direction as he starts to speak. "Last night, my parents told me that they liked Olivia and were disappointed I ended things with her. That having a steady girlfriend shows my maturity."

"Oh …" I say, piecing things together. "Is that why you told them about me?"

"It doesn't matter what I do. If I were still with her, they would say she was a distraction from school. Nothing is ever good enough. But I shut them up when I said that I actually do have a girlfriend and that you'd be there with me. I'm sorry."

Harry pushes his hands through his blond hair, and it's easy to see he's upset with himself.

"Don't worry about it. I did say that I would be your date," I reply, wanting to perk him up. Even though he lied to his parents about us dating, I understand why he did it. "I just don't want to make it more confusing for us, you know?"

"I know." Harry nods. "Part of me hoped that I'd be the boy who got his shit together for a girl. Now, I'm starting to wonder if I'll be forced to do it for my father instead."

"You should do it for yourself."

"My dad couldn't hide his disappointment last night." Harry shakes his head. "All of this, it's my doing. We have to put on a show as a family because I couldn't keep my mouth shut. Because I didn't do a good enough job of hiding my discontentment."

"What did they want you to do?" I ask, growing upset. "Put makeup over your black eye? Not tell your mom the severity of the situation?"

Harry lets out a sad laugh. "Mum sat there the entire time, agreeing with every single thing my father said."

"I thought this was just a show for her too? I thought she was on your side?"

"Apparently not. I shouldn't have expected differently, and I never should have trusted her. Now, I wish I had never told her. At least things would be normal then," Harry admits as the bell goes off.

"Normal isn't good, Harry."

"The worst fucking part is, tonight, I'm sure my dad will wrap his arm around my shoulders, acting like we're close. I've stood in front of the mirror, pretending he's there with his arm around me. Practicing not to flinch. He'll praise me, laugh at jokes I never spoke." Harry swallows, looking down at the desk. "And part of me is scared I'll want that affection. What if I like it? It's what I've always wanted, right? I know that it's a lie, but I lied about you. What does that say about me?"

Harry looks at me, his eyes swirling with confusion.

I can see the conflict all over his face.

He's scared that his dad will give him attention and that he will actually like it.

That in some messed up way, he'll justify it to himself.

I grab on to Harry's hand.

"It says that you're human. You're someone who wants to be loved by his parents. It makes you normal," I reply.

Harry gives me a sad smile and quickly squeezes my hand before pulling back. He puts his palms on my shoulders, turning me toward the front of the classroom as Mr. Pritchard starts class.

Harry continues our conversation, now whispering in my ear, "I'm not normal though. I'm a Brooks. And in exchange for my name, I had to give up the expectation of love. Everything in my family is a business deal. A transaction. Nothing is a gift or given freely. I've had to learn that."

"But you have us," I say, glancing back at him. "And we'll be there for you. Always."

"I know," Harry whispers back. "It's the only thing that keeps me sane, honestly."

I nod but don't say anything because Mr. Pritchard glances in our direction. I seal my lips shut, drop my gaze back down to my notebook, and try not to think about tonight.

What I want.
YOGA

"OH MY GOD, I've been dying to talk to you alone all day," Naomi says, rushing up to me in the changing room before class.

"We just had Geography together." I laugh, forcing Harry and our conversation out of my mind.

"Yes. With *Harry*," Naomi says, like I should know better.

"Okay. What's up?" I ask, taking a sip of water.

"Mohammad kissed me," she blurts out.

I choke on the water in my mouth and end up in a coughing fit.

"What?!" I finally get out when my throat clears.

"Yes!" Naomi grins.

"When?" I ask, sitting down.

"This morning. When we were watching the sunrise," she

gushes. "It was *magical*."

"Magical?" I repeat, completely shocked.

"When you never came back, I wondered if it was going to be awkward. But it wasn't awkward at all! We started talking, and I finally went for it." Naomi grins.

"Wait, you kissed him?" I lean my back against the lockers, needing more support.

"Yeah." She glances around us, lowering her voice. "I know that Olivia's been telling you that if you feel something for Noah, you have to do something about it. That you have to tell him how you feel. So, I decided that her advice was right. If I fancy Mohammad, I might as well do something about it. I might as well kiss him. Show him what I want."

"I'm so proud of you for making the first move." I smile, melting a little at her words.

"I'm glad too. Mohammad seemed surprised at first. I could tell he was hesitant. I was too." She flushes. "But then he started kissing me back, and *oh!* It was perfect. He has the lushest lips."

She's practically radiating.

"I'm so excited to see him tonight," she goes on, moving to her locker.

She pulls open her gym bag and starts to change, but suddenly, all I can think about is tonight. And how Mohammad's mom will be there. And that he already has a date.

"Have you two talked about tonight?" I ask, hoping that he told her.

She shakes her head. "Since Olivia's family wasn't invited, I didn't want to bring it up."

"Is she upset about that?" I don't know why I feel so guilty that she won't be there, but I do.

I know it's Harry's decision on who he invites, but I wish that he would just let her come. Everyone else is going to be there, and I can't imagine it being easy for her, knowing that. But at the same time, as Harry said, this isn't just *some* party. This is a show his family is putting on, and he only wants us there for support.

"I think she was surprised. And hurt," Naomi admits. "But it's probably better this way. I think she wants to move on, and the more that they're pushed together, the harder that will be for her."

"That's probably true," I agree. "Where is Olivia anyway?"

"She had an appointment she forgot about. Left after Geography," Naomi explains as we change.

"Did you tell her that you and Mohammad kissed?" I ask, pulling on my yoga pants.

Naomi nods, her whole face radiating again. "I told her right after we left your hotel."

"Was she proud of you?" I grin.

"She actually was." Naomi smiles back at me.

Slightly defenseless.
DETENTION

YOGA GOES BY quickly with Olivia gone, and after class, I rush to change back into my uniform for detention. I look around for Naomi but don't find her. Which is probably for the best. I think if I saw her again, I might spill about Mohammad having a date tonight. Not because I want to hurt her feelings, but because I want her to know that Mohammad likes her back. That he's been asking about her for days. But it's also not my place. And if I told her, it would probably just make things worse. It would make Mohammad look like he's lying—which he sort of is, but still, I understand why.

I grab my bag and am in the library in no time. Mrs. Bateson isn't at her desk, so I head straight to the staff room. Noah isn't here yet, but I find Mrs. Bateson hunched over a cart filled with books.

When the door closes behind me, her head snaps up.

"Good afternoon." I smile and set my bag down on the desk.

"I've got quite the load for you," she replies. And she actually sounds excited.

I walk over to the overly full cart.

"Lots of returns?" I ask.

"We've been gifted a private collection," Mrs. Bateson explains, proudly looking over the books.

"That's great," I say as the door creaks open. I look toward the sound and watch as Noah joins us.

His brown hair is still wet from a shower. Apart from his hair, he looks just like he did before he had football.

His tie is set tightly at his neck, and he has his blazer on over his white button-down. There isn't a single part of him that is out of place. Noah's eyes meet mine before moving to Mrs. Bateson.

"I was just telling Miss James that the library has received a rather generous donation of books to add to its collection," Mrs. Bateson says to Noah. "We added them to the system this morning, and I'd like for you to double-check the information before you shelve them."

"Okay," Noah replies.

Mrs. Bateson nods approvingly.

"Come by the desk when you're finished, and you'll be done for the day," she says before leaving.

Noah's quick to move, and I watch as he rolls the cart close enough to the desk to start scanning the books.

"Someone seems motivated," I say, pulling out the chair next to his.

"I don't really care about this," Noah admits, looking over the information on the computer screen.

"But you've been so meticulous about getting our tasks done all week."

I take the book after he's checked the information and start a pile on the floor.

"Nothing better to do. It keeps my mind occupied and stops it from wandering," Noah says, keeping his eyes on the screen.

"What, are you afraid of what you might think about?" I tease as he hands me another book.

Noah's eyes come to meet mine for a brief moment, and there isn't any hint of amusement in them. "Sometimes."

I chew on my lip, surprised by his seriousness.

"How come?" I ask as he grabs another book and scans it.

He double-checks the information before handing it to me. But when I try to grab it, he keeps it in his grip. We both sit, holding on to the book.

"Because I'm stuck here with you. And I'm coming to realize that I'm slightly defenseless."

"In regard to me?" I laugh nervously.

"Are you laughing at me?" Noah asks, his mouth falling open.

"Yeah, I am." I grin.

"I see that." He shakes his head and finally lets go of the book.

"So, why are you defenseless?" I ask seriously, adding the book to the stack.

Noah glances at me, but he doesn't say anything.

He doesn't look like he's going to crack.

"I thought we said we'd talk," I push, shoving his words

back at him.

Noah rolls his eyes as he grabs another book.

"It's like I've had an equation floating through my mind, and just when I think I have solved it, I realize that I underestimated some variables and their impact."

I raise my eyebrows at him.

Noah thinks so differently from anyone I've ever met, and the way he explains his thoughts is both beautiful and unique. But it can also be a little confusing.

"So, what variable did you underestimate?" I ask as he hands me another book.

"It's not so much a question of what, but who," Noah replies.

"So, your equation is about people?"

I stand up and make Noah switch seats with me, so I can check the information.

"I guess."

"I thought you were the one who told me people couldn't be put into boxes. I'm assuming that means they also don't fit into equations."

Noah's forehead creases at my statement. But a second later, his mouth is curling up into a smile. It spreads all the way up to his eyes, causing them to crease.

"You really do surprise me sometimes." He chuckles.

"Sometimes, I surprise myself. Who knew I was so full of wisdom?" I laugh too.

AFTER WE GET all the books checked, we load them back onto the cart.

"You're Harry's date tonight," Noah says as we leave the staff room.

My stomach does a flip at his words.

"I am because he asked," I explain, glancing at Noah.

"I know." Noah pushes the cart down an aisle and starts to unload it. "I wasn't surprised he asked you."

"You knew he would?"

Noah shrugs. "I thought he might."

I grab a book, flipping it over in my hands. "Harry told his parents that I was his girlfriend. I'm not, but he explained that his mom asked about Olivia and was disappointed when she heard they broke up. I guess one thing led to another."

"I think the idea of dating someone who his mum felt comfortable calling and trying to influence spooked Harry," Noah admits.

"It would freak me out," I agree.

"So, are you saying that my mum hasn't rung you to try and straighten me out?" Noah says, his voice lightening.

"Do you need to be straightened out?" I laugh.

"Nope," Noah says, pushing out his lips as he shakes his head.

I smile at him.

"Mmhmm. Say what you want, but we both know that you do." I shake my head and shelve a book.

"I don't know what you're talking about, Mal. I'm a good boy, aren't I?" Noah says, encroaching on my space. He's wearing a knowing smile on his face as he looks down at me.

"Depends on the day," I fire back.

"That's probably fair."

"So, are you nervous about tonight?" I ask, my mind moving to Harry.

To meeting his family.

"Not really. Are you?"

I swallow, trying to push down my anxiety.

"Yeah, a bit. I'm nervous to meet his parents. To come face-to-face with his dad. It's going to be hard."

Noah runs his hand back through his hair, his lips pulling

into a flat line. "You just have to focus on being there to support Harry. Don't worry about anything other than him. At least, that's what I try to remind myself to do," Noah says.

"You're right. It just feels wrong. I don't know if I can think of one good thing about tonight."

"We'll all be there," Noah offers.

"We were all at lunch together," I counter.

Noah's eyes shift up to the corners as he thinks. "What about ... seeing me in a suit?"

"I'm going to see you in a suit?"

"Mmhmm." Noah nods. "Mum had it pressed yesterday."

"What color is it?"

"Black," Noah answers.

"I remember when you wore all black at Harry's that one night. It was a little unearthly." I laugh, grabbing another book.

"That was an interesting night," Noah reflects.

And it was. It was the night that I thought Harry and I would sleep together.

It was the night that Noah asked me not to.

"What do you remember about it?" I ask him.

"Besides getting plastered, sulking, and admitting a few feelings?" Noah says easily, walking around the cart to grab a few more books.

"Besides that."

"Probably finding that lingerie." Noah's eyes flick to mine.

"It wasn't for you though," I reply, feeling slightly guilty about him having found it. And for lying about wearing it.

"I've got a good imagination." Noah grins at me.

"Well, I'm glad you have that good imagination. Because I don't plan on having you see me in lingerie anytime soon."

Noah's hand comes up to my shoulder, pushing a piece of

hair away from my face.

"You're right." Noah nods adamantly. "I think we should skip the lingerie altogether and get straight to it."

"Noah," I gasp, pushing him against the bookshelf. "Are you telling me that if you had the chance to see me in lingerie, you wouldn't want to?"

"I thought you said it wasn't for me?" Noah points out, his gaze falling down to my lips.

"It wasn't for you."

"Mal, it doesn't matter what you wear," Noah says, pulling me toward him by my wrists. "At some point, it will just come off."

"What about last night?" I ask.

"What about it?"

"We never …"

"Kissed?" Noah finishes.

"No."

"Can I ask you something, Mal?" Noah says, still holding on to my wrists.

"Sure."

I search his face, my heart speeding up in my chest.

"How often do you think people come across this?"

"Come across what?"

Noah's eyes slip down toward his hands. They're still on my arms, and he gently slides them across my skin.

"Love is abundant. I won't deny that. Connections are too. But us? It's different than that, isn't it? It's … more. A lot more."

Noah's eyes come to mine as he waits for my answer.

And for the first time, it feels like he's looking at me for guidance.

I move my eyes over his defined cheekbones, to his straight nose, and down to his rounded lips. But finally, I come back up to his eyes.

To him.

"It's one plus one equals three," I barely get out.

Noah nods. "We're tangible. I feel it so clearly when we come together. There's no denying it."

And I know what he means.

Something else is between us when we're together. There's something else there. It isn't him. It isn't me. It isn't just a connection linking us.

"Why haven't we figured out a way to … come together then?"

Noah looks down at me and swallows. "Because we're scared."

"But what about Friday? Weren't you scared then? When you told Harry how you … felt?" I ask.

Noah's lips pull to the side, and he drops my arms. "I couldn't let you leave without exploring this. Without feeling all of you. We were powerful before we ever touched. I couldn't imagine what it would be like as more."

"You think about what we would be like together?"

"Yes," he replies.

"But I thought that you … couldn't do that?" I look to Noah, confused.

"Do what?"

"Be with me."

"Because I've been upset," Noah says, understanding what I mean. He grabs the cart, moving it to the next aisle.

"Noah, Harry told me something," I say hesitantly, trying to work up the courage to finish.

Noah nods, urging me to continue.

"He told me that he thinks we should *explore* what we have."

Noah stops the cart and stares directly at me. "Do you

want that?"

I grab a book, fidgeting with it in my hands. "It seems almost overwhelming," I admit.

"That's because we've got a lot of energy set aside for one another, I think."

I put the book on the shelf as Noah grabs a stack from the cart, handing me another one.

"You mean, pent-up sexual energy?" I laugh.

"Maybe a bit." Noah grins. And it's a wide, deep grin that I don't want to look away from.

"I don't want to just hook up," I say, wanting to be clear.

Noah's brown eyes stay with me, but my stomach feels like it's going to fall out of me if he doesn't say something soon.

Finally, he says, "Neither do I."

"I don't want to hurt anyone."

"Too late for that," Noah comments, still holding my eyes.

"So …"

"So?" Noah repeats, his face softening.

I flush, not at all sure what to say or do next. I want to ask him if we should try. And what trying would even mean. What any of this means.

Noah gives me a quick smile before his gaze slips down to my legs. "Have I told you I like your tights?"

"Really?" I look down at my tights and move my leg around. Because they really aren't anything special.

"Yeah. They're cute on you." Noah nods, still looking toward the ground.

"Thanks." I smile up to him.

"You're welcome." Noah moves closer to me.

He brings his hands to my shoulders before his fingers slide up to either side of my neck. My head grows heavier in his hands, wanting to fall back. But I don't let it.

"Do you want to play a game?" I ask, flicking my eyes up to his. And I can see the disappointment in them. I know what he was going to do.

He was going to kiss me.

But I can't kiss Noah without knowing if he'll be happy or upset about it after. I need to be sure. We both need to be ready.

Because I want our next kiss to be the start of something for us. I want it to be the action that shows we belong to one another. I don't want it to be an action that seals us in the past. And I certainly don't want it to be a secret we keep hidden in the library.

"I thought we were done with games?" Noah says.

"I meant, a real game. Like Truth or Dare," I reply as I take a step back.

Noah pulls his hands off my skin, glancing around the library.

"Aren't we kind of limited here?" He smiles.

"We'll make it work," I reply.

I grab on to the cart, moving it to the last section. We only have a few books left to put away, but I don't want to leave.

"All right," he agrees.

"You first. Truth or dare?"

Noah puts a book away and says, "Truth."

I lean my back against a bookshelf, bringing my finger up to my chin as I think. "Is it true that you ... are good at chess?"

"I'm decent. But you already knew that." Noah raises his eyebrows at me.

"I was just checking to see if you'd actually be honest. All right, my turn." I grin.

"Truth or dare?" Noah asks.

"Truth."

"You were supposed to pick dare," Noah says, gently placing his hand on my back as he moves past me.

"Not up to you."

I watch as Noah squats down, finding the spot where the book belongs and then standing back up and facing me.

"Okay. What was your nightmare about?" he asks.

I turn away from him, my fears coming back.

He must have been able to see the distress on my face because he says, "You don't have to tell me."

"It was about you."

"About me?" Noah asks, his thick brows weaving together. "You had a nightmare about me?"

"Yes." I glance down to my shoes, embarrassed that I'm telling him this. I should have just lied. Or not answered. Or asked him for a dare instead.

"You've been down lately," Noah says, stepping in front of me.

"So have you," I comment.

"So, the nightmare?" Noah questions.

I move to rest my head against Noah's chest and wrap my arms around him.

He stands still for a moment but then quickly wraps his arms around me.

"It was terrible. I kept trying to find you, but I couldn't. And the worst part was, when I finally found you, it was like you didn't see me. You just looked at me like I was some memory. Like I was glass." My voice breaks with my words, but at least I said them.

Noah hugs me tighter. "That sounds … scary."

I nod against his chest. Noah pulls back and kisses me on the forehead.

"It was. But it's okay now," I say, looking up at him.

But Noah's not looking back at me like he did in the dream. He's looking back at me like he can see me. Like he hears me. Like he cares.

"Your turn," Noah says, his eyes never leaving mine.

"Truth or dare?" I ask.

"Dare," Noah says, surprising me. His fingers shift from my back down to my waist.

"I dare you to ..."

"To what?" Noah asks, looking down at me through his thick lashes.

All I can feel are his fingers pressing against my sides, and I feel like there isn't any free air in the room.

"I dare you to put a book in the wrong place."

Noah's hands slip off of my waist, but he smiles.

"Are you trying to get me into more trouble? What would Mrs. Bateson say if she saw a book out of place?" Noah says lightly.

"Do you want a truth instead?" I offer.

"Nah. I'll do it." Noah holds out a book in front of me and then sticks it into a random spot.

I smile, looking at the book. But then I read the label on the side.

"Wait, Noah. It's only out of place by, like, one spot," I say pointedly.

"Someone someday might actually want to read this book. Who am I to take that away from them?" Noah replies disapprovingly when someone walks past our aisle, pulling me out of the game.

It's then that I realize our cart is empty. We're done.

Noah must notice too.

"Do you want to finish the game later?" he asks, bringing his hands to the cart. "At the party?"

"Still some truths you want to get out of me?" I tease, grabbing the cart from him. I start pushing it toward the staff room.

"That," Noah replies after we grab our bags, "or maybe I'm just waiting for you to give me another dare."

"I just gave you a dare." I laugh, shaking my head.

"A pretty pathetic one," Noah says, tilting his head back.

"What kind of dare were you looking for?" I ask as we leave the library. I give Mrs. Bateson a wave, but she doesn't acknowledge us.

"Something more ... active," Noah says at my side.

"Active? Like what, running?" I ask when we get out of school.

"Running?" Noah laughs.

I whip my head in his direction and glare at him.

"Why don't you just tell me what you want then?" I grumble, crossing my arms over my chest. *Because if he has a better idea, then by all means, let's hear it!*

Noah moves in front of me with a smile on his lips. He uncrosses my arms and looks down at me.

"I was thinking something that involved you and me, Mal," Noah says, searching my face.

As his words settle in, my eyes fly open. I look up at him, my heartbeat speeding up in my chest.

Noah gives me a smirk. "I'll see you later for that dare, yeah?" he says, taking a backstep in the direction of his house.

I open my mouth to reply, but nothing comes out. I just stand there with my mouth hanging open, looking like a complete idiot.

Kill me.

"Uh-huh," I squeak out, my voice not cooperating. I bring my hand to my throat, trying to get it to calm down.

"Cool." Noah gives me a half-smile and then walks off.

"Cool!" I shout when my voice finally starts working again. And I instantly want to smack myself.

Because, cool?

I bring my hand up to my face, mortified. But when Noah looks back over his shoulder at me, he's still smiling.

"Cool!" he calls back.

A crazy day.
5:03PM

I WALK TO my hotel in a daze. Because tonight, I'm going to see Noah.

And Harry.

And meet Harry's parents.

And meet Mohammad's date.

And see how Naomi reacts to Mohammad having a date.

And I'm going to be Harry's date and pretend to be his girlfriend when I meet his parents, which means I'm going to have to pretend that's what we are for the entire party even though Noah will be there and he just asked me to give him a better dare that involved both of us and hopefully our bodies …

I feel like my eyes are going to pop out of my head, just thinking about tonight.

And everything that could go wrong.

Before I realize it, I'm back at the hotel.

I drop my backpack on the floor when I get to my room and have to fight off the urge to fall face-first onto my bed and pass out. Mohammad said he was coming over to get ready for the party, and who knows when he'll show up?

I pull out my phone. It's five fifteen. We're supposed to

be at Harry's at seven.

That gives me just under two hours to eat, get ready, and mentally prepare myself for the party. The mental preparation is the most important part, so I decide to do what Mohammad would do.

I draw a bath.

Last night, when I was flipping through Mohammad's book of *advice*, I came across a page that said, *When your nerves are about to get the best of you, soak them away in a bath.*

And I decide he might be right.

I fill the bath with warm water, clip my hair up, and strip off my uniform. I even light a candle for a little ambiance. But just as I sit down in the tub, my phone goes off.

Ugh.

I stand back up and grab my phone off the counter in case it's Harry or Mohammad calling. But one look at my screen tells me it isn't.

"Hey, Mom," I answer, getting back into the bath.

"Hi, sweetie. How are you?"

"Good. You?"

"Very well actually. I wanted to call and tell you that your father and I put in an offer on the penthouse I told you about," she says excitedly.

"Wait, really?" I ask, sitting up straighter in the tub.

"Yes. And we'd love for you to go see it this weekend. Do you think you'll have time for that?"

"Yeah, of course. That would be great." I smile to myself. Because if they've put in an offer, that means my parents will be here soon. And I won't have to stay in this hotel forever. Not that it's a bad thing or that I'm ever really alone. But after living at Noah's, I sort of miss living with a family.

"Good. We'll get something scheduled with the realtor and keep you posted. I've also decided we'll join the club through the spa at the Bvlgari. I'll arrange it all once we're there," she continues.

"That's exciting."

"Yes. You have been using the spa, haven't you? The gym? Pool?"

"Um, not really yet. I'm pretty busy with school. And then I have yoga class at school twice a week for exercise."

There's a long silence, and I know my mom isn't thrilled with my answer.

"Once I'm there, we'll do a consultation with one of the trainers," she replies like she's somehow fixing my situation.

Whatever situation that is.

"Okay," I agree.

"So, what are your plans? How was school today?"

"School is fine. I'm a little tired, but there's a party I'm going to tonight. I'm in the bath right now and then going to get ready here in a bit."

"Whose party?"

"Harry's parents are throwing it. It's not a big thing," I fib.

"Do you know what you'll wear?"

"Harry's sending over a dress," I answer before thinking better of it.

"Oh, darling!" my mom coos. "How thoughtful. And this is the boy you're dating, correct?"

This is the boy you're dating, correct? My mom's question echoes in my head.

"Actually, we're not together anymore. But I am going as his date tonight," I explain.

Didn't my dad tell her what happened? Shouldn't she know?

"Don't you think that sends the wrong message?" she says disapprovingly.

"And what message is that?" I ask, frustrated.

"I've got to run, dear, but have a good night. I'll have your father call you with details later." She rushes through her sentence and barely lets me say good-bye before ending the call.

I toss my phone onto my towel and sink down into the tub.

"SEE, THIS IS why I needed a key."

I open my eyes, finding Mohammad in the bathroom.

"Mohammad!" I yell, waking up with a startle.

I scramble to cover myself, but Mohammad throws me a hand towel before turning around to give me privacy. I blink a few times, trying to slow down my heart as I lay the towel across the front of me.

"I think I fell asleep," I say more to myself than Mohammad.

"Hasn't anyone ever told you that you're not supposed to sleep in the tub? You could have drowned," Mohammad scolds, peeking over his shoulder to see if I'm covered.

"Hasn't anyone told you it's polite to knock?" I reply, leaning my head back against the tub.

"I *did* knock. *You* didn't answer."

He walks out of the bathroom but is back a second later, unloading his toiletries onto the counter. He lines up his toothbrush, toothpaste, and floss. He's also got two types of cologne, hair gel, lip balm, deodorant, and who knows what else. By the time he's done, half of my counter is filled.

"Wait, what time is it?" I ask, scrambling to get out of the bath. Because if he's already here and I fell asleep …

"Whoa, whoa!" Mohammad holds his hands up in front of his face, shielding his eyes. I still have the towel covering me as I stand, but apparently, Mohammad isn't taking any chances. "It's six. You've got an hour."

I let out a breath and try to relax. But then I hear a knock at my door.

"Can you get that?" I ask.

"Yeah, but hurry up. We need to eat and then get ready!" Mohammad says before leaving the bathroom.

I step out of the bath, wrap a fluffy towel around me, and drain the water. I pat my body dry and throw on a robe.

"Did you order food?" I call out, joining him in the sitting room.

"Brought it. I didn't think we'd have time to eat out. Actually, that's not true. I knew we would, but I didn't want to be rushed," Mohammad corrects.

"Sounds more accurate." I grin as Mohammad comes back from the door with a garment bag in his hand.

My eyes light up with recognition.

"What is this?" Mohammad asks, holding up the bag.

"My dress for tonight. Harry said he would send over something for me to wear," I explain.

"He messengered you a dress?" Mohammad asks, his brows shooting up.

"Yeah. He said since I was going as his date, he thought it was the least he could do." I grab the bag, eager to see what's in it.

"That's not fair," Mohammad groans. "Why couldn't he send me over a new suit?"

"If I recall, you just got a new suit for tonight."

"And you're telling me you didn't have a dress you could wear?" he fires back.

"All right, fine. I probably do. But I wasn't about to argue with him. It was thoughtful."

Mohammad tilts his head, weighing my statement.

"It was," I insist.

I take the bag into my bedroom and lay it out on my bed.

There's a tag attached at the top with a note.

Can't wait to see you.
Harry x

I tuck the note into my pocket and unzip the bag, carefully freeing the dress from its encasement, and hold it out to Mohammad.

"Wow," I whisper.

It's a strapless gray-blue organza minidress with dainty silver stripes cutting across it. The top curves out in a sweetheart neckline before cinching in at the waist. It's modern but classic.

And very, very beautiful.

"Whoa," Mohammad says, eyeing the dress.

"I know."

Mohammad touches the fabric, and he looks impressed. But then he gets a determined look on his face and turns to me, clapping his hands together. "All right, game plan. Let's eat now and then get ready, so there's no chance of stains."

"Sounds like a plan," I agree, hanging up the dress.

I follow Mohammad into the sitting room. He has a takeout bag on the table, and I start emptying it out while he opens up containers and lays out the silverware. He's working with speed and precision. And he's practically glowing.

"You're buzzing. I thought Harry told us not to get excited about tonight?"

"I'm not excited about the party," Mohammad replies, pointing between two boxes. "Chicken or pasta?"

"You're not?" I ask, looking at the food. "Chicken."

"Good choice," Mohammad says, handing me the container. "And no, I'm not. Mum will be there. Harry's parents too. But I am excited to see Naomi."

"Speaking of Naomi …" I start to say, but as I take a bite

of chicken, the flavors overtake my mouth. *Am I in heaven?* "Oh my god, Mohammad. Where did you get this?"

I stare down at the delicious chicken. It's covered with a delicate lemon caper sauce, and there are roasted potatoes on the side.

"One of our restaurants," Mohammad answers, taking a bite of his pasta.

"You're going to have to be more specific," I say, inhaling another bite. "I'm talking name, location, hours, and menu."

Mohammad laughs before stealing a bite of my chicken. He pops it into his mouth, nodding in approval.

"Anyway, Naomi," I say, getting back to the conversation. I glance up to Mohammad and almost drop my fork.

Because he's blushing.

"She told you?" he asked.

"I can't believe you didn't tell me!" I reply, setting down my fork.

"It's been a crazy day," Mohammad says, like that's somehow an explanation.

"I don't know how you could just forget to mention that." I gape at him.

"It's sort of like how you forgot to mention that you're going to pretend to be Harry's girlfriend tonight," he replies.

And it takes me by complete surprise.

"Did Harry tell you that?" I ask, my forehead creasing.

"Harry and Noah," he answers.

I let out a deep sigh. "I didn't agree to *pretend* to be Harry's girlfriend."

"Then, what did you agree to?"

"Under pressure, Harry told his parents last night that I was his girlfriend. I said I was fine with him telling them that as long as it didn't make things confusing between us. I made it clear that we aren't together."

Mohammad nods, but the look of concern doesn't leave his face.

"Have you talked to Harry?" I ask, my stomach doing a flip.

"Yeah, Harry called. He asked if I would still be there tonight. He seems nervous. Noah rang too. Said he'd see us there. Asked if I was still coming here before." Mohammad takes a bite of his pasta, his eyes flicking up to mine. "So, even though you told Harry that you aren't together, have things changed? Do you think you want to be?"

I stab a potato and pop it into my mouth as I think.

"I'm doing this as his friend. And I told him that. But honestly, I'm kind of worried about it."

"You should be. Sometimes, I think you're too nice." Mohammad shakes his head at me.

"What was I supposed to do? Say, *Oh, sorry, Harry. I actually am not okay with you lying to your parents about us being together, so even though I agreed to be your date tonight I want you to tell your parents we aren't a couple on top of everything else*?" I roll my eyes. "It's not the best situation, but it couldn't be helped."

"That would have gone over terribly." Mohammad laughs, deflating the tension in the room.

I chew on another piece of potato, a smile forming on my mouth. Mohammad grins back at me before checking his watch.

"Shit. It's half past six. We need to get ready!"

Mohammad grabs the fork from my hand and pulls me up from the table and into the bathroom.

I stand next to him, doing my hair and makeup while he gets ready. I decide that with the necklace Harry gave me for my birthday and the gorgeous dress, I can't really go simple with my makeup tonight. I take extra time on my foundation, adding highlights to my cheeks and nose. On my eyes, I blend in a dark blue shadow across the lid and add a shimmering silver to the inner eye. I line them in black and take care when putting on an extra coat of mascara. I finish it all off with a creamy nude lipstick that makes my eyes really pop.

"What do you think?" I ask, turning toward Mohammad.

He's brushing his hair, but he stops to look at me.

His eyes critically scan my entire face before he replies, "It looks good. Well done."

"Good." I grin, clapping my hands together in front of me.

I decide to run the straightener over my hair and add a little shine cream to the ends. I let Mohammad change in the bathroom while I change in my room.

As I shimmy into the dress, I keep my fingers crossed that it fits.

And it does.

It fits perfectly.

I zip it up and then go out to the living room. I am sitting on the couch, pulling on my heels, as Mohammad struts out from the bathroom in his new suit.

"What do you think?" he asks, spinning in front of me. His dark hair is parted and brushed back, and his suit is perfectly tailored.

"You look dashing," I say with a grin.

"It's Mr. Bond to you," he says, his pearly whites on full display.

He shoots me a wink, looking way too happy with himself. But I have to give it to him—he looks great.

"Well, Mr. Bond," I say, standing up, "you're going to have more than a few women swooning for you tonight, looking like that."

"What can I say?" Mohammad's beaming.

I go into the closet and pull the necklace Harry got me out of the safe. I bring it back to the bedroom and open the velvet box.

"Can you do the clasp for me?" I ask Mohammad.

I step in front of the mirror and hold it up to my neck. Mohammad comes in the room and hooks it into place before looking up at my reflection. But when he finally does, his eyes go wide.

"Whoa," Mohammad says, looking me over.

"*Yeah.*" I look at my reflection.

The dress alone is beautiful. It highlights my waist, and the silver and blue threads in the dress bring out the color of my eyes. They look large and engaging with the eyeliner and extra mascara. My hair sits perfectly at my shoulders, and with the diamond necklace brushing my collarbone, I look ... captivating.

"You look stunning."

"Thank you. Harry really knows how to pick out a dress," I reply, turning to Mohammad.

"And the necklace? I haven't seen it before."

"It was a birthday gift." I shrug.

"A birthday gift? Wait ..." Mohammad sucks in a breath, examining it closer. "From Harry? That had to have cost a small fortune. It's all diamonds, right?!"

I swat Mohammad's hand away from the necklace.

"I know. I told him it was too much, but he wouldn't listen."

Mohammad looks from the necklace up to me but then glances away like he's thinking of something. His face flashes with recognition, and he pulls his eyes back to mine.

"Shit, I forgot to tell you. Not that you need it now, but I cracked Noah's locker combination," Mohammad says.

"Really?" I ask, my whole face lighting up.

"Yeah."

"So, you finally won over Ms. Adams?"

"Oh, that. No," he says, waving me off. "I gave up on her. Apparently, my sultry eyes aren't foolproof. Anyway, I followed Noah to his locker and watched. So, here's his combo."

Mohammad reaches into his pocket before handing me a piece of paper with the combination written on it.

"You're amazing," I reply, taking the paper from him.

"I know." He smiles back at me.

"Wait, why don't you think I'll need it now? Did Noah say something to you?"

"You just saw yourself in the mirror, right? If Noah doesn't crack tonight, I don't think any amount of granola bars stuffed into his locker will fix things."

"By crack, you mean …"

"I mean, make a move. It's obvious you won't," Mohammad says knowingly.

Too knowingly.

"Did he tell you that?" I say, my mouth falling open.

Mohammad gets an evil grin on his face, but he doesn't answer.

"Like you're one to talk!" I exclaim. "Naomi had to kiss you because you were too chicken. Have you even told her about your date tonight?"

"For your information, no, I haven't. But it's part of my plan," he says coolly, checking his hair in the mirror.

I roll my eyes before grabbing my jacket and a small evening bag.

"So, you have a plan now?" I ask Mohammad.

"Yes. Well, sort of."

"Okay. Let's hear it then," I say, moving to stand in front of him.

"The plan is, I'll bounce between them. I'll appease my mum and also ask Naomi out on a date. Since she's going to be there with her family tonight, it should be fine." Mohammad nods like he actually believes it.

I force my eyes shut and rub at my temples. "That's a *really* bad plan."

"Well, at least it's a plan. You, Miss America, don't even have one."

"Actually, I do."

"Really?" Mohammad questions, surprise flashing across his face.

"Really." I nod. "Things will be great tonight. We are going there to support Harry, so that's what I'm going to do. See, I have a plan."

"That's not a plan! That's one of those naive things people tell themselves when they can't face reality."

"What is my reality then?" I ask, holding out my hands. "Lay it on me."

"You look too good in that outfit for you to fool yourself into thinking that neither Harry nor Noah will notice. Because they will. And that means you'd better be careful about what type of *support* you show Harry. Especially if you feel for Noah the way I think you do." Mohammad gives me a serious look, and his tone reminds me of my mother's.

I let out a huff. "Should I change?"

Mohammad smashes his eyes shut, shakes his head at me like I'm an idiot, and then leaves me standing in the bedroom.

"I'm serious!" I call out.

I cross my arms over my chest, but Mohammad doesn't reply.

Understated.
7:10PM

EVEN THOUGH HARRY'S house isn't far, I'm not about to walk the distance in heels. Especially because we're running a little late. Mohammad texts Harry to let him know our ETA as the doorman flags down a black cab for us.

"Thank you," I tell him, getting into the car.

The ride to Harry's is short, and quickly, we're pulling onto his street. The entire road is lined with cars, and there's a steady stream of people entering his house. The cab driver pulls to a stop.

"I just messaged that we're here," Mohammad says, getting out.

A valet opens the door for me, and by the time I'm up and standing, Mohammad is at my side, ushering me into the house.

The large circular table in the entryway is filled with flowers, and the scent of them hits me the second I walk through the door. Candles are lit and bunched together on every free surface. Mohammad's mouth falls open as he looks around. I do a full circle, taking in the enchanting glow.

"Wow," I breathe out.

"Think Harry's mum might have overdone it a little," Mohammad comments.

I give him a halfhearted smile before my attention slips to a woman approaching us. She has a clipboard in her hand and clicks her pen in like she's ready to write us up and send us to detention.

"Name?" she asks.

I'm about to answer her when I hear familiar footsteps

moving down the stairs. I look up, my eyes connecting with Harry's. He rushes down the stairs, his eyes focused down on the next step in front of him. He has on a gorgeous navy suit with a white dress shirt underneath. His hair is gelled back like Mohammad's, making him look much older than he really is.

He looks perfect.

"They're my guests," Harry says, approaching us.

The woman nods once and then turns her attention to someone else coming in. Harry's blue eyes meet mine, and I can see the relief in them.

He gives me a kiss on the cheek before pulling Mohammad into an embrace. But then his jaw sets.

"Right. Let's go upstairs," Harry says, putting his hand on either of our shoulders.

He leads us up the stairs, weaving past maids and staff on the way there. When we get to the billiards room, he pulls the door shut behind us and clicks the lock into place. He practically throws himself against the door, his head falling back as his eyes slip shut.

"Are you all right?" I ask, noticing that Harry already looks completely overwhelmed.

"I'm fine. Everything's fine," he replies, his eyes pulling open. Instead of looking at me or Mohammad, he heads straight to the liquor cabinet.

Mohammad elbows me, flaring his eyes like he wants me to do something. I throw my hands up in response.

Because what am I supposed to do?

Harry pulls out the whiskey, uncorking it without effort. Mohammad gives me a worried glance before joining Harry at the bar. I watch as they line up four glasses.

Four glasses.

Which means Noah's here.

I move my gaze across the room until I find Noah. He's

seated on the couch, one leg crossed over the other. He has on a dark suit, like he said. The band collar shirt underneath buttons up all the way to his neck in European fashion, and he already has a shot glass in his hand. A bottle of alcohol stands alone on the table in front of him.

Apparently they've already started.

When I move to take off my coat, Noah finally looks at me. I pull the jacket off, letting it slip down over my arms. The air is cool on my skin, but Noah's gaze almost burns me. He sucks in his cheeks, tilting his head back as I get my coat off.

His eyes are all over me.

I can hear Mohammad adding ice to the glasses as Harry pours in the liquid. I should move. Help them. Do anything other than stand here. But I can't.

Noah's eyes move from my exposed legs up to my waist. His gaze rises to my collarbone and then to my necklace. They stop for a brief moment before finally making their way up to my eyes. And when they do, they're as dark as his suit.

I shift slightly and set my bag on the end table as I consider moving to the couch, but just as I think about it, Noah stands up. His dark eyelashes flutter as he looks down over himself, adjusting his suit.

I swallow, my throat feeling hot.

Noah walks toward me in long, eloquent strides. His presence hits me like a wall as he stands in front of me. I let my eyes take in his frame. His suit is beautiful. It rounds over his shoulders and cuts in at his waist.

It's dark. Understated.

And very, very sexy.

It's the type of outfit that screams, *I'm not asking for your attention; I'm demanding it.* It's completely annoying. And completely Noah.

"You look beautiful," Noah says, his voice breaking into my thoughts.

I glance up to him, trying to pull myself together.

"Thanks. And you look—" I start, but Harry interrupts us.

"Sorry about that," Harry says, clearing his throat. "Drink?"

Noah's still looking at me, but I break my eyes away from him and focus on Harry. Which is a good thing because he doesn't look any better than before. A thick crease is set on his forehead, and his mouth is turned down in a frown.

"Sure." I smile at him and try to be encouraging, but Harry's hand is visibly shaking as he hands me the glass. I take it from him, steadying his hand before letting go.

Mohammad follows with two more glasses and hands one to Noah.

"Cheers, mate," Noah replies.

Harry holds out his glass, skipping the toast. We all clink our glasses together.

I take two large gulps, the liquid burning. Noah does the same, his Adam's apple bobbing as he swallows. Harry finishes off his entire glass before licking his lips.

"Fuck, that's good," Harry breathes out with relief.

"It is," Mohammad agrees, taking another sip.

"Mohammad, can you put on some music? Something operatic tonight," Harry asks.

"I'm on it," Mohammad agrees.

Noah glances between Harry and me and then follows Mohammad to the couch. They both dip their heads down and look at Mohammad's phone.

"Drink up," Harry insists.

He brings my glass up to my lips, and I finish off the drink.

When it's empty, he takes the glass from me. He sets it down on the bar before coming and standing in front of me.

"Now, let me look at you," Harry says, giving me his full attention.

He takes my hand and spins me in a circle. The first one is slow and torturous because I know his eyes are all over me. But then Harry spins me again, quicker this time. I let out a stream of giggles and look up at him.

"Have fun?" Harry's smile reaches his eyes, and he beams at me.

"It *was* pretty fun," I agree with a grin.

Harry's blue eyes move from my face, down over my dress, and then back up again. "You look stunning tonight."

"I'm glad you like it. It would have been awkward if you didn't, seeing as you picked it out," I tease.

Harry bites his lip, his blue eyes squinting as he smiles.

"Could you imagine? It would have been a disaster," Harry says, going along with it.

I glance down at our outfits, realizing something.

"It actually would have been. Did you notice we match?"

"I did." Harry nods. "Coordinating outfits is an important part of being a *good boyfriend*, apparently. Or so says our stylist." He raises his eyebrows, his lips pulling flat.

"So, your stylist helped pick this out?" I glance down to my dress.

"I told her about you. She gave me a few different options appropriate for tonight, and I picked one." Harry's blue eyes stay with mine, and my heart melts a little bit.

He went to a lot of trouble to make me feel special tonight. *The necklace. The dress.*

I know he's trying to show me that he appreciates me being here.

Being his date.

But he didn't have to do this. Any of it.

I would be here with him regardless. I'm about to tell him that when Mohammad finally turns on the music. It's eerie and dramatic. Harry's expression changes as the woman's voice fills the room. He diverts his eyes, like he's being sucked into the song. Like he's being sucked away from me.

"Come," Harry says.

He places his hand on my back and leads me to the couch. As I sit down, he goes back to the liquor cabinet. He brings over our empty glasses and the entire crystal decanter of whiskey and pours everyone a refill.

"So, what happened last night?" Noah asks once we all have fresh drinks.

"He didn't tell you yet?" Mohammad asks. His question sounds judgmental, but I know he's just surprised.

"No. And if you had been here on time, you'd know that," Noah replies grumpily.

I narrow my eyes at him, not sure where the attitude is coming from.

"Seriously?" Mohammad says back. And the tension is palpable in the room.

Everyone is on edge.

"Enough," Harry booms, and we all snap our heads in his direction. "I couldn't say this twice."

Harry looks between us.

Mohammad glances at me and then sits up straighter. Noah's brows pull in so close that they almost look like they're one. I stare at Harry, my nerves getting the best of me. Because Harry looks worried.

"My parents said to get used to *this*," he says, motioning around us. But I think he's referring to everything going on downstairs. "That this party is just the start."

"Seriously?" Mohammad says with disbelief.

"Yeah. They're courting a possible client who could take things to the next level for the company. It's just another excuse though. The possible client will be here tonight as well as members of the board. They're trying to show that our *family life* is intact. Dad has meetings scheduled through early next week, but then … we're going to Shanghai."

"*We're?*" Noah repeats, his face going white.

"Apparently, that includes me," Harry says. "It's just to visit. They want me to spend part of my holiday with them there, doing the same fucking shit. They want to put on a show."

"Are you serious? What about a separation?" I ask.

"They didn't even say. They already live separate lives. What's a little longer?" Harry shrugs and takes a large drink.

"I thought your mom was going to use what happened as fuel in the divorce? Did you ask her about that?" I ask, trying to grasp at something.

Anything.

"My dad gave her a better offer. A larger percentage of the company when they split amicably."

"Harry …"

"I didn't expect anything different," he replies.

"So, you're going to Shanghai next week." Noah looks at Harry like he can't believe this is happening.

"Doesn't sound like I have a choice."

"Why do they need you there? Wouldn't it be better for them to leave you and go as a team? Or whatever they are," Mohammad mutters.

"That's the best part." Harry shakes his head, and he looks like he could cry. "They want me to take a meeting with upper management while I'm there. Dad is requiring that I work there over the summer holiday. He said it will be good for our company image and give me a chance to *grow the fuck up.*"

"Are you serious?!" Mohammad shouts.

My eyes flick over to him. I've never heard him shout before or seen him look this upset.

It causes my stomach to roll.

"Yeah, that was basically my reaction," Harry responds.

"I thought you would intern here, if anything," Noah comments, like he's trying to piece this news together in his head.

I want to tell him that you can't make sense of this, but I keep my mouth closed.

"I figured he'd make me intern after school or some shit like that or insist that I study business at uni. But no, he's sending me sooner. They'll probably divorce while I'm gone. Or he'll join me in Shanghai. Let me follow in his footsteps." Harry visibly flinches.

"I don't understand why they're rushing this. You were supposed to have a gap year," I say, finding my voice.

"Mum said that if I wasn't constantly stepping out of line, we wouldn't be in this situation." Harry's blue eyes flick up to mine. They are filled with hurt and instantly make me want to run downstairs and strangle his mother.

"Well, there goes my respect for your mom," I say through gritted teeth.

"It's grooming, I suppose. If they're going to convince people that our family is stable, then I need to be stable. I'm the future of the company after all." Harry's voice is hollow and empty.

I shake my head and let out an unsteady breath.

I need to do what Noah said.

I need to stay calm for Harry.

I need to be here for Harry.

I need to focus on him and how he's doing.

Not on myself. Not on my anger toward his parents. Toward this situation.

"Harry, how do you feel about all of this?" I ask hesitantly.

"I'm …" Harry struggles.

"Please don't say fine," Noah cuts in.

Harry glances up to him and nods.

"I feel … like I've been strung up, and I'm being pulled in every which direction. Fuck my parents and what they want. It's bollocks, what they're asking of me. To lie. To pretend our family is fine. But what can I do? What if I ruin everything to spite them? What if I ruin my future? I have to go along with it—at least for now." Harry works through his thoughts as he says the words, and we all listen intently.

Noah finally nods, and my heart wants to break for Harry. Because I know that he's going to accept this.

But he shouldn't.

And I know that Noah, being Noah, is going to be there for Harry.

And that he's going to ask that of me too.

Be there for Harry. No matter what.

But the fact that he's in this situation, it makes me want to break in two.

A tear slips from the corner of Harry's eye, and a second later, Noah is sitting between us, hugging him. Mohammad looks to me, choked up himself. I force my eyes to remain dry, keeping myself composed.

When Noah pulls away, he stands up and pulls Harry and me with him. He motions for Mohammad to get up, too, and drags us all together into a hug.

"No matter what, you have this." Noah presses his forehead against Harry's as we all wrap our arms tighter around one another.

"What a fucking disaster." Harry sniffles. He wipes his nose with the back of his hand, glancing away.

"Can't argue with you there," Noah agrees.

Mohammad stays silent. I give him a quick smile, hoping that he's all right. He smiles back at me, but it isn't up to his usual brightness. And I can't blame him for not mustering up a better smile.

"What's the time?" Harry asks.

Mohammad grabs his phone, breaking us apart. "Eight o'clock."

"All right, boys," Harry says, "the time has come. We're about to embark on our greatest act as of yet. So, put on your charming smiles and ready yourselves to mingle. And in honor of the great illusion we are about to propel forward, I say we do another shot."

"Thank god," I breathe out. And I think my words break the tension because Harry and Noah both chuckle as my chest deflates and Mohammad gives me an honest smile.

Harry raises his glass. "To the act," he says.

"To the act," we all repeat, downing our drinks.

After Mohammad finishes off his drink, he quickly takes a shot.

"Whoa. All right there?" I ask.

"I can't drink in front of Mum," Mohammad explains. "She'd murder me."

"She would," Noah agrees.

"So, I'll do one more shot for good measure, and then I've got to cover up the scent of alcohol on my breath," Mohammad replies, taking a smaller swig this time straight from the bottle. He pinches his lips together and shakes his head as the shot hits him.

"You could eat something," I offer.

"I'm going to rinse my mouth out just to be sure," Mohammad says, slapping Harry on the shoulder.

"Wait, are we allowed to drink downstairs?" I ask.

"I fucking am," Harry replies.

He already looks less tense than when we arrived, and it puts my own anxiety at bay.

"Yeah, it's fine," Noah agrees.

"Such bollocks," Mohammad grumbles. "Mum's fine with you two drinking, but if she found a drink in my hand, she'd drag me out of the party."

I pull my lips back in a straight line. *Poor Mohammad.*

"See you down there," Mohammad says as he heads toward the door to the billiards room.

"See you in a minute," I reply.

Harry turns to Noah and lets out a long, shaky breath.

"Everything good?" Harry asks, looking down at himself.

Noah examines him before slightly adjusting Harry's suit.

"Perfect," Noah replies.

Harry nods. "Okay then."

The rest of us descend the stairs together, entering back into the glowing entryway, the black-and-white marble floor glistening in the candlelight. Harry comes to stand at my right and Noah at my left.

"Together?" Harry asks Noah and me.

"Together," Noah replies.

I lace my arms through both of theirs as we make our way through Harry's house to the main living space. There are people mingling everywhere on the main floor. Every room has candles and flowers, and waiters move throughout the rooms with trays filled with hors d'oeuvres and champagne.

Both Harry and Noah are silent as we enter the room, where the majority of the guests seem to be. There's classical music playing in the background and vibrant chatter.

But when Harry enters into the room, everyone turns

their attention toward him.

I even look at him.

"A beautiful prison," I mumble, remembering what Harry said when first describing his house. And here, tonight, it really is.

Everyone is beautiful.

Their hands are filled with champagne and appetizers, glasses clinking together. But I can't find a single smile. At least, not one that looks real.

Harry's arm flexes under my hand, and I know he's uncomfortable.

"Told you the scent of flowers would strangle you," he says, tugging at his collar.

I hold on to Noah and Harry, not sure when I should let go of their arms. Or if I even want to. I look to Noah, but his eyes are focused on someone approaching us. I turn my head toward Harry, seeing his square jaw lock as a woman glides up to us. He clears his throat and stands up straighter.

"There you are," the woman snaps. "Your father and I have been looking for you." She tilts her head robotically, plastering on the kind of smile that shows the guests all is well while still telling Harry that he's in trouble.

She quickly moves her eyes from Harry, skipping over me, and goes straight to Noah.

"Noah, darling, I like the new look," she comments. "Very European."

Noah looks down his nose at her. His face is pale and unmoving, like stone. It makes me wonder when he will crack.

"Mia brought the shirt back from Greece," Noah replies.

"Oh, yes ..." Harry's mom hesitates.

She has no clue what he's talking about. And Noah knows it.

"She went on a student exchange there. Had a great

time," Noah says, filling her in.

I take the chance to really look at Harry's mom. She has on a black cowl-neck cocktail dress. Her thin blonde hair sits, curled, on her shoulders. Everything about her says understated and collected.

Well, apart from her jewelry.

She's wearing oversize diamond drop earrings that shimmer in the light and a thick diamond bracelet on her wrist. On the other hand is her wedding ring. And it features a massive stone.

"Good for her," she replies, her gaze flicking over me again to land on Harry.

"Mum," Harry says, clearing his throat, "this is Mallory."

Harry looks from his mom to me, and her eyes follow.

"The new girlfriend," she states.

"It's nice to meet you," I say.

"Harry's told us all about you," she says, that tilt in her head coming back.

I don't know why she does it. Maybe it's her tell. Or maybe she just thinks she looks endearing.

"Did he?" I prompt. "He's told me all about you too."

I give her my best glowing smile and try not to attack her.

"Right," she drawls out. She doesn't say anything else but looks between the three of us. Her eyes focusing in on our interlinked arms.

"I'll take her to meet Dad then," Harry says, breaking the awkwardness and ushering us forward.

Noah drops my arm.

And Harry's words finally register.

It feels like my feet aren't working as we walk. It's like I'm floating *slowly* toward hell. Toward something, someone I don't want to meet.

Noah's still at my side, and I glance at him.

"Introductions?" Noah asks Harry, placing his hand on my free elbow.

"Yeah," Harry replies.

"Together then," Noah agrees.

"Dad," Harry says, walking up to a man in the middle of a conversation.

He's wearing a three-piece suit that looks like silk is woven through it. It's beautiful. The man is tall, but not intimidating. It isn't until he turns to me that I almost stop walking. I scan his face, noticing immediately how much he looks like Harry. The blue eyes. The square jaw. He looks from me to Harry, his mouth set in a frown.

"I'd like to introduce you to someone," Harry says, bringing me forward with him. "Dad, this is Mallory James. Mallory, this is my father, Ashford Brooks."

"It's a pleasure to meet you, Miss James," his dad says, extending his hand out to me.

My first reaction is not to take it. But Noah shoves his shoulder against mine, and I move my hand forward.

"My son just recently informed us of your relationship. I'm glad you were able to attend tonight's event," he says warmly.

"I wouldn't have missed it," I hear myself reply.

I lace my arm through Harry's, desperate to hold on to him.

Harry's dad lets out a deep, authentic laugh. I furrow my brows, confused by what's going on. Because Harry's dad hits him. He drinks too much.

He isn't supposed to be laughing and shaking my hand and … being nice.

It doesn't make sense.

But then it does.

Harry's dad is putting on a show.

For everyone.

And everyone includes me.

"Excuse me," Ashford says, placing his hand on his chest as he collects himself. "I'm sure you'd all rather be out tonight, but it's good that you're here. Family is everything. And please, don't forget there are many distinguished guests with us tonight. The key to your future could be walking through this room."

"And you'll always be there to remind us of that, I'm sure," Harry says, offering his dad a closed-lip smile and a nod.

And then I finally see it.

The *real* him.

Mr. Brooks frowns again, shifting his gaze from Harry to someone on the other side of the room.

"Harry, if you'll come with me, there are a few people I'd like to introduce you to. I'm afraid you and your date will have to part for a bit. Though I'm sure we'll be leaving her in capable hands." Mr. Brooks's piercing blue eyes land on Noah. "Good to see you, Noah."

"And you, sir," Noah replies.

"Of course," Harry says flatly.

I drop Harry's arm, wishing that he wouldn't go with his dad.

Noah and I stand together, watching them walk up to another two men who are in the midst of a conversation. Harry's dad lets out a forced laugh, looking between Harry and the men before patting Harry firmly on the back.

It makes me feel sick.

"You did good," Noah says to me.

I force my eyes shut and let out an unsteady breath. "So did you."

Noah rubs his hand against my arm, comforting me. I

smile at him and try to perk myself up.

"Have you seen Mohammad yet?" I ask.

Noah searches the room and then nods. "He's talking to his mum."

Noah spins me, so I'm facing them.

"Has Naomi arrived yet?"

"I haven't seen her," Noah replies.

"What about his date?"

Noah shrugs.

"Sometimes, I swear. Useless. Useless. Useless," I tease.

Noah grins at me, his skin getting its color back. "You're talking to the wrong guy. I don't keep up on that stuff."

"Well … want to know something?" I ask before glancing back to Mohammad.

"Is it gossip or an actual fact?" Noah questions.

I roll my eyes at him.

"All right, what?" Noah says, giving in.

"Naomi and Mohammad kissed," I whisper.

I keep my eyes peeled wide open, waiting for his reaction. Excitement? Surprise?

But instead of reacting, Noah gapes at me.

"I thought I told you not to meddle." He frowns.

"I didn't. I promise."

I extend out my pinkie finger to show him I'm serious. Noah examines it before bringing his gaze back to mine, seemingly not convinced. I drop my hand.

"They did it all on their own."

"I have trouble believing that," Noah replies.

"*Anyway* … I think he's spazzing because Naomi will be here with her family. And he's got his date," I explain.

"Mohammad's pretty good at making a mess out of things," Noah says back to me.

"You know for my birthday, he gave me a book of advice."

Noah's face lights up with interest, his thick brows rising. "Did he really?"

"Yeah." I laugh. "It says things like, *What would Mohammad do?*"

Noah closes his eyes and lets out a deep laugh. "You have to show it to me."

"I will." I grin at him.

I'm not sure if the alcohol has set in on Noah yet, but he seems relaxed. Maybe it's because we've already spoken to Harry's parents. Or maybe it's because I made him laugh. But he looks good. *Happier.* His cheeks are the same color as his lips again.

"Should we go say hi?" Noah asks.

"To who?" I ask blankly.

Noah smiles at me. "To Mohammad and his mum." He places his hand on my back, leading us over to them before I can say anything.

Meera smiles widely as we approach her.

"Oh, Noah," she says fondly, hugging him. She places a kiss on each of his cheeks. She's beaming.

I look at Mohammad, whose eyes are rolling back at the interaction.

"It's nice to see you, Mallory," Meera says, moving her gaze to me. "You look lovely."

"You as well." I smile at her. "Where's Samar?"

"Making the rounds," she replies. "We know quite a few people here. It's one of the things I love about London. It's really a small town."

"Mohammad finally brought me food from one of your restaurants," I say, trying to make conversation. "It was amazing."

"Thank you," Meera replies brightly. "Samar works very

closely with the chefs on designing the menus."

"Whereas Mum is obsessed with restaurant concept and design," Mohammad adds.

Noah clears his throat, capturing all of our attention.

"I was just telling Mallory about that the other day," Noah says.

"Oh?" Meera asks.

"She wants to get into real estate one day," Noah explains, glancing over at me. "I was trying to convince her to consider selling commercial space."

"That is hot property in London," Meera agrees.

"Do you work with the same realtor each time, or does it depend on the property?" I ask Meera.

"We typically work with the same salesperson. She has her own firm. And she charges quite a large fee. I've always told Samar if we were to ever expand, I want to incorporate real estate and chefs directly into the business. No middle-*woman*."

"Smart." I grin at her, but I'm quickly distracted by a girl approaching us.

She has on a beautiful gold cocktail dress, her skin glowing against it. She looks at Meera with shy brown eyes.

"Sara," Meera says, greeting her.

I look to Mohammad and flare my eyes.

Because this must be his date!

I elbow Noah and motion toward her. He looks at me like I'm crazy, but I can't help it. This is exciting!

And Sara is gorgeous. Really gorgeous.

Meera pats Sara's hand and then looks between Mohammad, Noah, and me.

"I'd like you to all meet Sara. Sara, these are Mohammad's friends, Mallory and Noah."

"Nice to meet you," she says with a blush.

"You too," I reply.

"Mohammad, why don't you and Sara go get a drink?" Meera directs, pointing to a bar in the far corner.

At first, I'm surprised because Mohammad said he couldn't drink, but on closer inspection of the bar, it looks like they're just serving water and sodas.

"Sure," Mohammad agrees, nodding for Sara to come along with him.

And she does.

Meera leans toward Noah and me as they walk off. "Do encourage him. Sara is a very lucky find. Brilliant. Wonderful family. Plans on studying electrical engineering."

"I ... will?" I ask more than reply.

Meera nods, agreeing with whatever answer or question I just gave her. Her eyes stay on Mohammad the entire time.

Both Noah and I watch them talk awkwardly, and I have to bite my lip to keep from laughing.

Because Mohammad is blowing it.

He keeps rubbing the back of his neck and glancing at her and then away from her. Though maybe that's his goal.

Harry sneaks up on me, wrapping his arms around my waist. I smile at him as he releases me, giving Meera a kiss on the cheek.

"Nice to see you here," Harry says before he takes a sip from a heavy crystal glass in his hand.

Meera looks at the glass with concern but replies, "It's good to see you too, Harry."

"Everything all right?" I ask.

"Absolutely," Harry replies, downing his drink. "Sorry to steal them away, but there are a few people I'd like to introduce them to." He looks at Meera apologetically.

"Go. Mingle," Meera replies, waving us off.

Harry gives her a full smile before motioning for Noah

and me to follow him.

"Who are we meeting?" I ask when we get to the hallway.

Harry stops, looking at Noah with a smile.

Noah lets out a chuckle, his eyes coming to mine.

"That was an excuse, wasn't it?" I ask, crossing my arms over my chest at them.

"Yes," Harry replies warmly. "And apparently, a convincing one."

I follow Harry and Noah. We only stop to each grab a champagne flute off of a tray passing by. They lead me into a room less full, and I instantly recognize it. It's the room that we found Harry in, drunk. The fireplace is crackling, just like it was that night.

But things couldn't be any more different.

"Feel like I can finally fucking breathe again," Harry says quietly, loosening his tie.

There are only two other couples in here, and I search the room for a distraction.

"Want to play chess?" I offer. It's the only thing I can find.

"You know how?" Harry asks, taking a sip of his champagne.

"I meant, you and Noah," I clarify, glancing from Noah to the chessboard.

Noah follows my gaze and then turns to Harry. He wraps his arm around Harry's shoulders and grins at him.

"Let's play," Noah insists. "Or are you scared to lose?"

Harry's whole face lights up. "You're a prick. And I'm not going to lose."

A one-time snog.
8:45PM

TWENTY MINUTES LATER, we've moved the chessboard to the center of the room, and Noah and Harry are seated on opposite couches. A small crowd of partygoers has gathered around to watch, and both of their champagne glasses are now empty. Mohammad and Sara stand next to me.

Harry makes the final move.

"Checkmate," he says tentatively. He's watching Noah.

Noah's brows are drawn in, and he stares at the board for a minute before his shoulders slump.

"Bloody hell," Noah mutters loudly, standing up.

Harry takes the move as his victory and stands up to a handful of applause.

"You're on a winning streak," I congratulate. "What's your secret?"

"It's not about being ahead. It's about knowing your opponent." Harry smirks before ruffling Noah's hair.

"How could you know his next move?" I question, placing my hands on my hips.

Harry bends toward me, the smell of champagne moving in the air.

"I guessed his next move," Harry whispers. "And I'm always a good guess."

Harry's tongue slides down over his lip as another wide smile sets on his face.

"So, no game theory there." I laugh, watching them.

"Nah. Just Noah theory," he replies, hugging Noah.

They're both grinning from ear to ear, but Noah's grin quickly slips off his face. His eyes move to the door, and I turn to see Harry's dad.

"Harry," Mr. Brooks says, joining us.

"Did you see that, Dad?" Harry says with excitement. "I won. And Noah's no easy opponent."

"There are more important things going on tonight than chess," his dad says with a frown. "We're moving into the study for a smoke. Come join us."

Harry's face falls, but he nods. He gives the three of us an apologetic smile before following his dad out of the room.

"Wanker," Mohammad says under his breath.

Noah starts to put the pieces back in their places, and I watch as Mohammad helps him. I glance around, not seeing Mohammad's date.

"Mohammad"—I place my hand on his arm, tugging him up—"where's Sara?"

Mohammad spins in a full circle, his eyes going from relaxed to frantic.

"Fuck. Good question." Mohammad bolts out of the room, leaving Noah and me alone with the chessboard.

Noah puts back the final piece in its place.

"The pieces fell, and Harry won," Noah comments as he finishes.

The room empties out, and both Noah and I sit down on the couch.

"Why'd you let him win?" I ask.

"I didn't," Noah replies.

I shift on the couch, turning slightly to face him.

"I know how the game works. I saw you, Noah. I've seen you play before. You let him win."

Noah drops my gaze and shakes his head.

"I don't let him win," Noah disagrees.

"Not normally, no. But today, you did."

"Forget about chess," Noah says. But he doesn't deny it.

He leans forward slightly and pulls off his suit jacket, laying it next to him. My eyes wander across his black shirt. It pulls across his chest and hugs his shoulders and arms.

Noah brings his hand up on the back of the couch and looks at me. "How are you feeling?"

"I'm feeling a little annoyed that you won't answer my question about the game," I reply, flashing my eyes up to his.

"You're going to stay salty about that?" Noah asks, amused.

"Probably not," I sigh, letting my head fall back against the cushion.

"That's good. You look beautiful tonight, Mal. Too beautiful to be upset with me. The dress is nice. Really nice."

I glance down at my dress, my heart speeding up in my chest. "Thank you. Harry had it sent over."

"The necklace is new, right?"

"Yeah." I bring my hand to the necklace, my stomach flipping.

"It's very shiny," Noah observes.

"It is."

"You received a lot of birthday gifts then?" Noah asks, his brown eyes meeting mine.

I nod at him, holding his gaze.

"And yet my favorite are some raggedy sweats. Kind of funny, isn't it?" I ask, my cheeks warming.

"I don't think it's funny at all. It's sweet actually," Noah replies.

"Who would have thought?" I smile at Noah.

"I don't know … someone once told me that those sweats were loose and comfy. Maybe I had trouble parting with them after all." Noah raises his eyebrows at me, his lips in a playful grin.

"I'm sure it was a dramatic departure," I tease.

"It was," Noah agrees, nodding enthusiastically. He even pushes out his bottom lip into a very fake sad pout. "I think I might need to be cheered up."

"Oh yeah?" I smile, my eyes slipping down to his lips.

Noah's eyes sparkle as they move across my face. He doesn't say anything, just nods slightly.

Before I realize what I'm doing, I'm leaning toward him. Our faces are inches apart when I hear my name being called.

I freeze at my name, my body in shock at what I was about to do. About who could have seen.

I recover quickly and turn as Naomi plops down on the couch next to us.

"Hey," I squeak out.

"Hi," Naomi replies, leaning in to give me a kiss on the cheek. "Have you seen Mohammad?"

"No," I say at the same time that Noah says, "Yes."

"Uh …" Naomi shifts her eyes between the two of us, a thick line forming between her brow. "What's going on?"

"We have, but I don't know where he is now," I clarify. "I think he went to find his mom."

Naomi nods, apparently understanding.

"I'm going to go find him," she says breezily. "Also, you look beautiful. I'll see you later!"

Naomi gives me a little wave before floating out of the room.

"Why did you do that?" I gape at Noah, batting him on the chest.

"What? Tell the truth?" he asks, grabbing my hand.

"Yes! Because if Naomi actually finds him, there's a real chance Sara's going to be with him."

And good luck explaining that one.

"Such a terrible thing to do. Tell the truth," Noah retorts.

I roll my eyes.

"Well, it's up to Mohammad now," I say, relaxing back into the couch. "I'm not getting involved in any unnecessary drama tonight. There's already too much going on."

"I didn't think you were going to shake Harry's dad's hand back there," Noah comments.

"I didn't want to." I look at Noah, hoping for some guidance.

"You feel a lot, and you don't always stay in control of it. I'm surprised you were able to," Noah admits, tilting his head at me.

"His dad took me by surprise. He was nice at first. Plus, I *usually* can keep myself in check," I say dryly.

"That's debatable." Noah smirks. "The perfect storm, remember?"

"You really need to get better analogies for me. Storm. *Bulldozer.* Can't I be something ... softer? Sweeter?" I offer, hoping I can convince him.

"Nope," Noah declares.

"Why not?" I pout.

"You were this huge storm that came rolling into my life. Into my house," Noah says. "And that was before your first day of classes when I found out you already knew Harry."

My whole body feels like it's floating with Noah's words. I remember meeting him for the first time in his room. I remember how upset he was when he found out I knew Harry. I remember how he answered the bathroom door in that tiny little towel.

I bring my eyes up to his.

"We never finished our Truth or Dare, you know," Noah says.

"Tell me a truth."

Noah presses his lips together, his eyelashes fluttering as he thinks. "I miss you in my house," he finally says.

"Did you like having me there?"

Noah nods. "Hearing you a room over. Your smell. Finding your hair on my bed. Lying next to you."

Noah licks his lips, drawing my attention to them. They're so plump and perfect.

"Noah," I mumble.

His mouth moves, and I watch as his lips form a word.

I see Noah say it, but it sounds like it's coming from a different room. Or maybe it's coming from within me. It's hard to tell where his voice ends and I begin. Where the lines are between us.

"*Yeah?*"

I bring my eyes to his and watch as he looks over my shoulder.

"There you guys are," Mohammad says breathlessly, joining us on the couch. "I just saw Naomi. And my date. This is a disaster."

"Oh?" Noah says hazily.

I peel my eyes away from Noah and turn to Mohammad. His head is resting on the back of the couch, and he's looking up at the ceiling like he's in a therapist's chair.

I let out a sigh.

"What are you going to do?" I ask.

"Why don't you two talk?" Noah offers. "I'm going to go find Mia."

"She's here?" I ask Noah as he gets up.

"I saw Sophia earlier, so Mia should be around somewhere," he explains.

"Okay." I nod.

When Noah's out of the room, I scowl at Mohammad.

"You had to choose that moment. Noah was in the middle of searing off my underwear!" I throw my head back with a groan and stare at the ceiling.

Mohammad lazily rolls his head in my direction and makes a gagging gesture. "Too much information. And I'm in trouble here!" He covers his face with his hands, dragging his fingers down over his skin. "*Ughhh.*"

"What's the problem? I thought you said you liked girls fighting over you," I tease.

Well, sort of tease.

Because this is his doing!

"No. I said I wanted a sweet and busty girl. That's it," Mohammad corrects.

"Well, I don't know about Sara, but I do know one girl here who is excited to see you," I offer.

"And I'm avoiding her." Mohammad pouts. "Kill me."

"What are you going to do?"

"I have no idea. And she smells so good," Mohammad says, letting out a sigh.

"What?" I ask, leaning up to grab my champagne glass. I lay my head back against the couch and bring it to my lips.

"She smells like peaches," Mohammad says.

I roll my head toward him and watch as he licks his lips.

"Okay, enough," I whine.

Mohammad grabs my champagne glass, finishing off the drink. My mouth falls open at his bold move.

"You're telling me that you can say that Noah's *searing off your knickers*, but I can't say the word *peach*?" Mohammad scowls.

"Right. You're right," I reply, trying to gain some perspective. "But why did you down my drink? What about your mom?"

"I know I'm right. And things are headed south anyway," Mohammad says with a shrug.

"Well then … why don't you gush?" I ask, wanting to be supportive.

"Gush?"

"About Naomi."

Mohammad sits up, and I can tell he's taking this seriously.

"She's so hot. Smells like sugar and peaches. And her hair," he says dreamily. "Her lips too. She looks banging tonight."

"Way to leave out her personality," I tease. "But yeah, Naomi always looks beautiful."

Mohammad rolls his eyes. "Her personality is what takes her from a one-time snog to maybe more," he replies.

"Oh?" I grin.

"We'll see. No rush, right? I mean ..." Mohammad says, starting to sound nervous.

"No rush," I agree.

"We can date. Keep it casual. I'm a free bird," Mohammad states more to himself than to me.

"Definitely a free bird."

"Just one who keeps circling back around the same tree."

"Exactly." I nod. "Wait, what?"

Mohammad diverts his eyes as he thinks. "Well, the tree is nice. Good views, soft branches. Who wouldn't want to make a home in that tree? No one would blame the bird," he explains.

"I thought girls were birds?"

"No, I'm the bird," he clarifies.

"And Naomi is a tree?" I ask, finally understanding.

"I guess," Mohammad says. And he looks completely confused.

"Hmm. Don't tell Naomi that."

"Wasn't planning on it," Mohammad says.

"So ... what about your date?" I ask him.

"Fuck. Right. I should probably go find her."

"Good idea!" I agree, ushering him up.

Mohammad's up and off the couch before I have a chance to ask him if he needs help. I debate going after him, but I think this is something he probably needs to deal with on his own.

I look around the sitting room. There are a few people talking, and a couple is seated on the opposite couch, but not much is happening.

I get up, deciding to explore.

I grab a fresh glass of champagne off a passing tray and pop a mushroom cap into my mouth. I enter the oversize dining room and quickly spot Mia and Sophia. I'm about to go say hi when I see Noah. He's in the corner of the room with his back to the wall. He's watching them, and a smile dances across his lips.

I walk up to him and lean my back against the wall, mimicking him.

"Having fun?" I ask, taking a sip of champagne.

"Mia looks happy," Noah comments.

"She does," I agree. Another waiter circles through the room, and I grab two more mushroom caps, handing one to Noah. "You know your sister thought it was *hilarious* that I was jealous of Sophia. Finally made sense when she told me why."

"I tried to tell you I wasn't into Sophia," Noah says after finishing the appetizer.

"Well, you did a bad job of it," I reply.

"All we do is talk." Noah laughs. "I tried to tell you, but you wouldn't listen. Sometimes, you're too stubborn."

I laugh along with him because he's probably right. Noah looks from me and back to Mia and Sophia. Sophia has one of the mushrooms in her hand and is trying to feed it to Mia. But every time she gets close, Mia moves her head back.

Noah lets out a chuckle.

"Do you like seeing Mia with someone, or are you protective of your sister?"

"I just want her happy," Noah says.

"She looks happy."

"She does," Noah says, but his tone seems hesitant.

"But?" I ask.

Noah looks back at me, his lips pulling to the side. "But she and Sophia have been friends forever. I think the transition to *more* will be hard for them. I just don't know if they're suited, long-term."

I glance back at them. They look happy.

"You can't tell them that," I say.

"I wouldn't," Noah replies.

"Mia told me that she missed Sophia when she was in Greece. If they've been friends forever, why do you think they aren't suited?"

Noah crosses his arms, his eyes shifting as he thinks. "I think Sophia is going to stay in London. I could see her working her way up at a big theater company here. Mia is a bit more of a free spirit. I never thought she'd be exclusive with anyone, honestly."

"Really?"

"She kind of has a love for life. As well as people." Noah smiles.

"Well, time will tell." I take another sip of champagne, feeling more relaxed.

Seeing Mia and Sophia happy makes me happy. I smile, watching them.

"Time does have a way of doing that," Noah says. And it quickly pulls me out of my happy, floating bubble.

"You should be an expert on it," I agree, looking up to Noah. "I swear, every day with you, it's all about *time, time,*

time. Right time, wrong time, not enough time …"

Noah pushes off the wall and shifts toward me.

"Has anyone told you that you're impatient?" he asks.

"Yes. You have."

Noah shakes his head, but he's smiling. I grin back at him.

"Do you want to find some food?"

"Are you hungry?"

"I ate earlier, but …"

"But then again, you can always eat." I laugh.

"Pretty much."

"Sure," I say.

We search around, but the only food we can find is what's rotating around the room on trays. Noah and I both take a few appetizers.

"Have you seen Harry?" I ask, spotting his mom.

She's got her hand on someone's arm, listening to them like what they're saying is the most important thing in the world.

"No. We should probably go find him though," Noah replies, grabbing another appetizer from my hand.

We wander around until we find Harry in the study, and I instantly feel silly for not remembering what Harry's dad said about smoking.

The room is dark and filled with men. The music is different from the rest of the house. It's the same classical opera music that Harry asked Mohammad to play earlier.

I waft the air in front of me, feeling suffocated.

By the smoke.

By the blazing fireplace.

The whole thing reminds me of when we found Harry here, drunk.

It's a different room but the same effect.

The music.

The drink.

The ashtray.

The pain on Harry's face.

Except this time, Mr. Brooks is standing behind Harry's chair, his hand resting on his shoulder.

Harry is staring at the fire, ignoring the conversation. He looks trapped. And it makes me want to vomit.

"Should we go over?" I ask Noah when Harry turns. He quickly spots us.

Noah motions for him to come to us, but Harry shakes his head slightly. But he mouths the word *five*, which I'm assuming means five more minutes.

I watch Harry as he breaks our gaze, turning his head up to look at his dad.

"Come on," Noah whispers, moving me out of the study.

We walk around a corner to an empty hallway, and I down the rest of my champagne. Noah leans his back against the wall, looking upset.

"This is … ridiculous. I'm so frustrated with all of this. Harry's parents. This party," I say.

"I am too," Noah agrees. "We'll be able to leave soon though."

"I'm worried about Harry."

"We're doing everything we can," Noah replies, pushing off the wall.

He rakes his hand through his chestnut hair. It isn't gelled like Harry's or Mohammad's, and it slips easily through his fingers. When he brings his face back to mine, I see doubt in his eyes.

"What does this mean for us?" Noah's voice strains as he places his hand on my necklace.

"For us?" I choke out.

"Yes. You're Harry's date."

Noah keeps his hand on my chest, trailing his fingers away from the necklace to my skin. Goose bumps crawl down my arms.

"I'm here to support him," I answer, trying to think straight.

"Is this what you want?" Noah asks. He moves his fingers off my skin and taps against my necklace.

"What? The necklace?" I ask.

"No. Being needed. Harry, he needs you," Noah says seriously.

"And I'm here for him."

"You like to be needed. You like putting others' needs before your own," Noah says, his finger moving back to my collarbone. My eyes flutter at the sensation. "But sometimes, it's okay to put yourself first."

"It's hard for me," I struggle to say. Struggle to speak.

"How do you feel about being Harry's date?" Noah asks, stepping away from me. He leans back against the opposite wall.

"How do you feel about it?"

"I don't like it."

"I didn't think you would."

"Yet you agreed anyway," Noah says, shaking his head.

"Last time we were here, you told me that you liked me. You grabbed my hand."

Noah leans off the wall and walks back to me. He runs his hand across mine, his other hand coming to rest on the wall beside me. "Like this?"

"Yes." I nod, my lips parting.

Noah plays with my fingers, joining our hands together.

"Do you want me to say it again?" Noah asks, his eyes on me.

"If you want."

Noah's face grows serious as he dips his head closer to mine. "I like you, Mal. A lot."

"And you're happy that I stayed?" I push, wanting him to finally admit it.

"Silly question," he replies. "You said your life was here."

"I feel like it is," I agree.

Noah unwraps his hand from mine, scraping his fingers up my side. My body trembles at the motion, begging to be closer to him.

"Isn't it?" Noah asks, holding my gaze.

He drops his hand and licks his lips. I think he's about to kiss me when I see movement out of the corner of my eye. I turn my head, looking past Noah's arm to see Harry's dad.

He's stopped, his head tilted to the side. His blue eyes are exactly the same as Harry's, and they are on us. A shiver runs through me. His mouth curls into a wicked smile as he eyes Noah. And then me.

Noah follows my gaze, spotting Harry's dad. He doesn't flinch or move away from me; instead, he holds his gaze. When Mr. Brooks is finally out of sight, I feel like all the air had been removed from my lungs.

"I'll be right back. Bathroom," I stutter, pushing past Noah.

I run to the bathroom in a haze and grasp on to the counter when I'm finally alone. I let my head fall as I suck in a gulp of air.

Why do I keep hesitating with Noah?

He just told me he liked me.

Is it because of Harry?

Or am I just using Harry as an excuse?

I look at myself in the mirror and try to clear my head.

The bathroom door starts to open when I realize that I

forgot to lock it.

"Sorry, I'm …" I start, but then I'm greeted by Harry's face.

I tilt my head, trying to read his expression. He isn't angry. Or upset. It looks like he's trying to calculate what to do.

"Fuck," he whispers, pacing.

My stomach drops.

"What's wrong?" I ask, walking to him.

"Mum invited Natalia."

"Natalia?" I ask.

"An odious girl," Harry remarks. "But the second Mum heard that Olivia and I ended things, she started plotting."

"Does she really have time for that?" I ask, my eyebrows shooting up.

"One wouldn't think," Harry says, looking annoyed. "She invited her here even though I told her that you were my date. My girlfriend."

Harry's eyes come up to mine, and he stops pacing.

"Why would she do that?"

"Natalia's family was one of the families that joined us at our house in the country. My father's invitation was given to solidify a deal at the time. Anyway, her family was invited round, and a few drinks later, we were snogging."

"Oh …" I reply, caught off guard.

"It was a decision I made when I was pissed," Harry explains. "Noah and Mohammad weren't there."

"Do you regret it or something?" I ask, not really understanding the problem.

"She's a bit possessive," Harry responds.

"Was this before Olivia?"

"During one of our off moments," Harry answers.

"Now, I'm seeing the big picture," I reply.

"She made a beeline for me the moment I left the study. I hadn't even known she'd be here. Walked straight up to me and whispered …" Harry frowns.

"Whispered what?" I ask.

"Rather dirty things in my ear."

"I thought you liked that sort of thing?"

"Usually, sure. When I'm in the right mood. Or with the right girl. Neither of which is now or her," Harry says. "I told her to leave it be. We'd fooled around, and it's in the past. She didn't seem thrilled."

"I'm not getting into another fight over you," I clarify.

"I wouldn't dare ask." Harry grins. He moves in front of me and sets his hand on my waist. "I'm sorry about earlier with my dad. Business talk is, well, business talk. Mind-numbing yet never-ending."

"It's fine," I reply, focusing on him. I bring my hands onto his arms and nod. "And if Natalia is bothering you, I'll go along with being your girlfriend out there. Tonight, I'm here for you."

Because tonight isn't about my feelings.

It's not about me and Noah.

Harry pulls me into a hug.

"But if you two hooked up when you *maybe* had a girlfriend, why would she care about me being here?"

"I don't want to fend her off tonight. And I wasn't with Olivia then. I'm hoping if she sees us together, she'll back off," Harry replies. And he seems upset.

"It's not a big deal. I mean, I can't blame her for being interested in you." I give Harry a smile, wanting him to relax.

"It's not that. It's … Mum knew what happened between me and Natalia. I was younger, and we used to talk. I told her it was a mistake. Her family has no reason to be here tonight, yet they were invited. Why?"

Harry wears a pained expression on his face, and I try not to flinch at it.

"Okay." I nod.

"Okay?" Harry asks.

I grab Harry's hand and lace his fingers through mine.

Getting caught together.
9:30PM

WHEN WE GET back to the party, I quickly spot the girl Harry must be talking about. She's our age, beautiful, and staring at Harry when Mohammad walks up to us. He glances at our hands but doesn't say anything.

One look at him though tells me something's off.

"Are you okay?" I ask.

"I just snogged Naomi," Mohammad blurts out.

Harry grins. "About time, mate."

"I'm so proud of you." I smile, equally thrilled.

"It was so hot," Mohammad admits. "I pulled her into a free room. Couldn't keep my hands off her."

"Wait, what free room?" Harry asks.

"Uh …" Mohammad draws out. "Your room."

Harry sticks out his tongue and gives Mohammad a high five. "Get any action?"

"Nah, but she was sexy. Pressed me up against the door." Mohammad waggles his eyebrows.

"Wait, what about your date?" I search the room but don't find Mohammad's mom or Sara.

"Turns out, she has a boyfriend. Parents made her come too," Mohammad says with relief.

"Did you find that out *before or after* snogging Naomi?" I

ask pointedly.

"Details." Mohammad waves off my question, and I shake my head at him. "Besides, I told Naomi she was my cousin."

"Mohammad!" I scold.

He drops his mouth open and stares at me. "I wasn't about to let my mum fuck up the possibility of future sexscapades with Naomi Fleming."

Harry chuckles, a huge grin on his face.

I want to tell Mohammad he shouldn't lie to get what he wants, but Harry's too happy for me to ruin it. I catch his eye, and he gives my hand a squeeze in return.

"So, what's with the hands?" Mohammad asks, pointing between us as Noah joins us.

"Mum decided to invite Natalia. I told you about her— from the country house—yeah?" Harry offers as an explanation.

"For fuck's sake," Noah growls. He roughly pushes his hand through his hair again.

"Yeah," Harry agrees. "I wouldn't have put two and two together until Mum had asked if I'd seen Natalia yet. It was then that I realized she'd specifically invited her."

"Which one is she?" Mohammad asks, scanning the crowd.

Harry doesn't get a chance to answer before Mohammad lets out a low whistle.

"She's fit," Mohammad says, looking at Harry like he's crazy.

"And psycho," Harry mumbles.

"She *is* staring," Noah agrees, glancing over at her.

"More like eye-fucking you. The girl's intense," Mohammad says approvingly.

"Yeah. Not quite sure she's getting the hint," Harry says, looking down at our interlaced hands.

Noah looks at our hands, too, and swallows hard.

"Anyone want a drink?" Noah asks.

"Cheers, mate." Harry nods, but I can tell his focus is still on Natalia. And his mom.

"Sure," I agree.

"Mohammad?" Noah asks.

"Mum left, so definitely," Mohammad says with a grin.

Noah stomps off, and Mohammad is quick to follow him. Harry and I stay standing in the middle of the room, and I can feel multiple sets of eyes on us. Harry nods to someone passing by and gets a pat on the shoulder in return.

"I feel like I'm under a microscope," I admit, looking up at Harry.

Harry brings his attention to me, stepping in front of me and lacing both of our hands together. "Can you blame them for staring? You're the most stunning girl in the room."

I squeeze his hands.

I'm proud of him for being so strong.

"I've got nothing on you. And I can't blame Natalia for staring," I tell him.

"Maybe you're right," Harry says, thinking. "Maybe we need to move into phase two."

I let out a surprised laugh. "You're starting to sound like Mohammad," I tease.

Harry taps me on the nose, not finding my statement all that amusing.

"Wait, what's phase two?"

"Getting caught together," he replies.

"*At your parents' party?*" I gape at him. "Because that sounds like a terrible idea."

"Not by everyone. We just want to give Natalia a glimpse," Harry corrects.

"Harry, I can't do that."

"Trust me?" Harry asks, his blue eyes pleading with me.

I don't say no. But I don't say yes either.

"Let me see what I can find out," Harry replies as Noah and Mohammad return.

"All right," I agree.

Noah offers Harry a drink, and he accepts it, giving Noah an excited kiss on the cheek.

"The best," he says before rushing away.

"Where's he off to?" Noah asks, watching Harry move easily through the thinning crowd.

I'm about to reply when my gaze lands on Mohammad's mom. *And Naomi.*

"Mohammad," I say, pulling at his sleeve, "I think Naomi has found your mom …"

Mohammad follows my gaze and then jumps. He moves to hide behind me while simultaneously shoving his half-empty champagne flute into my hand.

"Shit. Shit. Shit. I thought she'd left!" he says, scrambling.

"You didn't make sure?" I ask, trying to keep cool as I spin around toward him.

"I need a mint!" he says frantically.

Noah holds up his hands to show that all he has is a glass of champagne.

Mohammad stares at me.

"Where would I put a mint?" I ask, looking down at my dress.

"Oh my god," he says, rushing off in the opposite direction.

"What a way to spend a Thursday night," I say to Noah as I set down both of the champagne glasses.

"I'd rather be at home," Noah admits.

"Tell me about it," I agree. "I miss your mom."

Noah shakes his head before releasing a deep laugh. It

bounces out of him and into me, and I find myself laughing too.

"Ouch," he says, placing his hand over his heart.

"It's true," I tease, still laughing. I don't even know why I'm still laughing. But I am. It feels like the longest night of my life, and the end isn't even in sight.

"What else do you miss?" Noah questions, his eyes sparkling.

I raise my hands up, not bothering to fight off answering. "Uh … I miss having coffee brought to me in the morning."

"You have room service," Noah counters.

"I miss … massages," I continue.

"You have a spa at the hotel."

I raise an eyebrow at him. "Someone's being picky." I tap my finger on my chin, thinking. "I miss your mom's cooking. And yours too, surprisingly."

"Yet you have what I'm sure is a great restaurant at the hotel." Noah smirks. And it's obvious he's pleased with himself.

"Noah …" I roll my eyes.

"What else do you miss?" he asks, egging me on.

"I miss … running."

"Yet I saw you running," Noah replies, tilting his head back.

He looks down at me through dark lashes, and I feel like my heart might actually stop.

"Fine. I give. I miss … you."

Noah smiles, his Adam's apple bobbing as he swallows.

"Prove it," he says, looking down at me.

"What?"

"I said, prove it. Show me." Noah's hand slides around my waist, and then he pulls me toward him with a firm grip.

"Prove it how?" I ask, my eyes connecting to his.

"There's a lot of ways to show these things," he says. "You could be creative."

"I feel like this is another game to you," I almost whisper as his face—and his lips—move closer toward mine.

"There's nothing about this that's a game. I'm telling you that if you miss me like you said you do, then you should show me, Mal. Show me."

And I know what Noah wants.

He wants me to kiss him.

Here.

Now.

In front of everyone.

He wants me to show him that I'm his. That I belong to no one else.

And it's too much.

Because Harry is somewhere. Maybe even in this room. And probably Harry's mom. Not to mention, Mohammad. Naomi.

They're all here.

Our lunchroom kiss comes rushing back to me.

How I hurt everyone in that moment.

And I can't—won't—break Harry's heart again.

I can't do that to him. I can't hurt him like I did before. No matter how much I want Noah, I can't have him like this.

I need Harry to be happy. I *need* to know that he's okay. That he's *really* okay. Only then can I be happy.

"That's what I thought," Noah says, trying to pull away from me.

I don't let him.

"I can't break Harry's heart again. I won't allow myself this—you—if it hurts him. I thought you of all people would understand."

"I'm not asking you to break his heart. I'm asking you not

to break mine." Noah's voice cracks.

"I'm not trying to," I say, stumbling over my words.

"I shouldn't have expected for things to be different. I shouldn't have hoped that you would … feel the same. I shouldn't have thought that you were mine," Noah says softly.

"But I am," I say, still holding on to him.

"Not fully." Noah shakes his head. "And what did I tell you? That when I have you—"

"You'll demand nothing short of everything," I finish.

"You always remember my words," he says with a smile.

I smile back. "Well, they're usually wise, but I can't kiss you here. Not in front of him. His family. I couldn't do that."

"That's not what I was asking," Noah replies, seemingly frustrated.

"What were you asking?"

Noah sighs. "I don't know."

"Can I ask you something?" I ask.

"Go ahead."

"Do you really want *everything* from me, Noah? Do you really want *all of it*?"

Noah gazes at my face, and I feel my heart in my throat. But then his eyes leave mine, moving up over my shoulder.

I turn and see Harry approach us. Noah drops his hand from my waist as Harry drapes his arm around Noah's shoulders.

"Noah, can I borrow you?" Harry asks. "One of dad's old friends heard that you're good at Maths. He wants to meet you."

Noah doesn't look at him. He just stares at me for a beat.

"Sure," he says to Harry, but Harry's focus is elsewhere, searching through the swarm of people.

Noah's eyes find mine again. "Yes," he says to me. "The answer is yes."

As they walk off, Noah looks back over his shoulder at me. I stare at him, feeling like I could pass out.

Because Noah just said yes.

He said yes.

I search for Mohammad. For Naomi. But they aren't here. They aren't in this room.

And I can't move. I'm frozen in this spot.

When Harry finally comes back, he's alone. He grabs my hand without saying anything and leads us out of the room.

I feel dazed, still thinking about Noah's words, not really paying attention to what Harry is saying.

"I overheard her talking about powdering her nose," Harry says quickly. "She should be here any minute."

"Harry," I say, shaking my head. "Did she say something else to you?"

Harry's face flushes, and it snaps me back into the moment.

"Fuck," I mutter.

Harry is leading me to the closest bathroom. When we get inside, he doesn't lock the door. Instead, he places his hands on my waist. Then, he picks me up and sets me down on the counter in one seamless motion.

"Wrap your legs around my waist," Harry instructs as he quickly undoes a few buttons on his shirt and moves my hands to his neck.

Harry's looking down at me through his blond lashes, his lips parting. I do as instructed, causing him to move closer, situating himself between my thighs.

And suddenly, this feels *too* familiar.

Too real.

Especially when he slides my butt toward him, keeping his face in front of mine. And when his hands come up onto my shoulders, falling down over my exposed arms, my heart quickens in my chest.

Being here, in this spot, with Harry feels familiar. And I care about him.

But after what Noah just said …

"This is too much, Harry," I say, wanting to end this charade. Because I can't deal with it right now.

"You have feelings for me, Mallory," Harry says steadily, keeping his palms on my shoulders.

"Harry," I say, shaking my head.

Harry's forehead creases, his blue eyes flashing with concern. He looks down at me.

"Look, just because Noah loves you doesn't mean that I don't. I know that you love Noah. I do too. But I think the three of us need time, like you said. We need to let things settle. Let things stay how they are now. Loose. No pressure. No … restrictions."

"No restrictions?" I repeat, looking up to him.

"Noah told me you two haven't, uh … explored your feelings yet."

"He told you that?"

"I understand if you need to. But I know that it's different now. You don't live there. You're not sucked into his life as much maybe?" Harry asks.

"He has a presence," I agree.

"He has a pull. It's Noah. He pulls everyone to him."

"Harry, what are you trying to say?"

"If you need to explore things with him, then you should. But my feelings haven't changed. I care about you, Mallory. Noah understands that. We're young. Who knows what's going to happen today? Tomorrow? Nothing is guaranteed."

"Then, why are we in here? Go talk to Natalia. If things are what they are, then why …" I start, but Harry shakes his head.

"I don't want her," he says, dropping his hands. "I'm talking about us."

"I don't know what to say."

"You don't have to say anything. I can see it. I see what you and Noah have—I do. But this—us—it feels good too."

"Being between my legs?" I ask, glancing down.

"I'm not complaining about that." Harry grins. "But what I meant was, me and you."

"You really are a romantic," I reply, shaking my head.

"I'm not sure about that," Harry says, moving his palms to rest on my thighs.

I suck in a breath at his touch.

"You still get the same look, you know," he says seriously.

"What look?"

Harry leans in, his mouth at my ear. "When you get turned on, your lips part, and your pupils dilate. I can tell that you're focused on me. On how I make you feel."

I force my eyes shut. "Harry, I can't."

Harry pulls back, cupping my cheeks in his hands. I open my eyes, relief flooding through me as I do.

Because it's just Harry looking back at me.

"I'm not trying anything. I promise. I'm just telling you that I can still see it. That there's still something between us, no matter what there is with you and Noah."

"I never said there wasn't, but …"

"I don't think either of us knows exactly what it is," Harry says, dropping my gaze.

"Maybe it's friendship? We're close."

"Maybe it's just me, but generally, I don't snog my mates. Or think about them naked." Harry smirks. "Or let my fingers explore between …"

I roll my eyes, but a smile comes onto my face.

"I get the point. We have a connection. I'm not denying

it. I'm not sure what it means though, Harry. But ... I do have feelings for Noah."

"I know you do. And you don't need to know what they mean yet," Harry insists. "I just ..."

"You what?"

"I just want to make sure that you don't forget it. I know things are fucking mad out there. I've been pulled around all night. But you're ..." Harry stops when the sound of heels clicking against the marble floor echoes into the bathroom. "Shit, I think she's coming."

"Harry, what are you going to do?" I ask.

But suddenly, his lips are pressed gently on my neck. His hands find my waist just as Natalia opens the door and then jumps back in surprise. She takes in the scene—Harry's mouth on my neck, my legs wrapped around his waist— before storming away.

"I think she got the point," I mumble.

Harry breaks his lips from my skin and starts to pull away from my neck when more movement from the door catches my attention. I look up and find Noah staring at us in the open doorway.

He goes white.

Harry's hands rest on my thighs as he pulls his head away from me. I can see the corner of Harry's face, a wide smile pulling at his lips.

"That was effective." He laughs, but his voice feels like it's rooms away.

I unwrap my legs from around his waist, moving away from him. I need there to be space between us.

I need to be able to think straight.

Noah's eyes are glued to me, and I feel like I've been hit with a wall of cold water. Like up until this point, I knew what I was doing. It was for Harry. I always go along with him. Because he asks me to. Because part of me wants to. But seeing Noah, frozen in the doorway, makes me realize in one complete moment that I have to stop.

That Noah was right.

I put Harry before him. I put Harry's needs before Noah's. I do it because Harry needs us.

Harry needs me.

And Noah, despite how I feel about him, can take care of himself. I know he can stand on his own two feet, like he's always telling me to do. *Be your own hero.*

But Harry, he needs one. And maybe I like being that for him. I've always liked being needed, just like Noah said. But at what cost?

I stare at Noah, feeling my stomach drop within me. Because this is the cost.

Hollowed eyes.

A pale face.

A hurt, pained expression.

Noah's mouth is slightly open, his cheeks sucked in. It's like he drew in a surprised breath that he hasn't been able to let back out yet.

Harry must notice that my eyes are fixed on the doorway, and I feel him turn in front of me, his eyes landing on Noah. Noah's intense gaze breaks from mine, and he moves his attention to Harry.

"Oh my god, that was fucking brilliant!" Harry says with a laugh as he strides toward Noah. He wraps his arm around his neck, pulling him into the bathroom.

I slide off the counter, adjusting my dress as they both come back to stand in front of me.

Noah clears his throat, his brows drawing in.

"What's up?" Noah asks, looking at Harry.

"I had to get Natalia off my case," Harry explains, dropping his arm. He looks from Noah to the mirror and messes with a piece of his hair.

Noah flicks his gaze at me before frowning.

"You two weren't …" Noah says.

Harry doesn't break his gaze in the mirror as a small chuckle escapes his lips.

"No. It was all for effect," he replies.

"Well, you two did a good job of looking convincing," Noah says flatly.

"That was the point, mate. Wanted to get Mum off my back and Natalia away from me," Harry says, turning back to us. "Come on. I'm going to tell my parents we're leaving."

I snap my head in Harry's direction. "What?" I ask.

"I made the rounds. Put on a smile. I think my job is done," Harry replies.

I look to Noah, wondering if he's going to say anything. But he doesn't. He just nods once at Harry.

"Meet me out front in five. I'll find Mohammad and tell Mum we're leaving. I want to go to the club." Harry gives me a quick kiss on the cheek and then turns to Noah.

Noah nods in agreement, and Harry firmly pats him on the shoulder before walking out of the bathroom.

I look around the bathroom, wondering what to do.

What to say.

I clear my throat and look up at Noah. "Well …" I start.

Noah looks back at me, his expression unreadable.

"That was rather unfortunate," I say, letting a stream of air out of my chest. I lean back against the counter and cross my arms over my chest.

"All for show, huh?" Noah asks, not moving from his spot.

"Apparently," I mumble.

Noah starts to walk out of the bathroom, but I push off

the counter and grab on to his arm.

"Before I knew what was happening, Harry was dragging me in here with a plan to …"

"To what?" Noah snaps.

"His mom invited Natalia here even though he told her I was his date. Harry felt hurt and wanted to, I don't know, get the point across to Natalia that he isn't interested."

"You're not something to be used, Mal."

Noah glances away from me, anger flashing across his face. I grab on to his hand.

"I'm sorry. I shouldn't have come in here with him. I shouldn't have gone along with it."

Noah blinks at the ground, but I see his shoulders relax. Eventually, his thumb moves, rubbing back and forth across my hand.

"We're both here for him tonight though, aren't we?" Noah finally says.

"Yes," I answer. "But that came close to crossing the line for me. Outwardly, Harry is so put together. But inwardly … I know he is struggling."

"We should probably go with him then," Noah exhales.

"To the club?"

"Yeah."

I glance away from Noah, thinking. I need to tell him or show him that I understand how he's feeling. That I'm not unaware of how it looked.

"Well, if you go, then I'll go," I say, looking back at him.

"And if I go home?" Noah starts, but I cut him off.

"Then I'll leave too."

"You would let Harry go alone?" Noah asks, tilting his head to the side.

I squeeze Noah's hand tighter. "I'm … I'm starting to realize the cost of being there for Harry."

Noah steps toward me, his gaze softening. "And what is the cost?"

"You. Seeing you look hurt was terrible."

Noah's mouth pulls at the corner, but before I have a chance to see if he smiles or frowns, he brings me into a hug. I grasp on to him, grateful to be in his embrace.

"Come on," Noah says into my ear. "Let's go get our coats."

"Remember what I said. If you go, I'll go. If not ..." I trail off, but Noah places his palm on my cheek.

"Let's go. You can make fun of my terrible dance moves. It'll get us out of this party and keep Harry and Mohammad happy, yeah?"

I nod and smile at Noah. "Yeah."

This music is slow.
10:45PM

"WHO'S READY TO hit up the club?!" Mohammad chants when we get out front of Harry's house.

Naomi is standing next to Mohammad, her hand wrapped around his. I look at their interlaced fingers and then to Noah, raising my eyebrows at him before giving my attention back to Mohammad.

"I am," I reply, going along with his excitement. "Where's Harry?"

I glance around, seeing it's just the four of us out front.

"Here," Harry says, walking out the front door.

He's pulling on a camel coat, having already removed his suit jacket and unbuttoned the top button of his shirt. Everything about him seems lighter, and I love seeing his big smile and bright eyes.

"Good to go?" Noah asks from my side.

"Ready to get this fucking party started," Harry says with a grin.

Harry wraps his arm around Noah's shoulders and starts guiding us up the street, away from his house. With the growing space between us and the house—*the party*—I feel better too.

There's no more pretending.

I'm not Harry's girlfriend.

I don't have to worry about leaving Harry alone with his parents.

Mohammad and Naomi seem better than good.

And Noah and I are okay.

We can move forward like the party was just a bad blemish on an otherwise normal week.

I walk in step with Mohammad and Naomi.

"I'm sorry I didn't get to meet your parents," I say to Naomi. In all of the chaos of the night, they're the one set of parents that I didn't meet.

"Don't worry about it," Naomi says. She glances at Mohammad, a smile playing on her lips. "I thought I was going to die of boredom, going round and saying hello to everyone, before Mohammad came and saved me."

Mohammad grins, like he's now some knight in shining armor.

"Speaking of parents, did yours finally leave?" I ask Mohammad.

"Nah. They're still in there. Mum and Dad are talking to some investor who's interested in their business."

"That's actually pretty cool. And they were fine with you leaving?" I ask, remembering Mohammad telling me that he told his parents he was spending the night at Harry's.

"Definitely not," he replies matter-of-factly. "I lied. Told them I was going to walk you back to your hotel."

"You lied to your mum?" Naomi asks, her brows drawing up.

"I didn't exactly lie," Mohammad says quickly. "I just avoided concerning her. Mum gets pretty worked up over the small stuff. Figured it was best to let her stay at the party and not worry about me."

"And she believed you?" Naomi laughs.

"Obviously." He beams. "I have a trustworthy face. Gave her a kiss on the cheek and told her that by the time I got back to stay at Harry's, she'd probably already be home."

"You're seriously going to get caught one of these days," I say, shaking my head.

We walk for a good ten minutes before we finally get to the club, and it's surprisingly busy for a Thursday night. We all check our coats, and then Harry goes to get us drinks with Noah while Mohammad drags both me and Naomi out onto the dance floor.

"This is so much fun." Naomi laughs, throwing her hands into the air.

Mohammad sings along with the song as Noah and Harry find us.

I'm handed a cup, and I take a sip of something … brown.

And strong.

It burns, going down, but I don't really mind.

"How'd you get alcohol?" I ask.

"We've got fakes," Harry says into my ear.

Mohammad downs his drink and encourages Naomi to do the same, but she dances, holding her cup up in the air as she does.

It seems like a recipe for disaster with all the bodies and

movement, but she manages not to spill a drop. I take a sip of my drink, glancing around.

"You're not dancing," Harry says, standing in front of me.

"I'm not really in the mood," I reply.

"Come on. You can't make a lad dance alone. It isn't right," Harry says, pushing out a pout.

He holds out his hand to me. I roll my eyes but take it, letting him twirl me around. After the second twirl, I let out a laugh and relax.

"All right, all right. I give," I reply, taking my hand back as I start dancing.

We all dance together, sort of in one big circle.

And it's fun.

"Told you you'd get to see my dance moves tonight," Noah calls out to me.

"A true gift." Harry laughs.

I grin at them.

"I'm so proud of you. Letting loose!" I tease Noah, finishing off my drink. And it makes me feel better.

Harry flits off to the bar again. Someone else joins our group. It's fun.

I get to dance with Naomi and Mohammad.

When Harry comes back from the bar, he's got his phone in his hand, looking down at the screen.

"What's up?" I ask.

"One of my mates from The Arrington messaged. Said he heard Dad was back in town and was checking in. He's actually at a pub just up the road. Wants me to come by," Harry says to me.

"Are you going then?" I ask, confused. I thought he wanted to hang out with us.

"Yeah, I should. I'll just drop by for a pint, and then let's meet back up," Harry says, looking between all of us now.

"Are you sure?" Mohammad asks.

"We can come with," I offer.

"Nah. Stay and party," Harry says. "Let's meet at your hotel though. In an hour?"

"We should all just head home," Noah says, checking the time. "It's getting late anyway."

"Oh no, no, no," Harry says, shaking his head at Noah. "You're not getting out of this one. Besides, Mallory promised us a dip in her hotel pool!"

"The pool isn't even open." I laugh.

"I'll see you there in one hour," Harry says, pointing his finger first at Noah. Then, he moves it to me, Mohammad, and Naomi, trying to keep a serious expression on his face.

"Mate, thanks for tonight. I love you," Harry says, kissing Noah on the cheek before moving to Mohammad.

"I'll see you in an hour," he says to Mohammad.

"And, Naomi," Harry says, saluting her, "always a pleasure."

Naomi waves him off, and after, I watch Harry push through the crowd to leave.

I turn and look at Noah.

"Do you think it's a good idea?" I ask, wondering if we should go after him.

Noah dips his head closer, so I can hear him. "Harry always does as he pleases. Case in point, at the party."

"I didn't know he was going to …"

"What? Kiss your neck?" Noah shakes his head. "Harry will always need you. And you love being needed. You're always going to be there for him."

"I didn't want to be there for him, not in that way."

"What, as his date? Why not tell him then?"

"Because," I say, trying to figure it all out. "You … you wouldn't talk to me for days because I hurt him. I thought if I hurt him by saying no or by saying how I felt, you would be even more upset. We both care about him, but ..."

"You did it for me?" Noah asks. His eyes go wide, but someone bumps into his back, shoving him forward and out of his train of thought.

"Dance!" Mohammad says, grabbing on to my hand. He extends it up over my head and spins me around in a circle. The motion forces a smile onto my face. "Harry will be fine. We'll meet up with him later."

I roll my eyes but decide to listen to Mohammad.

And try to relax.

We dance. Moving to the beat. All of us dancing around one another.

I smile at Mohammad, who now has both of his hands up in the air. Naomi is doing her own thing but seems to keep one eye on him. Even Noah seems to be having fun, swaying to the song.

But then the energy in the room shifts as a slow, heavy beat echoes throughout the club.

Naomi wraps her arm around Mohammad's neck and moves her body in close to his.

I nervously glance around the club, trying to look anywhere other than at the boy who is next to me.

At Noah.

Because he's at my side.

And this music is slow.

And sexy.

Before, we were all dancing together. But now ...

I glance at Noah, my heart pounding. He's staring back at me. His golden eyes almost lighting up the club.

But then someone moves in front of me. He cocks his head at me and grins, a nonverbal way of asking if I want to dance. I take a step back from the guy and run into a hard body behind me. Firm fingers steady me at the waist. The guy looks over my shoulder, shrugs, and then turns around, dancing off in someone else's direction.

I look over my shoulder at Noah.

I push back against him, unsure if I get relief or more nervous from his touch.

I don't know why I'm so scared to be in his arms.

To have his hands on me.

I think it's that I worry once we start, we won't be able to stop. That, all along, he's been right. Once we kiss—*actually kiss*—I won't want to stop. I will be his, fully.

And feeling that way, falling for someone like that, it's scary.

Because I know that he could actually hurt me. That he has the power to.

"Are you all right?" Noah asks, dipping his head down to my ear.

And it's then that I realize I've been standing here, frozen, pushed up against him. That I haven't moved, but I haven't pulled away either.

"Uh, I'm fine," I reply, shaking my head.

I pull out from his hold and give him a smile. And it's a terrible smile. It feels awkward and forced. It doesn't reach my eyes, and I know that he can tell.

Noah looks back at me, confused, his brows creasing in.

"Come on. Let's go to the restroom," Naomi says, saving me. She laces her fingers through mine, pulling me away from Noah and Mohammad.

"You looked stricken back there," Naomi says when we get to the line.

"It's a bit weird," I admit.

Naomi searches my eyes before putting her hand on her hip. "Well, it doesn't have to be. You can dance however you want. With whomever you want. Dancing is just dancing. It's why we go out," she says with a smile.

"Yeah, but you and Mohammad are cute," I reply. "And maybe dating?"

"And you and Noah?"

"Are complicated."

"There isn't anything complicated about the way he looks at you," she counters, pushing me ahead of her in line.

I'm up next, and I decide I might as well go.

"You know what I think you need?" Naomi says from the next stall over.

"What?"

"A shot." She giggles.

"We're going to feel terrible tomorrow." I laugh as I come out of the stall and wash my hands.

"Who cares? It's our last day of school before break. Besides, we're better off having a drink and dancing a little longer. That way when we go to bed, we'll crash." She comes out of the stall and washes her hands next to me.

"Sound logic." I grin.

"So, deal then? We drink and then actually dance?" she asks pointedly.

"I'll do my best," I say as she pulls me out of the restroom.

She drags me to the bar, orders two doubles, flashes her own fake, and makes us down them right then and there. I purse my lips at the strong taste.

As quickly as we got there, we leave the bar and go back to the dance floor. I get bumped in the crowd and have to grasp on to Noah's arm when I get back to him.

"You smell like …"

"Vodka," I clarify.

"Sneaking some booze in the restroom?" Noah asks, looking from me to Naomi with an easy smile.

"Naomi insisted. Said I needed to loosen up and have fun."

"Are you not having fun?"

"Sometimes, it's hard to let go with you around," I say.

"Shouldn't I make it easy to let go?"

I shake my head. "I feel like you're watching my every move. It's unnerving."

"I am." Noah shrugs. "It isn't a bad thing. I like watching you."

"How about we dance instead?" Naomi calls out.

She wraps her arms around Mohammad's neck. I stand and watch them for a second. He's singing the song. She's swaying back and forth, a huge smile on her face.

But then Noah shifts me back around to face him. His hands slip around my waist, and he pulls me toward him. I place my palms on his shoulders. We move back and forth, shifting from one foot to the other.

And it's probably the most awkward dance of my life.

"I feel like I'm at prom," I mumble to Noah, completely breaking the tension between us.

He lets out a warm laugh before grabbing my arms and pulling them higher up around his neck, so his chest is against mine.

"Better?" he asks, tightening his hands at my waist.

"Better."

I hold on to Noah, leaning into him. I can see everyone around us jumping and singing out, but Noah and I don't do that. We stay pressed against one another for a long time.

"MOHAMMAD, I NEED to get a cab home," Naomi says, loud enough to grab my attention.

I pull away from Noah.

Naomi smiles at us before giving me a quick kiss on the cheek. "Mum's going to kill me. It's so late! But I had so much fun!"

I smile at her, but Noah's fingers are still holding on to my waist, making it hard for me to focus on anything else.

"I'll walk you out," Mohammad says, placing his hand on her back before guiding her through the crowd.

"Wait, are you coming back?" I call out, feeling slightly abandoned.

And wholly terrified.

Mohammad shoots me a nod that I'm not sure is an answer.

"Sometimes, I wonder if you're afraid to be alone with me," Noah says, shaking his head.

"I'm not afraid."

"That's good. I never want you to feel like that with me," Noah says, concern evident in his voice.

"I don't. I just … I'm feeling our drinks."

"Then, relax."

"Relax into what? We're in the middle of a dance floor," I say, motioning around us.

"Into me. We can just dance for a bit until Mohammad gets back, and then we'll go."

"You hate dancing."

"I like swaying. Especially with you. And swaying isn't really dancing. So, we won't be dancing." He gives me a sweet smile.

"We will be swaying?"

Noah pulls me closer to him. And being back in this position—with his hands on me, his fingers pressing into my skin—it's overwhelming. I lace my fingers around his torso, holding on to him like I'm hugging him. It feels safer than wrapping my hands around his neck, where our faces would be so close.

I try to focus solely on swaying. But focusing on that means I feel everything. The way his body is pressed against mine.

I rest my head against his chest. It seems like a sweet gesture, but really, it allows me not to look at him. Not to have our mouths close.

After the kiss in the lunchroom, the thought of kissing Noah again gives me anxiety. And I'm not sure this is where it should happen.

So, I'm going to avoid his lips.

I just keep moving back and forth and try to fall into the flow of it.

Even though Noah says he's a bad dancer, he isn't.

At least, not when he's dancing like this.

With me.

"Do you feel better?" Noah asks.

I nod against his chest. Because I do. I've had a moment to stop thinking and freaking out, and I allow myself to start feeling.

"Good," he replies.

I slowly unpeel myself from him, bringing my hands up onto his chest.

Noah watches me, his eyes finding my hands as my palms slide up his chest, across his collarbone, and onto his shoulders before wrapping around his neck.

The process holds all of my attention, like it might be the most important thing I've ever done.

And when I finally lace my fingers together, I feel like they will never come apart.

Noah pulls me against him and stops swaying. He just stands there, looking down at me. His mouth slips open as his eyes dilate. They always turn from the softest brown to a few shades darker and get larger when we are this close, and it's hard to look away when his eyes do that. They just pull me in.

He pulls me in.

"We're supposed to be dancing," I whisper.

"We are dancing," Noah replies, his voice heavy.

He shifts again, his hands moving from my waist down onto my hips. When his fingers press into my skin, I practically jump at the sensation.

Noah's lips pull up at the corner, his eyes softening. "I told you you're jumpy," he says as his hands move from my lower hips to my backside, pushing his hips into mine.

I practically shudder at the sensation, my eyes fluttering.

"I'm not jumpy. I'm just …"

"Just what?"

"Overwhelmed," I admit.

And I am. By his touch. By the way he smells. By how close we are.

Noah bites his lip and slowly nods his head. "That's good. Just stop thinking about it and feel it."

I want to tell him that I've been trying to do that, but he spins me around and then grinds into me.

"Close your eyes," Noah insists.

So, I do.

I push everything out of my mind. Harry. Mohammad. What this all means.

I forget everything and just focus on Noah.

On his body.

On how it feels, having his hands on me.

How it's possible that I feel so turned on.

I press my palms on the back of his hands and then move them from my hips, down over my thighs, and back up again.

"I like when you stop thinking," Noah whispers with a shaky breath.

I turn toward him. His cheeks are sucked in, and I can visibly see his chest rising and falling.

I smile at him. "It reminds me of when you rubbed my back in bed. When you held on to my hands. I could feel all of you against my back. You were …" I say, my smile leaving.

Because I can only think of one word.

"I was what?" Noah asks, his voice clear. His eyes search mine as his hands rest on top of my shoulders.

"Consuming," I finally get out.

Noah nods once but then grows serious. "You're just now realizing this, aren't you?"

I glance at the floor, feeling my cheeks grow flushed. "I've always known it, Noah. I've always felt it. You have a way of pulling people in."

"I don't care about anyone else."

"You do," I correct.

"I do. But I …" Noah says, his expression growing serious.

"You what?"

"You're different. And I know you know that. This," he says, grasping on to my hands, "feels right. It feels good to me. Like our normal."

"It's not our normal though," I reply. "It's a big deal."

"Holding hands is a big deal?" Noah asks, an amused smile sneaking onto his face.

"Monumental." I smile back.

"You like it though."

"You're missing my point."

"What is your point then?"

"There is no coming back from you. Once we do this, everything is over."

"Hand-holding has never sounded so tragic," Noah says, his forehead creasing.

"You know what I mean."

"You mean, you don't know. You still aren't sure, but once you hold my hand, then you've decided?" Noah asks, sounding hurt.

"No, Noah. It's just … so hard."

"Nothing with us is hard, Mal. Why are you making it so hard?" Noah asks with frustration.

"Flirting with you, talking, dancing—it's all easy. I told you, you absorb people. *It's who you are.* The only thing keeping me grounded is not giving in to the physical. Once we start that, there's no stopping it."

Noah looks at me, perplexed.

"Well, why would you want to?" His confused expression twists into a silly grin, and he raises his eyebrows at me. "I mean, it doesn't sound so bad, if you ask me. Giving in."

"You can't flirt with me right now. I have to be serious. I have to think all this through," I reply, crossing my arms over my chest.

Noah uncrosses them and smiles at me. "You really don't."

"I really do," I insist.

Noah rolls his eyes but then pulls me back against him. "Sometimes, you really do surprise me. You've begged me to kiss you before, and yet now, you can't even hold my hand without freaking out."

"It's because it means something to me, Noah. And I would think it does to you too. It's not just hand-holding. It's not just dancing. It's way, way more."

"You're being a little silly tonight," Noah says with a smirk.

"Silly?"

"Silly." He nods. "You asked me last night for things to go back to normal. For us to be friends. Over and over, this shows me that I can't just be your friend. I'm always going to want more. Want this. Want us."

I feel like my heart might break out of my chest.

"I thought you meant that you *couldn't even* be my friend. That it would be too much for you. That you still, somewhere deep down, hadn't forgiven me."

Noah shakes his head. "Not what I meant. I didn't think I could only be your friend. I'm still not sure I can. I tried today, but you were sad, and then …"

"And then you flirted with me."

"It's hard for me not to. But if you aren't ready, if this isn't what you want, well, I would try not to."

"I don't want to be *just* friends either," I say, my voice shaky.

"But?"

"But … relationships are about more than just amazing chemistry."

"You still don't trust me."

"I … I trust you. I just don't know if we want the same things."

"Tell me what you want then."

I shake my head, feeling like I could cry. Because I want this. *Him.* And I'm sabotaging it.

I know I am.

But I'm terrified.

"There you guys are," Mohammad says, joining us and interrupting our conversation. "Harry texted and said to head to the hotel."

Before either Noah or I have a chance to say anything, Mohammad's already walking back out of the club.

"Come on. I'll walk you back." Noah takes my hand and leads us to the coat check.

And even after we get our coats and meet Mohammad out

front, Noah doesn't drop my hand.

And I like that.

"So, can you stay with us?" I ask Noah when we get back to my hotel.

We're standing out front, and Mohammad is glancing around, looking for Harry.

Noah lets go of my hand and shakes his head. "Mum wants me home tonight. Detention after school and all that."

"Helen's got you on a short leash for that one," Harry says.

I snap my head in the direction of his voice and am quickly swept up into a hug.

"I wasn't sure you were coming." I smile at him, relief flooding through me. I was worried he'd go on some crazy bender like he has in the past after dealing with his parents.

Harry's blue eyes find mine, and he smiles at me. "I did one better. Got us food," he says, holding up a bag of takeout.

"What'd you get?" Mohammad asks, excitement flashing across his face.

"Falafel and chips." Harry grins back at him.

"Ooh, yes," Mohammad moans out, his eyes rolling back.

"Sound good?" I laugh.

"I'm not sure there are words to describe how happy I am right now," Mohammad says, eyeing the takeout bag. "So, are we ready?"

It's obvious he's eager to go up and dig into the food.

"Are you sure I can't convince you to stay?" Harry says to Noah. "I'll message Helen. I'll even give you the extra salt and vinegar packs I got for the chips."

Noah smiles but shakes his head. "Mum wants me home, but I wanted to make sure you were staying here tonight," Noah tells Harry.

"Always worrying about me," Harry says, pulling Noah

into a quick hug.

When Harry pulls back, he places a kiss on Noah's cheek. Mohammad holds out his fist for Noah to bump, his eyes still on the bag of food.

Noah gives him a fist bump and a pat on the shoulder before turning his attention to me.

He moves toward me and slowly wraps his hand around my waist as he pulls me into a tight side hug. I wrap my arm around his back and bring my free palm to rest on his chest. While the side hug is typically considered less invasive, this one feels intimate. It's soft and slow. Like time is moving around us and we're stuck in a moment alone.

Noah leans his head down by my ear. "I'll see you at school tomorrow," he whispers before kissing me on the cheek.

I hold my breath as his lips find my skin.

It's a quick, friendly kiss, but that doesn't stop a flush from spreading across my cheeks.

When he pulls away, I look up at him dreamily. "See you tomorrow," I reply.

Noah holds my gaze for a brief moment before looking between Harry and Mohammad. His lips turn up into the slightest smile before he turns and walks off.

Harry wraps his arm around my shoulders and grins at me. "Ready?" he asks.

"Ready," I reply as we walk into the hotel.

Bath Kingdom.
12:30AM

WHEN THE ELEVATOR dings as we reach my floor, Mohammad looks across Harry to me with a naughty smirk. He narrows his eyes into serious slits as he prepares himself for the door to open.

I know exactly what's about to happen and quickly kick off my heels in preparation. When the elevator opens, Mohammad bursts into the hallway and starts sprinting to my room.

I chase after him. I give it my all, but it's not quite enough to catch him.

Mohammad is practically radiating when I get to the door.

"You're such a brat!" I say.

I suck in a gulp of air, resting my hands on my hips.

"I won. I won," Mohammad chants, waving his room key like it's his prize.

"You cheated! You should have warned me it was coming," I disagree, folding my arms across my chest.

I want to rip that key out of his hand, but Mohammad looks too happy for me to take that away from him.

"Sorry, Miss America. That's on you. You've always got to be prepared." He nods firmly, agreeing with himself.

"Prepared? I was in heels!"

"And no one thought to tell me what was going on?!" Harry says, aghast, looking between Mohammad and me as he joins us.

"I couldn't chance you dropping the food," Mohammad says, like that's somehow justification enough.

"You two about gave me a bloody heart attack!" Harry says, wide-eyed. "And I'm too young and beautiful to die."

Mohammad chuckles, but Harry really does look worried.

"Well, apparently, we were both unprepared," I say sympathetically, giving Harry's arm a squeeze.

"Unprepared *and* losers," Mohammad says, sticking his

tongue out at us as he inserts his key, letting us into my room.

"Insult upon injury," Harry says, ushering me through the door. "I'm thinking I might have to hold your falafel and chips hostage until I get a proper apology."

Harry looks to Mohammad, a gleam in his eye.

Mohammad rolls his eyes in response.

"I'm sorry that I'm so quick that I not only almost gave you a heart attack at sixteen, but that I also beat Mallory fair and square despite her disagreement. My speed amazes me too," Mohammad banters back.

Harry pushes out his lips into a pout but then nods his head firmly. "That's good enough for me."

I roll my eyes at both of them.

Only Harry would think *that* was an apology, and only Mohammad would find a way to flatter himself in the process of saying sorry.

"Mallory, how about for you?" Harry asks as Mohammad kicks off his shoes.

I watch as he closes the curtains before stripping off his suit jacket and laying it over the arm of the couch. It's obvious he's not paying attention to our conversation because a second later, he's walking over to the mini fridge.

I shrug at Harry. "I'm easily offended, so I think my answer is no."

"Huh. Well, maybe this will take the edge off of your defeat." Harry smirks, pulling a flask out of his pocket and handing it to me.

"How are you always prepared?" I laugh, taking a drink before handing it back to him. I drop my heels onto the floor and strip off my coat.

"Someone has to be," Harry says, bringing the flask up to his lips.

"We don't need that," Mohammad says. "We've got

champagne." He pulls the bottle out from the mini fridge and holds it up to show us.

"How?" I ask.

Because last time I looked in the mini fridge, it was empty. Mohammad's drained me of soda and juice during his many visits.

"Had the girls stash one for us," Mohammad replies triumphantly.

His grin is contagious, and I can't help but smile back at him.

"Brilliant," Harry says, dropping the carryout bag and flask onto the table as he goes to help Mohammad.

I push my hair away from my face as I watch them. Harry's careful to pop open the champagne without spilling any. Mohammad unbuttons his shirt as Harry brings the bottle over to me.

"Ladies first."

I grab it, taking a sip of champagne straight from the bottle. I lick my lips, the cold liquid and bubbles tasting much better than whatever was in Harry's flask.

"Good?" Harry asks, his eyes lingering on my lips.

"Delicious."

"So much better," Mohammad says. He's shirtless now but still in his slacks.

"Were you over the suit?"

"I was over the suit when we went dancing. I got sweaty," he replies, scrunching up is nose.

"Speaking of dancing," I say, turning back to Harry, "I can't believe you ditched us!"

"Aww. Someone felt abandoned?" Harry asks, pulling me into a hug.

I rest my head against his chest, and it's actually nice.

"Slightly, yes."

"What can I say? I'm downright devious sometimes. It's why you all love me though." Harry grins at us.

"Yes, leaving your friends in the club is just one of your many charms," I say.

"Speaking of devious actions … who is ready to check out the pool?" Harry asks.

I shake my head, pulling away from him. "It's not open."

Harry grunts once, pushing his hand back through his blond hair.

"Next best option then," he says. "If I remember correctly, someone has a bathtub that is highly praised."

Harry and Mohammad share a knowing glance before rushing to my bathroom with huge grins.

"Oh, no, no, no," I say, chasing after them.

"*Oh, yes,*" Harry says, looking at the bathtub with approval.

I glance at Mohammad, wondering if he'll agree with me. But he's got the champagne bottle to his lips, and I know I'm not going to get any support from him on this one.

"This bathtub is *not* big enough for three people," I say, trying to state the obvious.

"It's either this or I'm sneaking into the pool," Harry says to me. "I'm in desperate need of a soak."

"Ring the front desk," Mohammad says to me. "All Harry would have to say is that Mr. Brooks is requesting use of the pool."

"They know your father here?" I ask with surprise.

"Everyone knows his father," Mohammad answers.

"That simple, huh?" I say as Mohammad hands me the champagne.

"That simple," Harry agrees. "Or you could call. You are staying in one of their nicest suites. Maybe it's time you use that card."

I roll my eyes, realizing I'm not getting out of this.

"Fine, the tub it is," I say, giving in. Because I won't call down and ask about the pool. Despite being a guest of the hotel, I wouldn't feel comfortable, asking for special treatment. It's not me.

"I'll get it ready," Mohammad says excitedly. He closes the drain and turns on the water before finding a candle and lighting it.

I laugh, watching him work.

"Let's turn on the telly," Harry says, finding the remote. He clicks it on and flips through a few channels before finding an old show.

"Wait, what about our food?" I ask. Because food sounds way better than a bath right now.

"I'll bring it in," Mohammad says, leaving the bathroom in a flash.

"Grab us water too," I call out.

"Got it," Mohammad says back.

The sound of the water running fills up the bathroom, and I sit down on the stool, waiting for Mohammad. Harry is leaning over the counter, looking through the bath products. He must find what he wants because he tosses me a plastic bottle.

"It's not a proper bath without bubbles," he says.

I get up from the stool, drain the bottle, and watch as the bubbles form in the water.

"Nice," Mohammad says approvingly, coming back into the bathroom. He's got the takeout in one hand and bottles of water in the other.

Harry sets the champagne down on the floor by the tub while Mohammad sets the food on the stool, moving it so we can reach it from inside the tub.

"I think that's everything," Mohammad says, scanning the

setup.

"In we go!" Harry agrees, stripping off his shirt.

Mohammad does the same, moving to the button of his pants when I freeze.

"Whoa, whoa, whoa." I hold up my hand, stopping them. I push my shoulders back and narrow my eyes in on them. "Underwear stays on."

"Afraid to see us knicker-less?" Mohammad teases, pulling off his pants.

"Terrified," I reply, flaring my eyes at him. But I crack a grin.

"Deal," Mohammad agrees. "It's for the best anyway. Anyone who lays eyes on my naked figure might be rendered speechless."

I raise my eyebrows at him as Harry lets out a chuckle. Mohammad walks over to the bath in his underwear, turns off the water, and then hops into the tub.

"And on that note, I'll go get my swimsuit." I turn to walk to my closet, but then I remember that my dress has a back zipper. I glance at Mohammad, but his hands are already wet and bubbly.

I move my gaze to Harry, who's still undressing. My cheeks flush at the sight of his shirtless torso. His hands are on the button at his waist when I interrupt him.

"Can you unzip the back?"

"It would be my pleasure." Harry smirks.

I roll my eyes but am surprised when he simply turns me around, brushes my hair off to the side, and unzips my dress.

"Thanks." I sneak off to my closet and change into my swimsuit before heading back to the bathroom.

Harry and Mohammad are both in the tub now, and my eyes bulge at the little amount of room that's left.

This is going to be interesting.

I grab a clip from the counter and pin my hair up before joining them.

"We barely fit." I laugh, trying to wedge myself between Harry and Mohammad.

"We fit fine," Mohammad says, waving off my comment.

"It's a squeeze, but we'll manage," Harry adds.

I'm checking to make sure all of my hair is up when my hand slides against my necklace. "Shit. Can someone take this off? I probably shouldn't get bubbles on it."

"Keep it on. You look regal," Harry says, grabbing the bottle of champagne off the floor.

"Really?" I laugh.

"Basically," Mohammad agrees, shoving an entire falafel into his mouth. "But I'm pretty sure that was the intended effect."

"It was." Harry nods in agreement before passing me the bottle of champagne.

I try to sit crisscross but end up letting my feet hang out over the edge of the tub.

I take a swig.

"Maybe you should start calling me Queen then," I tease. "Or Princess."

"You'll always be Miss America!" Mohammad shouts.

"If she's to be a princess, then we have to do it up properly," Harry says, looking at Mohammad. "Go grab her birthday crown. Then, she can be Princess of the Bathtub!"

"Of the entire Bath Kingdom." Mohammad laughs.

"Not the crown," I say, adamantly shaking my head.

"You can't be a princess without a crown," Harry points out.

"I don't want to be one. I was just teasing."

"Too late!" Mohammad says, standing up. He gets out of the bath, dragging water and bubbles across the bathroom floor.

I glare at Harry, but he just laughs.

Mohammad comes back into the bathroom and rejoins us in the tub. He tosses the crown to Harry, who quickly places it on my head.

"Your Highness," Harry says before giving me a small bow.

I roll my eyes at him before turning to Mohammad.

I adjust my hair and the crown and then give him my best smile. "Well, how do I look?"

"Like a woman who is wearing a birthday crown, a swimsuit, and a crazy-expensive necklace in a bubble bath," Mohammad says before blatantly laughing at me.

I push out a pout, turning to Harry.

"You look like a princess," Harry corrects.

I smile at him, happy with his answer. Harry hands Mohammad the champagne before reaching over the edge of the tub and pulling out his phone from his pants pocket.

"And I'll always cherish this," Harry says, opening up his camera.

I shake my head and partially cover my face with my hand.

"Please?" Harry asks, giving me puppy-dog eyes.

I let out a huff, but then Mohammad hands me back the champagne. I take another sip, feeling really relaxed. And really happy.

Harry's still looking at me, so I nod.

"Say ... princess." He laughs, getting ready to take the photo.

I straighten my crown and hold up the champagne bottle, smiling. Harry snaps the photo and then hands his phone to Mohammad.

"Screen-saver material, for sure," Mohammad says, admiring the photo. He hands him back the phone and then steals my crown.

"Hey!" I laugh, trying to grab it back, but Mohammad already has it on. He offers me a handful of chips instead.

"You two look mad." Harry laughs, looking us over. "You're eating chips in the tub, and Mohammad has on a *Birthday Girl* crown."

And I know he's right.

This is ridiculous.

But it's sort of fun. And I have to give it to them; the bath, the food—it wasn't the worst idea they'd ever had. But then I notice that Harry doesn't have on anything special. No crown. No necklace.

"You need something too," I say, thinking about what I could do. "Ah, I know."

I get out of the tub, go to the counter, and grab my black eyeliner. I get back into the tub and sit so that I'm facing Harry. I pull his head closer to mine and turn it slightly, so I have the perfect canvas.

"What are you doing?" Mohammad asks, watching over my shoulder.

Harry doesn't say anything. He just goes along with it.

"I'm giving him something special," I reply.

I draw a little heart on his cheek and then pull my hand back. "Perfect."

"I want one," Mohammad says.

"What'd you give me?" Harry asks, touching his cheek.

"A heart," I reply, turning toward Mohammad. I bring my hand up and draw on his skin. "And for you, a star."

"Fitting." Mohammad grins proudly.

"And for you," Harry says, grabbing the eyeliner from my hand.

"Nothing dirty," I say sternly, but he's already writing

something on my cheek. "What does it say?"

"It's my name," Harry says, putting the cap on the eyeliner.

"Aww." I smile at Harry, but then bubbles come up to the surface of the water. "What the …"

Mohammad bursts out laughing.

"Ah, mate. Seriously?" Harry's face flashes with horror.

"What?" Mohammad laughs, wiping at his eyes. "I'm just making us some bubbles. It's all the champagne."

"Bubbles … with your farts?" I breathe out, trying to figure out how boys can be so gross and yet so pleased with themselves. It just doesn't make sense.

"Try it. It's fun," Mohammad says to Harry.

And I can tell he's considering it.

I shake my head at Mohammad, snatching back the crown from him. I turn to Harry.

"If I'm Princess of the Bathtub, then you have to follow my rules."

"And what are your rules?" Harry asks, amused.

I press my lips together, thinking. "Rule number one: no farting. Rule number two: no getting my hair wet." I narrow my eyes, wondering if I've missed anything. "Yeah, I think that's it." I give him a confirming nod.

"She said nothing about being naked!" Harry laughs, moving to stand up like he's about to strip out of his underwear.

"Rule three!" I shout. "Knickers. Stay. On."

"No fun," Harry says, splashing me.

He dries off his hands with a towel before grabbing a box with a falafel wrap and chips in it. Mohammad leans his head back against the tub, taking a sip of his water. He blinks up at the ceiling, looking relaxed.

"Tonight was …" he starts.

"Tonight is perfect," Harry says.

I look between them and smile.

Harry takes a swig of champagne before feeding me a chip. He digs into the wrap, handing me bits of it. First, there's a bite of falafel. Then a cucumber. Then another fry. I lick the sauce off my fingers before looking to Mohammad.

"I can't believe you kissed Naomi tonight," I say, reflecting.

"I can't believe you kissed ... no one." Mohammad laughs.

I roll my eyes and flick a bubble at him.

"I can't believe we actually got through it," Harry says with a relaxed sigh.

"Do you feel relieved?" I ask him.

"I feel ... nothing. Which is exactly what I was going for." He grins at me.

I smile back before thinking about the party. "Did you see that Mia and Sophia are together?"

"Seriously?" Mohammad asks, his eyes going wide.

"Yep," I reply. "They looked happy."

"I always thought Sophia had a thing for Noah," Mohammad says, looking perplexed.

"Nope, wrong sibling." I smile.

"Hmm," Mohammad huffs.

"Hmm what?" I ask.

"I can't believe I was so off," Mohammad says, visibly pouting.

I hand him one of Harry's chips in consolation.

"It's understandable you didn't know. They just took that step," I explain.

"The shagging step," Harry says with an excited grin.

I swat at him. "No. The friends-to-more step," I clarify.

"Boring," Harry drones out.

"Not boring. It's sweet."

"Are you sure?" Mohammad asks, his forehead creasing.

"Positive."

"Hmm … that changes things," Mohammad replies.

"Changes what?" Harry asks.

"Maybe I shouldn't become a matchmaker," Mohammad says, looking conflicted. "But it's just one couple. You can't be right about them all."

It's easy to see he's taking this news hard.

"I forgot you consider yourself a part-time matchmaker," I say, finally realizing what this is about.

"I didn't see Naomi and me either," Mohammad says, growing even more worried. "I guess I'll have to find a different future occupation."

"You already have one, Mr. Bond," I say, holding my finger up as a gun before blowing out the fake smoke.

"You're right." Mohammad nods, looking more certain.

Harry laughs and finishes off the bottle of champagne.

We eat all of the chips and falafel and empty a few bottles of water before dragging ourselves out of the tub.

"I didn't bring clothes," Harry says, patting himself dry with a towel.

I grin at him, standing up in the tub.

"You can wear my pajamas," I offer.

"How *hilarious*."

"I'm sleeping naked!" Mohammad declares, stripping off his underwear before running naked into my room.

"Shh! I don't want to get into trouble." I laugh. "And you can't sleep naked. Remember my rules."

"You know rules are meant to be broken," Harry says, his blue eyes sparkling at me.

"Not this rule," I disagree.

"Don't worry; I brought clothes," Mohammad says, popping his head back into the bathroom to show us his pajama pants.

"Of course you did." I laugh, wrapping a towel around me.

Harry extends his hand, helping me out of the tub.

"I didn't," he says, tilting his head at me. "So, does that mean I can sleep naked?"

He grins at me again, looking way too eager.

"As fun as that sounds, nope. Follow me, Mr. Brooks." I grab on to his arm and pull him into the closet with me.

"Someone has a plan." Harry laughs, watching me.

"Someone does." I open up one of my drawers, sifting through it until I find what I'm looking for. "I'm thinking the purple pajamas shorts," I say, holding them up for him to see.

Harry's eyes go wide when his gaze lands on my skimpy shorts.

"Absolutely not," Harry says, shaking his head.

"They're your only option—unless you want to sleep naked and alone on the couch," I point out.

Harry shakes his head. "You play dirty," he says, suddenly tickling me. His fingers brush across my arms and down over my towel.

I drop the shorts, defending myself from his tickle attack, and let out a stream of giggles.

Harry gives me a defeated sigh, reaching down to grab the shorts. "If you insist," he says, still looking unconvinced.

Harry leaves me in the closet, so I can change. I quickly strip off my wet swimsuit and pull on Noah's sweatpants and a T-shirt. I know that I should have let Harry wear them, but the thought of seeing him in my tiny purple pajama shorts was too much of a temptation to pass up.

Besides, I want to be comfortable.

And covered.

And Harry's wearing my only other set of pajamas. Well, apart from the pajamas that Naomi gave me. Although I'd rather sleep naked than in those horrifying things. I'd probably suffocate to death in them. They're too fuzzy.

And way too embarrassing.

When I come out, changed, Mohammad's already in bed with fresh water bottles on the bedside table for us. I crawl into bed with him as I hear the bathroom door squeak open.

"Well, what do we think?" Harry asks, strutting out of the bathroom in my shorts. They're way too small on him and very revealing.

"Gorgeous," Mohammad says, trying to sound serious. But a second later, he bursts out laughing.

Harry puts his hand on the doorframe, posing for us. The purple shorts are basically as tight as underwear on him, but they have frilly lace lining the bottom, which sort of makes them cute. He is barely covered, but he's grinning.

"Oh my." I laugh, bringing my hand up to my mouth.

"I'm not sure if I should feel degraded by the clothing option provided or if I should feel victorious in the fact that you obviously wanted to see me as close to naked as you could get me," Harry says, pushing off the wall.

"When in doubt, always go with the compliment," I offer.

"Hey, you quoted my advice!" Mohammad beams.

I nod, thinking about his birthday gift to me. Harry walks toward the bed, but I stop him.

"Wait, can you flip off the lights? And turn on the fan, please." I smile up at him, trying not to sound bossy.

"Whatever the princess wishes," he replies.

Harry flicks off the lights, but Mohammad turns on a lamp at the same time. Harry falls down next to me on the bed, lying flat on his back.

I adjust myself between them and scoot down, so I can

stare up at the ceiling.

Exhaustion washes over me.

"Mohammad, you probably need to set an alarm." I yawn, trying to think straight.

"We'll skip," Harry disagrees, rolling over to look at us.

"I'll set it," Mohammad says, clicking on his phone before plugging it in.

I listen as he cracks open another water bottle and takes a drink.

He hands me the bottle.

I lean up and take a small sip before passing it to Harry. He finishes off the bottle and sets it down on the bedside table next to him.

"I wish Noah were here," Harry says, sliding under the covers.

I bring my hands down to his sweatpants, feeling like, in some way, he is here. "Me too."

"Same," Mohammad says before turning off the lamp.

I roll onto my side, getting comfortable. I fluff the pillow under my head. Between the food, the bath, the warm covers, and the cool fan on my face, I feel like I'm in heaven.

Plus, I have Harry and Mohammad here with me.

And a little piece of Noah too.

"I think skipping tomorrow is a good idea," I mumble out.

"We'll skip," Harry says back.

And then I think I fall asleep.

FRIDAY, OCTOBER 18TH
A heart on your cheek.
6:30AM

I WAKE UP, hungover.

With my face buried in a chest.

And with two hands set at my waist.

I pull my head back from Harry's chest and glance down to see that Mohammad and Harry have their hands resting on top of one another's.

On top of me.

A beeping noise vaguely registers, and I try to push the sound out of my head. I feel like I'm in a groggy, alternate universe, which means that the best thing I can do is go back to sleep and wake up on my own.

I ignore the hands at my waist and close my eyes. The beeping fades, and I'm almost back asleep when Harry stirs.

"Mohammad," Harry mumbles, "turn it off."

I ignore Harry since he obviously isn't talking to me and keep my eyes shut. I feel like I'm floating on a cloud, slowly moving further and further into a dream.

But I keep being pulled out of it.

"I know," Mohammad moans.

One of the hands leaves my waist. It must be Mohammad's because Harry pulls me closer.

"Alarm," Mohammad says, finally rousing me.

I blink my eyes open again, squinting at Harry.

He barely looks awake, his blond brows woven together in disapproval.

"Let's blow it off," he mumbles.

"We can't," Mohammad says, his voice clearer this time.

"This is shit." Harry pouts.

I wipe at my eyes and push my hair away from my face, trying to wake myself up.

"It's not the end of the world," I finally say.

Because Harry's face is still pouting even though his eyes are shut. And it's kind of cute.

His lip curls into a smile, and he opens one eye, peeking over at me.

"It could be. And if it were, wouldn't you feel rather silly, having dragged me to school?" He raises an eyebrow at me, and I let out an easy laugh.

"I'm going to go shower," Mohammad says.

I roll over and watch him get out of bed. He's slow to stand at first, but once he's up, I can practically see him recharge right in front of me. He stretches out like a cat before bounding into the bathroom like he isn't the slightest bit hungover.

"That was … an eventful night," Harry says, recapturing my attention.

His hand is still draped over me. I roll toward him and bring my hands under my cheek. Harry's own cheeks are pink from sleep, but other than that, he looks the exact same as he always does.

"We took a bath," I reply, the memory coming back to me.

"We cuddled," Harry replies, wiping the sleep out of his eyes before connecting his gaze to mine.

I look away quickly. "You and Mohammad maybe."

"That's not exactly true."

"Harry." I bring my eyes back up to his, wanting him to stop there.

The weight of his hand is suddenly heavy on me. Harry must understand because he smiles and lets out a warm breath.

"Well, can you blame a man for wanting to be held in the middle of the night? After all, it was like a blizzard in here. What are you doing, trying to freeze us out? Have you decided we're taking our year off now and are sending us up the Himalayas from your room?"

I grin at him. "That's exactly what I was trying to do."

"You're terrible." Harry smirks, but then his face pinches in pain. "And I'm hungover."

"That makes two of us."

I lay my head flat against the pillow, listening as Mohammad turns on the shower. I let out a long, slow grumble and cup my hands at my chest.

I just want to curl up into a little ball and fall back to sleep.

"You could sound a bit more excited, you know," Harry says, rolling onto his side.

"About what?"

"Well, you did happen to wake up in bed with me. I might feel a little offended if you keep groaning over there."

I shake my head and give him a small push. "I'm not groaning."

"I mean, moaning would be one thing," he says with a smirk. "But groaning in discontent? Now, that's just unacceptable."

"Harry …" I whine. "You are being way too much of a morning person for me right now. And too witty. I am tired and hungover and can't keep up."

I push out my lips in a pout and roll fully onto my side. Harry gives me a small pout back, acknowledging my hungover-ness before pulling me to him. I wrap my arms around him, grateful for the warmth on his chest. He strokes the back of my hair as we both lie on our sides.

"Better?"

"Mmhmm," I mumble.

Harry rubs my arm, and I burrow myself against him.

"This is nice."

"It is," I agree.

I pull back slightly and look at Harry.

"You have a heart on your cheek," I comment, my finger finding his skin. I move through my memories, trying to remember how it got there. I narrow my eyes. "Did I draw that?"

"A Mallory James original." Harry nods. "Should I keep it?"

I smile. "Definitely."

"I won't wash mine if you won't wash yours," Harry says brightly.

And loudly.

"Shh." I hold my finger up to my lips and push out another sad pout.

"Aww, babe. Seriously, let's skip."

"I mean … it's not the worst idea," I admit.

"Although I might have to find my own bed. You're a bit of a bed hog, you know."

"And you snore," I fire back.

"Really?" Harry asks, like he has no clue.

"Hasn't anyone told you that before?"

Harry looks at me with surprise. "Actually, no."

"I remember when you slept over at Noah's and I walked past his room. You and Mohammad were so loud that I couldn't believe anyone in the house was able to sleep through it." I laugh.

"So, it isn't just me. Mohammad snores too then," Harry points out.

"I guess so. Although honestly, I barely remember getting into bed last night."

Harry rolls onto his back, taking me with him. My head stays on his chest, and I rest my hand on his stomach, warmth flooding through me.

"I wouldn't try to. I'm pretty sure it was only a few hours ago that we actually did."

"All right, time to switch," Mohammad says, bounding out of the bathroom.

I try to get my head to move in his direction, but it won't budge.

Harry sighs, and his stomach flexes under my palm as he sits up. "No showers for us. We're all skipping."

"We're not," Mohammad says.

I listen to his footsteps as he walks around the bed and then pulls Harry up and out of it. I slip off his chest, my head helplessly falling onto the bed.

Harry grumbles but gets up. And when he's standing, I can't help but notice that he's in my pajama shorts.

My eyes instantly go wide.

Harry's long, lean body is fully on display. Harry looks down over himself, blatantly checking himself out. I watch as he flexes his abs, seemingly amused at the action.

"Like the new look?" he asks me.

He's beaming. I roll my eyes and try to swat at him, but I end up only swatting at the air because he's too far away. And each time I scoot closer toward the edge of the bed to get him, he moves a step back.

It would probably help if I was willing to move my body

off the bed and sit up, but I'm too lazy this morning. I finally give up, my arm hanging defeatedly over the edge.

"Hurry up and shower. If you're not quick, then I won't have enough time to get ready. Then, I really will be skipping."

"You're not skipping," Mohammad says, moving out of eyesight. "I'll order room service. Any requests?"

"Coffee," I say, my voice scratchy.

Mohammad nods, and I think I hear him flipping through the room service menu.

"It would be quicker if we showered together," Harry offers, sticking his tongue out at me. But he doesn't wait for an answer before going into the bathroom.

"Harry, you want the usual?" Mohammad calls out.

"Yeah," Harry replies.

When I hear the water come on, I pull the covers up and over my head. I listen as Mohammad starts to order us breakfast and doze happily back to sleep.

THE SPACE IN bed next to me gives, and I squint my eyes open.

Again.

"All right, your turn." Harry's voice sneaks in through the sheets.

"No," I mumble, trying to scoot further down on the bed to hide.

But Harry finds me and pulls me out from under the covers.

"If you don't get in there, I'm going to drink the cappuccino with a double shot I ordered just for you," Mohammad says.

My mouth falls open, and I snap my head in his direction. His eyes are sparkling, but his words sounded serious.

"So mean," I grumble.

But his threat is enough to pull me out of bed. Because without my coffee, I have no chance of getting through today.

Harry helps me up and out of bed, waiting to let go of my hand until I'm up. He's wearing one of the hotel robes, his hair wet from the shower.

When I feel steady enough to walk, I let go of his hand and make my way to the bathroom.

My legs are wobbly, but my head doesn't hurt as much as I expected it to with the change in direction.

When I get into the bathroom, I glance at my reflection.

And the damage is there.

Leftover makeup.

Wild hair.

I don't take a second glance before turning on the water. I brush my teeth and strip off my shirt, my fingers moving to the waistband of my pants.

Of my sweats.

I pull my eyes down, realizing that I'm in Noah's sweatpants. I take in a large gulp of air, my heart rate speeding up. Because last night comes rushing back to me. The party. The club. Dancing with Noah. What he said. *Yes. The answer is yes.*

I swallow and look back up at my reflection. I don't have anything else on, except for Noah's sweats.

Even without being here, he's here.

He's always with me.

I take a step toward the mirror as it starts to fog over, something black on my cheek catching my attention. I bring my hand up to my cheekbone, running my finger along it.

Harry.

"Food should be here in twenty," Mohammad says, banging on the bathroom door.

I drop my hand and quickly leave the mirror. I strip out

of Noah's sweats and toss them onto the stool before hopping into the shower.

I scrub at my cheek.

My hair.

I focus on waking up. On shampooing and conditioning. Knowing that in twenty minutes, I need to be ready to eat and then go to school. I don't let thoughts of Noah or Harry or the fact that I woke up, buried in Harry's chest while wearing Noah's sweats, creep into my mind. I shut it all out.

AFTER I SHOWER, I slip on a bathrobe and go to my closet to change.

By the time I join the boys in the living room, our food has arrived, and both Harry and Mohammad are in their uniforms. I drag myself to the couch and sit down next to Mohammad. Our food is spread out on the coffee table, and Mohammad hands me my cappuccino.

I take a sip and give him a grateful smile.

Harry is seated on the chair opposite us. He's looking down at his eggs like they've somehow offended him. He stabs at them, taking a small bite.

"Not hungry?" I ask, having another sip of coffee.

"Eating before nine o'clock is ridiculous." He gives up on the eggs and grabs a piece of toast instead. "It's why they invented brunch."

"You like brunch?" I ask, glancing at the food.

"Brunch is ideal. It lets you sleep in, includes hair of the dog, and offers a breakfast-lunch combination," Harry replies.

I give him an encouraging smile.

He smiles back, but it's quickly replaced by a frown, directed at his half-eaten piece of toast.

"Breakfast is either supposed to soak up the alcohol with its sheer weight or offset your upset stomach with something else. Like grease," Mohammad replies knowingly. And he really is taking his own advice.

His plate is packed full, and he seems to have no problem eating this morning.

I look across the food, deciding I should probably try to eat.

I grab a piece of toast, jam, and some eggs, bringing the plate to my lap.

I stare at my food and take another sip of my coffee.

"You need to eat," Mohammad says disapprovingly as he chows his food.

I put jam on my bread and bite into the piece of toast, trying to keep my nose plugged from the smell. I hold up the bitten toast to show Mohammad.

He nods in approval.

I glance back to Harry, realizing he's in his uniform. But he didn't bring anything with him last night.

"Did Mohammad bring you an extra uniform?" I ask him.

"I had it messengered over," Harry replies, finishing off his toast. He licks a piece of butter off his finger, more awake from the food. Harry leans forward, his blue eyes scanning my face. "You got rid of my name."

I take a bite of the toast before looking back at Harry.

"And you got rid of my heart," I point out, his bare skin reflecting mine.

"Hmm," Harry huffs, crossing his arms over his chest before leaning back into the chair.

Mohammad looks up from his food, glancing between Harry and me.

"And I got rid of the star," Mohammad says, jabbing at his food. "Sometimes, you just have to move on."

I let out a surprised laugh, covering my mouth with my hand.

"Mohammad," I comment, shaking my head at him.

"What? It's the truth."

"Nothing like a dose of cold, hard truth in the morning to make me want to crawl back into bed," Harry adds.

"Well, next time, do something more permanent," Mohammad shoots back.

"Like a tattoo." Harry beams.

"It's a solid option." Mohammad nods in agreement.

I glance at him, my mouth falling open.

"Tattoos are not an option," I disagree. "Besides, anything you like today, you'll probably change your mind about tomorrow. People are always changing, and once you get it, you're stuck with it."

"You're just scared of the pain," Mohammad replies.

"I'm sure it doesn't feel good. Wait, do you have any tattoos?" I ask Mohammad.

"Mum would murder me. But one day, I'll get one."

I glance over to Harry. "Harry, do you …" I start but quickly clamp my mouth shut.

Because I know the answer.

No.

Unlike Mohammad, I've seen all of Harry naked before. And I'm pretty sure I would remember if I saw a tattoo. Harry's eyes are dancing with amusement, but he doesn't say anything. I flush and look back at Mohammad to find him checking his watch.

"Shit, we need to get going, or we're going to be late," Mohammad says, clearing his plate.

"I have to clip up my hair, and then I'll be ready." I stand up slowly, my head pounding.

I finish off my coffee as Harry and Mohammad clean up the food.

I move into the bathroom and grip the edge of the counter, wishing I could let the boys go to school and crawl back into bed, alone. The coffee was delicious, but I need some time to myself.

To think.

To sleep.

But Mohammad isn't going to let that happen. And I'm better off giving in to his demands and going to school than trying to talk him into going without me.

Which I know would be a useless cause.

I fumble through my drawer, looking for a hair clip when something catches my eye. I look down at the floor to Noah's sweatpants and notice there's something white sticking out of the pocket. I grab the sweats, realizing it's a note.

I start to unfold the piece of paper when Mohammad calls out impatiently, "Hurry up!"

I quickly grab the clip from the drawer and pin up my hair before flicking off the bathroom light. I get my coat and backpack, shove the note inside, and meet Harry and Mohammad in the sitting room.

"Ready?" Harry asks, pulling on his coat.

"Ready."

Jam in your hair.
STATISTICS

TWENTY MINUTES LATER, it feels like it took all my effort just to get here. The second I get to my desk, I drop my backpack and lay my head down on the desk. Mohammad had us speed-walking, and somehow, he managed to get us to school before the warning bell went off. I'm one of the first students in the classroom and surprisingly grateful that I have a few minutes to sit and nap before class starts.

I close my eyes, listening to the voices in the classroom grow louder.

I hear students unzipping their backpacks, their chairs creaking. Pens start to click, and notebook pages are flipped. I can hear the students' voices, too, but they sound distant, like background noise. My focus is on all of the other annoying noises. Paper moving, pens scribbling, someone clearing their throat, someone dropping a stack of textbooks.

I let out a groan.

"Morning." Noah's voice cuts clearly through the noise.

I quickly pull myself up off the desk. But I immediately regret it, forcing my eyes shut.

"Morning," I mumble back, bringing my fingers up to my temples.

"Feeling good this morning?" Noah teases.

I peel my eyes open, taking in his easy expression. I glance across him, feeling light-headed. He smells like a shower and laundry. There's a slight shadow under his eyes, probably from being up so late, but other than that, he looks good. Really good.

Bright eyes.

Fresh face.

Pink lips.

Someone clicks a pen, pulling my attention away from Noah. The noise is piercing, and I squint at the sound.

"Feeling hungover actually," I admit.

"You and Harry both," Noah replies, pulling his textbook from his backpack and setting it on his desk.

"I'm sore too," I admit, my whole body feeling stiff.

Noah's eyes shift back to mine, his brows pulling in. "From?"

"Dancing. Heels. Hours and hours of plastering a fake

smile on my face," I say, trying to crack a joke. I try to smile at Noah but just end up pouting. Because my head hurts and I know it was a terrible joke.

"Let me feel," Noah says.

"My face?" I ask.

Noah shakes his head and brings his palm to rest on my back between my shoulders. I straighten out at his touch.

"You're tense," Noah comments, pushing his fingers into my shoulders.

"You touched me," I reply as he hits a small knot. I bite my lip at the tenderness.

"Shouldn't that relax you?" Noah chuckles, his fingers moving to a different spot. "I think you need a massage."

"I'm always getting massages from you." I smile.

"Mmhmm. You love it when I touch you," he barely whispers.

I let out an unsteady breath before looking toward the front of the room. Noah's hand is warm on my back, but the pressure feels like too much. It's that line between pleasure and pain.

And right now, a back rub mixed with feeling nauseous probably isn't a good idea.

"I do," I finally get out. "But I think if you keep at it, I might puke."

Noah retracts his hand, his lips pulling into a flat line.

"How about another time?" he offers.

With the pressure gone, I instantly feel better. But I also notice the absence of his hand.

And I don't like it.

"I feel like you're just getting out of it now." I smile at him.

"Yeah? What do you want then?" Noah turns himself sideways in his seat, so he's facing me.

"You can rub my shoulders. Just gently," I reply, keeping my eyes on him.

Noah starts again, and I let my head rest on the desk. He's gentle and light, his fingers tickling my skin through my shirt more than anything.

And it feels good. Really good.

But then Noah stops.

I lift my head off the desk to see where his hand went when I see Noah looking at the front of the classroom. I follow his gaze and find Mr. Johnson eyeing us. One of his eyebrows is raised, and I drop his gaze as the bell goes off.

"Wait, is that jam in your hair?" Noah asks, pointing to a piece of my hair that fell out of my clip.

I glance down and see that there actually is jam in my hair. Noah's fingers land on the strand of hair, and I look up to him, mortified.

"Oh my god," I mumble, pulling the piece of hair from him. "I rushed through breakfast."

"I can see that." Noah laughs as Mr. Johnson closes the classroom door. "Speaking of food, will you sit with me at lunch today?"

"Yeah. I mean, I did before," I reply, pulling out my notebook.

"I packed you food. I thought you might need something filling after last night," Noah explains.

"Harry's right. You are always prepared."

"So?" he asks.

"Yeah, I will." I nod.

"Cool."

"Wait, today's the soccer field, right?"

Because it's Friday.

And normally, on Fridays, we go outside to watch Noah practice.

"Shit, yeah. Okay, well, we can play some football," Noah says, startled, like he somehow forgot his tradition.

I glance at him, wondering why he looks so flustered.

"I'm not sure I'm in a state to play," I reply.

"Because you're hungover," Noah says more than asks.

"Because of that, and because … well, you're pretty good at football. And I'm not sure I could handle being hungover *and* losing to you at lunch." I smile at him.

Noah grins back. "It's one of the nicest days we've had in weeks. How about you get some sun and watch me practice instead?"

I bring my eyes to his, getting lost in pools of golden brown.

"Is it really?" I ask, distracted.

Noah lets out a warm laugh. "Didn't you notice on your way to school how nice it was?"

"I was more concerned with Mohammad leaving me in the dust. He speed-walks like a mom in a grocery store." I flare my eyes at Noah.

"See, even hungover you haven't lost your sense of humor."

"Thank god for that." I smile. "Anyway, sounds like a plan. Lunch."

I glance to the front of the classroom, seeing Mr. Johnson standing at the side of his desk. He's collecting a stack of papers in his hands as he looks out at us.

"All right, everyone, settle down." He clears his throat. "Over break, you won't be assigned any coursework; however, I am passing out a review. It's the first half of the review for your final exam at the end of term. You'll be required to complete this and submit it before your final exam. It's up to your discretion when you do, but if I were you, I'd take the break to catch up to where we are while the formulas are fresh in your mind."

Mr. Johnson walks around the classroom, handing out the thick review packets.

I flare my eyes at it.

This can't only be the first half.

"So, did you have fun last night?" Noah asks as Mr. Johnson continues passing out the reviews.

"I don't know about fun. I guess after the party, I did."

Noah nods, looking me over.

"I wish I could have stayed. But Mia's been going on a bit about equality in the household, and Mum ..." Noah says.

"I got that impression from her hair meltdown."

Noah's forehead creases, and he adjusts his tie at his neck. "And my parents, I guess the whole cocktail party put them on edge."

"That's understandable."

I can't blame Noah's parents for wanting him home last night or for not attending.

"Harry seemed ... okay?" Noah asks, bringing his eyes to mine.

"He seemed happier once we left. He was definitely in a good mood when we got back to the hotel. I think the pressure was off him at least."

"That's good."

I chew on my lip. I want to say more to Noah. I want to tell him about last night even though it's a little foggy still. And about this morning. I want to tell him that I woke up in Harry's arms. That it didn't mean anything. That it felt good to be Harry's friend again. Things finally feel right with us.

But that I woke up in *his* sweats. I'm not sure what it all means, but I know that I have to say something.

"About last night," I start, swallowing.

"Which part?" Noah asks.

"Uh ..." I stutter.

That's a great question.

Which part?

The part where I almost kissed him. The part where he saw Harry and me together in the bathroom. The part where he said that he wanted everything from me. The part where he held my hand. The part where we danced. The part where I chickened out of kissing him. *Again.* The part where Harry stayed over and he didn't.

"Look, Mal, I'm not going to make you pick Harry or me. I won't ask you not to be friends; not to be there for him," Noah says, shaking his head.

And he looks uncomfortable.

"Noah, it's not a choice."

"It's more of a choice than you realize, I think. More than I realized."

"No, Noah. Sometimes ... I guess I just feel like I've been swept up into this spiral of ..."

"Of what?" Noah asks, but his eyes shift to the front of the room.

Mr. Johnson has finished passing out the reviews and started the lecture.

"Of you," I whisper. "The way you see the world. The way ... the way you make me feel ... how you talk about Art. Love. *Math.*"

Noah's eyes fall to his desk. "Did I push you last night?" he asks quietly.

I shake my head. "I got scared."

Noah shifts in his seat. "I know. I felt it."

I chew on my lip, wishing there were something else I could say. Something that would bring a smile back to Noah's face. Something that would take away his frown. But with Mr. Johnson speaking and the silence in the room, I don't want to chance getting in trouble for talking. And I really don't want someone to overhear us.

I pull out a piece of paper from my notebook and write Noah a note before I chicken out.

I wore your sweats to bed last night.

I pass the note to Noah before I lose my nerve, dropping it into his lap. Noah looks from me to the note, disapproval apparent on his face. I eye the note, urging him to read it. He unfolds it, scanning my words. He glances at me, his chestnut hair falling into his eyes.

Noah looks back down at the note, grabs his pencil, writes something, folds the paper, and hands it back to me. I hold on to it, not reading it while Mr. Johnson is talking to us. But when he turns his back to the class, I quickly unfold it.

How did they make you feel?

I smile. Of course that would be the question Noah asks. I want to write something sassy back, but Noah looks too serious to entertain that right now.

Well, they don't exactly compare to you.

I hand him back the note, my heart speeding up in my chest. As Noah reads the words, his lips curl up at the corner. He forces them together to keep from grinning, but I can see that he's happy about what I wrote. Relief washes over me. He smirks, writes something out, and then tosses it back to me.

Missing me in bed?

Noah watches me read the note. I look at him and see his eyebrows rise in question. He can't hide his grin now. I roll my eyes and write back.

In your dreams.

I toss him back the note and then nod my head in Mr. Johnson's direction. We need to focus on class now. Especially because Noah looks way too happy, reading over the note in his hand, and if Mr. Johnson were to glance at him, he'd know that Noah was doing something he shouldn't be. Because no one grins at their statistics notebook like that.

I'm watching Mr. Johnson write on the whiteboard when Noah slides the note back into my lap. I look from the note to him, shaking my head slightly so he knows that we need to stop.

Noah shrugs indifferently.

I unfold the note, keeping it in my lap.

Nah, I think in yours. The real question is, when do you plan on letting me make that dream come true?

I reread the note, my mind instantly moving to Noah and me together.

In bed.

My face flushes at the thought. But then I read it again, realizing he didn't ask *if* I planned on making my dream come true. No, he asked *when.*

When!

As though it were obvious that I was going to end up in his bed. Or he was going to end up in mine. I look over at him, shock flashing across my face. Noah looks back at me, his face completely relaxed. He sucks in his cheeks and looks at me in question, his head tilting to the side.

I make a show of putting the note away in my notebook, letting him know that he isn't going to get an answer from me.

Noah just smirks.

I try to focus on Mr. Johnson.

On Statistics.

I rest my chin in my hand, my eyes growing heavy in my palm as Mr. Johnson drones on.

I close my eyes, wondering about what Noah said. I imagine myself pushing my worries to the side and falling into bed with him. I imagine how it would feel to have him kiss me.

He'd take me back to his house after school. Up to his room.

I imagine what it would be like to have his hands trail over my skin when we were finally alone.

He'd undo his tie.

Unbutton his shirt.

His mouth would only leave mine to find my neck. My throat.

He'd strip off my shirt, his palm landing on my chest. My stomach.

But I know Noah. If we got to that point, he wouldn't stop there. I wouldn't either. He'd want more of me.

He'd strip off my stockings, his palms pushing up my thighs until his hands found their way under my skirt. I'd be frozen, waiting for him to move. Wondering if he'd actually do it.

Take that next step.

And then he finally would. His fingers would push aside my underwear as he kissed me again before—

My eyes fly open.

My chin is still resting in my palm, but my whole body is pounding.

I don't move an inch as I glance around the classroom. I must have fallen asleep.

Or was I daydreaming?

Either way, it doesn't matter. Because I'm in class!

In school.

I'm sitting right next to Noah, having a sex dream about him.

I blink, trying to calm my thoughts. I force myself to sit up, hoping to feel more awake. Because I cannot fall asleep again.

And I definitely can't let my dream pick up where it left off.

An English rose.
LATIN

EVEN AFTER ALL the *excitement* in Statistics, I ended up falling asleep again in class.

Luckily, the second time was sex-dream free. I think I was too tired—and mortified—to let myself go there. Even subconsciously.

I'm still exhausted though, and I don't have high hopes that I'll make it through Latin. I fall into my seat, already ready for class to be over.

And it hasn't even started yet.

But the moment that Mohammad sits down next to me, I know any chance of peace and quiet before class went right out the door.

"Can you believe last night?" Mohammad says, putting his textbooks on his desk.

I glance over at him. His eyes are lit up. He looks starry-eyed.

"Last night was fun. Probably too much fun," I reply, my

headache a constant reminder.

"After that party, we deserved to get plastered," Mohammad says seriously.

"That's true."

"I got to snog Naomi. Dance with her. It was a pretty epic night for me," Mohammad admits, nodding along with his words.

"You're happy?"

Mohammad grins, his pearly whites coming out. And I think that just about answers my question.

"Why wouldn't I be? I appeased my mum. Got, like, a million points for going on a date she'd set up. I got to make out with Naomi. Even felt her up a bit when we were dancing."

He waggles his eyebrows at me, and I force myself to sit up, giving him my full attention.

Mohammad's in too good of a mood for me to not encourage it.

"Score," I say, holding up my palm for him to high five, which he does with obvious excitement.

"Speaking of the night, how did things go for you?"

Hmm?

How did things go?

I want to tell him what Noah told me last night. That his answer was yes. That he wants me. That I want him. I want to tell him about how I almost kissed Noah—more than a few times—at the party. How conflicted I felt, trying to balance being there for both Noah and Harry. About my almost sex dream in class. But I can't tell Mohammad any of that. At least, not until I talk to Noah.

And I *definitely* can't have that kind of conversation with him at school.

If Mohammad has taught me anything, it's that there are

eyes and ears *everywhere*. The last thing I want to do is spill my guts to Mohammad or talk to Noah about last night and be overheard.

"Miss America?" Mohammad whistles, bringing me back to his question.

"Things are becoming … clearer."

"Now that you've met Harry's parents?" Mohammad nods.

"What? No." I laugh.

"Then, how have things become clearer?" he asks, looking confused.

"Well … you pointed out once that I'm a grade-A chicken, and that was clarified last night," I say, trying to answer his question without, well, actually answering his question.

"Feathers and all," Mohammad agrees.

"Basically."

Mohammad swivels toward me, his knees jutting out into the aisle. "You know, Naomi asked me to walk her out of the club, so you and Noah would have a chance to be alone."

"She told you that?"

He nods. "I tried to tell her that I didn't think anything would happen, seeing as you've got serious chicken in your lineage. Or did it?"

"Unfortunately, the chicken in my DNA took over. I froze." I flush, feeling ridiculous about it. "I mean, of course we danced, but—"

Mohammad cuts me off with a wave.

"Well, dancing these days is basically shagging with clothes on, so at least Noah finally got a little action," Mohammad teases.

I flare my eyes at him but crack a smile.

"Don't worry. I'm sure one of these days I'll work up the courage to overcome the chicken within and finally get some action too."

"Miss America! Are you telling me that you've thought about getting it on with our little English rose?"

"Are you calling Noah an English rose?" I ask, furrowing my brows.

"Obviously. And the title's fitting since he's never been with anyone."

I slap my hand over Mohammad's mouth, trying not to freak out.

"Mohammad!" I say through gritted teeth. "You shouldn't talk about people or their sex lives like that."

Mohammad rolls his eyes before pulling my hand off his mouth. "I'm sorry. I'm just buzzing today. Despite the hangover."

"I'm happy you're happy." I smile at him as the bell goes off.

I look toward our professor. He gets up and starts writing across the board, his back to us.

"Thank you. I was worried how things would go, but everything worked out. It was brilliant. Mum won't be on my case now. Naomi is totally into me," Mohammad says, but then his forehead creases. "And I was pretty worried about Harry. Especially after he told us about the internship last night."

"Yeah, that was pretty big news."

"Huge," Mohammad agrees. "I didn't expect that."

I nod, fidgeting with my skirt. "At least he has almost a year, you know?"

Mohammad tilts his head, uncertainty flashing across his face. "The whole thing feels off though," he whispers.

"That's because it is," I agree.

I open up my notebook and start copying down the words and definitions being written out on the board, but something keeps nagging at my mind.

"Mohammad, can I ask you something?"

"Shoot."

"Was it weird for you, seeing Noah and me dance together? Were you mad?" I watch his expression, unsure of how he's going to react.

"Mad? If anything, I should be thanking you. Because of you two, Naomi dragged me outside and snogged me for a good fifteen minutes before she finally left."

I smile at Mohammad before looking back down at my notes. I think when it comes to Mohammad, that was basically the same thing as him giving me his approval.

Halfway through class, Mohammad shoves a note into my lap. I glance up to make sure our professor isn't looking at me before opening it.

Guess what?

I look at Mohammad, but he's smiling to himself, and he motions for me to write back. I scribble on the paper.

What?

I toss it back to him. He writes something and then slides it into my hand.

Two more classes, and then we're out for break.

I reread the note, realization settling in. Because he's right. Two more classes, and then we have a week off. A week of no school, no uniforms, no homework. A full week of freedom. I smile down at the note before turning to Mohammad.

I mouth, *Two more to go,* and give him a thumbs-up.

Grass and sweat and sun.
LUNCH

THE EXCITEMENT OF only having two more classes for the day is short-lived. By the time class is over, I didn't get in another nap, like I had been hoping for, and the realization that we're actually going to have homework over the break sets in.

Well, at least Latin homework.

Our professor took the entire class to list out new vocabulary terms and explain their definitions. I happily copied them down until he told us that our first class back after break, we'd have a quiz over them.

And then I wasn't so happy.

"I can't believe he just did that to us." I look over to Mohammad for confirmation when we get out into the hallway after class.

"Latin has a way of sucking the joy out of most things," Mohammad replies, flaring his nostrils.

"Out of *everything*," I correct.

I want to toss my Latin notes in the air and let them scatter forever, but I think that probably would come back to haunt me when I failed our quiz after break.

"Why are you walking so slow?" Mohammad asks when we get a few paces away from the classroom.

"My head hurts, and I'm annoyed. How else should I be walking?" I glare at him. I am officially tired now, and my hangover seems to be getting worse rather than better.

"Don't get mad, jeez. I was merely suggesting you up your pace."

"This is the pace today. Take it or leave it."

Mohammad mumbles to himself, and I shoot him another glare. He doesn't say anything else, but I can tell he's annoyed with how slow I am.

When we turn the corner, moving into the hallway that leads out to the football field, I can't help but groan. Because the hallway is long.

Extremely long.

I quickly grow disheartened about making it out to the field before lunch is over. Mohammad was right. At my pace, we might as well start walking back to our classes. Maybe it was the toast or the shower this morning, but I had a lot easier of a time getting myself to school than walking down this hallway.

"It's useless," I reply, pushing out a pout.

"Hop up," Mohammad says, stopping.

"What?" I ask, turning to him.

He squats down and motions for me to get on his back.

"We'll get in trouble."

Mohammad makes a show of looking around us at the empty hallway.

"What are they going to do? Kick us out?"

"Yes, exactly."

"Well, too bad," Mohammad replies. "Now, hop on, you nugget. You're going for a ride."

"I'll get on if you promise to never call me a nugget again," I say pointedly.

Mohammad moves his head back and forth, like he's weighing his options.

"Deal," he finally says.

"This is a bad idea," I tell him.

But I hop onto Mohammad's back anyway, hoping that no one sees us. Because I'm pretty sure at this point, Headmaster Compton would take any reason he could get to send me to detention again.

"All right, hold on!" Mohammad laughs and starts running down the hallway.

And suddenly, I don't feel good.

I don't feel good at all.

"Mohammad, you have to walk!" I squeeze him, trying to push back my nausea.

"Oh shit," Mohammad says, glancing over his shoulder to me. "You look a little green."

"Mmhmm," I mumble back, my stomach doing a flip.

Mohammad slows down, and he walks steadily to the end of the hallway.

We make it outside without being noticed, and Mohammad keeps me on his back until we get to the field. I unwrap my legs from his waist and fall onto the grass in a heap.

"That was very thoughtful of you," I say, laying my head back in the grass.

"I was just trying to get you out here before the bell went off and lunch was over."

I wave him off. "I wasn't walking *that* slow."

"I disagree. It was pretty bad," Mohammad says, pulling lunch out from his backpack.

"Are those leftovers from breakfast?" I ask as he pops open a tub.

"Yep. Toast and cold eggs. Harry's bringing food for us from the cafeteria too," Mohammad says, offering me a piece of toast.

I shake my head.

"Noah's bringing food too," I say.

Mohammad takes two pieces of toast and smashes the eggs between them to make a cold sandwich. I watch Mohammad eat, my stomach twisting. He barely swallows his food before taking another bite.

I raise my eyebrows at him.

"You know, your girlfriend might consider sitting with us at lunch if you didn't eat like you were constantly starving."

Mohammad gives me an unamused look.

"Have you ever thought that I actually am starving?" he fires back. "Besides, maybe I'm a slob at the table because I don't want her to sit with me. This is our time. The boys' club, you know?"

"That's sort of sweet," I say, a smile forming on my lips.

"It is," Noah says, joining us. He drops his backpack on the ground and sits down next to us in the grass. He pulls out two brown bags, handing me one.

"Thanks." I smile at him and slowly sit up before peeking into the bag.

"Besides, the boys' club has to have rules," Mohammad continues.

"I wouldn't think you'd like rules," I comment, watching Noah take a bite of his sandwich.

"Maybe *rules* is the wrong word," Mohammad replies, thinking.

"Tradition," Noah offers, glancing between us.

"Exactly," Mohammad says brightly. "I could deal with having Naomi and Olivia join us for lunch a few times a week, but I could never see them coming out here. It's our tradition, you know? You can't mess with that."

"Speaking of tradition, where's Harry?" I ask, taking a bite out of the apple that Noah packed me. I chew hesitantly, wondering how my stomach will react to it. But the second the sweet, crisp taste hits my tongue, I realize it's good.

"Running late," Mohammad answers. "But he'll be here."

I nod and focus on my food. I eat part of my sandwich, feeling a little better with the food in my stomach.

But overall, I still feel like crap.

Noah quickly finishes his lunch and then gets up to practice. I prop myself up onto my elbows to watch him. The sun is warm on my face.

Noah was right.

It's a beautiful day out. I have to squint my eyes to see him, but I don't mind.

"And he's dribbling the ball," Mohammad yells, commentating.

I listen as he calls out Noah's moves with excitement. But he just keeps getting louder and louder.

"Mohammad, come closer," I say, pushing away my food. "And stop yelling."

"But I'm announcing!" he says excitedly, his eyes never leaving Noah.

I fall back down into the grass and look up at the sky. Mohammad continues yelling, and all I want to do is cry. Or fall asleep. Or ask Mohammad to be quiet.

"Noah!" I call out, rolling my head to the side to see him.

Noah turns at my voice, stopping the ball with his foot. He kicks it to Mohammad before walking over to us. His shadow falls over me before his voice does.

"Yeah?" he asks, squatting down next to me.

I look up at him and push out a pout. "Can I use you as a pillow?"

"Well, that's pathetic," Mohammad says, rolling his eyes. He stands up and kicks the ball around, announcing all of his moves as he does.

Noah lets out a chuckle before looking back down at me. "Sure."

He sits down next to me, at first propping himself up onto his elbows so he can watch Mohammad. But I'm not sure how to use him as a pillow when he's leaning up at an angle. I draw my brows in, looking over him for a solution.

"Come here," Noah says, lying all the way down on the grass.

I scoot closer to him.

I put my head on his firm chest as he wraps his arm around me, his hand coming to my waist. I grab on to him, feeling myself relax in the sun. It feels good to be here. To be tucked against him. He doesn't smell clean anymore, like he does in the mornings.

He finally smells like him. Like grass and sweat and sun.

"You're warm," I comment, feeling the heat rising from his chest.

"Are you cold?" Noah asks.

"Mmhmm."

Noah pulls me closer until my knees are touching his leg. I close my eyes, shutting everything out, except for the warmth. From Noah. From the sun. I listen to his heartbeat, trying to match my breathing to it.

I'm almost asleep when a shadow falls over me, blocking out the sunlight for a moment. A second later, it's moved though, and I listen as someone sits down next to us in the grass.

"Hey," Harry says.

I open my eyes, peering over at him. He lies down next to Noah, dropping a can of soda and a bag of crisps on the grass.

"Hey," Noah replies as I bring my head up off his chest.

I smile at Harry. "Hi."

He smiles back.

"I feel like shit," I admit before bringing my head back down onto Noah's chest.

"Same," Harry replies, splaying himself out.

"I feel left out," Mohammad complains, jogging over to us before falling down next to Harry.

"Well, come on. Get in here," Noah says, waving Harry

and Mohammad toward us.

They scoot closer until we're all packed together on the grass.

"I could fall asleep," I say, rolling my head to watch the clouds.

Noah strokes my back, his fingers light, like the breeze.

"I told you we should have skipped," Harry says.

"Where have you been?" Noah asks, rolling his head to glance at Harry.

"Snagging us some brownies from the lunchroom." Harry grins and pulls out napkins that he shoved into his pants pockets.

I glance across Harry to Mohammad. He's watching Harry, too, and it isn't until Harry opens the napkins that I realize that's where he stashed the brownies.

Mohammad's eyes light up.

"They're all smushed," I comment.

"Who cares?" Mohammad says, looking like he hit the jackpot.

Harry hands him one of the brownies and then offers the other one to Noah. Noah takes it from him, holding it out to me. I shake my head against his chest.

Noah sets it down in the grass as Harry opens up his bag of crisps.

I watch as he drops one chip into his mouth, chewing.

"This is nice," Harry says, looking content.

"It is," I mumble back in agreement.

"I'm so happy it's almost break," Mohammad chimes in between bites of brownie. "No school. No homework. We'll be free!"

"For a week." Noah laughs, causing his entire chest to vibrate under me.

I grasp on to his shirt, trying to keep from moving.

"Some of us will be free," Harry says with a dramatic sigh.

I watch as he drops another crisp into his open mouth.

"We'll have plenty of time to chill before you leave," Noah says, patting Harry's hand.

"That's true," Harry agrees. "And I think we were off to a good start last night."

"You never said who you met up with," I comment, thinking back to last night.

"Ah, just a bloke I know from the club," Harry says carelessly.

"Tell us your best and worst," Mohammad says, finishing off his brownie.

"Best and worst what?" I ask.

"The best part of the night and the worst part of the night," Noah answers.

"That's easy," Harry says. "Worst part: the entire party. The best part ... I'd have to say, the bath."

"The bath?" Noah asks, tensing under me.

"Oh yeah, it was fucking hilarious," Harry agrees.

"The three of us got into the bathtub," Mohammad explains.

"We barely fit," I add.

"Drank more. Ate chips and falafel," Harry continues. "Found ourselves a princess too. It was a solid ending to what had started out as a shitty night."

"You were in the bath together?" Noah asks, trying to clarify.

"Yeah." I clear my throat. "Harry threw a fit that we couldn't swim in the pool even though I told him it was closed. That was the next best option."

"Shit, I forgot about the Bath Kingdom." Mohammad laughs, glancing over at me.

I flare my eyes at him, wanting him to stop going down

last night's memory lane.

"Bath Kingdom?" Noah asks, confused.

Harry opens his mouth, but I cut him off. I push up off Noah's chest and look down at him.

"Mohammad farted and made tons of bubbles. It was disgusting," I blurt out.

"Sounds … fun," Noah says, looking bewildered.

I nod once before lying back down. I'm not sure if I should keep my head on his chest, but Noah doesn't give me an option. He brings his fingers to my hair clip, playing with a strand that got loose.

I relax against him.

"So, what did your mum think of the party?" Harry asks Mohammad. He still has his head lying flat in the grass, his eyes closed as he finishes off his bag of crisps.

"Who knows? But I've got to convince her into letting me get out of tutoring lessons for the week," he says, sounding annoyed.

"Tutoring lessons?" I ask. Because I don't remember Mohammad ever mentioning them before.

"Yeah, Mum went on about how, apparently, all my knowledge could go down the drain in a week and told me that she was going to hire a tutor to keep me in check," Mohammad explains.

"Seriously?" I gape at him.

"Yep."

"So, how are you going to get out of it?" Harry asks with interest.

"If you needed help, you should have told me," Noah says, dropping the strand of my hair he was playing with and glancing over to Mohammad.

"I have a brilliant plan," Mohammad says, sitting up. "I'm going to tell her the girl she set me up with last night had a boyfriend and that I was heartbroken over it all day. I'll guilt her so much that she'll be forced to give in to my demands."

"Mohammad, that's terrible!" I swat my hand out at him, but he's too far away, and I end up just swatting the air.

"I'm just working with what I got," he disagrees.

"Huh," is all Noah says.

And I'm not sure if he's worried or impressed.

"Think she'll go for it?" Harry asks.

"Let's hope so," Mohammad replies. "There's rarely anything I can hold over my mum. Which means if all goes according to plan, I'll be free over break."

"Cheers to your plan, mate," Harry says, cracking open his soda and holding it up in the air in a toast.

All sticky.
ART

EVENTUALLY, WE ALL have to force ourselves up from the grass and back into school. Maybe it was lying in the sunshine or being with Noah, Harry, and Mohammad, but I feel better.

More awake.

Less hungover.

As I walk into class, Mia almost runs straight into me.

"Oh," I say, reeling back in surprise.

"There you are," she says quickly, pushing her hair behind her ear. "Here, try my cookie." Her voice is firm, and it's more of a demand than a request.

I look at the cookie resting in her outstretched hand.

"What?" I ask, trying to follow along.

"Will you just try it?" she says, handing me the cookie with a light-brown frosting, resting on a napkin.

"There's something wrong with it, isn't there?" I ask, shifting past her to my seat. I drop my backpack and place the suspect cookie on the table.

"There's nothing wrong with it." She laughs as she sits on the desk, letting her legs swing over the side. "I've been baking. And since Mum let me keep my purple hair, I thought I might surprise her with them after work. But I'm not sure they're good. I can eat pretty much anything."

I look from Mia to the cookie, examining it.

"It's pumpkin with a maple syrup frosting on top," she explains.

I raise an eyebrow at her but pick up the cookie. "Why'd you bring me one? I mean, I'm sure Noah or Gene would have been more than willing to test it out for you."

"Enough chatting, more chewing," Mia says, motioning with her hand at me. "Anyway, Noah was in a healthy mood this morning, and Dad left for work early."

"And Sophia?" I ask curiously, taking my first bite.

"She's my best friend. I don't trust her to be objective," Mia says matter-of-factly.

"Oh," I say, taking another bite. "Mia, wow. This is good." My eyes widen as I chew, and I lick my lips to get the delicious frosting off of them.

"Really?" Mia smiles proudly. "That's a relief. Mum and I are reading Sherlock Holmes right now, which is perfect for fall. When I was at the farmers market on Sunday, I bought a pumpkin. I didn't know what I'd make with it until today."

"Did you bake these this morning?" I ask, taking another wonderful bite.

"If I can't sleep, I bake."

"I'm glad you and your mom are getting along. She missed you, you know."

Mia flushes. "I know. She's come around to the purple

hair too. Even complimented me on it."

"She's got good taste then." I smile. "And, Mia, really, this is delicious. You should bake all the time. And then let me sample it." I hold my hand out under the cookie as I take another bite, catching a few crumbs.

"I will." She gives me a happy grin.

"So, I saw you and Sophia last night. I'm sorry I didn't say hi; it was just a busy night."

"You saw us?" Mia asks, her legs stilling.

"Yeah. You looked really happy," I say, wondering why Mia seems suddenly nervous.

"We've decided to test it out. I'm calling it our trial period though. That way, if things don't go well, we can go back to being friends. No harm done. I didn't plan on, well, showing that off last night." Her cheeks flush.

"You're worried it won't work?"

Mia's forehead creases as she thinks. "I don't know. But I'm happy right now," she says, her eyes flashing to mine. "And what about you and Noah?"

I stick my finger into the maple syrup frosting, thinking about how to answer that.

What about me and Noah?

But before I have a chance to reply, Noah comes into the classroom. Mia follows my gaze, looking back at me with understanding.

"We'll finish this later, yeah?"

"Are you sure you want to know?" I tease, licking the icing off my finger.

"Everything, except the dirty details," she replies before hopping down off the desk and walking to her seat.

I swipe another dollop of frosting onto my finger before finishing off the cookie.

"Hey," I say to Noah as he gets to our table.

"Hey," he replies.

He drops his bag, running his hand through his hair before taking a seat.

His sleeves are rolled, and his tie isn't set straight. It's easy to tell that he rushed changing back into his uniform. I bring my gaze to his white button-down.

"You're one button off." I notice.

I reach out to show him, but Noah grabs my hand, holding it up to examine it.

"What's on your finger?" he asks, his brows drawing in.

"Frosting."

Noah looks at the frosting like he isn't sure about it, but he runs his fingers over my hand. "You're all sticky," he says with a frown.

"Mia insisted that I try her pumpkin cookie. She put a bunch of maple syrup in the frosting, so it kind of comes with the territory," I explain.

Noah raises his eyebrows in acknowledgment. But then he pulls my finger into his mouth and sucks off the frosting. My mouth falls open, and I jerk my finger back.

"You brat!" I glare at him. "I swiped that off and was saving the best part for last."

"Well, you're slow." Noah laughs, licking his lips. "And you're right. That probably was the best part."

I bring my hand up to cover my eyes, disbelief washing over me that he actually just did that.

I'm partly mad about the frosting, partly shocked, and partly turned on.

And I don't know which part is worse.

I uncover my eyes and flick my gaze up to Noah's. "You can't do that."

"Why not?" Noah tilts his head in question.

"Because." I wipe my finger against my shirt, my cheeks

flushing.

"Because," Noah teasingly repeats. "You're being bossy today. *Come be my pillow. Don't take my frosting.*"

Noah grabs my hand from my lap and runs his fingers down over mine again. It's like he's exploring them. Feeling which ones are sticky. Which ones are clean.

"And you're being a bad rule-follower," I fire back.

"You have a lot of rules," Noah says, placing my hand back down. He brings his brown eyes up to mine. "It's kind of funny. I don't really believe in rules. And you've got, like, a million."

"That's true." I can't help but agree.

Because he sort of has a point.

"What do you think that means for us?" He sets his chin in his palm, propping his elbow on the desk.

"I think if anyone can manage it, we can."

"True."

"So, Mia said you wouldn't try her cookies this morning. Why wouldn't you? I know you love sweets."

Noah rolls his eyes before looking over his shoulder at Mia.

"She practically attacked me the second I walked into the kitchen, trying to get me to eat her cookie. I hadn't even had breakfast yet." He laughs. "Besides, I thought you'd like to try it more than me."

I shift my gaze from Mia to Noah with surprise. "Wait, you told her to have me try it?"

"It was a suggestion," Noah answers.

I can't help but grin at him.

"I think that might be one of the sweetest things you've ever done for me," I coo.

"Really?" Noah says, sounding pleased.

"Yep. I mean, apart from being my pillow on the football

field, bringing me lunch, and ... yeah, I think that's it. At least for today."

Noah lets out a deep, warm laugh. "I think I spoil you."

"Maybe just a bit." I hold up my fingers to show him the small amount as the bell goes off. "So, Mohammad is really looking forward to break. Are you ready for it?"

"I don't care too much either way. School doesn't really bother me."

"You're the only person who would be so casual about a week off of school."

Noah smirks, his eyes coming up to mine. "Are you excited?"

"I am. It will be nice to have a break."

"Will your parents be arriving soon?" Noah questions.

"I don't know. They told me yesterday they put in an offer on a penthouse somewhere in the city. They want me to go see it this weekend."

"That's exciting," Noah says encouragingly.

"Yeah, it kind of is. I mean, it will be fun to see the place they chose at least."

"What do you think it will be like?"

I pull my lips to the side as I think. "Modern, I'm sure. My parents made it sound like it was even nicer than our last place, which, honestly, is hard to imagine. My mom's thrilled, and even my dad seems happy about it all."

Noah nods. "I'm sure you've missed your parents."

"I guess. I mean, it'll be great to have my own room again. It beats living in a hotel."

"Mal."

"All right, fine, I've missed them," I admit. "But it's just sort of hard to imagine."

"What is?" Noah asks as he shifts toward me on his stool.

"Having my parents here. Like actually living in London.

I know New York and London are both big cities, but my parents are quintessential New Yorkers. What happens if things change when they get here, you know? It's going to be different. I'll have my own room and a curfew. Well, probably not. But they're going to want to meet everyone and go on outings. I don't know …"

"Change is a part of life," Noah says, his gaze softening. "You'll create new memories here. It won't be exactly the same as before, but that doesn't mean it won't be good."

"You're being too wise for me right now," I reply with a sigh. But I give Noah a small smile. "You know, Mohammad's actually excited to meet my mom. He wants to help me restock my wardrobe. I think they might actually get along."

Noah chuckles as Mrs. Jones stands up to address the class.

"Good afternoon," Mrs. Jones starts. "I'm going to come around and pass out clay again today. I'd like for you to finish your chapter and start thinking about your project. The sculpting tools are laid out on the far-right table, as usual."

I bump Noah's arm with mine and whisper, "Don't forget about your promise. No mermaids."

"No promises," he whispers back, a shadow of a smile falling onto his lips.

"As for your coursework over break, the only thing I expect of you is to be prepared to start your project on Monday. That means, I want a sketch with a clear vision. You'll be expected to turn this in at the beginning of class."

Mrs. Jones nods her head at us before having a few students help her pass out the clay to our tables.

Noah goes to grab us tools, so I sit and play with the clay in my hand.

Normally, the texture and tackiness would bother me, but Noah was right. My hands are already sticky from the cookie, and at this point, a little clay won't kill me.

"So, your parents," Noah says when he's back to the table. "Tell me more about them."

I watch as he lines up the tools for us before sitting back down.

"Well, my dad is ... I guess he's a lot like me. He's a straight shooter. He talks fast. He's witty but not in an obnoxious way. He likes to run with me in the morning and pretends that my mom isn't his other half. He jokes with me. Can always pick out a great restaurant. And he likes to get out, especially on the weekends. Museums, coffee, walking in the park, visiting friends. I know he has a stressful job, but he works hard at not letting it interfere with our life."

"You're a daddy's girl," Noah says, glancing at me.

"Maybe a bit." I flush.

"He sounds like a great dad," Noah adds. "And your mum?"

I press my knuckles into the clay and think about my mom.

"My mom is very social. She's on a ton of charity boards and involved in women's leagues in the city. She's always busy. She runs the house, supports my dad. She cares about appearances and can be a little one-track-minded, but I know she means well. She loves decorating and lunching and stuff like that. She can get pretty swept up in her world, and my dad, well, he always indulges her," I explain.

"They sound well suited."

"They surprisingly are."

Noah pulls his textbook out of his backpack, opening up to the correct chapter. He flips the page, scanning to find where we left off yesterday. He marks the paragraph with his finger before looking back over to me.

"And are you looking forward to having your own room

again?"

"I guess. Although I have my own space now at the hotel. And the benefit of no parents." I smirk.

"That's true." Noah smiles. "It's something to consider, isn't it?"

"What, taking advantage of it?" I laugh. "I think I already have. Between my birthday brunch, my birthday party, last night, and Mohammad's multiple *bath visits*, I think I've gotten my use out of it."

I pick up one of the tools—a pointy scraper—and start poking at the clay. It easily pierces through it.

Noah glances over to watch me.

"We haven't though," he says, licking his lips. "Have you thought about my note from Stats? My question?"

His question …

His question about being in bed. Together.

"Oh."

My eyes come up to his the same time that my hand slips. I accidentally slide the scraper along my finger, wincing at the pain. Noah and I both look down to see a line of blood pooling over a fresh cut.

"Oh my god," I say, freezing at the sight of my blood and bringing my eyes up to Noah's.

Because I'm panicking.

My heartbeat speeds up in my chest. My eyes keep widening as my finger starts to throb.

"Shit," Noah finally says.

"Noah, I don't like blood," I say quickly, keeping my chin securely tilted up.

I watch Noah look across the table, searching for something to do. A second later though, he's grabbing the cookie napkin.

"You're careless," Noah says, wrapping my finger up in

the napkin.

"I am not! I was just—" I start, but Noah cuts me off.

"Distracted?" Noah tilts his head to the side before shaking it disapprovingly. "I can see that."

He glances up to Mrs. Jones before grabbing on to my arm and pulling me up and out of my seat. He drags me up to Mrs. Jones's desk, his grip firm.

"Mrs. Jones, I need to escort Mallory to the infirmary. She sliced her finger. It's not bad, but I think the nurse should put some ointment on it."

Mrs. Jones's face flashes with surprise, and she quickly stands up. "Oh dear, of course. Thank you for offering to do that, Noah."

She gives me a sympathetic smile and hands Noah the hall pass. I don't have a chance to say anything back before Noah has us out of the classroom.

We're out in the hallway and down the main stairs before I decide to glance in the direction of my finger.

The second I do, I regret it. Because the thin napkin wrapped around my finger is already stained red.

"My finger is throbbing," I say, my brows pinching in.

"Well, that's what you get for not paying attention." Noah's face is set firmly, but when he glances over at me, I can see the concern in his eyes.

"Noah," I whine. Because I don't need a lecture right now.

Noah pulls me closer to him and keeps his hand on my arm. He looks down to my finger, his eyes growing wide. I immediately get nervous.

"Talk to me. Take my mind off it," I say as we move down the hall.

"What do you want to talk about?"

I rack my brain for something, but all I can think about is

Art and clay and …

"What are you going to do your project on, really?" I ask.

Noah glances at me, a smirk on his lips. "I still like the idea of a mermaid. Although now, maybe she'll need to be an injured mermaid."

I glare at him.

"Then, I'm committing to Medusa," I say back.

"You know, for someone feeling ill, you're being slightly ungrateful for the help," he replies.

"Thanks for saying an *injured mermaid* and not *cut*. That word freaks me out," I say, a shiver running down my spine.

"Then, why are you saying it?"

"That's a good point. I don't know. I talk when I'm nervous. Cut is just an … icky word. You know? Cuts imply warmth and oozing and blood and infections—"

"Mal," Noah cuts me off, pulling us to a stop.

I look up to him. He looks paler than before.

"Yeah?"

"Stop talking."

"Right," I agree.

He starts off again, keeping me at his side until we get to the nurse's office.

"Here we are," Noah says. He holds the door open, pushing me inside.

The room is sparse and strikingly white. It has that bleached effect to it that makes the whole room feel unnaturally clean. Noah puts his hand on my lower back, moving me forward as he lets the door swing closed behind us.

The noise causes a woman to pop her head out from an adjoining room. She's leaning back in a swivel chair in what must be her office. When she sees us, she quickly stands up and greets us.

I stare at her blankly.

"Mrs. Richards," Noah says, causing me to glance over my shoulder at him. "Mallory sliced her finger in class. Would you mind taking a look at it?"

I hold up my hand, showing her the bloodied napkin wrapped around my finger. Mrs. Richards's eyebrows shoot up in understanding.

"Of course," she replies, motioning for me to take a seat.

Noah stays standing by the door. I keep my eyes on him while Mrs. Richards moves busily around me.

Noah nervously bounces his leg. He brings his gaze to mine before moving it to my finger.

He quickly goes green.

"May I sit down?" Noah asks the nurse, his brows pulling together.

"Oh dear. Are you all right?" Mrs. Richards asks Noah.

"Fine. Slightly light-headed, is all," he replies, pulling at his tie. He takes a seat in the waiting chair opposite me, his eyes staying focused on the ground.

I look from him to my finger to Mrs. Richards, my heart rate quickening.

"Noah!" I squeak out his name.

Because he looks sick. And if he's sick, that means he can't be here for me. Which means that I won't have anyone to distract me while she does whatever she is about to do to my finger. My eyes feel like they're about to pop out of my head again.

Noah glances up to me.

"This is your fault. All that talk of ooze and infection," Noah says, his mouth pulling back into a sour expression.

"Text Mohammad," I beg as Mrs. Richards unwraps the napkin from around my finger.

"Phones are not allowed in school," she says, examining it.

I flare my eyes at Noah. He must realize how serious I am

because he pulls out his phone while her focus is on me.

"It's not a deep cut," Mrs. Richards says. "You're just a bleeder."

"Oh," I say, looking the opposite direction.

"I'm going to put some antiseptic on it and a plaster, and then you'll be on your way," she says.

"Okay," I mumble in response.

She leaves the room, walking back into her office. When she's out of earshot, I look to Noah, and I am freaked out.

"Noah," I whisper frantically, "what's a *plaster*?"

"What?" Noah asks, glancing up at me.

"Is she saying I need a cast?" I ask, swallowing hard.

"A cast?" Noah looks at me, confused. "No, it's a plaster. A covering."

"Wait, like a Band-Aid?"

But before Noah has a chance to answer, Mrs. Richards is back with the antiseptic. She's using a Q-tip to lather the cut when the door flies open and Mohammad walks in. He looks from Noah to me with questioning eyes.

Mrs. Richards doesn't even glance up before asking, "What can I help you with?"

"I've got a splitting headache," Mohammad replies, rubbing at his temples.

Mrs. Richards huffs next to me.

"Take a seat," she says. She puts the Band-Aid on my finger and then lets out an appeased sigh. "Brand-new."

I hold up my finger, realizing it doesn't hurt that bad anymore. It's just a dull ache. My gaze moves from my finger to Mohammad and Noah. Mohammad has his hands on either side of his head, looking pathetic.

And Noah's no better.

He's looking down at his shoes, slouched over in the chair. Mrs. Richards follows my gaze.

"I'll be back with a few waters," she mumbles before leaving us.

I expect Mohammad to stop faking his headache when she leaves, but he doesn't.

"Do you actually have a headache?" I ask him.

"I do," Mohammad replies, glancing to Noah. He gently pats him on the back. "All right there?"

Noah nods. "Fine. I'll be fine," he says.

But he never looks up at either of us.

I want to scream at the two of them. Because they're supposed to be here to comfort me. But no, they both just sit there, looking at the floor and sighing in unison.

Mrs. Richards comes back with two paper cups in her hands.

"One paracetamol for you," she says, handing Mohammad one cup. "And a water for you."

Noah takes the water. Mohammad takes the paracetamol.

Whatever that is.

Noah drinks the water gratefully, and Mohammad pops the pill into his mouth. Noah gives him the rest of his water to swallow it down with.

Mrs. Richards stands there for a moment and then smiles at them. "All right, out with the lot of you. Get back to class."

I slide off the table as she ushers Noah and Mohammad up from their seats.

She practically throws us out of her office.

"So much for *caring*," I mumble under my breath. I look between Mohammad and Noah. "I don't understand. I thought Noah texted you to come because I needed you. You didn't seem hungover at lunch?"

"It was a coursework headache. Not a hangover headache," Mohammad replies.

I frown, not understanding.

"Mallory, there was no headache," Noah says, loosening his tie.

I snap my head in Mohammad's direction. "Seriously?" I ask.

"Seriously," Mohammad replies.

I blink, impressed.

"Wow. You're a good liar," I tell him.

"*Actor*," Mohammad corrects. "So, Art was dangerous today?"

He looks between Noah and me brightly, interest flashing across his face.

"Apparently," I mumble.

Mohammad frowns at me but then pulls me into a hug. I let out a sigh in his arms and hug him back before finally pulling away.

"She was playing with the tool like it was a toy," Noah informs him as we start walking back to class.

I roll my eyes and lace my arm through Mohammad's as we walk. Mohammad takes us all the way back to the art room before dropping it.

"Try to keep the rest of your fingers intact." Mohammad winks. He gives us a wave before heading back to the stairwell and off to his class.

I glance at Noah but don't bother saying anything before going back into class.

"Are you all right?" Mrs. Jones asks the moment Noah and I are through the door.

"I'm fine." I nod and give her a sympathetic smile.

Because she looks flustered.

Relief flashes across her face, but she's still frowning at me as I walk back to my desk.

By the time we're back in our seats, class is pretty much over. Our tools and clay are still on the table, and Noah takes the remaining minutes to clean them off and then put them away.

When he's walking back to our table, the bell goes off.

Noah's gaze lands on me.

"Be more careful in Geography," he says before grabbing his backpack and walking out the door.

Battle scar.
GEOGRAPHY

AFTER THE WEIRDNESS that was art class, I'm grateful to only have Geography left for the day. I walk to my locker and check my phone before class and see that my dad texted me.

> **Dad:** *Call us after your classes. I've got news. I'd also like a sweatshirt from your school. Need to show that I'm a proud Kensington School parent!*
>
> **Me:** *If you want a sweatshirt, does that mean I'm going to see you soon? Or will I have to ship it internationally?*

As I wait for my dad to text back, I grab my geography textbook and notebook and then slam my locker shut. My phone vibrates again.

> **Dad:** *You shouldn't be texting in school.*
>
> **Me:** *You started it.*
>
> **Dad:** *Turn your phone off. Then call us after school.*
>
> **Me:** *Love you too.*

I roll my eyes, turn my phone off, and walk to Geography. When I get to the doorway, Naomi comes bounding up to me, Olivia at her side.

"Hey!" Naomi says brightly.

I wince at the high pitch of her voice. She looks perfect today, her blonde hair in soft, loose curls.

"Can you take it down a notch?" I ask, hugging her.

"Hungover?" Olivia asks, arching an eyebrow at me.

"At this point, who knows?" I reply. "It's been a yo-yo day for me."

"I hate hangovers," Naomi says, wrinkling her nose as we walk into class.

I follow behind her, Olivia at my side. She's wearing a sweater over her uniform today, and her hair is pulled back into a sleek bun that shows off her full lips and lined eyes. She looks beautiful.

"Yet this one is partially your fault," I say to Naomi as we walk to our seats.

"I gave you a double. The rest is on you," Naomi points out. "Sit with us?"

I glance away from Olivia and Naomi, finding Harry already in his seat.

"Yeah, give me a second," I reply, nodding over at Harry.

Olivia doesn't acknowledge me, but Naomi nods in return. I move across the room and walk down the aisle toward him. His blue eyes come up to mine, a smile on his lips.

I hold up my hand, showing him my Band-Aid. "Battle scar from Art."

Harry's smile falters, and he takes my hand in his as concern flashes across his face. "You all right? What happened?"

"I'm fine. It was a minor injury," I say with a smile. "I wanted to see how you were. The girls want me to sit with them today."

"I'm sure Olivia just wants the gossip," Harry says, his

eyes flicking over to her.

"Maybe they just like my friendship," I offer instead, not liking the frown on Harry's face.

Harry brings his gaze back to me, his shoulders visibly relaxing.

"Can't blame them for that," he replies. "Besides, I intend to spend this class time usefully."

"Really?" I laugh, wondering if that means he's actually going to pay attention.

Harry nods. "I've decided I'm utterly sour at Mohammad for dragging us to school today, so I'm going to come up with an equally traitorous payback."

I raise an eyebrow at Harry. Because it's not the worst idea he's ever had.

"Let me know what you come up with after class," I tell him.

"I will. And you'll tell me about the finger?"

I nod before walking back over to the girls. Olivia is fussing with her bun as I drop down into the open seat next to her. Naomi is sitting in front of her and turns in her chair, so she can talk to us.

"So, you and Noah," Naomi says, her voice filled with excitement.

My eyes widen in shock.

"Let's *not* talk about that," I say, shaking my head at her.

"Then, tell me about last night," Olivia offers. "Was Harry all right?"

Olivia glances over at Harry. I look, too, watching as he writes quickly in his notebook. It makes me smile, knowing that he's writing out ways to get back at Mohammad. It reminds me of when I first got here. When Harry said that he used to go over to wake Noah up early and mess with him.

I bring my attention back to Olivia.

"He did great actually," I reply, thinking about the party. But Olivia doesn't look convinced.

"He's good at putting on a show. How was he *actually*?"

I glance to Naomi, wondering why Olivia didn't just ask Naomi.

Naomi was there. I'm sure she saw Harry and knows enough about what went on at the party to satisfy Olivia's questions. But then I realize that they aren't just questions.

She's worried. She still cares about Harry, and she wants to know how he actually is. She isn't just looking for a run-through of the night.

"It wasn't fun for him. But he'll get through it. He has to," I say, chewing on my lip. "You know, Olivia, I'm sure Harry would talk to you about it if you—"

Before I have a chance to finish, Olivia cuts me off.

"Naomi, tell us more about Mohammad," she says, changing the subject.

I seal my lips shut as the bell goes off. I wish she and Harry would just talk and make up. At least pick up the pieces of their friendship. I know they both care. It's obvious in the questions that she asks. The look in her eyes. And it's obvious with how hurt Harry was about everything.

If he didn't care, it wouldn't have hurt so much.

"We need to get together this weekend and talk about it," Naomi says, sternly looking between Olivia and me.

I don't dare disagree. "Sure," I reply.

"Of course," Olivia agrees.

When Naomi turns back, appeased, Olivia sneaks a glance at me and widens her eyes in amusement.

I let out a soft laugh.

MR. PRITCHARD LECTURES for the entire class. I sneak a glance at Harry, who's dozed off.

I can tell he's done with school, and honestly, so am I.

I fidget in my seat, ready for the day to be over. To go back to the hotel, take another shower, and then fall into bed and sleep.

And sleep and sleep.

The thought of my hotel room sends a jolt through me.

I remember this morning, being in the bathroom, pulling out a piece of paper from Noah's sweats.

I sneak a glance over to Olivia. She's looking down at the phone in her lap. Naomi is listening, but she's doodling in the notebook in front of her. I grab the note out of my bag, unfolding it with shaky hands.

When I finally get it open flat, I stick it into my notebook and shut it. I look up to Mr. Pritchard, making sure that he isn't watching me. That he won't come over and take it, thinking that it's a note we're passing around.

After a few minutes, I open up the notebook and look over the paper.

It's definitely Noah's handwriting.

"What's that?" Olivia whispers, nodding at the note.

"Art homework," I lie, caught off guard. I roll my eyes and flip back to my geography notes, my stomach doing a flip.

Olivia scowls at the mention of *homework* and looks back down to her phone.

I let out an unsteady breath and try to focus on class.

Cosmic.
DETENTION

I'M NERVOUS TO see Noah in detention. I know I shouldn't be, but I am. Between the question he asked in Statistics to my lying on his chest in the grass, I feel like I'm a ticking time bomb, waiting to blow.

And that doesn't even include the fantasy I had about him this morning.

But I'm also sort of annoyed with him. He could have been slightly nicer about the whole cutting-my-finger incident. I know I was dramatic about it, but I was in pain.

And I really don't like blood.

But more than anything, the tone of disapproval in his voice made me feel embarrassed. Because I know I was being silly. And I was distracted. And in the midst of staring off into, well, *him*, I injured myself.

And that's kind of mortifying.

When I get to the library, Mrs. Bateson isn't at her desk, so I go back to the staff room, where I find her and Noah looking at a stack of books.

Mrs. Bateson eyes me, her curling gray hair pulled back into a wispy bun.

"We received another donation," she informs me.

I join them at the table, looking over the books.

"You'll need to scan them, check their labels, and then shelve them."

"We can do that." I nod in understanding.

Mrs. Bateson gives me a smile, pats me on the shoulder, and then walks very slowly out of the door.

I glance over to Noah, and his eyebrows are raised in interest at her slow, shifting pace. But the second she's out the door, his attention turns toward me.

I clear my throat and fidget with my hair.

"We should get started," he says as he takes a stack of books over to the scanner and sits down in front of the computer.

I move the rest of the books over, so he can easily scan

them, and then I take a seat on his right, so he can hand me the book when he's done. The screen's still black when I sit down, and I catch a glimpse of my reflection in it.

I flare my eyes and bring my hands back up into my hair.

"My hair's a disaster today," I comment.

"Your hair looks fine."

"I know it doesn't," I reply, making conversation as we wait. "I threw it up, so we wouldn't be late. And since then, it's seen jam, and grass, and the nurse's office."

Noah lets out a deep laugh.

"We've all had a long day. But you shouldn't worry about that stuff." He turns and brings his hand to my hair. "Besides, you've got nice hair. It's shiny. Soft."

Noah examines a piece that's fallen out of my clip.

"You like it?" I ask.

"Mmhmm."

"And … what about my smell?" I tease.

"Well, that's just another story," Noah says, a warm smile coming onto his face.

"Compared to yours, it is."

Noah raises his eyebrows, his golden eyes lighting up. "You talking shit about my manly musk?" he says in a deep voice, puffing out his chest.

I giggle, watching him.

"No. You smell nice. Like sweat and grass and a locker room." I stick my tongue out at him.

"I'll be sure to shower after school then. I'm sure Mum would appreciate it at least."

"A warm shower sounds nice. Honestly, I could use a warm bed and a nap."

"Are you cold?" Noah asks.

"A bit."

I'm not sure why the library is chillier than usual today.

Noah shifts in his chair and turns, so our knees are touching. He rubs his hands up and down my arms quickly, trying to warm me up. I smile at him, already feeling warmer.

But then he drops his hands down to my thighs. His gaze flicks up to mine before moving down to my tights.

He rubs from my knees up to the hem of my skirt.

I suck in a breath, my face flushing.

Noah brings one palm on my thigh, the other coming up to catch my hand.

"How's your finger feeling?" he asks, looking at the Band-Aid.

"Much better."

He brings my finger up to his lips and then gently kisses it. "I was worried about you."

I keep my eyes on his lips for a moment before pushing out a little laugh.

"Worried about me? I was worried about you. I thought you were going to faint."

Noah laughs. "I considered it," he admits.

"Luckily for us, Mohammad saved the day."

"He has a way of coming through on stuff like that. I still can't believe you actually thought he had a headache." Noah drops his eyes, folding my hand into his. "I'm sorry I was hard on you. I just didn't like seeing you hurt."

I bring his chin up, so he has to look at me.

"It's all right. I appreciated you walking me to the nurse's office. And for having the strength not to pass out on me."

I smile at him. Noah shakes his head but smiles back.

He drops my hand and lets go of my leg, turning to scan the first book.

Once he's checked the information, he hands it to me.

"You know, my dad texted me before geography class."

"Yeah? What'd he say?"

"They want me to call after school. But from the sound of it, they closed on the apartment."

"That's great news."

"It is," I agree. "You know, I was thinking about our parents."

"Yeah?" Noah says as he hands me another book.

"Yeah. And I was wondering something. Your mom is traditional. She wants a man to *be a man*. But really, your dad is soft and smart and kind. It had me thinking … what do you want to be?"

"Like, as a partner?" Noah asks.

"I don't know. Do you think we always end up like our parents?"

"Nah. We can. It's the easiest route really because it's the environment that we were raised in."

"Is it a bad thing?"

"Of course not. Unless you've got shit parents."

"So, do you want to be like your parents?" I ask, thinking about Helen and Gene.

They're kind and loving. It's obvious they love each other. They care for their children. And I know my parents care for each other too. They care about me.

Noah's voice pulls me out of my thoughts. "Mostly maybe. I mean, I think relationships can be taken a step further. They can be … more."

I look at him, confused. "More? More of what?"

"More of everything," he says, handing me another book. "My parents care for one another. They care for me and Mia. But I don't want a love that's ordinary. And I'm not saying that theirs is …" Noah's brows pull in.

"You want a love that's … cosmic, right?"

"If I'm going to have it, it might as well be, right?" Noah asks, looking over to me.

I drop his gaze and fidget with my finger. "I guess."

"And you, what do you want?"

"Honestly, that scares me a bit."

"You're afraid," Noah states.

"Yeah."

He lets out a slow breath. "Well, that's living, isn't it? Fear. Love. These are tricky and scary things. Trappings really." Noah grins, leaning back in his chair.

"Noah," I say seriously.

"I'm serious. You're best off, staying away from it all. I'll make you a little box to crawl under," he says playfully.

"You're being mean."

"I'm teasing."

"So, no box?" I ask.

Noah thinks about the question, his eyes shifting up to the corners.

"I wouldn't want you to do that, but if it made you happy …"

"Why wouldn't you want me in a box?" I laugh, realizing how weird this conversation is getting.

Noah picks up the last book, scanning it.

"Because you'd hurt yourself. You'd lose out on something beautiful because of it. And … well, it might make my life a bit more torturous," he says with a smirk.

"Because?" I ask as Noah hands me the book.

"Well, if you were under a box, then I'd have to go and find a box to crawl under too. And I'm not really that flexible, so I would be smushed in an uncomfortable position."

I set the book down on the cart, thinking.

"So, beauty. Love. It's worth the risk?"

"You tell me," Noah replies, his hand coming up to gently caress my cheek.

I bring my eyes to his. "Probably."

Noah's lips curl slightly. He holds my gaze for a moment and then stands. He pulls me up with him and then pushes the cart out into the library. I watch in silence as he starts to shelve books. He's so meticulous about it. So thoughtful. It's like every decision is thought out in his mind before he ever does it. But at the same time, he never picks a book I expect him to. Every time he goes back to the cart, he approaches it in a new way.

That's what makes Noah so confusing.

He's unpredictable.

"Have you ever felt like you could see your future, your destruction, in the midst of heaven?" I ask as he squats down, sliding a book into place.

Noah glances up at me, looking confused. "I can see the horizon, if that's what you mean. The possibilities."

"I feel like I'm standing under a rainbow, and all I can think about are the storm clouds I can see."

"You're talking in code," Noah says, standing up.

"You're sort of the rainbow in this analogy," I admit.

Noah shifts in front of me, a smile on his lips.

"Then, look at the rainbow and forget about the storm, silly girl. What's wrong with you?" Noah says, pulling me toward him.

Pulling me into a hug.

I wrap my arms around his neck, letting my fear slip away.

I fold into him, knowing he's right. Everyone's right.

This.

Him.

It's what I want.

Noah pulls back and looks down at me. "Speaking of rainbows, are you looking forward to our veg day over break?"

"How is that speaking of rainbows?" I ask, breaking our

bodies apart.

"Well, since I'm the rainbow, I figured it sort of worked."

Noah walks back to the cart, and I follow him around the corner to a different section of books.

"Hmm," I comment. "Yeah, I am. Are you?"

"Definitely." Noah nods, his brown hair flopping. "I'm just wondering if we did it at my house, how much of a nuisance Mia would be."

"She's never a nuisance!" I laugh, pressing against his shoulder in disapproval. "Plus, she'd probably bake for us."

"That's true." Noah weighs his head back and forth.

"But I see your point. Maybe we should do it at my place instead then," I offer.

"Agreed. Who knows? If we wait until your parents are here, we could be having it at your new house. Your new room."

The thought of having my day with Noah spoiled by my parents makes me shake my head.

"Let's make sure to do it before they get here, okay?"

"Sounds good. You'll let me know when?" he asks, placing the last book on the shelf before looking at me.

"I'll let you know."

Noah smiles as he stands up.

"So, it's a date?" he asks, tilting his head at me.

I look up at him, knowing that this is my chance.

This is my chance to say yes too.

To a date.

To him.

I can't help but smile.

And say, "It's a date."

Raging storm.
5:03PM

AFTER DETENTION, I decide to give my dad a call while walking to the school's spirit shop. I figure if I don't go and get him the sweatshirt now—well, one, I'll forget. And two, with the school being closed, the shop will be closed too. Which means my dad would get here and, to his disappointment, not be able to announce that he's a Kensington School parent with his sweatshirt.

The horror.

The phone only rings for a second before my dad picks up.

"Hey, Dad," I say.

"Hey, sweetie!" His voice is thick with enthusiasm that fills up the phone.

"So, what's the news? Is Mom pregnant?" I tease.

"Let's hope not!" my father bellows.

I have to pull the phone away from my ear. *He really is in a good mood.*

"No, no. The news, sweetheart, is, your mother and I have closed on the apartment."

"Aww, Dad." I smile into the phone. "Congrats."

"Congrats to all of us," he replies quickly. "And at seven thirty—actually, I should say, at half past seven. That's the British way of saying it, right?"

"Uh, I think you should stick with the American way." I cringe.

"Not for long, honey. We're going to be Londoners soon!"

"Please." I laugh into the phone. "You're New Yorkers

through and through."

"Maybe all the tea will convert me."

"God, I hope not."

My dad chuckles into the phone.

"I'm not sure I've ever heard you so excited. I mean, apart from when you told me you got the job."

"I have a feeling you'll be as excited as your mother and I are once you see the new digs."

"You've got to stop saying *digs*, Dad. It stopped being a thing, like, thirty years ago."

"Do you prefer *pad*?" he counters.

I cover my face with my other hand and shake my head.

"*Anyway*, what's going on at seven thirty?" I say, trying to get him back on track.

"I've set up an appointment for you to view the house. The realtor will meet you there and show you the place."

"Really?" I ask, excitement bubbling in me.

"Really," my dad confirms.

"Wow, Dad. I can't wait." I smile against the phone.

"I'm glad to hear your enthusiasm, Mal. I hate to run, but I've got to head to a meeting. I'll have my secretary email you the address and the realtor's name."

"Sounds good. Have a good day, Dad."

"You too!"

My dad hangs up, and I throw my phone into my bag before heading into the school shop.

AFTER SEARCHING THROUGH a few racks of spirit wear, I finally decide on a sweater I think my dad will like. It's a zip-up with the school logo on the left side of the chest. It's the perfect mix of dressy and casual. He could wear it out to dinner with jeans or throw it on in his office if he gets cold.

I slide it onto the counter and pull out my wallet when a

piece of paper sticking out of my notebook jogs my memory. It's the note that I was going to read in Geography. The one I'd found in Noah's sweats.

I pay for the sweatshirt and leave the shop. I walk a few blocks away from school before I find a bench. I sit down, pull out my notebook, and flip through it until I get to the note.

It's still creased, so I flatten it under my hand.

Noah's name is written out on the top-right corner.

I move my gaze down.

I would like to express what my project is through a few lines.

Raging storm.
The universe booms around me.
She approaches.
Frightfully, I stand.
Yes.
Stuck.
Stuck in wonderment.
Something so strong, so beautiful.
Swirling around me.
Will it absorb me?
Maybe.
Or might it pass by?
It could.
Rolling waves of rage and chaos.
Cracks of thunder echo in my chest.
I am in the storm now.
How?
Dancing in the wind.
In her chaos.
Can I become a part of her forever?
I must be able to.
This feeling, so wonderful.

Maybe she will only pass me by.
Leave me to fall from the sky?
I hope not.
This raging storm around me.
So dangerous.
So pure.
Nothing but nature in her utter glory.
Pushing me into motion.
I spin in the midst of her, taking in the power.
The walls of motion.
Confusion surrounds me.
Particles forcing together and cracking apart.
I'm frightful again, the noise overpowering me.
I hunch into a ball, scared of what will become of me.
Still suspended in the air.
But she silences.
The sky clears around me.
It must be the eye of the storm.
The center of everything.
The center of her.
Yes.
The sunshine blinds me.
I raise my hand to shield my face.
The silence a melody in my ear.
Ah, finally soothed.
How extraordinary this is, floating and rising.
It overcomes me.
This space.
Joy?
But then I feel the air shift.
The power making my hair rise.
And suddenly, I'm moving again.
She moves along.

This raging, rolling storm.
The air sucking me up and down.
Ripping me apart.
Spinning.
Spinning.
Spinning.
Fear consumes me again as the storm takes hold.
Confusion.
So much confusion.
I cry, thinking I might die.
But it's over.
I look at my hands.
My feet.
Back on the ground.
She rolls away.
Spinning beautifully onward.
My, the power.
But the question.
Always the question.
Do I love?
Do I hate?
Her beautiful, frightening glory.
My dear raging storm.

I drop the note into my lap. My hand comes up, covering my mouth in shock. I blink down at the note, trying to slow down my heart rate.

Because Noah wrote this.

He wrote all of this.

And he wrote it about me.

About how I make him feel.

I think back to his project. How he told me it was about me. The eye of the storm.

Chaos. Confusion. Awe.

I've spent the week thinking of ways to get Noah to forgive me. I asked for Mohammad's help. I got his locker combination. When Noah came to see me on my birthday, I wanted him. I wanted him to kiss me in the hallway. I wanted him to tell me that I was his.

Only his.

Like he did last night.

I wanted him to tell me how he felt.

I wanted him to show me.

But I was never quite ready for it.

I was always scared.

Mohammad and Noah were both right.

I'm a chicken.

But I don't have to be. Everyone says that I'm bold and sassy and strong, but sometimes, I don't feel like that. It's one of the reasons Harry and I grew close so quickly. He saw who I was under all of that, and I liked that he saw me. Saw my heart. But Harry only ever got glimpses.

Noah … knows me. He might even know me better than I know myself, which is confusing. And the thing is, he doesn't want a passing glimpse.

Noah wants to strip away every layer I've buried myself underneath.

One by one.

Layer after layer.

Gone.

Just for him.

He wants my heart.

He wants everything.

I stand up from the bench and walk back to my hotel in a daze. I press the notebook against my chest, Noah's words still spinning in my head.

WHEN I GET to the lobby, I start to head for the elevator, but I stop.

I'm not sure what to do. I look around and find an open chair. I sit down and decide to reread his poem.

I scan over it again and again.

Noah talks about feeling confused. And about being scared. He talks about feeling overpowered.

Consumed.

He isn't sure whether to be ecstatic or terrified.

And that's exactly how I feel.

For the first time, I feel like I'm not going through this alone. I know that Noah cares for me. But my feelings, they've always felt deeper. Scarier.

But now, I know I'm not alone in that.

I'm not alone in feeling frightened by whatever this is between us. Because at least if Noah asks for everything, I can ask for everything too.

I stand up, knowing what I need to do.

I need to find Noah.

Now.

I KNOCK ON his front door.

Actually, I bang on it.

Because everything—my mind, my heart, my body—is going frantic.

And I have to talk to Noah.

I need Helen to let me in.

Or Gene.

It doesn't matter.

I just need to get into that house and find Noah.

My heart, my blood, they're pounding. Everything is pounding.

Noah loves me.

At least, I'm pretty sure he does.

No. I know he does.

His poem showed me that.

And I have to know now. I've been thinking about it for hours. Days. Every day really. I have to know what it would be like to kiss him.

To kiss him and actually mean it.

To kiss him with love.

To kiss him softly.

Not out of anger.

I have to see him.

I have to kiss him.

The door pulls open, and it's not Gene. It's not Helen, like I expected.

It's Noah.

Standing in the doorway is the boy who gave me his sweats. Who tucked a piece of paper into the pocket, hoping I would find it. Hoping I would read it. Hoping I would understand.

He pulls open the door, his creamy skin confronting me. His musk hitting me like a wall. His lips part, his eyes finding mine. He stands there, frozen, unsure.

And I remain frozen too.

Because I thought I would have something to say.

I thought words would pour out of my mouth.

Like they always do.

But I can't decide what to say.

I read your poem.

Kiss me, now.

My fingers twitch, just in one hand. My right hand. The hand that's holding the folded-up notebook paper he gave me. His eyes flick down to my hand, and I watch as he sucks in a breath. His chest rises with a sharp intake of air. But then his neck pulls back, his head tilting up again. He keeps his eyes on me but closes the door to the house, so he's standing in front of me outside.

Just him and me.

And I know what I have to do.

What I need to do.

I need to kiss Noah Williams.

I TAKE A step toward him, my body reaching out to his when the front door is yanked open again.

"You're here!" Mia says over his shoulder, a huge grin on her face. Noah's eyes slide closed as Mia pushes him to the side and drags me into the house. "Want some tea?"

I kick off my shoes, looking frantically between Mia and Noah, who's still in the doorway.

"Uh … okay," I hear myself say.

Okay?

Okay?!

No. I don't want tea. I want my mouth on your brother's actually.

I let out a shallow breath, trying to slow my heart rate down.

Mia pulls me into the kitchen and turns on the kettle.

"This is a nice surprise," she says, moving her books off to the side of the table as she sets down two mugs.

I glance at the homework, realizing why she is so happy to see me.

I'm an excuse not to study.

"I was just complaining to Noah that I needed a break," Mia goes on, flaring her eyes. "So, your timing is perfect."

"Actually," I start to say as Noah joins us in the kitchen.

He looks down at my hand.

"I found your note," I tell him.

"What note?" Mia asks, breezing past us, tea bags in her hand.

"Your poem," I say to Noah.

Noah stands, frozen, his body rigid as understanding washes across his face.

"Mia, I think we're going to have to come back down for tea later," Noah says. He breaks the space between us, his hand finding my free one.

"Seriously?" Mia groans, her shoulders dropping. "You're supposed to be helping me with my Chemistry homework. If I fail another assignment …"

"You won't. I'll help you later," Noah says, pulling me out of the kitchen.

"You'd better keep your word!" Mia calls out.

Noah walks quickly up the stairs, pulling me behind him. When we get to his room, he closes the door and lets go of my hand.

"Sorry about that." He runs his hand through his hair, looking flustered.

"It's—" I was going to say *fine*, but my voice falls short. My heart is still pounding in my chest.

Because I wanted to kiss Noah.

Right then and there, before I lost my nerve.

But now, we're both flustered, and Noah is looking at the paper in my hand again.

He takes a step forward. "I was starting to wonder about that."

I set the poem down on his side table and take a seat on his bed.

"You put it there on purpose?" I ask, already knowing the answer but wanting to be sure.

"Well, I did tell you that you could have it, didn't I?" Noah says, shifting. He moves from his door to his desk chair, turning the chair to face me and taking a seat.

"I've been thinking about everything you said. I've read and reread this now …" I fumble over my words.

"You never let on," Noah states, eyeing me.

"You can't always read me, you know."

Noah's cheeks turn pink, his eyes slipping across my face. "I think you're wrong about that, but I will say, you did a good job of concealing that you'd read it."

"Noah, I didn't even find it until this morning."

Noah's face flashes with surprise.

"And I didn't read it until after school. After detention," I explain.

Noah folds his hands together in his lap. "What did you think?"

"I was surprised."

"You hate surprises."

"No, I just … I hadn't expected it. I hadn't expected how it would make me feel."

I chew on my lip, wishing that this weren't so hard to get out.

"How did it make you feel?" Noah asks with hesitation.

"Less scared."

Noah smiles, and my nerves melt a little.

"I wanted to … kiss you. Out front just now."

Noah's head tilts back, his eyes finding mine. "Really?"

"Yeah. But then Mia came out and …"

"That wasn't ideal."

"But maybe her timing wasn't the worst," I reply, letting out a heavy sigh.

"What do you mean?"

"I mean, there are a few things I think we should talk about. A few things I need you to answer before …" I trail off, my cheeks turning pink.

"Ask," Noah says coolly.

I look at him, concern bubbling in my stomach. "Are you sure?"

"Ask me."

I shift over the past few weeks in my mind. All of the questions between us. The moments we've shared. The times that Noah has made me question my feelings.

Made me question *him*.

I look across the room to him, knowing this isn't going to be easy.

"I made it clear that I cared for you before I was supposed to leave. You knew how I felt, what I wanted. But you always told me that I could never have that. Why did that change yesterday?"

"What exactly did you want, Mal?" he asks me.

My forehead creases. He should know the answer to this.

"*You*. Noah, I was happy before, with Harry. He wasn't you, but I cared about him. And he gave me something that you couldn't. But last night, you asked for … everything."

Noah nods. "I did."

"Well, that's why I'm confused. I didn't think you were able to give me that. I know at first, it was because of Harry. Then, you were upset that I didn't tell you I was staying," I reply, trying to make sense of this.

"What if I can?" he says.

"What if you can what?"

"Give you more."

My gaze flicks up to his. "What do you mean?"

"I mean, this whole time, you've said that Harry gave you something that I couldn't. What would happen if I gave you that? What is it that Harry gave you?"

I shake my head, stopping him.

"What was it, Mal?"

Noah stands up from the chair and moves toward me.

I want to squeeze my eyes shut and crawl under his covers. Because he doesn't want to know the answer to this question. Not really.

And I don't want to admit it.

I don't want to hurt him.

Noah sits down on the edge of the bed next to me. His eyes meet mine.

I suck in a breath and then force out, "Consistency."

"You think I'm not consistent?" Noah asks, sounding defeated.

"No."

"You think I don't love you?" he asks gently.

I tilt my head to the side, feeling stuck. "Noah …"

"Answer me, please."

"I don't know," I push out. "Maybe. Yes?"

"Maybe?" Noah repeats, his eyes flaring. He pushes his hands back through his hair.

"No. I mean, yes. But, Noah, your poem. It said it perfectly. *Do I love? Do I hate?*" I bring my eyes to his. In the poem, I found what I had been looking for. I found that I wasn't alone in my feeling out of control.

But I also found his uncertainty.

His conflict.

"I've made so many mistakes." Noah shakes his head, his eyes looking distant.

"Like what?" I ask.

"Like telling you that I hated you. I shouldn't have pushed you away."

"No, you shouldn't have."

Noah sucks in his cheeks and lets out a shallow breath. He turns to me, his eyes finding mine again. But then his hand moves, catching my attention. He presses our palms together before lacing his fingers through mine.

"Mal, I didn't tell Harry at first because you both deserved to be happy. I wanted to take myself out of the equation. I have a family. I have you both in a way. I didn't need that with you. I'm happy on my own. I don't need much. But then you were always there. I thought being friends would be easy. After all, there's only one limitation to friendship.

"But then time went on, and you stayed. And you made me feel things that I hadn't expected. And by the time I knew what I was feeling, you and Harry were so wrapped up in one another.

"Then, things started happening with his family. And I love Harry. But the way he treated you wasn't the best. And I was annoyed by it. Furious really. I was torn between being supportive of him or you. I didn't know what to do. You two started to break apart, not because of me. But there you were, too beautiful to feel hurt. Too loving to feel unloved. And I sort of let myself slip further."

I search Noah's face, my whole body coming alive at his words. "You're so big on talking. On communicating. On honesty. Why didn't you tell me any of this before?"

Noah absentmindedly slides his fingers in and out of mine.

"I suppose by the time I realized all that, our three weeks were up. I mean, you were leaving. And I was going to tell you I loved you? I was going to let you leave even more broken?"

"Why would that have broken me?"

"I know you too well, Mal," he says, shaking his head.

"Fine. It would have been … hard," I admit.

"Impossible. It would have been impossible. And you would have suffered. And then I would have suffered."

"So, your plan was to torture me instead? Almost kiss me?

Tell me that you wanted all of me and then let me leave? To go to New York like nothing happened? You made me feel like I was crazy. Like I was alone."

My hand shakes in his. All of those feelings and moments come rushing back to me in a blur. But the worst one is clear.

Noah telling me to forget about him.

He squeezes my hand.

"That wasn't my intention," he says. "I wasn't trying to hurt anyone."

"You were hurting me," I snap back.

"I—" Noah's brows draw in, pain flashing across his face.

This isn't what I wanted, I suddenly realize.

I don't want to keep going over our old wounds. I want things to be different between us. And I think that means we have to make a few things from our past right.

"Noah, ask me what I want."

Noah's still holding my hand, but his head is hanging down. "I'm not sure that's a good idea."

I pull my legs up onto the bed and sit crisscross before grabbing on to Noah's other hand. I force him to turn toward me. To sit face-to-face with me.

He pulls his lips to the side, looking conflicted. I squeeze his hands, holding them between us.

"Ask me, Noah."

"What are you asking for?" he says, his eyes finally coming up to mine.

"I'm asking for everything. From you," I say, my heart in my throat.

"Well, everything isn't that much," Noah says with a wry smile.

"Noah."

"Mallory, what do you want?"

"I want you," I breathe out. "And I want you to answer

my questions."

Noah pulls his chin back and lets out an uneasy breath.

But I need to hear his answers.

"No evasions. No tactics. No retreats. Sit here before me with an open heart, like I've sat before you so many times. Please."

Noah chews on his lips for a moment before saying, "Fine. Ask."

"Would you have stayed in contact with me if I had left?"

"I don't know."

"That's not an answer."

"Ask a different question," Noah offers.

"When is the first time you thought about kissing me?" I decide to ask.

Because Noah was hard to read. He still is.

"The moment I saw you."

My mouth falls open in surprise. Noah just holds my gaze.

"I was frustrated at the thought, honestly, pushed it away. But it was there," he adds.

"Do you think that I came here, that I'm staying … for a reason?"

"We were meant to find one another, if that's what you're asking," Noah says, playing with my fingers.

I try to ignore the sensation and focus on my questions.

"How do you feel about things between you, me, and Harry?"

"I feel … less confused than before. Things are clearer."

"Could you imagine us *together*?"

"Yes."

"In a nonsexual way?" I question.

"No," Noah says, still looking down at our hands.

My whole body stills at the next question that rises to my

mind.

"Do you promise to never abandon me, Noah?" I practically whisper.

Noah's wide eyes move up to mine. "You think I'll leave you?"

"I think you're always willing to sacrifice me."

"That's how I've made you feel?" he asks, his fingers stilling.

And I have to tell him the truth.

"Yes."

Noah flinches at my word.

"Last question," I say lightly.

"I'm not sure I can handle another," he replies.

I unlace our fingers, desperate to calm Noah down. I rub circles across his forearms, hoping he'll relax. I know this isn't easy for him. It's not easy for me either. But I'd rather have this conversation now than let any piece of our past find its way into the future.

Into *our* future.

"What do you want?" I finally say.

"I want to be with you," Noah replies, his eyes scanning over me. Over my body.

"I know—" I start, but Noah cuts me off.

"No, I want to date you."

I pull my head back and look up to him. "Date me? That's—" My eyes widen.

"A step for you. I know." He nods, and I know my face flashes with surprise.

Because date Noah? I always thought that's what he wasn't willing to give me. Because of Harry. Because of our circumstances. But then last night …

"Are you allowed to ask everything of someone and then just date them?" I mumble, caught off guard by his answer.

Noah's eyebrows rise up.

"Were you hoping for forever?" Noah smirks.

"I'm only sixteen," I start, shaking my head.

"Seventeen now." Noah chuckles.

"You heard all of my conversations with your mom, didn't you?" I flush, mortified that he actually heard that.

"I couldn't help myself. When my mum asked what you made of her son, I had to know what you thought of me," he says with a chuckle.

I roll my eyes at him before realization settles in again.

"I guess I never thought that we could actually date. I know Harry suggested it, but ..."

"I don't care for labels," Noah replies, growing serious again.

I continue rubbing his arms, letting the motion distract me.

"But you labeled it dating. So, what would dating include?"

"Anything you want. I just know how you are with your boxes."

"Well, what would you consider me?" I say, trying to wrap my mind around this.

Around us.

"I would say mine, but I don't really believe we could be anyone else's."

I bite my lip, letting my eyes slip across Noah. His dark hair. His warm eyes. His creamy skin.

"So, I would be ..." I ask.

"You would be Mallory, the woman I gifted my heart to." Noah brings his gaze to mine.

"And you would be the boy who—"

"Who you might consider gifting your heart to," he replies.

"That's big."

"Nah. Not really. Besides, I think we're further along in the gifting process than either one of us would like to admit," Noah says, a smile growing on his lips.

"Oh? You think you already have my heart?" I tease.

Noah licks his lip before smiling. "Well, if not yet, then hopefully one day."

I can't help but smile back at him.

"So, does Noah Williams do girlfriends?" I ask, trying to figure out exactly what he's getting at.

"Not normally."

"Oh?"

"But for you, I'd make an exception," he says, his lips curling up further.

My heart feels like it's going to break through my chest with his words.

"And you would do all of this even though we haven't kissed yet?" I ask him.

"We have kissed," Noah points out.

"Not properly," I disagree.

"Don't you think it's about time we fixed that?"

I look at Noah.

A warm smile envelops his face, and he raises his eyebrows at me. I can't help but finally grin as he leans toward me.

"I thought you said once we started, we wouldn't be able to stop?" I ask, barely able to breathe.

Because Noah's leaned into me before.

I've thought we would kiss so many times.

But now … now, I know that it's finally going to happen.

It's going to be good.

It's going to be right.

"I think I can stop myself. But one can't be sure until …" Noah teases, his nose dancing against mine as his mouth—

"You can't hoard Mallory, Noah," Mia says, throwing open the door.

Noah stops, his mouth never reaching mine. He pulls back, blinking his eyes like he's trying to remember we're still in his house. In his room.

On his bed.

He looks in Mia's direction, and a second later, he's off the bed, trying to usher her out.

"She just got here," Noah states.

He puts one hand on her back, leading her toward the door. I decide to stand up, but I can barely feel my legs. They feel like Jell-O.

"She got here *forty-five* minutes ago," Mia replies, pushing Noah off her.

"Shit, really?" I ask.

Because I can't have already been here for forty-five minutes. It feels like we've only been talking for maybe twenty minutes.

"Really," Mia replies, standing with her back to the doorway. She has her arms crossed over her chest, and she's looking directly at me. Well, more like pouting at me.

Her face is drawn down into a sad frown, and her lips are pushing out.

I let out a sigh, knowing that I'm going to have to give in to her.

I can already tell if I don't go with her, she's going to hold it against me.

I walk toward her, glancing at Noah. He holds my gaze, his eyes still darkened from earlier. The last thing I want to do right now is leave his room, but it seems like Noah's time is up.

Mia laces her arm through mine when I get to her before sticking out her tongue in Noah's direction with a grin.

"You're terrible." I laugh, shaking my head at her.

"And you're a bad friend. Ditching me for my brother," Mia replies in the hallway.

"You know I really like you, Mia. And I do cherish our friendship. But your timing was terrible," I say as she drags me into her room.

"I saw that," Mia says with a knowing smile. "Noah's going to be an absolute grump about it tonight, I'm sure. But it was kind of satisfying, walking in right at that moment."

"Mia!" I exclaim.

"What?" she replies, falling onto her bed. "Maybe if you two would just shag and stop talking so much, I wouldn't have to wait almost an hour to hang out with someone."

"Fair point," I comment, plopping down onto the bed next to her. I roll onto my back, looking up at the ceiling. "Want to hear something weird?"

"Absolutely."

"I think your brother and I are going to date."

"That's not weird. That's nice."

"It is nice." I smile.

She rolls over and looks at me. "Okay, it is a little weird, but it's about time. I know Noah cares about you."

"Speaking of caring … how are things between you and Sophia?"

Mia rolls her eyes. "One second, she's great. The next, not so much. I think she's mad that I left for Greece. But it was only three weeks. And when I got back, I told her that I missed her."

"I'm sure she just missed you."

"Probably …" Mia replies. "Women."

"Women," I agree.

"Anyway, it has more to do with the fact that I brought up going to art school there."

"Are you thinking about it?" I ask with interest.

"Was," Mia says, rolling her eyes. "But Sophia took it as a personal insult that I didn't think we'd still be friends or be together by then."

"Give her a chance," I tell her. "I'm sure it's hard for her, too, adjusting to being more with you."

"We'll work it out. Anyway, check this out. I've been working on this cover for the guy whose album I played for you before school. He had professional photos taken and wants me to make this cool, retro mixed-media cover for his album," she says, pulling out her laptop.

FOR THE NEXT thirty minutes, Mia shows me her different ideas, scrolling through various photos she might use and inspiration boards she created. By the time she's done, I have to use the bathroom.

And I need to move.

She had us lying out across her bed, and my arms fell asleep. I stand up, shaking them out.

"I've got to run to the bathroom."

"Hurry up," Mia calls out before I'm even out of the room.

I shake my head and smile, walking into the bathroom. I close the door, but a second later, it opens. And before I know it, Noah is in there with me.

I gasp, caught off guard at his suddenness. I half-expect him to push me against the door and kiss me.

But I don't want that.

I want it slow.

I want to know that it's coming.

I want to prepare.

Noah's hands slide up my arms, wrapping around my shoulders. His fingers tickle my skin. They barely touch me but still send goose bumps down my arms.

"Mia has terrible timing," Noah says, his eyes meeting mine.

I could stare into his brown eyes forever, picking out the flecks of gold, the darker brown. They suck me in, over and over. Sometimes, I wonder if I'm not as strong as I always thought.

Because looking into his eyes, it's like they hold me.

Not in some type of warm embrace.

No.

They are literally my fixed point. The axis around which I rotate. I never thought I was someone who would fall hard. Who would be absorbed by a person. I never considered myself a romantic.

But staring into Noah's eyes, well, I see the appeal.

I can feel every part of myself want to just rotate around him.

"She really does," I agree.

"You're staring again. Remember in class, when you tried to convince me you weren't?"

"You had me pinned to the door," I mumble, holding his eyes.

"And you wouldn't give in," he says, a hint of a smile on his mouth. "You always lose focus, watching me. You get lost."

"I like getting lost in you," I whisper.

Noah licks his lips, his face coming close to mine. His hands move to my neck, pressing against my skin.

I let my palms move to his chest, grasping at him.

"Last time we were in here together, you wouldn't kiss me," I barely breathe out.

"I won't make that mistake again," he says.

His eyes stay with mine until he's so close that I can't

hold them anymore. His nose dances against mine as his hot breath engulfs me. I let my nails press into his shoulders as I wait. He pulls me closer to him until his lips finally find mine. They press against me warmly before moving away. Noah turns his head, letting his lips tease me. He brushes his mouth over mine as I push myself closer to him.

Against him.

When his lips find mine again, he really kisses me. His mouth is hot and soft. All I feel is pressure. And warmth.

But it's nothing compared to when he opens his mouth and his tongue connects with mine.

It's like my whole life, I've been this empty well.

I never knew that I was empty. I always felt content.

Full.

But I had no idea.

I had no idea what I was missing.

Because Noah is the water. He comes rushing into me, filling me whole and then some. Noah finds every crack and seeps in. He flows over everything that I am. He slips into me without any notice and makes me float. He's kind of the opposite of fire. He takes all of my aches, frustrations, and energy and dissipates it.

There's so much peace when he kisses me.

You'd think it would be the opposite.

I always thought love was consuming. Annoyingly consuming. I thought it was for people who looked naively at one another, wearing blinders. It's why love always seemed so combustible. It was filled with energy and fire, and I didn't want that. Fire will burn you eventually if you're around it long enough. That never seemed like love.

But this? I could drown happily in this feeling.

In him.

In everything about Noah.

His smell. His smile. His eyes. His *mouth*.

Everything separate is manageable.

But together, all at once, it's like heaven.

I bring my palms from Noah's shoulders down across his collarbone. I can feel his body shiver as my fingers slip across him. His arms wrap around me, pushing me against the door. I feel breathless at the sensation, my lips falling open to him again. He kisses me deeply before breaking our lips apart and pushing our foreheads together.

Noah opens his eyes, looking down at me through his thick lashes.

I look back at him, my heart pounding.

His arms unwrap themselves, falling down until his hands find mine. I grasp on to his fingers as a smile pulls on his lips. He stares at me, his fingers drawing up over my wrists and caressing my forearms.

Noah's lip twitches when I suck in a breath. His fingers move up to my shoulders, slipping lightly over my neck until his hands are in my hair. He turns his head, gently kissing me on the cheek as I wrap my arms around his neck.

His fingers slide out of my hair and fall down onto my chest before slipping down across my stomach. He sucks in his cheeks the same time goose bumps rise up my arms. He glances down, looking at them.

"You love when I touch you." He smiles before looking back at me with clouded eyes.

I nod, keeping my gaze connected to his.

Because I can't think about anything other than having his lips—those perfect, full lips—back on mine.

Noah holds my gaze before dropping his head back down. When his mouth finds mine, his kisses are wetter. His mouth is more open, and his hands are more insistent. I practically moan into his mouth, my fingers pushing into his soft hair.

Noah pulls me away from the door, his hands sliding down my back to my butt. He doesn't pick me up, but he pulls me against him until there's no space between us.

My whole body is pounding.

All I want to do is rip off his clothing.

To be pushed up against him like this forever.

But Noah loosens his grip, breaking our mouths apart.

He sucks in a ragged breath and grabs on to my hands.

I try to slow down my heart rate, letting myself focus again. Noah pulls my hands up to his chest, pressing both of my palms against him, his hands resting on top of mine. Then, he gets a serious look on his face.

"Do you understand now?" he asks.

He stands up straighter, looking down at me. And it takes everything I have to stay standing up. Because being this close to him, I realize how tall he is.

How beautiful. How daunting.

All I can do is nod my head at him. *Yes. I understand.*

Noah nods back at me. "It's beautiful, isn't it?"

"What is?"

"Us. This," he replies, keeping my hands on his chest.

I glance down at them and can feel his heartbeat. It's soft and consistent, but I can feel it.

And I want to fall into the beat, the rhythm.

I shut my eyes, really experiencing Noah. Trying to understand these feelings. All of these different sensations and emotions.

Everything feels so clear.

But everything feels new too.

Noah squeezes my hands before pulling them to his lips and kissing them.

"How are you feeling now?" he asks.

I open my eyes and grin at him. "I'm happy."

"You don't sound convinced. I should fix that," he says, his mouth quickly back on mine. His fingers trail up my hips as he pulls me toward him again.

And this time, our kisses aren't slow.

They aren't controlled.

Noah opens his mouth up to mine, and I give him everything.

I push my fingers up through his soft hair.

He backs me up against the counter, and a second later, I'm seated on it as Noah wraps his arms around me.

My palms move down over his chest to the edge of his shirt, where my fingers find his bare skin. I pull up his shirt, so it's out of the way.

He lets out a moan that vibrates through my mouth and all the way down through my body.

Everything in me tingles.

"Better?" Noah asks, his fingers sliding across my cheek. He pushes them into my hair, curling it behind my ear.

I don't say anything back.

I can't speak.

I don't know if I remember how. So, I just smile and nod.

"You should get back to Mia, or she might come looking for you again."

"Wait, what about us? This?"

"Found your voice?" he says with a pleased smirk. "I'm not going anywhere. I promise."

"Say it again."

"I'm not going anywhere. I promise."

"You promise?"

"Triple pinkie swear," Noah says, raising his eyebrows at me.

"I'm holding you to it."

"That's a lot of pinkies to hold. But if anyone can manage

it, it's you." Noah chuckles.

After he leaves the bathroom, I slide down onto the floor like Jell-O. I feel like I just got put in a toaster. Or like I'm floating in pudding. I don't know how I'm feeling.

I don't know anything.

Except, well, now, I finally know what it's like to really kiss Noah Williams.

I POP MY head back into Mia's room, my gaze quickly falling on her clock. It's already seven.

"Shit," I mutter, pushing open her door.

"What?" Mia swivels around toward me, her eyebrows drawing up in interest.

"It's later than I thought," I reply, falling onto her bed.

Onto my old bed.

I look at the purple comforter, feeling time whiplash. Just last week, this was my room. Well, it wasn't really mine; it was always Mia's. But it felt like mine, and I got to pretend it was for a few weeks. And now, lying here again, I get the same comfort I did back then.

And I need it.

Because Noah and I kissed.

Really kissed.

And all I want to do is lie here and daydream about it while simultaneously running circles through Hyde Park, shouting, *Finally, finally, finally.*

Because it was intense.

And so much more than I'd thought it would be.

It was hot. And exciting. And scary.

It was perfect.

It was more than perfect.

"Have plans tonight?" Mia asks, breaking into my thoughts.

"Actually, yeah. I get to go see the place my parents just bought," I reply, propping myself up onto my elbows.

"That's exciting," Mia says encouragingly.

"Yeah, it is." I smile. "Tonight's going surprisingly well. I got to come here …" I trail off, thinking about Noah again. And his mouth.

"And make up with my brother? Or should I say, make out?" Mia says, sticking her tongue out at me.

My mouth starts to fall open, but I clamp it shut as my cheeks turn pink.

I throw a pillow from the bed at her and roll my eyes like her words are ridiculous.

"We *did* make up, and I *am* happy about it," I tell her, adding in a firm nod.

Mia laughs, tossing the pillow back to me. "I'm sure you are."

I know she wants me to admit that we kissed, but I'm not ready to admit that to anyone yet. I can barely wrap my own head around it. And right now, Mia just suspects. I need time to come to terms with things before I start blabbering to everyone that Noah and I kissed.

And that I'm probably, likely, pretty much in love with him.

I clear my throat, shaking the thoughts out of my mind.

"Anyway, where are your parents?" I ask Mia.

I put the pillow back into its place before getting off the bed.

"Out for a date night," she answers, her expression softening.

"Aw, that's sweet." I smile, thinking about Helen and Gene. "Sorry to cut this off, but I'm glad we got to hang out."

"I am too," Mia says, standing up. "Thanks for listening to me go on about Sophia."

She flares her eyes at me before pushing a curly strand of hair behind her ear.

"It's no problem. Maybe next time we hang out, we could try all three of us," I offer.

Mia's face lights up. She stands up from her desk and pulls me into a hug.

"Totally," she agrees.

I hug Mia back and then leave her room, deciding to say good-bye to Noah before I leave. I knock on his door, not wanting to just burst in. Usually, I would, but ...

"Come in." Noah's deep voice sends a jolt of energy through me, and I open his door. He's seated in his chair, his back rounded so that his elbows are resting on his knees. His hands are on his game controller, his eyes on the screen.

"Hey. I just wanted to say bye before I left."

I stay standing by the door, knowing that I can't linger. I can't get pulled into his room.

Pulled into his orbit.

Because if I do, I'm seriously going to be late.

Noah turns his head, his eyes finding mine. He quickly pauses the game, throwing the controller onto the ground.

"You're leaving?" he asks, walking toward me.

I nod, feeling my heart pick up speed in my chest. Noah stops right in front of me, barely a sliver of space between us.

"Come by my match tomorrow. We'll hang out after," he says.

"Yeah?" I smile.

"Yeah."

"I'll be there," I reply, trying not to grin.

"Cool. And you can tell me all about the new place. Show me the future bedroom." The corner of Noah's lips pulls up into a one-sided smile.

"I will."

Noah nods, his eyes leaving mine and running down across my body. I bite my lip, not sure what to do. *Do I hug him? Kiss him? Maybe I should offer him a handshake to be safe.*

No.

"Noah."

"Yeah?"

"Thank you." I look up at him, bringing his eyes back to mine.

"For what?" he asks, his forehead creasing.

"For everything. The poem …"

"Just the poem?" he asks, his head tilting to the side.

"The talk. The … kiss," I add, pressing my lips together.

"You never have to thank me for kissing you," Noah says, leaning in toward me.

"No?" I ask.

"Nope." Noah shakes his head before bringing his forehead against mine.

I wrap my arms around his shoulders and let him pull me into a hug.

"I'm glad we talked, too, you know," I say, running my fingers through his hair.

"I'm glad we *finally* stopped talking. You know you talk a lot, right?" Noah smirks.

I pull back, ready to say something, but Noah's lips crash onto mine.

I'm momentarily caught off guard, but when his arms tighten around me, my body finally catches up.

He's kissing me—again.

And I'm not going to question it.

So, I let my mind go silent.

And I let my body fold into his.

Really … I let myself fall.

In his arms.
7:45PM

"I'M SO SORRY I'm late," I say, rushing up to who I assume is my parents' realtor.

I push my hair off my shoulders, feeling beyond flustered.

I know I should have left sooner, and I'd planned to. But kissing Noah …

It's like a minute or a million minutes could have gone by! No one knows.

And no one can tell.

Because the truth is, time *definitely* goes by quicker when your lips are occupied. You might think that your brain would come to understand this. It can nag you all day … with worries. Random ideas. Kind reminders that you're probably going to fail a pop quiz. Sweet little references to the fact that your parents are actually letting their teenage daughter stay alone at a hotel in London. My mind—*so unkindly*—reminds me of all of that all day! But then, the one time I *actually* need it, it turns into a big bowl of mush. It shuts down!

I needed it to send out warning signals, reminder bells …

Hey, you, you're going to be late!

But no, what did it do? It let Noah kiss me for twenty more minutes and decided to stay quiet.

Thus, why I'm late.

And mad at my brain.

"That's all right, Mallory. I got your text," the realtor says, looking a little flustered. Maybe it's because I'm flustered.

I pull at my uniform skirt, annoyed with myself.

Maybe this is why adults are always saying to use your head at the same time that they are telling you to follow your heart. I never understood how you could give that advice to someone.

It always seemed contradicting.

But now ... it makes perfect sense! Follow your heart means, well, obviously, follow your heart. But at the same time, you have to force your brain to stay turned on. You can't get swept away by how his arms wrapped around your waist make you feel. Or by how good he smells. Or by the way his kisses send butterflies through your stomach.

No.

You have to use your head.

But what they don't tell you is that when a certain boy kisses you, your head shuts down involuntarily—and rudely—without your permission or knowledge.

Which is why I'm standing here, late, gulping for air.

"That's good," I finally respond. "I'm just never late. It's very out of character for me. I mean, I did run from the tube station, but I don't want you to think that I'm wasting your time or anything."

The realtor smiles. "I just got my closing fee from your parents," she says, looking amused. "The least I could do was wait fifteen minutes, so their daughter could view the place."

"Oh," I say, surprised and impressed by her forwardness.

She smiles, waving me toward the front door. "Come on. I'll take you up."

The realtor leads me into a tall glass building. The entrance is opulent.

"You have a private elevator for the penthouse," she says, whisking me into it and hitting the button to go up.

When the doors part, I'm greeted with light wood floors, neutral colors, and walls of windows overlooking the river.

I was expecting a very modern apartment, much like our place in New York, but this surprises me. Yes, the windows are contemporary in shape and feel, but the wood floors make it feel cozier. Less austere and more welcoming.

The living room is a grand two-story space with a beautiful chandelier that seems to meld modern style with a hint of antique.

"I know it's hard to visualize now," the realtor says, "but just imagine it during the day. The entire room will be flooded with light from the windows on all sides. And the view of the river is divine."

"It's really pretty now," I say, taking in the city around us.

She points. "You'll have a sitting area here, facing the windows," she says as she keeps moving, "and this is your enclosed deck." She shows off a beautiful outdoor space.

"I would love to sit out here when it's raining," I say, noting windows that partially cover the space to provide protection and security because we're so high up.

I follow her out through the sliding doors, listening to the city around us. Inside, it was silent, but out here, you can feel the cold night breeze. The sound of cars in the distance.

We make our way back inside.

"I've introduced your mother to a fantastic decorator," she tells me. "I understand that they're going to do what they are calling contemporary English style."

"My mom mentioned that," I reply.

I follow her through the rest of the space, finding a sleek kitchen and a dining room surrounded by more windows. The entire place is open and airy. I walk around the island, my eyes landing on a stainless steel wine fridge.

"Now, that looks like something my dad would approve of." And I can't help but smile.

I walk back across the main floor, finding another room. It connects to both the living room and the outdoor area and features a full wall of bookcases.

But the best part is the pool table centered in the room.

"This is the study," the realtor says. "It's got phenomenal views of the river, and it has its own door out onto the deck that you can open up to get a nice breeze in the summer."

I step into the room, distracted by the wall of dark wooden bookcases. But then I turn my attention to the large pool table in the center of the room.

"Is this staying?" I ask, confused. Because it's the only piece of furniture in the otherwise empty apartment.

"The former owners are hoping your parents might agree to keep the billiards table, so they have left it here for the time being."

I look at the table.

"Knowing my mom, the owners are going to be let down. She's not really a fun-in-the-house kind of woman."

My mom values aesthetics over practicality.

But as I run my hand along the felt, I can imagine Mohammad, Harry, Noah, and me here. I know they'd all think this was cool. It would be like an extension of the boys' club but at my house.

"From what your mother has shared, they haven't determined the function of this room yet," she replies with a knowing glance.

She then leads me to the main bedroom, which is large and clean. But the best part is the bathroom. It features a gorgeous copper soaking tub that is right up my mom's alley. And for my dad, there's a large jetted shower. I can already picture myself teasing him about it because it looks more like a car wash than a shower.

The closet is oversize, as expected. Even though my mom mentioned purging our house of clutter, I know that won't apply to her collection of designer clothing.

After seeing their bedroom, the realtor leads me up a steel

and glass sculptural staircase to two bedrooms, one of which should be mine.

"Did my mom say which one she wants me in?" I ask. Because at this point, I think she knows more than I do.

She smiles at me, leading me into the first bedroom.

"She said she'd let you pick. Personally, I think this is the one I'd choose."

I step into the room and look around. It's got pale cream paint with a slight pink tint to it that makes it feel warm but bright. Usually, anything with pink, I'd turn my nose up at, but it's understated and pretty. And anyway, I don't think anyone would notice the paint after getting a glance at the view. There's a huge window along the far wall that matches the windows in the rest of the house, except there's a built-in bench below it.

I take a seat and look out.

It's sort of like being in a fishbowl.

Or a tower.

A really, really beautiful tower.

And surprisingly, I actually like it.

I get up and go into the bathroom.

A counter runs along the wall with double sinks set into white marble. The opposite wall is textured stone, which gives off a cool effect when you see the reflection in the mirror.

"These windows provide amazing light," the realtor explains, bringing my attention to the bathtub.

And this isn't just any bathtub.

It's sleek oval shape draws your eye to it, but the most amazing part is that it's set up on a platform with an entire wall of windows behind it.

Mohammad is going to die when he sees this.

The realtor takes me into the second bedroom. It's smaller than the first one, and it doesn't have the built-in bench. It still has the wall of windows, but I can see why she recommended the other room for me.

My phone buzzes in my bag as I peek my head into the bathroom.

And then it buzzes again.

And again.

The realtor looks at me.

"Sorry." I flush, feeling rude as I pull out my phone. I've got four texts, all from Harry.

Harry: Hey.

Harry: I need to see you.

Harry: Are you at your hotel?

Harry: I'm coming by.

Shit, shit, shit.

Does he know? Did Noah tell him? It's not possible that he already knows and he's mad, is it?

My stomach does a flip at the possibilities. I text him back.

Me: I'm viewing our new apartment. Is everything okay?

A second later, Harry is calling me.

"Hey," I answer.

The realtor points to herself and then to the hallway, telling me she's going to give me some privacy before leaving me alone in the guest room.

"Sorry to interrupt. I'm on my way to Bvlgari. When are you done?" Harry asks quickly.

"I can probably be there in twenty. Is everything all right?" I ask with concern.

"I just need to see you. Family stuff." His voice is gravelly, and it causes a twinge in my stomach.

"I'm on my way," I tell him before hanging up.

I quickly throw my phone back into my bag and flip off the lights, leaving the room and heading back downstairs.

"Sorry about that," I say to the realtor. "Thank you for showing me the place. It's beautiful. You and my mom did a good job, picking it out."

"It's a great property. Is there anything else you'd like to look at again, or do you have any questions?"

I shake my head. "Actually, I've got to get going."

"Of course. It was nice to meet you, Mallory."

She extends her hand out to me, and I shake it.

"You too," I reply before hopping on the elevator.

I TRY NOT to rush out of the apartment, but my mind is racing about Harry. I hurry to the closest underground station and am grateful when I finally get off at the hotel's stop.

I run up the steps to the street and shove through a crowd of tourists out for a night stroll until I can see the hotel. It's easy to spot the dark entrance, the sleek facade, and the bellman standing beside the door.

And then I see Harry.

He's standing on the sidewalk with a large duffel in his hand. My eyes go wide, my mind running through different scenarios of what could have happened.

Did his dad do something?

Is he leaving for Shanghai now?

I stop on the sidewalk, feeling my heart come up into my throat. But then Harry sees me. He drops the duffel and starts walking toward me until he has me in his arms.

"Thank god you're here," Harry says, kissing me chastely on the lips before pulling me into a hug.

His hands wrap around my waist, and he picks me up off

the ground. My thoughts are spinning as he hugs me. He sounds worried. But he also sounds sort of excited.

What the hell is going on?

He sets me back down, and I steady myself, keeping my hands on his forearms.

"Harry, what's wrong?" I ask, searching his eyes.

"I had to leave. It was fucking ridiculous, honestly. And I've been thinking about last night. About this morning …" he says, his eyes wide and frantic now.

"Harry," I start, my stomach twisting.

Because this morning, I woke up in bed. With him.

In his arms.

"I told my parents that we need time together before I leave," Harry continues, his blue eyes on mine.

I break his gaze, nervously looking around us. "We, as in …"

"You and me," he clarifies.

"Harry, tell me what's going on."

"My parents agreed to let us stay at the country house through the weekend. I have to be back in the city Wednesday for our flight to Shanghai and …" Harry continues, but that's all I need to hear for the tension in my chest to deflate.

I immediately pull Harry back into a hug, wrapping my arms around his ribs.

"Oh," Harry says with surprise.

"I'm so relieved. I thought you were leaving now or something. When I saw the bag …" I say, worry thick in my voice.

"It's all right," Harry says, holding on to me.

"It's not. When you called, I … I thought the worst." I pull back to look up at him.

Harry nods, understanding. "I'm all right. I'm sorry I worried you. Look, the only condition is that Tuesday night, we have to go to some party at my parents' friend's house.

254

Otherwise, they're fine with us leaving." Harry runs his fingers back through his hair. "Do you still have that key?"

I blink up at him. "The key to your country house," I say more than ask.

"Yeah," Harry replies.

I bite my lip before reaching into my purse. I pull out my wallet and slide the key out of it, holding it out for him.

But he doesn't take it.

"So, you'll come with me?" he asks, his blue eyes holding mine.

"Will you tell me what this is about first?" I counter.

Because I know that something has happened. Maybe it isn't as bad as I first thought, but there's a reason he wants to leave.

I know there is.

Harry takes the key, shifting it back and forth between his fingers.

"After school, my father was at the house. My mum was there, too, which I found odd. They wanted to talk to me," Harry explains. "Apparently, everyone enjoyed my company so much at the party that they … suggested I pop into the office here in London more often."

I furrow my brows, not understanding. "To do what?"

"To start my internship early," Harry says flatly, his face expressionless.

"Like, here, with your dad?" I ask, my voice rising.

"Yes."

"No."

Harry's jaw tightens, and he looks away. "It wasn't a question. I'll be paraded around once a week from now until I'm sent off to Shanghai in the summer."

"Harry …"

"I just want to get away. Get out. It's all too much." His

voice breaks, and I grab on to his hands, lacing our fingers together. "Please. Will you come with me?"

I press my lips together and search Harry's face. He's looking down at me like everything depends on my answer.

"What am I supposed to wear?"

"Is that a yes?" Harry asks intently.

"We always said we'd go," I answer.

And just like that, Harry's worried expression falls away, and he smiles.

"There's a shop I want to take you to before we leave. I was thinking on the way over about—"

Before Harry can finish his sentence, I stop him.

"We can't go tonight. Noah has a match tomorrow," I tell him, thinking about Noah. About what happened between us tonight.

"Okay. We'll leave straight after," Harry agrees.

"Harry, who exactly is going?" I ask.

"I'm hoping all of us. Me. You. Noah. Mohammad."

"Do they know?" I question.

"Not yet. I figured I'd ask you first since it was something we talked about before."

Harry gives me a knowing look, and I nod in understanding. It's something we talked about doing when we were together.

A couple.

"I have to ask my parents," I tell him, trying to think this through.

"Call them," Harry instructs. And he sounds so serious that I grab my phone out of my bag.

Harry places his palm on my back, leading me out of the middle of the sidewalk. For a minute, I think he's going to usher me inside the hotel, but instead, we end up standing by the front of the building. Harry checks to make sure his duffel is with the bellman as I hit Call.

"Hey, sweetie!" my dad answers. "We've been wondering when you were going to call. Well, what did you think?"

"Think of what?" I ask, caught off guard by his chipper voice.

"Of the apartment!" my dad bellows.

"Oh … the place," I say, clearing my thoughts.

"Well?"

"It's huge, Dad."

"Come on, sweetie. We wouldn't move and not do it up right!" he says, his voice full of pride.

"It's gorgeous and modern. But it's so different from our apartment in New York," I say as Harry comes back, standing next to me.

He adjusts his jacket, looking down at me through his blond lashes.

"And do you like it?" Dad asks, urgency in his voice.

I look away from Harry, knowing that I'm going to have to talk up our place before I have any chance of getting my dad to focus on anything else.

"I love it!" I exclaim, hoping to make him happy. "It's so cool, Dad. But I was surprised. I figured it would have some of that old-world charm you love or even some of the classic '20s touches Mom likes."

Harry's eyebrows draw up, and I mute my phone.

"My dad's thrilled," I explain before unmuting my phone.

"We thought, *Why not try something new?* Plus, your mother couldn't turn down the view. Or the closet!" He chuckles.

I smile, happy that my dad is happy.

"It's really great, Dad. I love the window seat in my room too. You and Mom did a good job, picking it out."

"Not too shabby, right?"

"Anyway, Dad, I was wondering something …" I say, building myself to ask about going away with Harry.

"How much is it going to cost?" my dad says merrily.

"No." I laugh. "It's not like that. Actually, my friend Harry has a house in the country, and he's invited me to go away for a few days over the break. Would that be all right?"

I glance to Harry, worried he's going to flat-out say no.

"I'm glad to hear you two made amends. Your dad gives great advice, doesn't he?"

I widen my eyes, annoyed. His perkiness is getting on my nerves. Well, it's not really getting on my nerves. I like hearing happiness in his voice. But I kind of need him to be serious now.

"You do," I answer.

"So, you want to go on holiday with his family?" Dad clarifies.

"Yes! Well, technically, no. See, his parents are too busy in the city to leave. But Mohammad and Noah will be there," I say, trying to soften the news. "It was a last-minute decision. A guys' trip sort of thing, you know?"

"A guys' trip," my dad repeats.

"Well, plus me." I laugh nervously as Harry flashes me a *what the fuck* look. I wave him off, turning around so I can focus.

"But you're not one of the guys, Mal," my dad says, his voice wavering.

I clear my throat and take a few more steps away from Harry.

"Technically, no. But I might as well be. We're all friends. And I'm not dating Harry anymore. We broke up, remember?" I say, wondering if that's what this is about.

I can hear my dad adjust in his seat through the phone, the familiar sound of his favorite leather chair giving below him.

"Yes, I do. And if I recall, it was because of your feelings for another young man who will be there."

I suck in a breath at his words and end up in a coughing fit.

"Dad, I swear it's not like that," I say, trying to pull it together. "Look, Harry's leaving on Wednesday for Shanghai. His parents are making him go over the break, and this will be my only chance to see him before he leaves."

I turn, glancing at Harry. He must be able to hear me because he urges me on, waving his hand for me to keep going.

"Plus, what else am I supposed to do over break? I'm stuck in a hotel, and you and Mom aren't here. So, I either go with my friends, who are leaving with or without me, or I sit around all week. Alone. By myself."

"Mallory, I'm not sure about this," my dad says.

And I can hear it in his voice.

He isn't convinced.

"What will it take for you to say yes?" I ask matter-of-factly.

"Are you bargaining with me?"

"I am."

"Fine," my dad replies. "You said this is Harry's house, correct?"

"Yes."

"Is he with you now?"

I look up at Harry. "Uh … yeah," I say hesitantly.

"Great. Put him on the phone."

"Wait, what? Dad, seriously?"

"Seriously."

I dart my eyes back and forth, not sure what to do.

Maybe I could try and talk my way out of this one. Or I

could deepen my voice and pretend to be Harry. No. That wouldn't work.

"Okay … hang on." I put the phone on mute and look to Harry. "Uh, Harry."

"Yeah?"

"My, um, my dad, he wants to talk to you."

His eyebrows rise in surprise, but he quickly extends his hand and accepts the phone, unmuting it.

"Sir?" Harry says, a perplexed but amused expression now on his lips.

"Yes, sir. My parents have a house just an hour or so northwest of the city," Harry says, pausing. Then, he continues, "No, my father has to stay in the city for business. He and my mother have quite busy schedules, so they suggested we head out to the country house for some fresh air before we leave for Shanghai."

I can only hear one end of the conversation, but it's enough to follow along.

"I can't say that I wouldn't have liked to go as her boyfriend, sir, but fortunately enough, we remain friends. And of course, this will extend into the trip. You have my word."

My mouth drops open, and my eyes feel like they're going to pop out of my head.

Because did my dad just ask Harry of his intentions?

Oh my god …

"Of course. I'll make sure she rings you every day. Mallory mentioned you're arriving next week. Once I'm back from Shanghai, I'd love to formally be introduced. Have you heard of The Arrington club?"

There's a pause, and Harry's eyebrows shoot up.

"Really?" Harry says brightly, letting out a deep laugh. A smile forms on his lips. "Oh, wow."

I look at him, trying to figure out what is happening.

"My father's in exporting. Brooks Exporting." He listens before continuing. "Well, I'm sure we'll see you there often then."

There?

Where is there?

"Not that I indulge on my own, but in my father's company, I have had the pleasure of trying the Macallan 25. It would be the perfect drink to toast with upon your arrival."

I blink a few times, trying to follow along before holding out my hand for my phone.

"Right, well, it was a pleasure speaking with you, Mr. James, and I look forward to doing so in person. It seems Mallory would like her phone back now."

I grab the phone, mortified.

"Uh, Dad?"

"Mallory," my dad says brightly, "I think you spending some time out in the country is a great idea."

"You do?" I ask, looking at Harry.

"I do," my dad says, taking a long pause. "Harry seems like a great guy. Or should I say, *chap*?"

"He does?" I ask.

"He does."

"Okay."

"But you have to call every day and check in. Do we have a deal?"

"We have a deal," I agree, causing Harry to smile in accomplishment.

"So, you liked the apartment?"

"*Loved* the apartment," I correct.

"Good."

"So … I'll call you and Mom tomorrow. We're leaving after Noah's soccer game."

"Sounds good. And, Mal?"

"Yeah?"

"Have some fun. Just … not too much."

"I will. I mean, I won't," I stutter.

"Bye," my dad says.

"Bye."

I click End and look at Harry in amazement.

"I can go," I tell him, baffled.

"I didn't have a doubt about it," he says. And he's beaming.

"What were you two talking about?" I ask, putting my hand on my hip.

Because that went weirdly well.

It seemed more like a buddy-buddy conversation than a father-interrogating-his-daughter's-ex conversation.

"Well, apparently, your dad's been thinking about becoming a member at The Arrington with the permanent move. And as you know, I just so happen to be a member too."

"I can't believe you smooth-talked my dad!" I swat at his chest, annoyed and impressed at his skills.

"I can smooth-talk anyone," Harry says with a laugh, sidestepping my attack.

I roll my eyes and shake my head in disbelief.

"That's true," I reply. Because I have to give him some credit. "But my dad, he's a tough one."

"About as tough as you were the first time we met. You put up a good front, but charm has a way of tearing down any walls. I'm pretty sure I had you snogging me in under five minutes."

"Are you trying to tell me that's your goal with my dad?" I tease.

"Absolutely," Harry jokes back.

I shake my head at him. "And by the way, I think the kissing had a lot more to do with being alone in a new city and the cider than it did the charm."

"Either way." Harry smiles, draping his arm over my shoulders. "So, now that we've checked off *approval from your father* from the list, can I put my bag in your room? Then, I want to take you somewhere."

I look over at him. "Where are you staying tonight?"

"I'm going to crash at Mohammad's, so I can convince his mum to let him leave with us."

When we get to the lobby, Harry drops his arm and retrieves his duffel from the bellman, handing him a folded bill.

"And what about Noah?" I can't help but ask.

"I'll text him in the room," Harry answers, leading me inside and to the elevator.

I get out my key card and press the floor number.

"His parents should be fine with it. They're usually good with my last-minute plans. Mohammad's parents though, they often require some convincing."

"If anyone can do it, it's you." I laugh. "You know, if all else fails, you could go into sales. I think you could talk your way into getting just about anything."

"Well, when I'm desperate," Harry says, giving me a halfhearted smile.

"Harry, are you sure you're all right?" I ask, stepping out of the elevator and onto my floor.

Harry falters at my question, the elevator doors closing behind him. He shakes his head, clearing away any hesitation. "I'm fine now. Come on."

Harry leads me down the hallway, and I let us into my room. Harry quickly strips off his jacket, tossing his duffel on the floor.

"Have you eaten yet?" I ask, hunger suddenly hitting me.

"No. You?"

"Nope. But I'm hungry."

"Let's grab dinner after the shop," Harry suggests.

"That would be great."

I walk into the bedroom, throwing my bag on my bed. And when I pass the mirror hanging on the wall, I realize that I'm still in my uniform.

"I need to change first," I call out.

"I'm going to message Noah and make a call," Harry says back.

I smile, thinking about Noah.

About his poem.

About kissing him.

I walk into my closet and strip off my uniform, my mind occupied. But when I look at my hanging clothes, I know I need to refocus. I decide to dress up a little, putting on dark jeans, heeled black booties, and an off-the-shoulder, three-quarter-sleeved metallic top. I move into the bathroom, brush my hair and my teeth, and put on a spritz of perfume. I take in a deep inhale and smile.

It feels great to be out of my uniform.

I put my wallet into a small purse and grab a jacket as I leave the room.

"Okay," I say, coming out into the sitting room.

Harry's on the couch, his ankles crossed one over the other.

He looks up at me, his blue eyes moving up my legs to my exposed shoulder.

"You look stunning. Although I think I might prefer the schoolgirl look," Harry says with a naughty grin.

I can't help but laugh.

"Unfortunately, it's not a *look* when it's your required uniform," I reply, pulling him up off the couch.

"A few minor adjustments, and it would be," Harry says to me.

"A few less inches on the skirt. A few buttons gone," I agree, thinking about our uniforms. "Even though they're conservative and annoying sometimes, I think I've grown to like them. It's nice to just get up in the morning and know what you're going to wear."

"Makes rolling out of bed, hungover, and getting to school on time easier," Harry agrees.

"Like you're ever on time." I smirk.

Harry laughs. "I'd rather not show up at all. But I know Mohammad would get salty about it if I stopped coming to school."

"He would. I think going to school is the highlight of his day. At least the social aspect of it," I agree, pulling on my jacket.

Harry follows me to the door, and I check my purse, making sure I put my room key in it.

"It's true. He's a social butterfly," Harry replies.

I turn to him, making sure he's ready to go. He has his coat in his hand and looks ten times happier than when I first saw him outside the hotel.

Harry and I take the elevator down to the lobby. As we're about to leave the hotel, one of the bellmen catches my attention. It's the guy that I spoke to when I first arrived here. When I got the note from my parents, saying that we were moving to London. When I had a meltdown.

He glances across the lobby, his face flashing with recognition when he sees me.

I give him a small wave, walking up to him.

"Hey," I say.

"Good evening. Are you well?" he asks.

He's standing in the corner by the luggage carts, his hand resting casually on one.

"Much better now," I admit.

"Shock finally wore off?"

"It has." I laugh, thinking back to when I got here a week ago. "I wanted to say thank you for the other day. For the water. For the corner to freak out in." I smile at him.

"There's no need," he replies, going slightly pink.

"There is. I really appreciated it. Anyway, have a good night," I say before wrapping my hand through Harry's arm and leading us out of the hotel.

When we get outside and down the street, he asks, "So, what was that about?"

"He witnessed firsthand my meltdown when I found out I was staying in London," I admit.

"Really?"

I nod. "Yeah. I sat on his luggage cart for who knows how long. He went and got me a bottle of water and talked to me. Calmed me down. It was really nice."

"I would have loved to see that freak-out." Harry laughs.

"It was a sight, I'm sure."

"That's all right," Harry says, waving it off. "I've done worse in a hotel. Once, when I was younger, I got so drunk at a hotel bar that I ended up getting sick in the empty crisps bowl they had sitting on the counter."

"You did not!" I squeal, my eyes going wide.

"Oh, I absolutely did."

"All right, you have done worse then." I laugh. "So, are you going to tell me where we're headed? Please tell me it's a shop full of food."

"The food will have to wait. I have somewhere I want to take you first," Harry replies.

I push out my lips in a pout, my stomach not happy about the decision.

"We'll be in and out in no time," Harry says, a smile flashing across his face. "And then we'll get you some dinner."

"Promise?" I ask pointedly.

"Promise."

TEN MINUTES LATER, Harry and I stop in front of a closed shop on one of the main shopping streets in London. A steady flow of people is moving around, dodging us on the sidewalk. Most of the buildings are dark along the street, apart from their lit-up window displays. Harry looks up at the name on the shop, nodding his head in familiarity.

"I think they're closed," I say, pulling my lips to the side. "Should we try and come back tomorrow before we leave?"

Harry doesn't answer. Instead, he walks up to the door and hits the buzzer.

"Harry, that's not going to work." I laugh. "The sign says they're closed." I point to the sign displaying their hours, trying to show him.

"Closed to the public," Harry says just as the door swings open.

I take a step back, surprised by a man's sudden appearance. I look to Harry, confused.

"Harry, lovely to see you," the man says, shaking Harry's hand.

"You as well," Harry replies brightly before turning to me. "I asked Phil if he'd keep the shop open for us."

I raise my eyebrows, realizing that the store *was* closed.

It's just not closed to Harry.

"Please," Phil says, holding open the door for me.

I step inside, quickly noticing the dark wood cabinets that line the walls. Low lighting makes the whole place glow. I walk farther into the shop and let my fingers run across a table filled with cashmere sweaters. The shop has a musky, manly scent to it that makes it feel cozy and inviting.

There are rows of tailored shirts, dark jackets, thin vests, tapered pants, and tweed.

Lots and lots of tweed.

I twirl around, feeling like I've stepped out of London and into a quintessential English country village.

"Phil, I'd like to introduce you to Mallory," Harry says, now next to me. "Mallory, this is Phil."

I look at Phil, noticing his bald head and square glasses. I shake his hand, my eyes wandering across his beautiful three-piece tweed suit.

"It's nice to meet you," I say.

"And you," Phil replies before looking to Harry. "So, what are we looking for today?"

"We're headed out to the country for the weekend," Harry explains.

"Lovely." Phil nods, listening intently.

"And we'll be going clay pigeon shooting," Harry says.

I'm nodding along until his words register.

I turn to him. "We are?" I ask.

"It's bloody good fun. You just need the appropriate apparel for it."

I look between Harry and Phil, trying to imagine myself shooting a clay pigeon.

"And what does one wear while shooting clay pigeons?" I ask.

"More formal attire is worn if you're going shooting or hunting, but since you'll be sticking to clay pigeons, the attire isn't as formal," Phil explains. "However, you'll want to make sure you've got pants that don't bag, sturdy shoes, and a top that provides warmth but doesn't inhibit your range of motion."

"Do you want to pick out your boots first?" Harry asks me.

"Are you buying clothes too?"

Harry nods.

"Okay. Let's look."

Phil leads us farther back into the store.

"I'd recommend wellies. They'll keep your feet warm and dry in case of rain or mud, depending on the weather."

I nod, looking at the row of tall boots. The styles are all similar, but there are numerous colors.

"There are so many options."

"If you'd like, I can show you to the women's section. We have some great jackets and jumpers. Perhaps we can match the shoes after?"

"That sounds great," I agree but look to Harry for his input.

"Why don't you browse while Phil helps me? Then, we'll come back and see what you've found, yeah?"

"Yeah." I smile.

Phil leads me through the store, stopping when he gets to the women's section.

"I'd recommend a vest for your outing. It's breathable, classic, and it will be appropriate for the weather," Phil suggests before heading back to help Harry.

I let out a breath, grateful to finally be alone.

I like to shop, but when people are hovering, it feels like too much pressure.

I glance around, deciding to start with the sweaters. I take my time as I look around and pick up various sweaters to feel their thickness and texture. But after remembering what Phil said, I end up picking out a long-sleeved white undershirt and a navy vest.

EVENTUALLY, HARRY AND Phil work their way back to me. Harry has a smile on his face, and it's obvious he's changed in and out of clothes because his hair is disheveled and his collar isn't folded down all the way.

"What did you find?" Harry asks, eyeing the clothes in my hand.

I hold up the shirt and vest for them to see.

"Splendid. If you'll tell me your shoe size, I'll grab some wellies for you to try on," Phil says.

"Seven and a half."

Phil nods, leaving Harry and me alone. Harry walks around, stopping in front of a table to pick up a sweater.

"What about this?" he asks.

"I like it, but I've got plenty of sweaters," I reply, trying to be practical.

"Try it on," Harry insists, handing me the crewneck cable knit sweater. It's dusty blue and really beautiful.

"All right," I reply as Phil comes back, a pair of navy wellies in his hands.

"Let me know if the size doesn't work. I also brought you matching socks," he explains, leading me back to the dressing room.

"Thanks," I say, watching as he hangs up the clothes.

He sets the boots down on the floor, laying the socks out on a chair.

When he's gone, I take off my top and pull on the white undershirt before adding the navy vest over it. I sit down, kick off my shoes, and then slowly pull the socks up my legs. It's hard, trying to get them over the top of my jeans, but I figure they must wear them for warmth. The white socks hit me just below the knee. I pull on the wellies, struggling to get them up.

Because these things are no joke.

They're like a heavy-duty rain boot with no give.

When I finally get them on, I stand up and look at myself in the mirror. It's not something I'd wear normally, but it's

270

cute.

And from the sounds of it, it's perfect for the occasion.

I step out of the dressing room to show Phil and Harry my ensemble.

"Very smart," Phil says, his eyes lighting up behind his glasses. He shifts me in front of a mirror, adjusting the vest at my shoulders. "The fit is right."

Phil sounds pleased, but I look over my shoulder at Harry.

"What do you think?" I ask him.

"Gorgeous," Harry says, stepping up to my side. "I like the navy. It suits you."

"It does," Phil agrees.

"I like it too."

I head back to the dressing room and slip on the sweater that Harry picked out. It's comfortable and cute. I decide to show him and Phil, and they both give me looks of approval.

I quickly change back into my regular clothes and then take everything out that I tried on.

"I'll take that," Phil says, gathering the clothes and taking them to the sales counter.

"Right. I think that's everything then," Harry says.

"What did you end up deciding on?" I ask.

Harry shrugs. "Who knows? Phil puts me in whatever he fancies."

"Well, did you like what he suggested?" I ask, holding back a laugh.

"Phil always makes me look sharp," Harry says with a grin.

We walk to the front of the shop, and I immediately notice that Phil has everything bagged for us. I get out my wallet to pay, but Harry leans in toward me.

"It's already taken care of. He charged it to our account."

I look at Harry, trying to figure out if he's serious.

And from the looks of it, he is.

"Harry, I can't let you do that," I say, shaking my head.

"It's already done," he says before turning to address Phil. "Thank you for the help."

"It's always a pleasure, Harry," Phil replies.

He walks around the counter, handing both of the oversize bags to Harry.

"Mallory, it was wonderful meeting you. I hope you have fun on your holiday."

"Thanks," I say.

Harry leads me out of the shop, adjusting the bags so one is in each of his hands. I try to grab one of them, but he pulls it away.

"Harry! Let me hold one of the bags." I stop, crossing my arms over my chest so he knows I am actually serious. "And I want to pay you back."

Harry glances away before looking back at me, a shadow of a frown on his lips.

"This trip was my idea. And I thought you'd like Phil. He's a great bloke, and I enjoy supporting his shop. The least I can do is cover the expenses when I ask you to drop everything and leave." Harry's brows weave together, and he doesn't budge when I try to take the bag again.

I let out a huff, knowing that I'm not going to win this battle. I drop my hands to my sides. "At least accept a thank-you then."

Harry's face quickly lightens. "I'm listening." He smirks, sounding amused.

"Thank you." I smile up at Harry, hoping he can hear the sincerity in my voice. Because he really didn't need to do this.

"You're welcome. And speaking of things you'll need, Tuesday night will be formal," Harry says, his blue eyes searching the shops. "I didn't even think of it until now."

"For the dinner thing?" I ask.

"Yeah."

I think back to everything I packed.

What I've bought while I've been here.

"Actually, Harry, I think I've got something that will work," I say, remembering a dress I bought but haven't worn yet. I purchased it the same day that I went shopping to find something to wear on my and Harry's date. When he took me to The Arrington.

"Yeah?" Harry asks, relief washing across his face.

"Yeah." I nod. "I've been sort of saving it for a special occasion."

Harry glances away. "Well, a forced-upon-you dinner sounds like the winner. I'm sorry. You don't have to come with me. I'll lie to my parents. Tell them you got ill on the trip and had to stay in bed or something. I can go alone."

"You don't have to apologize. I'll go. It's just ..." I cross my arms over my chest, wishing that I didn't feel sick to my stomach at what I'm about to bring up.

"What?" Harry asks.

"I don't know if I could go without everyone else going. To your house, I mean. Of course I'll go to the party with you, but ..."

Surprise flashes across Harry's face.

"You mean, if it was just us going this weekend?" Harry asks.

"Yeah." I chew on my lip, thinking. "It's not that we can't hang out alone or anything like that. But a weekend alone, it might send the wrong message, you know?"

"And what message is that?"

"It's just something we talked about doing when we were a couple. And now ..."

"We aren't," Harry states.

I shake my head.

"I hate this. I hate having this conversation. But I don't want either of us to keep getting hurt. We have to be clear about things," I tell him.

Harry presses his lips together before clearing his throat. "I want it to be a friends thing, truly. It's why I came to see you first. I didn't want you to be uncomfortable."

"I really appreciate that, Harry." I nod. "But what about the kiss?"

"Outside the hotel?" Harry asks, looking confused.

"Yeah."

Harry looks at me blankly. "It was a friendly kiss. A thank-god-you're-here kiss. I kiss Noah and Mohammad too—you know that."

"I know. I just had to ask."

I push my hair behind my ear, feeling nervous. Harry must notice because he puts both of the bags in his left hand and puts his right arm around my shoulders.

"Come on. I know a place we can eat at around the corner."

Harry leads me down a side street, and before I know it, we're being seated at a small table in a darkly lit pub.

"It's not the most elegant place, but the food is unbelievable," Harry says, handing me a menu.

I flip through it, taking note of all the comfort foods. Soups, potpies, mashed potatoes.

Harry doesn't say anything until after we order.

"Last night, at the party, things got a little intense," Harry states. He rests his elbow on the table, running his fingers along his lips.

It's like he's hiding behind his hand.

"Yeah, they did," I agree, glancing away. "Being in the

bathroom with you. And this morning, waking up in your arms … I love you, Harry. And I love our friendship. But after everything …"

"You don't owe me an explanation. You don't," Harry says, stopping me.

"Sometimes, it's hard for me with you. Because we're friends. Because we have so much fun together. Because, well, you're a flirt." I crack a smile, trying to break the ice between us.

Harry looks at me, smiling "A huge flirt."

"That's why this is important to me. I hurt you once, and I don't want to do that again. And look, what I said earlier, about not being able to go without the guys this weekend …" I pause, looking up to Harry. "If you really need me, I would be there. Maybe it wouldn't have been a weekend away, but you have my support, always. You know that, right?"

"I know that." Harry nods. "And you've got mine. But I promise a weekend away will do us all some good."

"I know it will." I smile.

Harry smiles back before glancing across the table. His eyes fall on my hand, and he quickly looks up at me in recognition.

"Didn't you say you injured your finger today?" Harry asks, eyeing my Band-Aid.

"Yeah. It was terrible." The image of the cut flashes in my mind.

"What happened? You never said in Geography."

"It was traumatic. I cut my finger in Art, and Noah was so upset with me. He thought I was being careless. He insisted on taking me to the nurse's office. But then I started talking about blood, and he got all green. I thought he was going to pass out! He had to text Mohammad to come and save us," I tell him, happy to be talking about something else.

"Oh fuck. Did Noah faint?" Harry asks, eating up the story.

"Thankfully, no. But he came close." I laugh.

"How did you cut it?"

"We're working with clay right now. It was stupid. Noah distracted me, and next thing you know ..." I hold up my bandaged finger. "We've been prepping for our next project. We need to have our idea solidified when we get back from break."

"Any ideas yet?" Harry asks.

The image of Noah as Medusa flashes through my mind, but I decide to keep that idea to myself.

"A few, but nothing certain yet."

"You've got plenty of time to figure it out," Harry replies.

I smile, realizing he's right.

"It's kind of great, isn't it? No school. No professors. No crappy lunch food."

"I feel like I can finally breathe again," Harry admits. "I constantly feel like I'm choking. Between school and my parents and the party ..."

I look at Harry, suddenly feeling like I could cry. Because I hate that he feels this way.

All I want to do is make it better.

To fix things.

But I know the only thing I can do is be there for him. I can't change anything.

And sometimes, I wonder if he really can't either.

I squeeze his hand across the table and force a smile onto my lips.

"Then, this trip is perfect timing. Don't they always say something about the country doing you good? The fresh air and all that?" I ask, trying to cheer him up.

Harry looks up at me and nods, his face brightening a little. "We can get away from it all. It will just be me, you,

Mohammad, Noah, and the staff."

"The staff?" I laugh.

"Yep," Harry replies. "We've got a full-time staff to run the house. A gardener, house manager, cleaners, butler, and a cook. Mum's called ahead about our arrival tomorrow, so everything's ready."

"Is that going to be weird?" I ask.

"What, having the staff there?" Harry asks.

"Yeah."

"It's not for me, but I grew up with it. It's their job, you know?" Harry says as the food arrives.

"I always forget you have more than one house."

Harry said that they not only have homes in London and in the countryside, but also in Shanghai and New York.

"I really like our country house. It has a lot of good memories for me. A few bad but …"

"Well, we can change all that this weekend," I say, holding up my water glass to clink against his.

"Just like you always planned to do." Harry laughs, touching our glasses together. "Make my bad memories good."

"That's kind of the point of having friends."

"I guess so," he agrees, taking a bite of his food.

"Harry, can I ask you something?"

"What?"

"It's just something I've been thinking about lately. Do you think we're predestined for things? Like, are we going to become the people we're meant to be regardless of the choices we make? Or does every choice lead us down a slightly different path?"

Harry sets down his fork, his brows drawing in. "I don't believe we can run away from who we are or who we are meant to become."

"But we make those decisions, don't we? Or if we don't, shouldn't we?"

"What makes you ask?" Harry's blue eyes come up to meet mine.

"I guess I was thinking about your family. About mine too. It's weird, thinking that I live here now. Sometimes, it feels like fate. But honestly, I'm not sure I believe in that."

"There are always paths laid out for us. By family, by obligation, by God. I just wish this weren't mine sometimes."

"Then change it."

Harry's features soften as he smiles. "You can't change your destiny, Mallory," he says, shaking his head. "You were born to fulfill it."

I search his eyes, wishing that he didn't look so certain about his answer.

"Do you really believe that?"

"I know that my future is in the family business. I've accepted it. Because I won't walk away from it. And my parents know it too. I might stray, take some time for myself. But after everything, I'll come back to it. It's my name. My legacy."

"As long as it's what you want, I'll support you," I say. But all I can think about is what Olivia once said. That when she and Harry were together, he would go astray. But eventually, he would always go back to her. Even if it wasn't good for him, I guess it didn't matter.

Because she was there.

Because she loved him.

I look back at Harry. "All I want is for you to have a choice, Harry. I want you to know that, whatever you do, it's your decision. Your life—it's no one else's. Even if our paths are laid out for us, like you say, that doesn't mean we can't take risks along the way. Especially if it's a risk that will make you happy."

"I appreciate that," Harry says, a hint of a smile on his face. He holds my gaze, a full smile forming.

"What?" I tilt my head, trying to figure out what he's thinking.

"Nothing. It's just your optimism. It's refreshing. You really are an angel, you know." Harry breaks my gaze and looks down at his plate. He clears his throat. "Anyway, for now, it's nothing to worry about. Your parents aren't here yet, and I haven't left. Let's forget about all of it and just have some fun this weekend."

"Sounds like a plan." I smile at Harry, knowing that he's right.

We need to appreciate the little things.

Like friendship.

And weekends away without any parents.

"YOU WERE RIGHT; that food was amazing," I say as Harry walks me back to the hotel after dinner.

"I get carryout from there a lot," he replies, swinging the shopping bags in his hand.

"Mohammad told me the other day that his parents can get reservations basically anywhere. Do you ever go out to eat with them?"

"Not much. They're usually pretty busy," he admits. "With the four kids, it's sort of a madhouse there."

"Yeah, I could see that. I think that might be too much to deal with on a daily basis for me."

"Sometimes I wish I had a sibling," Harry says as we walk. "Although I sort of have it with the boys. And really, I rather like the attention of being an only child. Though it's not always good attention …"

"I used to want a sibling too," I say in understanding.

Harry looks over at me. "But I've got Noah. He's as much a brother to me as a blood one would be. Maybe even more so."

"I know he feels the same."

"It's probably for the best. If my parents had two children, let alone boys, we'd probably be raised to hate one another. They'd want us to compete. My father would make it a game about who deserved to inherit the business."

Harry pulls out a box of cigarettes, lighting one.

"Maybe family is who we make it to be," I offer.

Harry glances at me, smiling. "I like that."

We walk the rest of the way back to the hotel in silence. The weather is pleasant, and I like being in Harry's company.

WHEN WE GET to the front of the hotel, he turns to face me.

"So, just take your stuff to Noah's before his match tomorrow. Mohammad and I will meet you there."

"Okay."

Harry nods, glancing off into the distance. "All right. So, see you tomorrow?" he asks, flicking his gaze back to mine.

"See you tomorrow."

Harry nods again, his body rigid in front of me.

"Harry?"

"Yeah?" he asks, his blue eyes coming down to meet mine.

I pull him into a hug.

"It's going to be okay," I say, wishing that he were more sure of this.

Of himself.

But I know that he isn't. Maybe it's because of his dad. Maybe it's because of what I said about us. Or maybe he's just feeling lost.

Harry holds on to me, resting his chin against my shoulder. When he pulls back, he kisses me on the cheek. "Thank you, Mallory."

I smile, patting him on the shoulder for encouragement.

"You don't need to thank me," I say. "But what you do need to do is get over to Mohammad's house and make sure he can come tomorrow. Go put your charm to good use."

Harry grins, his blue eyes lighting up. "I will."

He starts to walk off, but after a few paces, he turns around.

"Shit. Forgot my duffel," he says, striding up to me. "And forgot to leave you with your bag."

"Come on." I laugh.

I lead us into the hotel and up to my room. Harry grabs his duffel, leaving my new clothes in the sitting room. When he's gone, I head into my room and start packing. I lay out the clothes we bought, the dress I saved for a special occasion, and the necklace Harry got me.

I slip into Noah's sweatpants and pull on a T-shirt, taking my purse and backpack to my bed. I dig my wallet out of my purse and pull out the key to Harry's country house. I hold it up, shifting it between my fingers. I place it on the bedside table, reaching for my backpack. I pull out the poem Noah wrote, gently unfolding it.

My heart speeds up when I see his handwriting.

Because tonight, Noah finally answered all of my questions. He showed me that I wasn't the only one who was scared.

He told me how he felt.

He kissed me.

I place the note into my lap and look over at Harry's key. It's sitting in front of the two photos I have on my bedside table. One of Harry and me. The other of Noah and his family. I set the poem next to the key and roll onto my side. I look at my side table, trying to figure out how I can be so happy and sad at the same time.

I'm always going to be there for Harry. Noah knows that. I care about him. But all I can think is that, somehow, I'm going to mess this up.

And I really, really don't want to.

SATURDAY, OCTOBER 19TH
Spazzing out.
9:00AM

WHEN I GET out of the cab, I try to sling my duffel over my shoulder. I want to have that *I'm going on a road trip* spring in my step. The one where you tie up your shoelaces, throw the bag over your shoulder, and march off into the unknown.

Except, well, I sort of know where I'm going. And where I am. And my duffel is too heavy to *actually* sling over my shoulder, and I have a suitcase in tow. I try to at least lift the duffel higher, so it's not practically dragging on the ground, but it's no use. I roll my eyes and walk up the front steps, lugging my bags behind me.

Number 32.

I hesitate for a moment, a mixture of excitement and nerves coursing through me. Because I haven't seen Noah since last night.

Since our talk.

Since he asked me to come to his match.

Since we kissed.

And I'm freaking out.

Well, more like spazzing out.

I can't wait to see him. And I can't wait for our weekend away. To hang out with Harry. To catch up with Mohammad. To have time alone with Noah.

But then doubt sets in.

What if Noah doesn't know I'm coming over this morning? Harry said he told him that we'd drop our bags here before his game, but can I rely on Harry? What if he forgot to tell Noah? What if he answers the door and looks at me with surprise?

I chew on my lip, wishing I had texted Noah before coming over. I should have called him this morning and told him about the trip. Made sure he knew all the details.

What if he's changed his mind about me, about us, since last night? Or worse, what if he notices the amount of luggage I have and decides right then and there that his previous decision was a rash one?

After all, who the hell needs a duffel and a suitcase for a spur-of-the-moment trip?!

Me.

The answer is me.

The girl who annoys Noah. Because of my bluntness and quick reactions. Because of the amount of clothing I own.

I don't know why any of this hasn't occurred to me until now. But with Noah, it's a real possibility that I'm about to make a huge mistake. He's always all over the place with his emotions. His feelings. What if they—*his emotions*—decide after a day that they're over me and my obnoxious amount of luggage?

No.

That isn't going to happen.

I shake out all of the crazy thoughts swirling around in my head and drop my duffel on the stoop. I ring the doorbell, butterflies erupting in my stomach.

A few seconds later, the door swings open. The smell of Noah's shower gel hits me immediately, and right after, the sight of his shirtless torso does.

"Hey." Noah smiles, stepping out onto the front stoop.

Black joggers sit low on his hips, and I suck in a gulp of air when my gaze slips from his pants to the line of dark hair rising up to his belly button.

It's sunny this morning, and I squint my eyes as Noah comes fully into the light. His pale, firm chest almost glows in front of me.

"Hi," I croak out. I bring my hand up to my throat and clear my voice.

My brows weave together as Noah moves closer.

Until his chest is just inches from mine.

I don't know how long I stand there and stare at him, but Noah must not mind. He looks down at me as I let my gaze sweep across his face. His eyes are bright this morning, and his hair has dried from the shower, but I can smell the soap on him.

Eventually, I smile back at him, and his own smile moves from his lips all the way up to his eyes. He leans down and picks my duffel up off the ground.

He keeps his eyes on me as he stands back up.

"Here, let me," Noah says, motioning to the suitcase next to me.

His hand moves to the handle that I'm still grasping, and his fingers brush against mine. I blink, not sure what to do.

But finally, my brain registers what's going on.

I need to let go.

He's trying to take my suitcase inside. *Obviously.*

I remove my hand and roll my eyes at myself. I need to stay focused and stop losing my senses when he's around.

Noah picks up the suitcase and carries both of my bags into the entryway of his house. I follow him inside, closing the door behind us.

Noah drops the duffel on the floor and sets the suitcase down next to it. I kick off my shoes and glance around the living room.

It's empty.

"Where's your …" I start, but Noah's already back, facing me, and it takes me momentarily by surprise.

"Who's that?" Helen's voice bounces out from the kitchen.

I try to lean around Noah to see her, but he holds up his finger in front of his lips, wanting me to be quiet.

"It's Mallory, Mum. She's going to help me with something," Noah replies, taking my hand in his.

He turns and leads us to the staircase as I gape in the direction of the kitchen.

Because at any moment, Helen could pop her head out of the room.

She'd have an excited smile on her face. But then she'd see Noah, shirtless, my flushed cheeks, and our interlocked hands, and she would definitely know something is up.

And did Noah just lie to his mom?

"Your father will be back soon, so be quick, dear. I want to chat over breakfast," Helen calls out from the kitchen.

I think I hear her set down her coffee cup with a sigh, but Noah already has us at the top of the staircase.

"Okay," Noah calls back, leading us to his room. He drops my hand before closing the door behind us.

"Were you trying to hide me from your mom?" I ask, spinning around toward him.

"What? No." Noah laughs, closing the distance between us. "I just didn't want her to drag you into the kitchen to talk."

"Why would that be …" I start, but quickly, I close my mouth. A flush spreads across my cheeks as I realize what Noah is saying.

That he didn't want me to talk to his mom in the kitchen.

That he wanted me here.

In his room.

Alone. With him.

I break Noah's gaze and take a moment to look around his room. It's kind of a disaster this morning. There's a gym bag half-packed on the ground, and Noah's backpack is open next to it. A few of his textbooks and binders are stacked on his desk, and they look like they're about to slide off onto the floor. I move toward them.

"So, Harry did tell you," I say, letting out a relieved sigh.

"That we're going to his house for the weekend?" Noah asks, moving next to me by the desk. "Yeah, he told me."

"I was worried he was just going to spring it on you at the match or something," I reply, flicking my eyes up to his.

"Nah, he called. Told me that you'd come by this morning."

"That's good." I nod, feeling my cheeks flush even more. I don't know why I'm so nervous.

Noah's hands come to rest at my waist, and he turns me to face him.

I stare up at him.

"Didn't you think I would have found it odd that you were standing in my doorway with luggage if I hadn't known?" He chuckles, his face lighting up.

"That didn't even cross my mind at the time," I reply. "Honestly, *if anything*, I thought you'd be mad about the luggage."

A quiet laugh escapes Noah's lips, but quickly, it falters off. Noah drops his hands from my waist and takes my hand in his. He pulls me away from his desk and toward his bed.

"What are you doing?" I ask. The words barely have a chance to get out of my mouth before I'm falling back onto his bed.

"What does it look like?" Noah grins.

I watch his abs flex as he bends down toward me.

His palms press into the bed on either side of me as he crawls on top of me. His face moves above mine, leaving me in a shadow below him. I look from his firm jaw up to his golden eyes before flicking my gaze down to his lips, watching as they part.

His forearms come to rest beside my head.

My cheeks flush as Noah looks over me, the corner of his mouth curling up as he smiles.

"You look good on my bed," he says, raising his eyebrows.

He shifts his weight to one side, his hand finding mine. His fingers dance across my palm, sending a shiver through my body. My heart feels like it's floating in my chest until Noah finally lowers his head.

Until his lips find mine.

I expect him to kiss me hesitantly. Like he isn't sure how I'll react. Like he wants to make sure that today, nothing has changed. Like he was worried about how things might be. But there's nothing hesitant about the way he kisses me. His mouth forms its way around mine, his lips drawing me in. He kisses me deeply, his tongue dipping into my mouth. At first, I'm surprised.

By the intensity of his kiss.

By how quickly my body responds.

Without thought, I let him in.

His tongue dances with mine as my body heats up. I lace our fingers together and grasp on to his hand.

Noah pulls back slightly, a smile on his face.

"I never thought you'd get here," he says, running soft kisses across my lips.

"Have you been waiting for me all morning?" I beam up at him.

Noah lets out a chuckle before bringing his lips down to my neck.

"Basically," he mumbles back, kissing along my jawline. The kisses are light and wispy.

"That tickles." I say, relaxing into his bed.

"Do you want me to stop?" he asks, but he keeps his lips on my neck.

I shake my head, my eyes slipping shut.

"You smell so good." Noah kisses down to my collarbone. His mouth is warm and wet and sends goose bumps rising on my arms.

I inhale, thinking about his smell. About how the second he opened the door, I knew it was him.

"You smell like shower gel. I noticed it right away."

"Too clean?" Noah mumbles against my skin.

"You know how much I love that Noah musk." I laugh.

"You're the strangest." He chuckles.

"Want to know something even stranger?" I ask, pulling my eyes open.

"Tell me."

"I sort of had an almost freak-out at your front door."

"What?" Noah asks, pulling his lips away from my skin. He rolls off me, propping himself up onto his elbow, and looks over at me. "Why?"

"Because," I reply, sitting up, "my first thought was, *Oh shit, what if he doesn't know I'm coming over?* And then I started to wonder if Harry actually told you about today. And then my mind slipped to, *What if he's changed his mind since yesterday and—*"

"Am I really that flighty?" Noah asks, wide-eyed.

"Slightly." I shrug. But I can't help and smile at him.

Noah's fingers find my sides, and they dance across my skin as his eyes meet mine.

"Well, does it seem like I've changed my mind?" he asks, his gaze never faltering.

I hold his eyes and shake my head no.

"Good, because I wouldn't want to confuse you," Noah says, bringing his lips back to mine. His lips are warm and soft. But they're also firm and in control.

Everything about Noah is like that.

A paradox.

I don't know how long he kisses me for, but it feels like hours. Or minutes. It's easy to get lost in this.

In him.

"Food's here." Helen's voice floats up the stairs and into Noah's room from the kitchen.

"Hmm," Noah grumbles. But he doesn't pull back.

"I'm not hungry. Are you?" I whisper against his lips.

"Nope. I think we should stay here," he replies, adamantly shaking his head.

"What would Helen say?"

"Good point."

"Besides, I know you. And you need to eat before your match."

"That is true," Noah agrees. "And Dad went to get bagels."

"Oh." I can't help but sit up at the prospect of bagels. But I can't really sit up because Noah's partially lying on top of me.

"Pique your interest?" Noah asks, licking his lips.

"Mmhmm. I hope he got the strawberry kind." I try to get up from the bed, but Noah presses me back down.

"That's your favorite," he says, his legs on either side of mine, keeping me pinned beneath him. He has my wrists in his hands as he sprinkles my neck with kisses again.

"I love it," I say breathlessly.

"Mmhmm. The strawberry and honey," Noah says heavily, his mouth trailing up my jaw to my lips.

"Exactly," I reply as he brushes his lips against mine, giving me another kiss.

And any thought I had about the bagels are gone when my fingers weave into Noah's hair. He presses his body against mine, his hands trailing down over my sides until his fingers find the sliver of skin where my jeans meet my shirt. His fingers send a jolt through me, and Noah must feel it.

Because his body reacts.

His legs stretch out, and he lets go of my hands before putting his hands around my waist, pulling me flush against him. My palms find his shoulders as he deepens our kiss. I dig my fingers into him, my heart jumping in my chest at the sensation of our stomachs touching.

My body pushes up toward him, wanting to be closer.

Anything to be closer to him.

When his fingers graze against my stomach again, I have to peel my eyes open. I let out a soft moan, knowing I need to get ahold of myself. Because if he keeps kissing me like this, I really will forget about the bagels. And the fact that Gene and Helen are downstairs, waiting for us.

"You're a little … intense this morning," I mumble, trying to think straight.

"I got a good night's sleep," he says easily. He rolls off of me, pulling me onto my side. And he's radiating. His entire face is lit up.

"Is that all it is?" I ask, touching his pink cheek.

Noah's nose scrunches up as he weighs his head back and forth.

"The only reason I'm happy." Noah nods, teasing. But he isn't very convincing.

I grin at him, pulling him back to my lips. He gives me a

slow, drawn-out kiss before looking at me from under his dark lashes.

"We should probably get downstairs."

I'm about to say probably *again*, agreeing with him. But before I have the chance, Noah pulls me up and off the bed. I am barely standing upright before he's dragging me to his door.

"Wait, Noah," I say, stopping him. "You're shirtless."

Noah turns back to me, his cheeks still flushed. "And?"

"And ... you can't eat breakfast, shirtless."

"Too distracting?" Noah tilts his head to the side, a wide grin settling on his face.

I roll my eyes in reply, but Noah pulls a shirt out of his drawer and then opens his door.

"You have some serious sass this morning." I laugh, stepping into the hallway with him.

"I'm in a good mood," Noah replies, his hand finding mine.

He's pulling his shirt over his head with the other when Mia's door swings open. She steps out into the hallway, and Noah runs right into her, his face covered with his shirt.

"*Whoa*," Mia says, her hands coming up in defense mode.

Her eyes narrow into slits at Noah's apparent assault, but then her attention turns to me. And those narrow slits widen until she's ogling me.

"Whoa," she says again.

But this time, it's a freaked-out whoa.

It's a whoa that means, *My brother was shirtless and with you.*

Noah finally gets his shirt on.

"Sorry about that," he says to Mia.

But Mia's eyes are still glued to me, making me want to crawl away and hide.

"You look a little … flushed," she says, examining me.

"Uh … really?" I laugh nervously, trying to sound like I have no idea what she's talking about. I break my hand from Noah's, who seems to be clueless. "I'll meet you down there."

Noah nods before heading downstairs. I open the bathroom door and flick on the lights.

"Oh my," I mutter.

Because Mia was right.

My cheeks are pink, my lips redder than normal. And my hair could *definitely* use a brush.

"I don't know if I should be horrified that you were snogging my brother or happy that you two at least aren't fighting anymore," Mia says, popping her head into the bathroom.

I pull back with surprise but quickly refocus on my reflection. I run my fingers through my hair, tilting my head to the side when …

Shit. Is that a hickey?

I turn my head more and lean closer to the mirror, letting out a sigh.

It was just a shadow.

"Relax. You look fine," Mia replies, pulling me out of the bathroom as I try to run my hands through my hair.

I follow her to the staircase and can hear voices floating up from the kitchen.

"Mia," I say, stopping her when we get halfway down the stairs.

She turns to me, her brown curls pulled back into a large clip, a few tendrils escaping.

"Noah and I …"

Mia laughs, waving me off. "Yeah, yeah, I know. You're just *friends*," she says, shooting me a wink.

Before I can say anything else, she's down the stairs and headed into the kitchen.

I shake my head to myself and then follow her, knowing this isn't going to be good.

"OH, MALLORY, WONDERFUL to see you," Gene says from the table. He's already seated and unpacking the bagels as Helen places plates on the table.

"It's nice to see you too." I smile at him.

His glasses slip down his nose, and he pushes them back up. His newspaper is open on the table and resting below a plate Helen must have sat atop it.

"Will you be joining us at the match?" Gene asks as I slide into an open chair.

Noah is already seated in his usual spot, and Mia has her head in the fridge.

"Yeah, I am," I reply before glancing up to Helen.

She's at the counter, pouring a cup of coffee.

The amazing smell hits me instantly.

Helen walks to the table and sets the cup down in front of me before pulling me into a hug.

"That's lovely to hear," she says, squeezing me. I smile and hug her back. "You know you're always welcome here. For Noah's matches. For dinner. I don't like that you're all alone at that hotel."

Helen's face sours as she takes her seat. Mia joins us at the table, a cup of creamy coffee in her hand.

"It's not that bad," I tell her as Gene finishes unboxing the bagels. The strawberry and honey bagel catches my eye, and my mouth starts to water. "I actually don't mind living alone. But I'm happy to be here. I would never want to miss Noah's match."

Or these bagels.

Mia goes straight for the pile, luckily grabbing one topped with cream cheese and chives.

"Here," Noah says, picking up the one I want from across the table. "Give me your plate."

He extends his hand out toward me, and I do as he asked. He places my bagel on it and then breaks off a piece of his bagel, setting it on my plate before handing it back to me.

"Thanks."

"You're welcome. I thought you might want to try mine. It's good too," Noah says, his eyes on me.

I nod, butterflies forming in my stomach as I look over at him. Because just a few minutes ago, those hands, those lips, were on me.

I flush at the memory.

"That was …" Helen says, her voice rising.

I glance up to see her watching me with interest. I quickly drop her eyes and do my best to ignore her stare.

But I know I've been caught.

And I panic.

Can she tell that we were kissing?

Does she know?

I peek back up at her, seeing her gaze fixed on Noah now. I look at him and want to groan.

Because he's beaming. He's smiling down at his bagel, his eyes glancing up toward me every so often. I slide down in my chair, trying to reach his foot under the table so I can kick him. Mia looks over her coffee cup at me like I'm crazy, her eyebrows rising. I kick my foot out, but it doesn't reach.

It's no use.

"Was what, dear?" Gene asks, biting into his bagel, his eyes never coming up from the paper.

"Nice. That was nice," Helen says, recovering.

She shakes her head before looking around the table like she forgot something. She gets back up, and I spot her own cup on the counter. I take the chance to flare my eyes at

Noah, but he doesn't seem fazed.

If anything, he seems amused by it.

He lets out an easy laugh, his whole face relaxing. Helen sits back down at the table, cup in hand.

"So, when are your parents arriving, Mallory?" Helen asks me.

"I think next week," I answer excitely.

"That's great news," Gene says, looking up from his paper again.

"It is," Helen agrees.

"We should have them round for dinner," Noah says, catching me off guard.

I snap my head in his direction.

Because did he just invite my parents over for dinner?

"That would be nice," Gene agrees with a satisfied nod.

"It would?" Helen's words sound more like a question than an agreement, and I glance at her. She's looking at Noah, her eyebrow raised in suspicion.

I clear my throat. "My dad loves wine, Gene, so I know you two will get along." I let out a chuckle, trying to take the attention off of Noah and his request.

"Anyone who loves wine is a friend of mine," Gene says wittily, a smile pulling across his face.

Helen bats her hand out at him, a laugh escaping.

"Maybe Mia could make us more of those pumpkin cookies too," Noah says, looking to his sister. "I'm sure everyone would enjoy them. I know Mallory couldn't stop talking about them in class."

He glances up to me, his eyes dancing with light. "She especially loved the frosting," he adds.

My mouth falls open at his words.

Because could he be more obvious?!

I snap my mouth shut and turn to Mia. "Uh, yes, I did,

Mia. They were delicious."

"Well, if you loved them that much, I guess I'll have to make them," she says flatly.

But then she smiles before biting into her bagel, and I know she didn't miss the compliment.

"Thanks," Noah says happily.

I watch Gene and Helen exchange a glance, which can't be good. A moment later, they're both looking at Noah like his happiness is something unknown and untrustworthy.

"You ready for your match then?" Gene asks Noah.

"Definitely." He nods, not bothering to look up. He takes another bite of his bagel, looking down at it as he chews.

"Do you think you'll win?" Helen pushes.

"I hope so." Noah laughs, looking up at her like her question is hilarious. "Coach has been killing us in practices lately. I think he's just worried about midterm break. Although I'm not sure why. With the added weight during practices and the fact that he has us all running in the mornings, everyone on the team is as cut as they've ever been. He could stand to relax a bit."

"Really?" Gene asks, surprise flashing across his face. Again.

"We're in top form this season. Don't you agree, Mal?" Noah says, turning to me.

I look up and meet his gaze, my eyes going wide.

"You're asking me?" I say, pointing to myself. I try to say it calmly and detached, but I can hear the rise in my voice.

Helen and Gene both look at me. I meet their gaze for a second before glancing back to Noah. He smirks, his brown eyes filling with silent amusement.

"Well, you've seen me practice. Been to the matches. What are your thoughts?" he asks, and I know what he's really referring to is how he looks shirtless, but I can play along.

"Uh … yeah. You look—I mean, *the team* looks like they're ready to play some football. You know, go team!" I nod continuously before clamping my mouth shut.

"Wow, this is weird," Mia says.

She shakes her head before shoving a ripped piece of bagel into her mouth.

Gene looks at me like I've lost my mind, and Helen just stares at Noah.

"Uh, so plans today?" Gene says, coming back to himself. "Mia?"

"Sophia and I are going to the Saatchi Gallery after the match, and then we might grab some food," Mia answers.

"Aww." I smile.

"So, this is a … date?" Gene asks.

"Dad …" Mia grumbles.

Gene throws his hands into the air. "Well, someone had to ask."

"Yes, it's a *date*." She flares her eyes at him and shifts her rings around on her fingers.

"Well then, you should take her flowers. Women love flowers." Gene nods, apparently confirming the fact.

"Women do," Helen agrees.

"I'm not taking her flowers. Where would she put them?" Mia laughs, looking baffled.

"Hmm. Well, whatever you do, make sure it's romantic," Gene says. "Even daytime dates can be special."

"What's with all the advice this morning?" Mia comments, raising an eyebrow at her dad. "This is the strangest family."

Gene visibly flushes.

I look to Helen, wondering what that's about.

"Our anniversary is coming up, dearest," Helen answers.

"Aww," both Mia and I say at the same time.

Noah glances up to them, his lip twitching.

"Speaking of love and friendship, it appears you two have made up then?" Helen says to me and Noah, coming right out with it.

I stare down at the table, wondering if I could disappear if I tried hard enough.

"Helen, honey," Gene says, immediately turning beet red.

"Yeah, we have." Noah nods, still unfazed.

I clear my throat.

"We are all good," I confirm with a scared-as-shit smile.

"Well, that's lovely to hear. I'm glad all of the weirdness is behind you. Friendships are too important to just give up on," Helen says, sounding pleased.

"Friendship." Mia laughs under her breath.

I keep the smile plastered on my face and try not to scream.

Maybe no one heard her.

I avoid Helen's eyes, but I can feel her staring at me. I finally give in and look at her. Her eyes are so wide that I jump back in my seat. Her gaze flicks from me, to Mia, and then to Noah. She opens her mouth like she wants to say something, but instead, she seals her lips shut.

Thankfully, Noah's phone goes off, interrupting her train of thought. I watch Helen relax in her chair as Noah pulls his phone out of his pocket. He reads a text before looking back up to us.

"Harry messaged. Said he'd be by to drop his stuff off before the match, but to head over without him and Mohammad for warm-ups."

"We'll leave the key under the mat then," Helen replies.

"Cool," Noah says back.

"Speaking of Harry, how was Thursday night?" Helen asks, looking between all three of us.

"Noah didn't tell you about it?" I ask.

Noah shrugs.

"Fine for me," Mia replies, finishing off her bagel.

"Noah?" Helen asks, trying to wrangle more information from him.

"Went as well as expected," he answers.

"I swear, my children are sticklers with the details." Helen sighs before turning toward me. "Mallory?"

"Uh, honestly, it was weird, meeting his parents. I hated it. But I also needed it, I think, to understand Harry better. His dad was nice and charming, which just confused me at first. But then I realized that it was just a show. His mom didn't exactly speak to me," I explain, thinking about how she looked me over. How she'd invited Natalia, knowing that I would be there.

Helen shakes her head, disgust flashing across her face. "I couldn't be there for that."

"I understand why you didn't go," Noah says to his mom.

"Did Noah tell you about Harry's trip next week?" I ask, hoping for something lighter.

"Yeah, I did. Shanghai next week," Noah reminds.

"That's awesome!" Mia says, her eyes lighting up.

Noah shakes his head at her. "Harry's not thrilled."

"I wouldn't be either," Helen says.

"I would be," Mia disagrees, looking at them like they're crazy.

"He doesn't have a choice," I explain.

"But we do what our families ask of us, don't we?" Gene says, looking between us all.

I've never felt this much weight in the air at the Williams' house, and it's almost stifling. It's obvious how much they care about Harry. About how much they don't like what he's going through either.

"I guess we have to," I reply.

Everyone is silent for a moment.

"Actually, why don't Gene and I stay until Harry arrives?" Helen says, slapping her hand down on the table with resolve.

"Mohammad's coming too," Noah comments.

"That's fine, dear. It will just give us a chance to talk to Harry."

"About everything?" I ask.

Helen nods. "To check in. See where his head's at."

"Does anyone ever know where Harry's head is at?" Mia laughs.

My lip curls up as the tension at the table eases.

"I'm sure he'll appreciate that," I tell Helen with a smile.

"More like appreciate the attention," Mia remarks.

Noah laughs easily.

"Thanks, Mum. He will appreciate that," Noah says to her.

"It's settled then," Gene says, bringing his coffee cup to his lips.

"You, Mallory, and Mia can head to the field, and Gene and I will head over with Harry and Mohammad," Helen says.

"I'll wait with you," Mia chimes in.

"Mia, you will go with your brother," Helen scolds.

Mia drops her shoulders as a pout forms on her mouth. "It's just warm-ups, Mum. It's no big deal."

"You aren't getting out of going," Helen states firmly, having a stare-off with Mia.

I watch, curious who's going to break first.

"I wouldn't dare," Mia says, rolling her eyes. "Besides, who wouldn't want to sit and watch boys running around for an hour, getting kicked in the shins, sweating on one another, and fighting like their lives depended on an inflated ball?"

"Oh, Mia," Gene says, shaking his head.

"That was unnecessary, young lady," Helen says firmly.

"Well, it's the truth. Football is boring," she whines.

Gene looks up from his paper, tilting his head at Mia. Helen is glaring at her. But when Mia meets her dad's eyes, I see her soften. She purses her lips before looking at Noah, a smile playing on her face.

"Don't worry though. Boring or not, I'll be there to support you. I always am," she says, lightly punching his shoulder.

"I appreciate the support." Noah laughs and stands up from the table. "I'll change, and then we can head out."

He looks to me, and I nod in reply.

Noah jogs up the stairs, and when we're all finished, I help Mia and Helen clear the table. Gene is engrossed in his paper and barely notices the movement in the kitchen.

Noah's back downstairs in a flash, and relief floods through me when he comes into the kitchen, dressed and ready to go.

"We'll see you there," Noah says to everyone.

I wipe my hands off on a towel and then toss it to Mia with a smile.

"See you soon," Helen replies, catching my eye.

And I can already see it in her eyes.

She knows.

She knows because of what Mia said, and at some point, she's going to bring it up.

Noah puts his hand on my back, ushering me to the front door. But I can't focus on anything other than Helen.

Is she happy for us?

Is she mad?

I know that Helen cares for me. She's become sort of like a mom to me. I can depend on her. And what if, because she knows me, she doesn't approve of us?

She knows me.

She knows I react quickly, that I overthink things, that I can be impulsive. What if she adds all of those things up and decides that as much as she likes me as a person, she doesn't want me with her son?

What if she's upset?

"Ready?" Noah asks, shifting his duffel on his shoulder as I fumble, pulling on my shoes. I almost fall over, but Noah steadies me.

"Yeah, I'm ready," I reply before swinging open the door and almost whacking Noah with it.

"Shit," he mumbles, barely avoiding it.

"Sorry." I flinch, shaking my head. I drag Noah outside and close the door behind us, trying to pull in a breath of fresh air.

When we get a few paces from the house, I finally open my mouth and say, "So, that was interesting." My mind is racing.

"It was just bagels," Noah comments, walking beside me.

"Forget the bagels. Did you hear what Mia said? And the way your mom looked at me? *She knows.*" I flare my eyes at him, wanting him to grasp the severity of this.

"Is it a secret?" Noah asks, glancing at me.

"I don't know. Is it? I mean, are we telling anyone? What happens if we tell her and she's mad? I can't disappoint your mom. And what about Harry? Oh my god, what are we going to tell your mom about this weekend? Will she still let you go if she knows?" I ask, starting to freak out.

Because I never considered that Noah wouldn't be able to go. And if Noah doesn't go, then do I go? And what if I go and it's just me, Mohammad, and Harry? And Harry's made it clear that he's still interested.

"Mal," Noah says, stopping us.

"Yeah?" I ask.

"We're good. I promise." He throws his arm over my shoulders before he starts walking again.

His arm is heavy on me, but the weight feels good. It makes me relax.

At least, a little bit.

"Oh, you promise, huh? What is with you? You're too chill. I'm spazzing out here."

"Spazzing out enough for the both of us. Besides, what Mum doesn't know won't hurt her."

"Are you going to lie to her?" I ask with surprise.

"Not lie. Omit. It's the only way," he answers.

"Would she actually make you stay home if she knew I was going?"

"No, but she'd make Dad have a talk with me about the birds and the bees, and I think I'm all up to date on that, so we're good."

"But that's what I'm trying to say, Noah. She already knows."

"You *think* she knows. And if she suspects, then she'll ask me about it."

"And what will you say? That we are still friends, just friends who are now kissing?" I roll my eyes.

"We're not just friends, Mal. We both know that. I would tell her the truth. That we're together."

"Together," I repeat. "And you don't think we should ease her into it? Like, say we're dating, then dating exclusively, and then finally together? Give people time to adjust?"

"People or you?" Noah asks.

"People."

"Mmhmm," Noah replies, unwrapping his arm from around me before adjusting his duffel.

WE WALK A few streets in silence, our hands dangling at our sides. I force the what-ifs out of my mind and trust that Noah's right. Everything will work out.

Every few steps, Noah's fingers graze against mine, but he never takes my hand. I chew on my lip, wondering if I'm really about to do this.

I take his hand in mine.

Noah looks over at me and smiles.

"Look at you, making the first move. I'm impressed," he teases.

I shake my head and give him a small shove. But I keep his hand in mine.

"What? It's true. I clearly remember a few nights ago when you thought holding my hand would be your destruction or something. And look at us now." Noah raises an eyebrow in my direction.

I let out a sigh in response, but hold on to his hand tighter.

Because he does make a fair point.

"Look, I'll take care of it. Let's just enjoy this."

Noah's fingers slide through mine, sending tingles up my arm. I close my eyes at the sensation, warmth flooding through me.

"Okay." I nod, butterflies in my stomach. "So, are you excited for your match?"

"Very. And I'm always overwhelmed with the support at home," Noah says easily.

I let out a laugh.

"Mia is ... *opinionated.*"

"She is," Noah replies fondly. "Sometimes, it gets her into trouble. Although my dad finds it more entertaining than insulting, I think."

"She walks the line."

"But I know she's just taking the piss. When it comes down to it, she always shows up," Noah says.

"That's what siblings are for, right? Teasing you?"

"Teasing you. Annoying you. Reminding you how lame you are. Sometimes, they even come into your bedroom and steal the girl right out of your bed. It's mad," Noah says, dramatically shaking his head in disappointment.

"I wasn't *thrilled* when Mia came in your room yesterday." I laugh, agreeing.

"Oh yeah?" Noah asks, his voice rising.

I glance at him, watching as he bites his lip before his eyes find mine. My stomach flips as I think about kissing him yesterday.

This morning.

At how much I want to kiss him now.

I still abruptly, pulling us to a stop on the sidewalk. I let go of his hand, causing Noah's face to flash with confusion. But before he has a chance to say anything, I grab on to his jersey and pull him down to my lips. Noah's mouth is firm against mine, probably from surprise. I let go of his jersey and bring both of my hands to his chest, letting them slide up to his shoulders. He must finally register what's going on because his mouth relaxes. His hands lace around my waist, and he pulls me closer as I kiss him. I bite gently on his lip before kissing him again, knowing I should pull away.

"Mal," Noah mumbles, his fingers grasping at my waist.

I break our lips apart but don't move away from him.

"What was that for?" he asks, breathless.

I slide my fingers down to his chest, feeling it rise and fall under my palms.

Because I finally can.

"Do I need a reason?" I ask, looking up at him.

"Never."

"It was ... for luck," I answer.

"Luck, huh?" he says, raising an eyebrow as he smiles at me.

"Luck," I repeat with a nod that I hope is convincing.

"It can't hurt," Noah agrees. He's still smiling as he grabs on to my hand and leads us to the field.

He's being cocky.
10:15AM

WHEN WE GET to the field, part of the football team is already there. There are a few parents and friends scattered across the sidelines, watching them collect together to start warm-ups. The field is familiar, the smell of cut grass registering immediately. Noah walks next to me, an easy expression resting on his face. The last time I saw him here though, he wasn't relaxed.

And it was one of the worst days of my life.

Walking to the field to meet him.

Saying what I thought was good-bye.

Seeing him so hurt.

Upset.

I glance up at him, realizing how much is different now. How so many things have changed.

When we get to the edge of the field, Noah slows his pace.

"Thanks for coming with me," he whispers, bumping his shoulder against mine.

A moment later, he's walking out onto the field toward the team. But he keeps sneaking glances back over his shoulder at me.

"Hey, Noah," I hear myself call out.

"Yeah?" he asks, turning back to look at me as he continues walking.

"Have fun out there." I smile at him.

"Don't worry; I plan to." He winks at me, his lips pulling up into a cocky grin.

Butterflies erupt in my stomach, and I can't stop myself from grinning too.

When he gets to the center of the field, he clasps hands with one of his teammates before being pulled into a side hug. He walks to the far side of the field, dropping his duffel. He quickly pulls out his cleats and changes shoes before running back onto the field.

The grass is dry, so I decide to sit down while he warms up.

I watch him bounce the ball between his knees in the middle of his teammates. I watch him stretch, his hands hooking around one foot before switching to the other. I try not to ogle. But it's hard not to.

Really hard.

Because I can't stop smiling.

Or staring.

Luckily, no one else is around. I don't have to worry about Helen or Gene, Harry or Mohammad. It's just me and Noah.

And in between jogging, talking to Coach Carson, and warming up, Noah glances at me every free moment he has. He smirks or raises his eyebrows, his lips curling at the corner.

I try not to grin back at him every time he looks at me, but I can't help it when my eyes brighten or when my cheeks flush. Because it's impossible not to react to him.

Not to smile back.

I bite my lip, knowing that I need to pull myself together. That I need to come down from the cloud that I'm on. But everything is finally settling in.

I got to kiss Noah this morning.

Again.

Which means yesterday wasn't just a fluke. It wasn't a mistake or a one-time thing. It's something that's going to continue.

The smiles, the glances, the kisses.

This is real.

There isn't any uncertainty in the way that I feel.

I smile down at the grass, mindlessly running my fingers through it when someone plops down next to me.

"Saving us the best seats?" Mohammad asks. He's wearing a green bomber jacket, light-wash jeans, sneakers, and a big grin.

"Only the best for you." I smile, wrapping my arms around him in a hug.

When I pull away, I look over my shoulder to see Harry, Gene, Mia, and Helen all walking in our direction. They've got folding chairs hanging over their shoulders, and they don't seem to be in any rush.

"What'd you do? Sprint over here when you saw me?" I ask, turning my attention back to Mohammad.

"Not my fault they're slow," he says, waving it off. "So, what do you make of practice? Are our boys going to kill it?"

I glance back to the players on the field. "They seem pumped up."

"Good." Mohammad excitedly rubs his hands together. "I'm ready to see Kensington kick some ass."

"I'm just ready to see Noah play better than last week," Mia chimes in, joining us.

"Last week's match was rather unfortunate," Mohammad agrees.

"He played so terribly that I actually felt bad for him."

Mia laughs, opening up her folding chair.

"Now, Mia," Helen scolds, overhearing her. She shakes her head as Gene and Harry join us.

I stand up and look at Harry. He's wearing his trench coat with the collar popped up, a blue polo, and jeans underneath. A bag with the chair in it is slung over his shoulder. His eyes find mine, and they seem brighter than they were last night.

He looks happier.

"Aww, you brought me a chair," I tease, pulling him into a hug.

Harry wraps his arm around my waist, hugging me back.

"Unfortunately, this isn't for you or me," Harry replies, raising an eyebrow at me. "Somehow, I got talked into carrying Mohammad's chair."

"I was in the middle of a story," Mohammad says, shaking his head.

"And continually getting distracted," Mia fires back before turning to me. "He was walking backward down the sidewalk and almost ran right into someone."

"It's not my fault they weren't looking where they were going," Mohammad scoffs.

"We're all here now in one piece, and that's all that matters," Gene says, cutting in.

"Agreed," I reply.

"Harry, dear," Helen says, handing her chair to Gene, "will you help me lay out this quilt?"

"Of course."

"We didn't have enough foldable chairs for everyone, so we brought the quilt for Harry and Mohammad," Helen explains while Gene and Mia get all the folding chairs set up.

"Oh, so I actually do get a chair?" I say, teasing Mohammad.

"If you want one," Helen answers.

"Mallory was already sitting in the grass," Mohammad grumbles, obviously pouting.

I laugh, waving him off. "How about you take my seat, and Harry and I can share the quilt? But promise me we can switch if my butt goes numb or something."

Harry laughs, taking a seat on top of the quilt.

"Deal!" Mohammad says.

Harry extends his hand out to me. I take it, and he quickly pulls me down with him.

"Hey!" I laugh, trying not to fall.

"Ace seats for us, don't you agree? I feel like one of the players. One with the grass." Harry smirks.

"You're right." I smile. "I think this is the best way to watch the match."

"You're both mad," Mohammad disagrees. But it doesn't stop him from dragging his chair over, getting as close to Harry and me as he can get.

"All right," Harry says, rubbing his hands together as the match starts.

Everyone stays quiet, except Mohammad, who's already munching away on trail mix. I glance at him as he scoops in a mouthful, a few pieces escaping and falling onto his shirt.

I laugh and then turn my attention back to the match, watching the ball being dribbled down the field by the opposing team.

Noah looks warmed up and focused, his eyes never leaving the ball.

In a flash, he steals the ball, kicking it to a teammate.

"Funny how so much can change in a week," Mia says, watching Noah intensely.

"Yeah," I agree, amazed at how quickly he seems to be moving.

"Anything—and I mean, anything—would be better than

last week," Mohammad says.

Harry shifts next to me after a few minutes, craning his neck to look down the sidelines.

"I'll be right back. I'm going to say hi to some guys," he says to me.

I nod, my eyes still on Noah.

"He's on form today," Mohammad mumbles to himself.

And a moment later, Kensington scores.

As everyone is cheering, Mohammad gets up from his chair and sits down next to me on the quilt.

"Don't you agree?" he questions, his brows weaving together.

"Well, obviously," I answer. "They just scored."

I glance over at Mohammad, but he's staring out at the field.

At Noah.

We watch as Kensington steals the ball again, leading it down the field.

"He's being … cocky," Mohammad says. "Look at him. He's practically taunting that guy."

And Noah is. He's grinning. He's dribbling the ball between his feet and enjoying it. They're only one goal ahead, but looking at Noah, it's like they've already won. He seems so relaxed. So sure of himself.

What's gotten into him?

I shrug at Mohammad.

"You never know with Noah," I reply as they score again.

Noah's smiling from ear to ear, and then he's searching the sidelines. When his eyes find mine, he winks. I have to bite my lip to keep from smiling back at him.

Mohammad whips his head in my direction. "So this is because of you!" he practically yells.

"Shh!" I scold, glancing over my shoulder at Gene, Helen,

and Mia, hoping they didn't hear. I turn back to Mohammad and narrow my eyes at him. "It is not about me."

"Oh, it is. It definitely is. He looks too happy out there. Way too happy. I saw the wink. You know I saw it," he says into my ear.

"Yes, okay. I saw the wink too. But it's not a big deal," I try to tell him.

"Not a big deal?" Mohammad shakes his head. "The wink. How he's playing ... holy shit! You gave him some pregame encouragement, didn't you? That's the only answer to this kind of change! Or was it the promise of some postgame action? You have to tell me."

Mohammad's whole face is lit up, his eyes the size of saucers.

"Mohammad!" I exclaim, glaring at him.

"I'm sorry, but it's true. He either got some already or is living on the promise of getting some soon. You see him out there, right? This is not normal."

I look back out at the field and watch Noah play. I smile to myself, but then I remember what Mohammad asked.

"Yes, I see him," I answer.

And Mohammad is right. This isn't normal for Noah.

He's good. Really good.

But today, he's extraordinary.

"Well, I have never seen him like this," Mohammad says. "He doesn't play around on the field. He doesn't taunt other players. He does his job, and he does it well—I'll give him that. But—"

"Would you relax?" I tell Mohammad. "He's just enjoying himself."

"Enjoying himself?!" he cries out. "He might as well be holding up a sign that says, I got some."

"*Oh. My. God.* He didn't get anything," I grumble.

"Fine, change it to *I'm getting*," Mohammad says, testing me.

"You're being silly," I tell him, hoping he'll just drop it. Because Noah and I haven't really defined what we are, and I'm not sure what I would even say to Mohammad.

"I'm just stating the obvious," he says, admiration in his voice.

"He is kind of magnificent out there," I agree.

"Ha! I knew it," Mohammad says, his eyes lighting up again.

"Knew what?" I ask, trying to stay focused on the match.

"I knew something happened. Now, it's just a matter of finding out what. You know I'm a detective, right? I'm going to find out. If you didn't hook up, what was it? Light flirting? A little above-the-shirt action?" Mohammad waggles his eyebrows at me with excitement.

I look back at him like he's crazy.

And it must make him second-guess himself because he adds, "Well, did someone spike his coffee this morning? Did he accidentally ingest speed on his way out the door?"

I roll my eyes. "If you promise to stop talking about this and to never mention it again—"

"Spill," Mohammad says.

I sit up straighter and lean closer to him, so my voice is a whisper. "He might have gotten a kiss."

Mohammad's eyes go wide. "Oh shit."

"Yep," I agree.

Mohammad draws his brows in, and I can tell he's trying to process the information.

"You're telling me that just a single kiss from you did that?" he says in disbelief, looking from me out to Noah.

"All right, fine." I shake my head, slightly embarrassed. "It might have been *more* than a single kiss. There were a few kisses."

"And?" Mohammad urges, holding his hand out for more.

"And maybe a little clothes-on grinding on his bed this morning. It's not a big deal," I say.

I glance down the sidelines, looking for Harry. He's talking to a few guys I recognize from school.

"Not a big deal?" Mohammad says, looking like his mind has just been blown. "It's a huge deal! For one, congratulations. You finally managed to get over your chicken-ness and seal the deal." I roll my eyes, but Mohammad continues, "And second, how did this even happen?"

"Look, Mohammad, I want to tell you everything. But not here. I don't even know how it happened exactly."

"Is this the start of you two?"

"I think so, yeah."

"Wow." Mohammad blinks, looking slightly freaked out.

"What? I thought this is what you wanted?" I ask, worried.

"Things are going to change."

"Nothing has to change," I disagree.

"Everything's already changed. You might as well have a big pink heart floating around you. And Noah—I can't even talk about him right now," Mohammad says, holding his hands out in front of him like he wants to be rid of this conversation. "He's untouchable on the field already. Who knows what being in love will do to him?"

"Usually, I'm the one who overthinks things, but right now, you're the one overthinking. It's just like you and Naomi. You two dating or not dating doesn't change things."

"It changes the group dynamics, which in turn, changes everything. It will be a process," Mohammad replies. "I'm happy for you though. So you know."

"Thanks." I smile. "And later today, I want to tell you

about yesterday. I showed up at Noah's house after school. That's how it all happened. See, he wrote me this note ... or poem. I don't know. It's a long story but—"

"I can't wait to hear it," Mohammad says, his pearly whites coming out.

"Have you told Naomi yet that you're going to be gone for the weekend?"

"I think she's going to be mad at me."

"Yeah, usually, girls aren't big on spur-of-the-moment decisions. Especially if they've been secretly hoping that you'll take them out."

"Yeah. I'm going to have to come up with a way to make up for that one. But I wouldn't miss this trip."

"Me neither. I was so worried when Harry messaged me. I couldn't believe when he showed up last night."

"He's excited to be going. I think it gives him something to do other than sit around, thinking about his future."

"Yeah," I agree, looking back out at the field. "Mohammad, can I ask you something?"

"Shoot."

"Do I really have a big pink heart floating around me now?" I ask, cringing. "Because I don't want to become one of those girls who obsesses over the guy they're with, you know? Those big emotions and goo-goo eyes freak me out a little."

He pats me on the knee. "Yes, you do," he answers, looking me over. "But it's always been there, hasn't it?"

I shrug, pulling my eyes away from him. "Maybe a little," I admit.

"Maybe a lot."

"All right, chap," Harry says, coming back over to us, "do you want your seat back, or is it open for the taking?"

Mohammad looks from the folding chair to me. "Sorry, Mallory. Chair wins!"

I laugh, waving him off.

"Figures." Harry chuckles before taking Mohammad's spot on the quilt.

A few guidelines.
12:30PM

BY THE TIME Noah's match is over, I think everyone on the sidelines is in mutual awe. Because Kensington won ... by a lot. I look around the sidelines, seeing everyone trying to come to terms with the win. Because they didn't just win.

They destroyed the other team.

It was likely their best match ever. At least, the best match I've ever seen them play. And one look at Mohammad's gaping mouth confirms it.

Noah comes running up to us. He's covered in grass stains and sweat, but he's beaming. When he gets to the sidelines, he stops in front of our quilt and shakes his wet hair over us like he's a dog.

"Eww." I laugh, trying to shield my face.

Noah laughs too, extending his hand out to Harry. He pulls him up off the ground and into a hug.

"You killed it out there!" Mohammad says, getting up from his folding chair.

"I was just having some fun." Noah grins, glancing at him. Then, he turns to me, pulling me up next.

"I think we all could see that," I reply, smiling at him.

Noah pulls me into a hug, wrapping his arms around my waist. He smells like sweat and grass. But his body is warm, and his chest is firm against mine. My cheeks flood with heat as I wrap my arms around his neck to hug him back.

"Fucking wicked," Harry says. His blue eyes are still

sparkling.

"Thanks. Coach was pleased," Noah says, breaking us apart.

I look toward Coach Carson.

"Did this match make up for detention?" I ask him.

Noah flushes, rubbing the back of his neck with his palm. "I think so," he says. "But he gave us a big speech during practice about training over the break."

"Fuck that. You deserve a few days off," Harry says, shaking his head.

"And apparently, to do twenty minutes of core a day," Noah replies with an eye roll.

"Are you going to work out on the trip?" I ask curiously.

Because knowing Noah, the answer is yes. One hundred percent.

"Hell no," Harry says the same time Noah says, "I have to."

"Great match," Mia says, cutting into the conversation.

"Thanks." Noah smiles at her.

"You were absolutely brilliant out there," Gene says, joining us. He has two folding chairs draped over his shoulder.

"Thanks, Dad."

"Oh, lovely, what a match!" Helen beams, handing Noah a bottle of water.

Noah grins at her before taking a gulp.

"It was better than last week's anyway," Mia says, sticking out her tongue.

"Glad you enjoyed it." Noah laughs.

"I did. I'm very proud of you. Now, give me a hug. I'm going to meet Sophia."

Noah pulls Mia into a hug, and I instantly want to melt.

I think we all simultaneously watch them with affection. Helen tilts her head to the side, a smile on her face. Gene has a twinkle in his eye. Harry's watching intently, and Mohammad's grinning.

"Thanks for coming, Mia," Noah says.

"Thanks for not sucking. Love you," she replies, patting him on the shoulder.

"Love you too," Noah says.

"Bye, Mallory. Mohammad. Harry," Mia says to all of us. She's already walking off when Gene calls out, "Don't forget to romance her!"

Mia turns back to look at us. And she's bright red.

"Oh, Gene," Helen says, covering her mouth with her hand.

"What?" Gene asks.

Noah and I burst out laughing while Harry and Mohammad just look confused.

"What did I say?" Gene asks again, but he doesn't get an answer.

Helen just waves him off, trying not to laugh herself.

"SERIOUSLY, THAT WAS legendary," Harry says when we get back to the house. He pulls off his trench coat and sits down on the couch.

"I know!" Mohammad agrees.

They're clearly still buzzing from the win. Mohammad follows Gene to the couch opposite Harry, and they both take a seat. I slip off my shoes in the entryway as Noah closes the door behind us, dropping his duffel on the floor. Helen's already snuck off somewhere. When my shoes are off, I make my way to the living room and am confronted with a huge pile of bags. There are at least two suitcases, three duffels, and two backpacks, all pushed together.

"What is all of this?" I ask, looking at the large pile in disbelief.

"Stuff for the trip," Mohammad answers.

"All of this is for you two?" I point between Mohammad and Harry. Because my suitcase and duffel aren't even included in this pile. And I thought what I packed was overkill.

"Yeah," Mohammad answers again.

"But last night, you only had one duffel," I say, looking at Harry, confused.

"After I left your place, I realized that I wasn't actually prepared for a weekend away. I'd left the house in a rush, so I had one of the maids pack me more luggage," Harry explains.

I raise my eyebrows in surprise. "Well, I don't feel so bad about having two bags then."

I move past the pile of luggage into the living room and take a seat.

"You all overpacked," Noah chimes in, kicking off his shoes in the entryway.

"I only packed necessities," I disagree.

"I didn't." Mohammad frowns. "Who knows what you'll need? You always have to be prepared."

Noah starts to walk into the living room when, suddenly, Helen comes swooping back into the room, a towel in hand.

Noah takes one look at her, and his shoulders drop.

"Mum," Noah whines, rolling his eyes.

"Don't sass me. You will not be dragging all of that grass through my house."

Noah lets out a groan.

"Harry dear, will you help Noah?"

"No problem." Harry gets up and holds the towel out as a makeshift curtain for Noah, so he can strip off his clothes.

I try not to look in their direction, but the clothes falling to the floor force my eyes there. When he's only in his underwear, Noah wraps the towel around his waist and then hands Helen the dirty clothes.

"Wasn't so hard, now was it?" Helen raises an eyebrow at him before heading to the laundry room.

Noah walks into the living room and sits down in one of the free chairs. He's wearing nothing but a towel around his waist, and I have to completely ignore him.

And his naked chest.

"Noah, you packed everything I'd asked?" Harry says, sitting back down.

"Yeah, I've got everything," Noah confirms.

"Good. I can't very well wear a three-piece suit and have you in joggers. I'd look ridiculous." Harry laughs.

"Like you'd care. You'd still wear it, and you know it." Noah smirks at him.

"Probably. Though there isn't much that stops me from doing whatever I want," Harry agrees.

"There's the Harry we know and love," Mohammad chimes in.

"You all did seem to pack quite a lot. Harry, are you sure the luggage will fit in the car?" Gene asks, pushing his glasses up his nose.

"I got us a stretch," Harry answers. "Figured we needed to travel in style."

"Very nice." Gene smiles approvingly.

"So, turns out, I might actually be the one who packed the least for this trip," I say, finally looking at Noah. "Are you impressed?"

"You did good." Noah chuckles. "At least, better than these two anyway." He looks between Mohammad and Harry.

"I was under pressure! Harry showed up and announced we were leaving. That didn't give me any prep time," Mohammad says, looking offended.

"Except you had all night to prep," I say, poking fun at him.

"Ha-ha." Mohammad rolls his eyes at me.

Harry and Gene both chuckle, and Noah leans his head back against the chair. I let myself sneak a peek at him. His pale skin is almost the same color as his towel, and a thin trail of dark hair runs from his belly button straight down, disappearing below his towel. I swallow, flicking my gaze up to his eyes. He's watching me, an easy smile on his lips. I can't help but smile back at him.

"You'll have a great time," Gene says, breaking into my thoughts.

"Thanks again for agreeing to let Noah come," Harry says. "I really need this weekend away."

"We know you do," Gene replies, a frown forming on his lips.

"Mallory dear, come help me in the kitchen?" Helen calls out.

I glance over to the kitchen, my stomach instantly flipping.

I look over to Noah, giving him the *I know she knows* look. He shakes his head slightly, like I'm wrong.

But I know I'm not.

"Sure!" I call back.

All right, stay calm.

And don't incriminate yourself.

I push my shoulders back and walk into the kitchen.

"Hey," I say to Helen.

She's seated at the table, a cup of steaming tea in her hand and a serious expression on her face. I instantly go white.

"So, you and Noah," she states.

"Yeah?" I squeak out.

"Mallory ..." Helen says, raising one eyebrow at me. And it isn't a friendly eyebrow. It's an eyebrow that says, *Do not lie to me.* At least, that's what it would say if eyebrows could talk.

"I promise to be good," I blurt out, my chest pounding.

Helen motions for me to sit down, so I do.

"Don't make promises you can't keep," she says seriously, holding her index finger up firmly.

Which is a bad sign.

"I swear, all we've done is kiss. Noah didn't want me to tell you, but I feel like we're too close to have secrets. Although, now that I'm thinking about it, you might not want to know *everything*."

The moment the words leave my mouth, my eyes go wide.

"But I promise there's nothing to tell. At least, not yet. I mean, hopefully, one day but …" I stumble over my words, wishing that Helen seemed more like a friend I could talk to than Noah's mom right now. But it's becoming obviously clear with this conversation that I'm officially talking to a mom.

"Slow down," Helen says with a flush.

"Sorry. Too much?" I ask, feeling sweaty.

"You're both young," Helen says, thinking through her words. "I expect that you treat my son well and that he respects you."

"I promise I will." I take in a deep breath, trying to calm down.

"Has he … told Harry yet?"

I bring my eyes up to meet hers. "We just decided to give this whole *us* thing a shot yesterday. So, not yet."

"And this trip?"

"It's not about that. Harry asked us all to go. It's a friends' trip," I tell her.

"Hmm," Helen says before taking a sip of her tea.

"I know you said not to make promises I can't keep, but I do promise that this weekend isn't going to be treated like a weekend away for the two of us or something. It's not. I need to get used to the idea of Noah and me, you know?"

Helen sets down her cup, her face softening. "I understand that, but I know you, dearest. You can be impulsive. So, I have a few guidelines."

"Guidelines?" I ask, trying not to slink down in my seat.

"If you want Noah to come—which I wouldn't want to stop him from spending time with you or his friends—I want to chat about a few things first."

"Okay …"

"First and foremost, be safe," Helen says.

"Be safe," I repeat.

I quickly realize what exactly she's referring to, and my eyes instantly go wide.

"Oh, you mean …"

"I meant, be safe, as in be safe," Helen says, going pink. She brings the back of her hand up to her forehead, looking flushed. "Oh dear. Just … be smart. With your hearts. With your feelings. With your … bodies."

Oh.

I flush, embarrassed.

"Listen, Helen, as much as I want to experience that … someday, I don't think we'll be taking that step so quickly."

Helen visibly exhales. "That's good to hear. You're both far too young."

"Yeah …" I say, deciding to agree with her even though I'm not sure that I do. Especially not after seeing Noah in a towel in the living room.

"Yeah?" Helen repeats, looking at me in question.

"I mean, we're not *that* young. Honestly, I have thought about it. But this—between Noah and me—it's new. Maybe my feelings aren't, but being able to do something about them is. And we've only ever kissed. And not that you need to know, but I've never been with anyone. So, it would be my first time. And not that it matters, but it would be Noah's too," I tell her. "I think girls want a slow, drawn-out process, you know? Usually, we want to see how much a guy loves us before we take that step. Maybe for boys, it's different. Once they have a girlfriend, they're just … ready to go. I don't know."

"That's a lot of information," Helen says, her brows creasing.

"Please don't tell Noah I told you that," I say, covering my mouth with my hand.

Helen looks like a deer caught in headlights, and her nervousness is making me nervous. And apparently, chattier. Which, in turn, is making her nerves even worse. The whole situation is just weird.

"It will stay between us," Helen agrees quickly. "Now, this weekend."

"Yes?"

Helen takes my hand. "Sex is something that should really be reserved for marriage. And as far as I can tell, you're both far too young for that."

"Marriage?" I gape at her. "We are *definitely* too young for marriage."

"Good. Then we agree." Helen nods firmly.

"Uh … well, sure."

Helen stands up and puts her hand on her hip, thinking.

"Maybe I should have Gene speak with Noah before you leave," she says more to herself than me.

"No, no, no," I say, shaking my head. "Please, that would be completely embarrassing. I promise you, there will be no sex this weekend."

Helen smiles at me. "Good."

I shake my head, trying to clear out everything that just happened.

"So, Mia made you cookies yesterday?" I ask, standing up. Because at this point, I'll take any conversation over the sex conversation.

Helen's whole face seems to brighten. "She did."

"She told me that you're reading Sherlock Holmes together. She even made me test the cookie out before giving it to you," I tell her.

"Oh, Mia," Helen says, almost to herself.

"It was nice of you to let her keep the purple hair. I know she appreciated it."

"It seemed like that was a battle I was going to lose," Helen reflects. "Between Noah's insistence upon how upset she was and Gene's indifference to the color, I was overruled."

"I don't blame you for being upset. I'm sure it was a shock."

"It was."

"But also, it looks really pretty on her."

"That's true too. When Noah told me I hurt her feelings, I wasn't happy about that. It's a parent's job to do what is right for their child. And sometimes, that means not being their friend. But in Mia's case, well, she's very sensitive about her creativity."

"If you ask me, she just cares what you think," I tell her. "Maybe she won't admit it, but she does. That's why she had me test out the cookie first."

I smile to Helen when Harry comes into the kitchen.

"I'm in search of food," he says brightly.

"There's leftover roast in the fridge," she replies, patting him on the shoulder.

"Oh, let's make sandwiches for the road," Mohammad says, joining us.

"Make me one too," Noah calls out from the living room.

Harry opens the fridge, and both he and Mohammad stick their heads in, looking around.

"Oh, boys." Helen laughs fondly before ushering them

aside. "Let me."

Mohammad and Harry move as Noah pops his head into the kitchen.

"I'm going to shower."

"Be quick," Harry tells him.

"All right," Noah agrees before heading upstairs.

"I'll be, um, back," I say, sneaking out of the kitchen.

I listen as Mohammad and Harry debate on what else they want to eat. Helen laughs as she opens up the pantry. Gene has moved into his usual chair, his paper open in his hands.

I follow Noah upstairs, my thoughts going a million miles a minute.

WHEN I GET upstairs, the bathroom door is still open. I look in, finding Noah's back to me as he turns on the shower. But then he turns around. When his eyes land on me in the doorway, his face lights up.

"Trying to join me?" He smirks, breaking the distance between us.

I swallow, the image of a naked Noah flashing in front of me.

But then I refocus.

"Join you?" I squeak. "I just had to promise your mom that we wouldn't have sex this weekend. She brought up marriage!"

"What?" Noah asks, shock registering on his face.

"Yes! It was mortifying."

Noah pulls me into the bathroom, closing the door behind us. I lean my back against the counter and rub at my temples.

Noah narrows his eyes in on me. "You cracked, didn't you?"

"We can talk about that later," I huff.

"Uh-huh."

So many thoughts are running through my mind, and I don't know what to say. Or where to even start. But then Helen's question flashes into my mind.

"Noah, do we tell Harry?" I ask.

Noah's face grows serious. "About … us?"

"Yeah. Your mom knows. Mia knows. Mohammad. Everyone knows, and I don't even know what there is to know, but I don't want this to …"

"Mallory."

"What?" I look up at Noah, trying to calm down.

"I will tell him."

"Oh."

Oh.

"Are you sure?" I ask.

"Yeah, of course."

"Okay." I nod.

"I'm sorry she gave you *the talk*." Noah rubs his hands up my arms.

"Don't worry; you'll get it too," I tell him.

"Mum won't talk to me about it. If anything, she'll make my dad do it."

"No, I meant, from me," I say, swatting at him. "I haven't told you half of what she said. But the basic rule for the weekend was well established—no sex."

"I thought we determined that I like breaking your rules?" Noah smirks, pinning me against the counter.

A breath escapes my lips at the motion. "I couldn't do that to your mom." I laugh.

"Last time I checked, sex was between two people," Noah points out.

"Apparently not in this household."

"Well ... we're in no rush anyway, so we'll cross that bridge when we get to it."

"God, not another bridge," I mumble. "Bridges and wings. I swear, I need some concrete-ness in my life."

Noah glances up, his brows drawing in.

"We could use a different analogy. I'll think about it," he says seriously.

I can't help but smile at him. "Thanks."

Noah nods, putting some space between us, but I grab on to his arms.

"You know, you really did do great out there. It was slightly impressive."

"Just slightly?"

"Maybe more than that. It was ..."

"Hot?" Noah asks, tilting his head to the side.

"Seriously." I laugh, pushing him away from me.

Noah grabs on to my wrists, keeping my palms firmly on his chest. "Just admit it. You liked watching me."

"And apparently, you liked performing for me," I say back, holding his gaze.

Noah stands taller. "I don't just like performing for you. I *love* it," he replies, causing me to blush. "I'll admit though, I might have had a little too much fun."

"Uh-huh. Just a little."

"Just a little," Noah repeats my words, but his eyes are all over me.

My heart picks up in my chest, and I let my hands slide up onto his shoulders. Noah licks his lips, and for a minute, I think he's going to kiss me. But he blinks and pulls back a little.

"Anyway, Mia was going on and on about us men chasing around an inflated ball, so I figured I should have a good time with it, you know? Wouldn't want her to get bored. All that shin-kicking and falling into the grass."

I laugh, my whole body shaking. "I can't believe she actually said that."

Noah smiles and laughs with me.

"I probably need to head downstairs," I say, realizing the bathroom is already full of steam. The wet air makes the room feel smaller, like everything is heavy and dense.

"Yeah. I need to shower."

"Hurry up, okay?" I say, wishing that I didn't have to leave.

Noah nods slowly.

I shift past him, opening up the bathroom door. The cool hallway air hits me instantly. I turn back to see Noah stripping off his towel. He's watching me as he does it, his lips curled up happily at the corners.

I have to peel my eyes away.

I close the door to the bathroom and listen as he steps into the shower. I can hear him moving under the water. I try to focus on our trip. And on Helen's warning. On lunch waiting downstairs. And on anything other than the fact that I get to spend a long weekend with Noah.

With no parents.

And hopefully, with as few clothes as possible.

"I'M STILL IMPRESSED with myself," Harry says, looking between Mohammad and me with a grin.

We've been sitting at the table for ten minutes, watching Helen willingly pack us lunch for the road.

"About what?" Noah asks, joining us in the kitchen. His hair is wet from the shower, and he's changed into jeans and a sweater for the trip.

"My charm and chat know no bounds," Harry boasts, getting up from the table. "To think that just yesterday, I had to convince two sets of parents to make this trip happen." He holds up two fingers for effect.

Mohammad rolls his eyes as he stands up from the table. "I would have convinced my mum all on my own, thank you very much," he says, pushing in his chair.

I get up too, knowing that we're all ready to go now.

"Well, not Mallory," Harry argues, grabbing the bag of food off the counter.

Noah looks at me with the mention of my name.

"What do you mean?" Mohammad asks, leading us all out into the living room.

Helen moves to the couch with a book, and Gene is in his usual chair, now asleep.

"I had to talk to Mr. James on the phone last night. Convince him to let our girl come with us for the weekend," Harry says, waggling his eyebrows.

"Harry talked to your dad?" Noah asks me, his eyes widening.

"Only for a minute."

"A minute was all it took, boys. He loves me. I wouldn't be surprised if when he arrives and meets me, he begs Mallory to take me back." Harry laughs.

"What?" I cough out. Because he's joking.

Right?

"We bonded, your father and I." Harry grins. "He's a lot like you actually. Very straightforward. A little hesitant but charmed easily enough. I think we'll get on."

I bring my hand up to my mouth, mortified.

"Oh. My. God," I mumble more to myself than anyone else.

Noah blinks a few times, looking stuck in his spot in the living room. And I know I need to fix it.

"Harry's just being dramatic," I say, trying to recover.

"My dad asked to speak to him on the phone last night before he'd agree to let me go."

"It was easy enough to convince him. You know they're joining the club?" Harry says, walking over to the front window. He moves the curtain, looking outside.

"Really?" Noah asks.

"I didn't know until he told Harry," I reply, pulling my lips to the side. "Small world, I guess."

"Exclusive world," Mohammad corrects, pulling on his jacket.

"Car's here," Harry says. "I'll be right back."

Harry goes out front, leaving me, Noah, and Mohammad in the entryway.

"I'll start taking out the cases," Mohammad says excitedly, moving past Noah and me.

"Noah, I'm sorry about that," I say when we're alone.

"There's nothing to be sorry about. It's a good thing if your dad likes your friends," he replies, his brown eyes softening.

"I know. But …"

"I know." Noah pushes a piece of hair behind my ear, and I grab on to his hand, squeezing it.

When Harry and Mohammad come back inside, Helen joins us in the entryway.

"All right, you four, listen up," she says.

Mohammad drops the bag in his hand, giving Helen his full attention.

"I don't want to hear about any trouble, you understand?" she says, looking at each of us sternly.

"Understood," Harry and Noah say.

"Yes," I reply.

"You won't," Mohammad agrees.

"Good," Helen says, studying us before looking directly at

me and asking pointedly, "And you'll behave yourself?"

"I will," I answer, giving her a firm nod.

"I second that," Mohammad says. "You have nothing to worry about."

Helen's eyes move from Mohammad to Noah.

"Yes, Mum," Noah concedes under her gaze.

"And, Harry, that leaves you," Helen says with a raised eyebrow.

"You know me—I always behave." Harry grins at her.

The tension deflates with Harry's words, and I can see Helen trying to hide her smile.

"All right. Off you go then," Helen says, trying to shoo us out of her house.

Harry grabs a few bags, taking them outside.

"We passed the final test," Noah says, leaning into me.

"Did we?" I ask, looking up at him.

"Mmhmm. This weekend should be fun," he says, his voice lower than before.

My stomach flutters with excitement.

Noah grabs two of the suitcases, carrying them out to the car. I follow him, Mohammad flying past me to grab more stuff.

"I think he's excited," I say to Harry as he joins me on the front stoop.

"He is," Harry agrees.

Mohammad flies past us again with the rest of the luggage. I watch Noah, Mohammad, and the driver all load the car.

Harry looks over at me.

"I hope you know that this weekend, I *absolutely* plan on misbehaving." Harry bumps his elbow against mine. "Which means you're going to have to misbehave too."

I laugh, shaking my head at him.

"I don't think this is a laughing matter," Harry says, amused, his blue eyes on me.

"You're the one who said this would be a fun, wholehearted friends' weekend," I point out.

"Did I say that?" Harry grins, bringing his hand up to his chin like he doesn't remember.

"Harry!" I laugh. "Yes, you did."

"I'm glad you get to come," he says, sounding more serious. "And I was telling the truth before. It will be a friends' weekend."

I smile at him.

"Being friends is good," he states. "Friends can have a lot of fun together."

"Fun? What kind of fun?"

"Any kind you want. I don't have rules about what friendship includes," Harry says, raising his eyebrows at me.

My lips part, but before I can say anything back, Harry walks down the steps to the car, leaving me alone.

I look around, my mind racing, but then I force myself to take in a steady breath and calm down. Because that's just Harry.

He makes suggestions like that to test the boundaries. And that's something we're going to have to figure out this weekend.

What our boundaries are.

What exactly Noah and I are.

And what Harry is to me.

I glance over my shoulder, seeing the entryway empty. I close the front door, and when I turn back out to face the street, I see Harry, Mohammad, and Noah, all ready to go.

All waiting for me.

I look at Harry, thinking about what he just said. About us being more than friends. He looks younger and happier than I've seen him in a while, like all his worries have disappeared. And that makes me happy. He has his back resting against the car and a devilish gleam in his eye. His lips curl up into a smile before he shoots me a wink. And leaning against the car in his polo, jeans, and trench coat, he looks just like he did that first day at the pub.

He looks like trouble.

Major, major trouble.

And I think he knows it.

I break Harry's gaze, looking over at Mohammad. His face is down in his phone. I have no doubt that he's scrolling through his songs, creating the perfect playlist for our trip. Or maybe he's texting Naomi, which, knowing him, means he's probably flirting with her.

I smile, my eyes leaving Mohammad and landing on Noah. His gaze moves from Mohammad to me, and I know he's been watching me. His brown eyes hold mine, causing my heart to speed up in my chest. I search his face, from his lips to his creamy cheeks and dark eyebrows. Looking at him makes me remember the way his mouth felt on mine this morning. It makes me remember the words we exchanged yesterday. The way he looked in the bathroom. He smiles and slightly nods his head for me to come down to them.

To him.

I smile and walk down the steps.

Noah bites his lip. Harry opens up the car door, letting me get in first.

"Ready?" Harry asks.

"Ready," I reply firmly.

Because what's the worst that could happen?

It's just a weekend away at Harry's country house with three boys, no parents, and absolutely zero rules.

What could go wrong?

ABOUT THE AUTHOR

Jillian Dodd® is a USA Today and Amazon Top 10 best-selling author. She writes fun binge-able romance series with characters her readers fall in love with—from the boy next door in the That Boy series to the daughter of a famous actress in The Keatyn Chronicles® to a spy who might save the world in the Spy Girl® series. Her newest series include London Prep, a prep school series about a drama filled three-week exchange, and the Sex in the City-ish chick lit series, Kitty Valentine.

Jillian is married to her college sweetheart, adores writing big fat happily ever afters, wears a lot of pink, buys way too many shoes, loves to travel, and is distracted by anything covered in glitter.

Made in the USA
Middletown, DE
09 November 2021

51942823R00203